THIRTEEN HOURS

THIRTEEN HOURS

DEON MEYER

Translated from Afrikaans by K. L. Seegers

HODDER &
STOUGHTON

First published in Great Britain in 2010 by Hodder & Stoughton
An Hachette UK company

1

A CIP catalogue record for this title is available from the British Library.

Hardback ISBN 978 0 340 95359 4
Trade Paperback ISBN 978 0 340 95360 0

Typeset in Plantin Light by Hewer Text UK Ltd, Edinburgh
Printed and bound by Clays Ltd, St Ives plc

Hodder & Stoughton policy is to use papers that are natural, renewable
and recyclable products and made from wood grown in sustainable forests.
The logging and manufacturing processes are expected to conform
to the environmental regulations of the country of origin.

Hodder & Stoughton Ltd
338 Euston Road
London NW1 3BH

www.hodder.co.uk

05:36–07:00

I

05:36: a girl runs up the steep slope of Lion's Head. The sound of her running shoes urgent on the broad footpath's gravel.

At this moment, as the sun's rays pick her out like a searchlight against the mountain, she is the image of carefree grace. Seen from behind, her dark plait bounces against the little rucksack. Her neck is deeply tanned against the powder blue of her T-shirt. There is energy in the rhythmic stride of her long legs in denim shorts. She personifies athletic youth – vigorous, healthy, focused.

Until she stops and looks back over her left shoulder. Then the illusion disintegrates. There is anxiety in her face. And utter exhaustion.

She does not see the impressive beauty of the city in the rising sun's soft light. Her frightened eyes search wildly for movement in the tall *fynbos* shrubbery behind her. She knows they are there, but not how near. Her breath races – from exertion, shock and fear. It is adrenaline, the fearsome urge to live, that drives her to run again, to keep going, despite her aching legs, the burning in her chest, the fatigue of a night without sleep and the disorientation of a strange city, a foreign country and an impenetrable continent.

Ahead of her the path forks. Instinct spurs her to the right, higher, closer to the Lion's rocky dome. She doesn't think, there is no plan. She runs blindly, her arms the pistons of a machine, driving her on.

Detective Inspector Benny Griessel was asleep.

He dreamed he was driving a huge tanker on a downhill stretch of the N1 between Parow and Plattekloof. Too fast and not quite in control. When his cell phone rang, the first shrill note was enough to draw him back to reality with a fleeting feeling of relief. He opened his eyes and checked the radio clock. It was 05:37.

He swung his feet off the single bed, dream forgotten. For an instant he perched motionless on the edge, like a man hovering on a cliff. Then he stood up and stumbled to the door, down the wooden stairs to the living room below, to where he had left his phone last night. His hair was unkempt, too long between trims. He wore only a pair of faded rugby shorts. His single thought was that a call at this time of the morning could only be bad news.

He didn't recognise the number on the phone's small screen.

'Griessel,' his voice betrayed him, hoarse with the first word of the day.

'Hey, Benny, it's Vusi. Sorry to wake you.'

He struggled to focus, his mind fuzzy. 'That's OK.'

'We've got a . . . body.'

'Where?'

'St Martini, the Lutheran church up in Long Street.'

'*In* the church?'

'No, she's lying outside.'

'I'll be there now.'

He ended the call and ran a hand through his hair.

She, Inspector Vusumuzi Ndabeni had said.

Probably just a *bergie*. Another tramp who had drunk too much of something or other. He put the phone down beside his brand new second-hand laptop.

He turned, still half asleep, and bashed his shin against the front wheel of the bicycle leaning against his pawnshop sofa. He grabbed it before it toppled. Then he went back upstairs. The bicycle was a vague reminder of his financial difficulties, but he didn't want to dwell on that now.

In the bedroom he took off his shorts and the musky scent of sex drifted up from his midriff.

Fuck.

The knowledge of good and evil suddenly weighed heavily on him. Along with the events of the previous night, it squeezed the last remaining drowsiness from his brain. Whatever had possessed him?

He tossed the shorts in an accusatory arc onto the bed and walked through to the bathroom.

Griessel lifted the toilet lid angrily, aimed and peed.

Suddenly she was on the tar of Signal Hill Road and spotted the woman and dog a hundred metres to the left. Her mouth shaped a cry, two words, but her voice was lost in the rasping of her breath.

She ran towards the woman and her dog. It was big, a Ridgeback. The woman looked about sixty, white, with a large pink sun hat, a walking stick and a small bag on her back.

The dog was unsettled now. Maybe it smelled her fear, sensed the panic inside her. Her soles slapped on the tar as she slowed. She stopped three metres from them.

'Help me,' said the girl. Her accent was strong.

'What's wrong?' There was concern in the woman's eyes. She stepped back. The dog growled and strained on the lead, to get closer to the girl.

'They're going to kill me.'

The woman looked around in fear. 'But there's nobody.'

The girl looked over her shoulder. 'They're coming.'

Then she took the measure of the woman and dog and knew they wouldn't make any difference. Not here on the open slope of the mountain. Not against them. She would put them all in danger.

'Call the police. Please. Just call the police,' she said and ran again, slowly at first, her body reluctant. The dog lunged forward and barked once. The woman pulled back on the lead.

'But why?'

'Please,' she said and jogged, feet dragging, down the tar road towards Table Mountain. 'Just call the police.'

She looked back once, about seventy paces on. The woman was still standing there bewildered, frozen to the spot.

Benny Griessel flushed the toilet and wondered why he hadn't seen last night coming. He hadn't gone looking for it, it had just happened. *Jissis*, he shouldn't feel so guilty, he was only human after all.

But he was married.

If you could call it a marriage. Separate beds, separate tables and separate homes. Damn it all, Anna couldn't have everything. She couldn't throw him out of his own house and expect him to support two households, expect him to be sober for six fucking months, and celibate on top of that.

At least he was sober. One hundred and fifty-six days now. More than five months of struggling against the bottle, day after day, hour after hour, till now.

God, Anna must never hear about last night. Not now. Less than a month before his term of exile was served, the punishment for his drinking. If Anna found out, he was fucked, all the struggle and suffering for nothing.

He sighed and stood in front of the mirrored cabinet to brush his teeth. Had a good look at himself. Greying at the temples, wrinkles at the corner of his eyes, the Slavic features. He had never been much of an oil painting.

He opened the cabinet and took out toothbrush and toothpaste.

Whatever had she seen in him, that Bella? There had been a moment last night when he wondered if she was sleeping with him because she felt sorry for him, but he had been too aroused, too bloody grateful for her soft voice and big breasts and her mouth, *jissis*, that mouth, he had a thing about mouths, that's where the trouble had started. No. It had begun with Lize Beekman, but like Anna would believe that?

Jissis.

Benny Griessel brushed his teeth hurriedly and urgently. Then he jumped under the shower and opened the taps on full, so he could wash all the accusing scents from his body.

It wasn't a *bergie*. Griessel's heart skipped a beat as he climbed over the spiked railings of the church wall and saw the girl lying there. The running shoes, khaki shorts, orange camisole and the shape of her arms and legs told him she was young. She reminded him of his daughter.

He walked down the narrow tarmac path, past tall palms and pine trees and a yellow notice board: STRICTLY AUTHORISED. CARS ONLY. AT OWNER'S OWN RISK, to the spot just left of the pretty grey church where, on the same tar, she lay stretched out.

He looked up at the perfect morning. Bright, with hardly any wind, just a faint breeze bearing fresh sea scents up the mountain. It was not a time to die.

Vusi stood beside her with Thick and Thin from Forensics, a police photographer and three men in SAPS uniform. Behind Griessel's back on the Long Street pavement there were more uniforms, at least four in the white shirts and black epaulettes of the Metro Police, all very self-important. Together with a group of bystanders they leaned their arms on the railings and stared at the motionless figure.

'Morning, Benny,' said Vusi Ndabeni in his quiet manner. He was of the same average height as Griessel, but seemed smaller. Lean and neat, the seams of his trousers sharply pressed, snow-white shirt with tie, shoes shined. His peppercorn hair was cut short and shaved in sharp angles, goatee impeccably clipped. He wore surgical rubber gloves. Griessel had been introduced to him for the first time last Thursday, along with the other five detectives he had been asked to 'mentor' throughout the coming year. That was the word that John Africa, Regional Commissioner: Detective Services and Criminal Intelligence, had used. But when Griessel was alone in Africa's office it was 'We're in the shit, Benny. We fucked up the Van der Vyver case, and now the brass say it's because we've just been having too much of a good time in the Cape and it's time to pull finger, but what can I do? I'm losing my best people and the new ones are clueless, totally green. Benny, can I count on you?'

An hour later he was in the Commissioner's large conference room, along with six of the best 'new' people looking singularly unimpressed, all seated in a row on grey government-issue chairs. This time John Africa toned down his message: 'Benny will be your mentor. He's been on the Force for twenty-five years; he was part of the old Murder and Robbery when most of you were still in primary school. What he's forgotten, you still have to learn. But understand this: he's not here to do your work for you. He's your advisor, your sounding board. And your mentor. According to the dictionary that is,' the Commissioner glanced at his notes, '. . . a wise and trusted counsellor or teacher. That's why I transferred him to the Provincial Task Force. Because Benny is wise and you can trust him, because I trust him. Too much knowledge is being lost, there are too many new people and we don't have to reinvent the wheel every time. Learn from him. You have been hand picked – not many will get this opportunity.' Griessel watched their faces. Four lean black men, one fat black woman, and one broad-shouldered coloured detective, all in their early thirties. There was not much ungrudging gratitude, with the exception of Vusumuzi ('but everyone calls me Vusi') Ndabeni. The coloured detective, Fransman Dekker, was openly antagonistic. But Griessel was already accustomed to the undercurrents in the new SAPS. He stood beside John Africa and told himself he ought to be grateful he still had a job after the dissolution of the Serious and Violent Crimes Unit. Grateful that he and his former commanding officer, Mat Joubert, hadn't been posted to a station like most of their colleagues. The new structures that were not new, it was like it was thirty years back, detectives at stations, because that was the way it was now done overseas, and the SAPS must copy them. At least he still had work and Joubert had put him up for promotion. If his luck held, if they could look past his history of drinking, and affirmative action and all the politics and shit, he would hear today whether he had made Captain.

Captain Benny Griessel. It sounded right to him. He needed the raise too.

Badly.

'Morning, Vusi,' he said.

'Hey, Benny,' Jimmy, the tall, skinny white coat from Forensics, greeted him. 'I hear they call you "The Oracle" now.'

'Like that aunty in *Lord of the Rings*,' said Arnold, the short, fat one. Collectively they were known in Cape police circles as Thick and Thin, usually in the tired crack 'Forensics will stand by you through Thick and Thin.'

'*The Matrix*, you ape,' said Jimmy.

'Whatever,' said Arnold.

'Morning,' said Griessel. He turned to the uniforms under the tree and took a deep breath, ready to tell them, 'This is a crime scene, get your butts to the other side of the wall,' and then he remembered that this was Vusi's case, he should shut up and mentor. He gave the uniforms a dirty look, with zero effect, and hunkered down to look at the body.

The girl lay on her belly with her head turned away from the street. Her blonde hair was very short. Across her back were two short horizontal cuts, matching left and right on her shoulder blades. But these were not the cause of death. That was the huge gash across her throat, deep enough to expose the oesophagus. Her face, chest and shoulders lay in the wide pool of blood. The smell of death was already there, as bitter as copper.

'*Jissis*,' said Griessel, all his fear and revulsion welling up in him and he had to breathe, slow and easy, as Doc Barkhuizen had taught him. He had to distance himself, *he must not internalise this*.

He shut his eyes for a second. Then he looked up at the trees. He was searching for objectivity, but this was a dreadful way to die. And his mind wanted to spool through the event as it had happened, the knife flashing and slicing, sliding deep through her tissues.

He got up quickly, pretending to look around. Thick and Thin were bickering over something, as usual. He tried to listen.

Lord, she looked so young. Eighteen, nineteen?

What kind of madness did it take to cut the throat of a child like this? What kind of perversion?

He forced the images out of his mind, thought of the facts, the implications. She was white. That spelled trouble. That meant media attention and the whole cycle of crime-getting-out-of-control criticism starting all over again. It meant huge pressure and long hours, too many people with a finger in the pie and everyone trying to cover their ass and he didn't have the heart for all that any more.

'Trouble,' he said quietly to Vusi.

'I know.'

'It would be better if the uniforms stayed behind the wall.'

Ndabeni nodded and went over to the uniformed policemen. He asked them to go out another way, around the back of the church. They were reluctant, wanting to be part of the action. But they went.

Vusi came to stand beside him, notebook and pen in hand. 'All the gates are locked. There's a gate for cars over there near the church office, and the main gate in front of the building here. She must have jumped over the railings – it's the only way in here.' Vusi spoke too fast. He pointed at a coloured man standing on the pavement on the other side of the wall. 'That *ou* there . . . James Dylan Fredericks, he found her. He's the day manager of Kauai Health Foods in Kloof Street. He says he comes in on the Golden Arrow bus from Mitchell's Plain and then he walks from the terminal. He went past here and something caught his eye. So he climbed over the wall, but when he saw the blood he went back and phoned the Caledon Square station because that's the number he has on speed dial for the shop.'

Griessel nodded. He suspected Ndabeni was nervous about his presence, as though he were here to evaluate the black man. He would have to put that right.

'I'm going to tell Fredericks he can go, we know where to find him.'

'That's fine, Vusi. You don't have to . . . I appreciate you giving me the details, but I don't want you to . . . you know . . .'

Ndabeni touched Griessel's arm as though to reassure him. 'It's OK, Benny. I want to learn . . .'

Vusi was silent for a while. Then he added: 'I don't want to blow this, Benny. I was in Khayelitsha for four years and I don't want to go back. But this is my first . . . white,' he said that carefully as if it might be a racist statement. 'This is another world . . .'

'It is.' Griessel was no good at this sort of thing, never knowing what the proper, politically correct words were.

Vusi came to his rescue. 'I tried to check if there was anything in her shorts pockets. For ID. There isn't anything. We're just waiting for the pathologist now.'

A bird twittered shrilly in the trees. Two pigeons landed near them and began peck-pecking. Griessel looked around him. There was one vehicle in the church grounds, a white Toyota Microbus standing on the south side against a two-metre brick wall. 'Adventure' was spelled in big red letters along the side of the vehicle.

Ndabeni followed his gaze. 'They probably park here for security,' and he indicated the high wall and locked gates. 'I think they have an office down in Long Street.'

'Could be.' Long Street was the hub of backpacker tourism in the Cape – young people, students from Europe, Australia and America looking for cheap lodgings and adventure.

Griessel squatted down beside the body again, but this time so that her face was turned away from him. He did not want to look at the dreadful wound, or her delicate features.

Please, don't let her be a foreign kid, he thought.

Things would really get out of hand then.

2

She ran over Kloofnek Road and stopped for a second, indecisive. She wanted to rest, she wanted to catch her breath and try to control her terror. She had to decide: right, away from the city, where the road sign said 'Camps Bay' and whatever lay that side of the mountain, or left, more or less back the way she had come. Her instinct was to go right, away, further from her pursuers, from the terrible events of the night.

But that was what they would expect, and it would take her deeper into the unknown, further away from Erin. She turned left without further thought, her running shoes loud on the tarred downhill gradient. She kept to the left of the double lane road for 400 metres and then swung right, scrambled down a stony slope, over a bit of veld to the normality of Higgo Road, a residential area high against the mountain, with large, expensive homes in dense gardens behind high walls. Hope flared that here she would find someone to help her, someone to offer shelter and protection.

All the gates were locked. Every house was a fort, the streets deserted this early in the morning. The road wound steeply up the mountain and her legs just wouldn't, couldn't work any more. She saw the open gate of the house to her right and her whole being ached for rest. She glanced over her shoulder and saw nobody. She ducked through the gateway. There was a short steep driveway, a garage and car port. To the right there were dense shrubs against the high wall, to the left was the house behind high metal railings and a locked gate. She crept deep into the shrubbery, right up to the plastered wall, to where she couldn't be seen from the street.

She dropped to her knees, the backpack against the wall. Her head drooped in utter weariness, her eyes closed. Then she slid down further until she was seated flat on the ground. She knew the damp in the bricks and the decaying leaf mould would stain her blue denim shorts, but she didn't care. She just wanted to rest.

The scene imprinted on her brain more than six hours ago suddenly played unbidden through her mind. Her body trembled with shock and her eyes flew open. She dared not think of that now. It was too . . . just too much. Through the curtain of dark green foliage and big bright red flowers she could see a car in the car port. She focused on that. It had an unusual shape, sleek and elegant and not new. What make was it? She tried to distract herself from the terror in her head with this thought. Her breathing calmed, but not her heart. Exhaustion was a great weight pressing on her, but she resisted; it was a luxury she could not afford.

At 06:27 she heard running steps in the street: more than one person, from the same direction she had come, and her heart raced again.

She heard them calling to each other in the street, in a language she did not understand. The footsteps slowed, went quiet. She shifted slightly forward, looking for a gap in the foliage, and stared at the open gate. One of them was standing there, barely visible, the pieces of the mosaic showing he was black.

She kept dead still.

The mosaic moved. He walked in through the gate, silent on his rubber soles. She knew he would look for hiding places, the house, the car in the car port.

The vague shape halved. Was he bending down? To look under the car?

The pieces of him doubled, the outline enlarged. He was approaching. Could he see her, right at the back?

'Hey!'

She was shocked by the voice, a hammer blow to her chest. She could not tell if she moved in that second.

The dark figure moved away, but without haste.

'What do you want?' The voice came from the house, up above. Someone was talking to the black man.

'Nothing.'

'Get the fuck off my property.'

No answer. He stood still, then moved, slowly, reluctantly, until his broken shape disappeared through the leaves.

The two detectives searched the church grounds from the southern side. Vusi began at the front, along the Long Street border with the spiked baroque railings. Griessel began at the back, along the high brick wall. He walked slowly, one step at a time, his head down and eyes moving back and forth. He battled to concentrate, there was a sense of discomfort in him, an elusive feeling, vague and formless. He had to focus here now, on the bare ground, the grass tufts around the base of the trees, the stretches of tarred pathway. He bent every now and then to pick up something and hold it in his fingers – the top of a beer bottle, two rings from cold drink cans, a rusty metal washer, an empty white plastic bag.

He worked his way around behind the church, where the street noise was suddenly muted. He glanced up at the steeple. There was a cross at the top. How many times had he driven past and never really looked? The church building was lovely, an architectural style he could not name. The garden was well cared for, with big palms, pines and oleanders, planted who knows how many years ago? He went around behind the small office building, where the sounds of the street returned. In the northern corner of the grounds he stopped and stood looking up and down Long Street. This was still the old Cape here, the buildings semi-Victorian, most only two storeys high, some painted now in bright colours, probably to appeal to the young. What was this vague unease he felt in him? It had nothing to do with last night. Nor was it the other issue that he had been avoiding for two, three weeks – about Anna and moving back in and whether it would ever work.

Was it the mentoring? To be at the scene of a murder, able to look but not touch? He would find it hard, he knew that now.

Maybe he should just get something to eat.

He looked south, towards the Orange Street crossing. Just before seven on a Tuesday morning and the street was busy – cars, buses, taxis, scooters, pedestrians. The energetic bustle of mid-January, schools reopening, holidays over, forgotten. On the pavement the murder audience had grown to a small crowd. Two press photographers had also arrived, camera bags over shoulders, long lenses held like weapons in front of them. He knew one of them, a bar-room buddy from his drinking days who had worked for the *Cape Times* for years and was now chasing sensation for a tabloid. One night in the Fireman's Arms he had said that if you were to lock up the press and the police on Robben Island for a week, the liquor industry in Cape Town would collapse.

He saw a cyclist weaving skilfully through the traffic on a racing bike, those incredibly thin wheels, the rider in tight black shorts, vivid shirt, shoes, crash helmet, the fucker was even wearing gloves. His gaze followed the cycle to the Orange Street traffic lights, knowing that he never wanted to look that silly. He felt stupid enough with the piss-pot helmet on his head. He wouldn't even have worn it if he hadn't got it for free, with the bicycle.

Doc Barkhuizen, his sponsor at Alcoholics Anonymous, had started the whole thing. Frustrated, Griessel had told Doc that the pull of the bottle was not diminishing. The first three months were long over, the so-called crisis period, and yet his desire was as great as it was on the first day. Doc had recited the 'one day at a time' rhyme, but Griessel said he needed more than that. Doc said 'You need a distraction, what do you do in the evenings?'

Evenings? Policemen had no 'evenings'. When he did get home early, wonder of wonders, he would write to his daughter Carla, or play one of his four CDs on the computer and pick up the bass guitar to play along.

'I'm busy in the evenings, Doc.'

'And mornings?'

'Sometimes I walk in the park. Up near the reservoir.'

'How often?'

'I don't know. Now and then. Once a week, perhaps less . . .'

The trouble with Doc was that he was eloquent. And enthusiastic. About everything. One of those 'the glass is half full' positive guys who would not rest until he had inspired you. 'About five years ago I started cycling, Benny. My knees can't take jogging, but the bicycle is soft on an old man's limbs. I started slowly, five or six kilos a day. Then the bug began to bite, because it's fun. The fresh air, the scents, the sun. You feel the heat and the cold, you see things from a new perspective, because you move at your own tempo, it feels as though your world is at peace. You have time to think . . .'

After Doc's third speech he was swept up by his enthusiasm and at the end of October he went looking for a bicycle, in his usual way – Benny Griessel, Bargain Hunter, as his son Fritz gently teased him. First he researched the price of new ones at the shops and realised two things – they were ridiculously expensive, and he preferred the chunky mountain bikes to the skinny, sissyboy racing ones. He did the rounds of the pawnshops, but all their stock was worn out, cheap Makro stuff, junk even when they were new. Then he studied the *Cape Ads* and found the fucking advert – a flowery description of a Giant Alias, twenty-seven gear, super-light aluminium frame, Shimano shifter and disc brakes, a free saddlebag with tools, free helmet and 'just one month old, original price R7,500, upgrading to DH', which the owner later explained to him meant 'Downhill', as though he would understand what that meant. But he thought, what the fuck, R3,500 was one hell of a bargain, and what had he bought for himself in the past six months since his wife kicked him out of the house? Not a thing. Just the lounge suite from Mohammed 'Love Lips' Faizal's pawnshop in Maitland. And the fridge. And the bass guitar he meant to give Fritz for Christmas, another Faizal bargain that he had stumbled on in September. That was all. Essential items. You couldn't count the laptop. How else would he keep in touch with Carla?

Then he thought about Christmas and all the expenses still to come. He argued the bicycle owner down another two hundred and then he went and drew the money and bought the thing and began riding every morning. He would wear his old rugby shorts, T-shirt and sandals and that ridiculous little helmet.

He soon realised that he did not live in the ideal neighbourhood for cycling. His flat was a quarter of the way up the slopes of Table Mountain. If you went down towards the sea, you had to ride back up the mountain eventually. You could head uphill first, towards Kloof Nek, in order to enjoy the ride home, but you would suffer going up. He almost gave up after a week. But then Doc Barkhuizen gave him the 'five-minute' tip.

'This is what I do, Benny. If I'm not in the mood, I tell myself "just five minutes, and if I don't feel like going on, I'll turn around and go home".'

He tried it – and never once did he turn around. Once you were going, you went on. Towards the end of November, it suddenly became a pleasure. He found a route that he enjoyed. Just after six in the morning he would ride down St John's Street, illegally cutting through the Company Gardens before the zealous security guards were on duty. Then he would turn into Adderley and wave at the flower sellers offloading stock from the bakkies at the Golden Acre and then to the bottom of Duncan Street to the harbour, see what ships had docked today. Then he would ride down the Waterkant, to Green Point – and all along the sea as far as the Sea Point swimming pool. He would look at the mountain and out over the sea and at the people, the pretty young women out jogging with long, tanned legs and bobbing breasts, pensioners walking with purpose, mothers with babies in pushchairs, other cyclists greeting him despite his primitive apparel. Then he would turn and ride back, sixteen kilometres in total and it made him feel good. About himself. And about the city – whose underbelly was all that he had seen for a very long time.

And about his smart purchase. Until his son came around two weeks before Christmas and said he'd decided bass was not for him any more. 'Lead guitar, Dad, *jissie*, Dad, we saw Zinkplaat on Friday and there's this lead, Basson Laubscher, awesome, Dad. Effortless. Genius. That's my dream.'

Zinkplaat.

He hadn't even known such a band existed.

Griessel had been hiding the bass guitar from Fritz for nearly two months. It was his Christmas present. So he had to go and see Hot Lips Faizal again and at such short notice he only had one guitar available, a fucking Fender, practically new and horribly expensive. Plus, what he gave to Fritz had to be matched by a gift to Carla in London. So he was financially stuffed, because Anna made him pay maintenance as though they were divorced. The way she made her calculations was a mystery to him and he had a strong feeling he was being milked, he was being sucked dry while she was earning good money as an assistant to the attorneys. But when he had something to say she would reply, 'You had money for booze, Benny, that was never a problem . . .'

The moral high ground. She had it and he did not. So he must pay. It was part of his punishment.

But that was not the thing churning in his guts.

Griessel sighed and walked back to the murder scene. As his mind focused on the growing crowd of onlookers who would need to be controlled, he recognised the new unease he was feeling.

It had nothing to do with his sex life, his finances, or hunger. It was a premonition. As if the day brought evil with it.

He shook his head. He had never allowed himself to be bothered by such tripe.

The Metro policemen were helping a young coloured woman over the railings with eager hands. She picked up her briefcase, nodded in thanks and came across to Griessel and Ndabeni. A new face to them.

'Tiffany October,' she said, holding out a small hand to Benny. He saw it trembling slightly. She was wearing glasses with narrow black rims. Traces of acne under the make-up. She was slim, slight under the white coat.

'Benny Griessel,' he said and gestured at the detective alongside him. 'This is Inspector Vusumuzi Ndabeni. This is his scene.'

'Call me Vusi.'

'Pleased to meet you,' she said and shook the black detective's hand.

They looked at her enquiringly. It took her a second to realise. 'I'm the pathologist.'

'You're new?' Vusi asked, after an uncomfortable silence.

'This is my first solo.' Tiffany October smiled nervously. Thick and Thin from Forensics came closer, curious to meet her. She shook each politely by the hand.

'Are you done?' Griessel asked them impatiently.

'We still have to do the path and the wall,' said Jimmy, the thin one. He gave his shorter colleague a look. 'Benny's not a morning person.'

Griessel ignored them. Always some chirp.

Tiffany October looked down at the body.

'*Ai*,' she said.

The detectives were quiet. They watched her open her case, take out gloves and kneel beside the girl.

Vusi came closer. 'Benny, I asked the photographer to take pictures that . . . don't show the damage. Pictures of her face. I want to show them around here in Long Street. We have to identify her. Maybe give them to the media as well.'

Griessel nodded. 'Good idea. But you will have to put pressure on the photographer. They're slow . . .'

'I will.' Ndabeni bent down to the pathologist. 'Doctor, if you could give me an idea of how long she has been dead . . .'

Tiffany October didn't look up. 'It's too soon . . .'

Griessel wondered where Prof Phil Pagel, the chief pathologist, was this morning. Pagel would have sat there and given them a calculated guess that would have been within thirty minutes of the actual time of death. He would have dipped a finger in the pool of blood, prodded the corpse here and there, saying it was the small muscles that displayed rigor mortis first, and he thought she had been dead for approximately so many hours, which he would later confirm. But Tiffany October did not have Pagel's experience.

'Give us a guess,' said Griessel.

'Really, I can't.'

She's afraid of getting it wrong, Griessel thought. He moved toward Vusi and spoke softly, close to his ear, so that she would not hear. 'She's been lying there a while, Vusi. The blood is black already.'

'How long?'

'Don't know. Four hours . . . maybe more. Five.'

'OK. So we'll have to get moving.'

Griessel nodded. 'Get those photos quickly. And talk to the Metro people, Vusi. They have video cameras monitoring the streets – in Long Street as well. Let's hope the stuff was working last night. The control centre is in Wale Street. There just might be something . . .'

'Thanks, Benny.'

She fell asleep, against the wall, behind the shrubbery.

She had wanted to rest for just a moment. She shut her eyes and sank back with her backpack against the wall and her legs stretched out in front of her, trying to escape the exhaustion and the tension for a little while. The events of the night were demons in her mind. To escape that, she had thought about her parents, what time it would be at home, but the calculation of time zones was too much for her. If it had been early morning in Lafayette her father would be sitting with the paper, the *Journal & Courier*, shaking his head over the comments of Joe Tiller, the Perdue football coach. Her mother would be late, as always, her heels clattering down the stairs, in too much of a hurry, the battered brown leather briefcase over her shoulder, 'I'm late, I'm late, how can I be late again?' and father and daughter would share their ritual smile over the kitchen table. This routine, this haven, the safety of her family home overwhelmed her with terrible longing and she wanted to phone them, right now, hear their voices, tell them how much she loved them. She carried on this imaginary conversation, with her father answering gently and calmly, until sleep crept up and overcame her.

3

Dr Tiffany October called them: 'Inspector . . .'

'Yes?'

'I could speculate a little . . .'

Griessel wondered if she had overheard him talking.

'Anything could help . . .'

'I think she died here, at the scene. The blood pattern shows that he cut her throat while she lay here. I think he held her flat on the ground, on her stomach, and then he cut her. There are no splash marks to show that she was standing.'

'Oh . . .' He had already worked all that out.

'And these two cuts . . .' She pointed at the two cuts on the girl's shoulder blades.

'Yes?'

'It seems as if they were inflicted post mortem.'

He nodded.

'These look like fibres here . . .' Dr October used a small pair of tweezers carefully around the wound. 'Synthetic material, a dark colour, totally different from her clothing . . .'

Ndabeni looked at the forensic team, now walking bent over along the pathway, heads together, eyes searching, mouths never still. 'Jimmy,' he called, 'here's something for you . . .' Then he crouched down with the pathologist.

She said: 'I think he cut something off her back. Something like a backpack, you know, the two shoulder straps . . .'

Jimmy knelt beside her. Tiffany October showed him the fibres. 'I'll wait until you've collected them.'

'OK,' said Jimmy. He and his partner took out instruments to collect the fibres. They continued an earlier conversation, as though there had been no interruption: 'I'm telling you it's Amoré.'

'It's not Amoré, it's Amor,' said fat Arnold and took a thin transparent plastic bag out of his bag. He kept it ready.

'What are you talking about?' asked Vusi.

'Joost's wife.'

'Joost who?'

'Van der Westhuizen.'

'Who's that?'

'The rugby player.'

'He was Springbok captain, Vusi.'

'I'm more of a soccer guy.'

'Anyway, she has this pair of . . .' Arnold used his hands to indicate big breasts. Tiffany October looked away, offended. 'I'm just stating a fact,' said Arnold defensively.

Carefully Jimmy pulled the fibres out of the wound with tweezers. 'Her name is Amoré,' he said.

'It's Amor, I'm telling you. So this *ou* climbs on the stage with her and . . .'

'What *ou*?' asked Vusi.

'I don't know. Some *ou* that went to see one of her shows. So he grabs the microphone and says "you've got the best tits in the business", he says to Amor and Joost was the *moer in*, heavily upset.'

'What was she doing on the stage?' asked Griessel.

'Jeez, Benny, don't you read the *You* magazine? She's a singer.'

'So Joost grabs him after the show and says, "You can't talk to my wife like that", and the *ou* says to Joost, "But she *has* got nice tits" . . .' Arnold laughed uproariously.

Jimmy hee-heed along. Tiffany October walked off towards the wall, clearly annoyed.

'What?' said the short one innocently after her. 'It's a true story . . .'

'You should say "bosom",' said Jimmy.

'But it's what the *ou* said.'

'Now why didn't Joost just *klap* him?'

'That's what I'd like to know. He tackled Jonah Lomu till his teeth rattled . . .'

'Jonah who?' asked Vusi.

'Jeez, Vusi, that huge New Zealand winger. Anyway, Joost breaks booms at security gates when he's the hell-in, he's hell on wheels on the rugby field, but he won't smack a guy that talks about his wife's t . . . uh, bosoms.'

'Let's be reasonable, how is he going to get that past the magistrate? The guy's lawyer just has to whip out a stack of *You* magazines and say "Your Honour, check this out, in every photo her exhibits are displayed, from Tittendale down to Naval Hill". What can you expect, the guys *will* talk about your wife's assets like they belong to them.'

'That's true. But I'm telling you, it's Amor.'

'Never.'

'You're thinking of Amoré Bekker, the DJ.'

'Nuh-uh. But let me tell you one thing: I wouldn't let my wife walk around like that.'

'Your wife doesn't have the best tits in the business. If you've got it, flaunt it . . .'

'Are you finished?' asked Benny.

'We have to finish the path and do the wall,' said Jimmy and got to his feet. Vusi called the photographer over. 'How soon can I get my pictures of the face?' The photographer, young, curly-haired, shrugged. 'I'll see what I can do.'

Tell him not a damn, thought Griessel. Vusi just nodded.

'No,' said Griessel. 'We need them before eight. It's not negotiable.'

The photographer walked away to the wall, not bothering to hide his attitude. Griessel looked after him with disgust. 'Thanks, Benny,' said Vusi quietly.

'Don't be too nice, Vusi.'

'I know . . .'

After an uncomfortable silence, he asked: 'Benny, what am I missing?'

Griessel kept his voice gentle, counselling. 'The backpack. It must have been robbery, Vusi. Her money, passport, cell phone . . .'

Ndabeni caught on quickly. 'You think they dumped the backpack somewhere.' Griessel couldn't stand around like this any more. He looked about him, at the pavement where the spectators were getting out of hand. 'I'll handle that, Vusi, let's give the Metro guys something to do.' He went up to the wall and called to the uniforms. 'Who's in charge here?'

They just looked at each other.

'This pavement is ours,' said a coloured Metro policeman in an impressive uniform, emblems of rank all over it. Field Marshal at the very least, Griessel mused.

'Yours?'

'That's right.'

He felt the anger rise. He had an issue with the whole concept of the city police, fucking traffic cops that didn't do their jobs, total absence of law enforcement on the roads. He restrained himself and pointed a finger at a SAPS Constable: 'I want you to seal off this pavement, from down there to up to here. If people want to stand around they can do it on the other side of the street.'

The Constable shook his head. 'We don't have any tape.'

'Then go and get some.'

The SAPS man did not like to be the one singled out, but he turned and went off through the crowd. From his left-hand side an ambulance approached with some difficulty through the crowd.

'This is our pavement,' said the heavily ranked Metro policeman stubbornly.

'Are you the chief in charge here?' Benny asked him.

'Yes.'

'What is your name?'

'Jeremy Oerson.'

'And the pavements are under your jurisdiction?'

'Yes.'

'Perfect,' said Griessel. 'Make sure that the ambulance parks here. Right here. And then I want you to inspect every pavement and alley within six blocks of here. Every dustbin, every nook and cranny, got that?'

The man gave him a long look. Probably weighing up the implications should he refuse. Then he nodded, sourly, and began barking orders at his men.

Griessel turned back to Vusi.

'You need to look at this,' the pathologist called from where she was crouched by the body.

They went over to her. With a pair of tweezers, she held up a clothing label, the one from the back of the girl's T-shirt.

'Broad Ripple Vintage, Indianapolis,' she said and gave them a meaningful look.

'What does that mean?' asked Vusi Ndabeni.

'I think she's American,' she said.

'Oh fuck,' said Benny Griessel. 'Are you sure?'

Tiffany October's eyes widened somewhat at his language and her tone of voice confirmed it: 'Pretty sure.'

'Trouble,' said Ndabeni. 'Big trouble.'

07:02–08:13

4

In the library of the big house in Brownlow Street, Tamboerskloof, the shrill, terrified screams of the maid shocked Alexandra Barnard from her sleep.

It was a surreal moment. She had no idea where she was, her limbs felt peculiar, stiff and unwieldy, and her thoughts were as sluggish as molasses. She lifted her head and tried to focus. She saw the plump woman at the door, mouth twisted in what she at first recognised as revulsion. Then the noise penetrated to the marrow.

Alexandra realised she was lying on her back on the Persian rug and wondered how she had come to be there. As she became aware of the horrible taste in her mouth and the fact that she had spent the night on the floor in a drunken stupor, she followed the gaze of Sylvia Buys: someone was lying beside the large brown leather armchair opposite her. She pushed herself up on her arms, wishing Sylvia would stop screaming. She couldn't recall anyone drinking with her last night. Who could it be? She sat upright, and with better perspective, recognised the figure. Adam. Her husband. He was wearing only one shoe, the other foot wore a drooping sock, as if he had been in the process of taking it off. Black trousers, and a white shirt smeared with black on the chest.

Then, as if someone had eventually focused the camera's lens, she realised that Adam was wounded. The black on the shirt was blood, the shirt itself was torn. She pressed her hands on the carpet to get up. She was confused, stunned. She saw the bottle and glass on the wooden table beside her. Her fingers touched something and she looked down and saw the firearm lying next to her. She recognised it, Adam's pistol. What was it doing here?

She got to her feet.

'Sylvia,' she said.

The coloured woman kept screaming.

'Sylvia!'

The sudden silence was a huge relief. Sylvia stood at the door with her hands over her mouth, and her eyes glued to the pistol.

Alexandra took a cautious step forward and stopped again. Adam was dead. She knew it now, from the sum of all the wounds and the way he was lying, but she couldn't understand it. Was it a dream?

'Why?' said Sylvia, approaching hysteria.

Alexandra looked at her.

'Why did you kill him?'

The pathologist and the two ambulance men manoeuvred the corpse carefully into a black zip-up bag. Griessel sat on the stone border of a palm tree bed. Vusi Ndabeni was on his cell phone talking to the station commander. 'I need at least four, Sup, for leg work . . . I understand, but it's an American tourist . . . Yes, we're pretty sure . . . I know . . . I know. No, nothing yet . . . Thanks, Sup, I'll wait for them.'

He came over to Benny. 'The SC says there's a protest of some or other labour union at Parliament and he can only send me two people.'

'There's always a fucking protest of some other union,' said Griessel and stood up. 'I'll help with the footwork, Vusi, until the photos arrive.' He couldn't sit around like this.

'Thanks, Benny. Would you like some coffee?'

'Are you going to send someone?'

'There's a place down the street. I'll go quickly.'

'Let me go.'

They filled the Caledon Square charge office, complainants, victims, witnesses and their hangers-on with stories of the night past. Over the sea of protesting and accusatory voices a telephone rang monotonously, on and on. A female Sergeant, weary after nine hours on her feet, ignored the scowling face across the counter and grabbed the receiver. 'Caledon Square, Sergeant Thanduxolo Nyathi speaking, how may I help you?'

It was a woman's voice, barely audible.

'You'll have to speak up, madam, I can't hear you.'

'I want to report something.'

'Yes, madam?'

'There was this girl . . .'

'Yes, madam?'

'This morning, at about six o'clock, on Signal Hill. She asked me to call the police because someone wanted to kill her.'

'One moment, madam.' She reached for a SAPS form and took a pen from her breast pocket. 'May I have your name?'

'Well, I just want to report it . . .'

'I know, madam, but I need a name.'

Silence.

'Madam?'

'My name is Sybil Gravett.'

'And your address?'

'I really can't see how this is pertinent. I saw the girl on Signal Hill. I was walking my dog.'

The Sergeant suppressed a sigh. 'And then what happened, madam?'

'Well, she came running up to me and she said I must call the police, someone was trying to kill her, and then she ran off again.'

'Did you see anybody following her?'

'I did. A few minutes later, they came running.'

'How many, ma'am?'

'Well, I didn't count them, but there must have been five or six.'

'Can you describe them?'

'They were, well, some were white and some were black. And they were quite young . . . I found that very disturbing, these young men, running with such intent . . .'

She was woken with a start by someone shouting at her. She tried to stand up in her panic, but her legs betrayed her and she stumbled and fell with her shoulder against the wall.

'You fucking druggie!' He stood on the other side of the shrubbery with his hands on his hips, the same voice that had shouted from the house earlier.

'Please,' she sobbed, and stood upright.

'Just get off my property,' he said pointing to the gate. 'What is it with you people? Snoring in my shrubs.'

She made her way through the plants. She saw he was wearing a dark suit, a businessman, middle-aged, furious. 'Please, I need your help . . .'

'No. You need to shoot up somewhere else. I'm sick and tired of this. Get out.'

She began to cry. She approached him. 'It's not what you think, please, I'm from the United—'

The man grabbed her by the arm and dragged her to the gate. 'I don't give a fuck where you come from.' He pulled her roughly. 'All I want is for you people to stop using my property for your filthy habits.' At the gate he shoved her towards the road. 'Now fuck off, before I call the police,' he said and turned and walked back to his house.

'Please, call them,' she said through sobs, shoulders jerking, her whole body trembling. He kept on walking, opened a metal gate, slammed it shut and disappeared. 'Oh, God.' She stood crying on the pavement, shivering. 'Oh, God.' Through the tears she looked instinctively up and down the street, first left, then right. Far off, just where the road curled over the flank of the mountain, stood two of them. Small, watchful figures, one with a cell phone to his ear. Frightened, she began walking in the opposite direction, the way she had come earlier. She didn't know whether they had seen her. She kept to the left, against the walls of the houses, looking back over her shoulder. They were no longer standing. They were running, towards her.

Despair dragged at her. One solution would be to stop, so that it could all be over, the inevitable could happen. She couldn't keep this up, her strength was gone. For a second that option seemed irresistible, the perfect way out, and it slowed her down. But in her mind she replayed the scene with Erin in the night, and the adrenaline gushed and she carried on, weeping as she ran.

The ambulance men were lifting the body over the wall on a stretcher as Griessel arrived with the coffee. The spectators crowded closer, up to the yellow crime scene tape that now cordoned off the pavement. Griessel had long ceased to wonder about humanity's macabre fascination with death. He passed one of the polystyrene cups to his colleague.

'Thanks, Benny.'

The aroma of coffee reminded Griessel that he hadn't had breakfast yet. Perhaps he could get back to the flat for a quick bowl of Weet-Bix before the photos arrived, it was only a kilometre away. He could check whether Carla had written to him. Because last night . . .

No, he wasn't going to think about last night.

Vusi said something in Xhosa that he couldn't understand, some exclamation of surprise. He followed the detective's gaze and saw three of the Metro policemen climbing the wall. Oerson, the one Griessel had argued with earlier, was carrying a blue rucksack. They marched up, full of bravado.

'*uNkulunkulu,*' Vusi said.

'Jesus,' said Benny Griessel.

'We found it,' said the self-satisfied Field Marshal and held out the rucksack to Vusi. The Xhosa man just shook his head and pulled his rubber gloves from his pocket.

'What?' said Oerson.

'Next time,' said Griessel in a reasonable voice, 'it would be better if you let us know you found it. Then we would bring in the forensic guys and cordon off the area before anyone touched it.'

'It was lying in a fucking doorway in Bloem Street. A thousand people could have touched it already. There's not much in it anyway.'

'You opened it?' asked Vusi, reaching for the bag. The two straps were cut, just as the pathologist had predicted.

'There might have been a bomb inside,' said Oerson defensively.

'Did you handle these items?' asked Vusi, taking out a make-up bag. He crouched down to put the contents on the tarred path.

'No,' said Oerson, but Griessel could tell he was lying.

Vusi took a Steers serviette out of the backpack. Next, a small wooden carving of a hippopotamus in dark wood, a white plastic spoon and a Petzl headlamp. 'That's all?'

'That's all,' said Oerson.

'Do me a favour, please?'

They didn't respond.

'Would you go back and see if there is anything else? Something that might have been thrown away. Anything. What I need most is some form of identification. A passport, a driver's licence, anything . . .'

Oerson was not keen. 'We can't help you all day.'

'I know,' said Vusi, quietly and patiently. 'But if you could just do that for me, please.'

'OK. I'll get some more people,' said Oerson. He turned away and went back over the wall.

Vusi's fingers explored the few small pockets on the sides of the backpack. The first one was empty. He pulled out something from the bottom of the second – a green cardboard card with a black and yellow logo: *Hodson's Bay Company*. In smaller type: *Bicycles, fitness, backpacking, camping, climbing gear, and technical clothing for all ages and abilities.* There was an address: 360 Brown Street, Levee Plaza, West Lafayette, IN 47906. There were two telephone numbers as well. The Xhosa man studied it and then passed it to Griessel. 'I think the IN stands for Indiana.'

'West Lafayette,' said Griessel dubiously.

'Probably a small place,' said Vusi. 'I've never heard of it.'

'Fax them a photo, Vusi. They might be able to identify her.'

'Great idea.'

Griessel's cell phone rang shrilly in his pocket. He took it out and answered.

'Griessel.'

'Benny, it's Mavis. An Inspector Fransman Dekker called. He said to tell you he has a murder at Forty-seven Brownlow Street in Tamboerskloof, if you want to mentor him.'

'If I want to?'

'That's what he said. Wound-up guy, bit of a *windgat*.'

'Thanks, Mavis. Forty-seven Brownlow?'

'That's right.'

'I'm on my way.' He ended the call and told Vusi, 'Another murder. Up in Tamboerskloof. Sorry, Vusi . . .'

'No problem. I'll call you when we find something.'

Griessel began to walk away. Ndabeni called after him: 'Benny . . .'

Griessel turned. Vusi came up to him. 'I just wanted to ask you . . . I . . . uh . . .'

'Ask me, Vusi.'

'The pathologist . . . She . . . Do you think . . . Would a coloured doctor go out with a darkie cop?'

It took him a few seconds to make the leap. 'Er . . . you asking the wrong guy, Vusi . . . but yes, why not? A man can only try . . .'

'Thanks, Benny.'

Griessel climbed over the wall. At the churchyard gate he saw a tall, sombre man unlocking it with an extremely worried frown. The *priest* had arrived, he thought, or did the Lutherans call their ministers something else?

5

The traffic was impossible now. It took fifteen minutes just to get from Long Street to Buitengracht. They were bumper to bumper up Buitesingel's hill. He drained the dregs of the sweet coffee. It would last him until he could get something to eat. But his plan to quickly download Carla's email was stuffed. It would just have to wait until tonight. He had been offline for a week already with that damn laptop – he could wait a few more hours. Carla would understand – he'd had problems with the stupid machine from the start. How was he to know there were laptops without internal modems? He had bought his for a knock-down price at a police auction of unclaimed stolen goods. Once Carla left for London, he needed to know how she was – his Carla who needed to 'sort her head out overseas' before she decided what to do with the rest of her life.

So how did vacuuming floors in a hotel in London sort out your head?

It had cost him R500 to get the laptop connected to the Internet. He had to buy a damn modem and get an Internet service provider. Then he spent three hours on the phone with a computer guy getting the fucking connection to work and then Microsoft Outlook Express was a nightmare to configure. That took another hour on the phone to sort out before he could send an email to Carla saying:

Here I am, how are you? I miss you and worry about you. There was an article in the Burger *that said South African kids in London drink a lot and cause trouble. Don't let anyone put pressure on you . . .*

Writing this, he discovered that putting in the Afrikaans punctuation symbols was just about impossible on these computer programmes.

> *Dear Daddy*
>
> *I have a job at the Gloucester Terrace Hotel near Marble Arch. It is a lovely part of London, near Hyde Park. I'm a cleaner. I work from ten in the morning to ten at night, six days a week, Mondays off. I don't know how long I will be able to do this, it's not very pleasant and the pay's not much, but at least it's something. The other girls are all Polish. The first thing they said when I told them I was South African was 'but you're white'.*
>
> *Daddy, you know I will never drink . . .*

When he read those words they burned right through him. A sharp reminder of the damage he had caused. Carla would never drink because her father was an alcoholic who had fucked up his whole family. He might have been sober for one hundred and fifty-six days, but he could never erase the past.

He hadn't known how to respond, his words dried up by his insensitive blunder. It took two days before he answered her, told her about his bicycle and his transfer to the Provincial Task Force. She encouraged him:

> *It's nice to know what you're doing, Daddy. Much more interesting things than I am. I work and sleep and eat. At least I was at Buckingham Palace on Monday . . .*

Their correspondence found a level both were comfortable with: a rhythm of two emails a week, four or five simple paragraphs. He looked forward to them more and more – both the receiving and the sending. He mapped out replies in his head during the day – he must tell Carla this or that. The words gave his small life a certain weight.

But a week ago his Internet connection stopped working. Mysteriously, suddenly, the computer geek on the phone, who made him do things to the laptop that he hadn't known were possible, was also at a loss. 'You'll have to take it to your dealer,' was the final diagnosis. But he didn't have a fucking dealer: ultimately, it was stolen goods. On Friday afternoon after work he bumped into Charmaine Watson-Smith on the way to his door. Charmaine was deep in her seventies and lived at number 106. Everyone's grandma, with her grey hair in a bun. Devious, generous, full of the joys of living, she knew everyone in the block of flats, and their business.

'How's your daughter?' Charmaine asked.

He told her about his computer troubles.

'Oh, I might just know someone who can help.'

'Who?'

'Just give me a day or so.'

Yesterday, Monday evening at half past six he was ironing clothes in his kitchen when Bella knocked on his door.

'Aunty Charmaine said I should take a look at your PC.'

He had seen her before, a young woman in an unattractive chunky grey uniform who went home to her flat on the other side of the building every evening. She had short blonde hair, glasses and always looked tired at the end of the day, carrying a briefcase in her hand.

He had hardly recognised her at his door: she looked pretty. Only the briefcase alerted him, because she had it at her side.

'Oh . . . come in.' He put down the iron.

'Bella van Breda. I'm from number sixty-four.' Just as uncomfortable as he was.

He shook her hand quickly. It was small and soft. 'Benny Griessel.' She was wearing jeans and a red blouse and red lipstick. Her eyes were shy behind the glasses, but from the first he was aware of her wide, full mouth.

'Aunty Charmaine is . . .' He searched for the right word. '. . . busy.'

'I know. But she's great.' Bella had spotted the laptop that he kept in the open-plan kitchen, his only worktop. 'Is this it?'

'Oh . . . yes.' He switched it on. 'My Internet connection won't . . . it just stopped working. Do you know computers?'

They stood close together watching the screen as it got going.

'I'm a PC technician,' she answered and put her briefcase to one side.

'Oh.'

'I know, most people think it's a man's job.'

'No, no, I . . . um, anyone who understands computers . . .'

'That's about all I understand. Can I . . . ?' She gestured at his machine.

'Please. He pulled up one of his bar stools for her. She sat down in front of the tin brain.

He realised she was slimmer than he had previously thought. Perhaps it was her two-piece uniform that had given him the wrong impression. Or perhaps it was her face. It was round, like that of a plumper woman.

She was in her late twenties. He could be her father.

'Is this your connection?' She had a menu open and the mouse pointer on an icon.

'Yes.'

'Can I put a shortcut on your desktop?'

It took him a while to work that one out.

'Yes, please.'

She clicked and looked and thought and said: 'It looks like you accidentally changed the dial-up number. There's one figure short here.'

'Oh.'

'Do you have the number somewhere?'

'I think so . . .' He took the pack of documents and manuals out of the cupboard where he kept them all together in a plastic bag and began to sort through them.

'Here . . .' He indicated it with his finger.

'OK. See, the eight is gone, you must have deleted it, it happens quite easily . . .' She typed the number in and clicked and suddenly the modem dialled up, making its complaining noises.

'Well, fuck me,' he said in genuine amazement. She laughed. With that mouth. So he asked her if she would like a cup of coffee. Or rooibos tea, like Carla always drank.

'That's all I have.'

'Coffee would be nice, thank you.'

He put on the kettle and she said, 'You're a detective,' and he said, 'What didn't Aunty Charmaine tell you?' and so they fell into conversation. Maybe it was purely because they each had a lonely Monday evening ahead. He had no intentions, God knows, he had taken the coffee to the sitting room knowing that in theory he could be her father, despite the mouth, even though by then he had become aware of her pale faultless skin and her breasts that, like her face, belonged to a fuller woman.

It was polite, slightly stilted conversation, strangers with a need to talk on a Monday night.

Two cups of coffee with sugar and Cremora later, he made his big mistake. Without thinking he picked up the top CD from his stack of four and pushed it into his laptop's CD player, because that was all he had apart from the portable Sony that only worked with earphones.

She said in surprise: 'You like Lize Beekman?' and he said in a moment of honesty: 'Very much.' Something changed in her eyes, as though it made her see him differently.

He had bought the CD after he had heard a Lize Beekman song on the car radio, '*My Suikerbos*'. There was something about the singer's voice – compassion, no, vulnerability, or was it the melancholy of the music? He didn't know, but he liked the arrangement, the delicate instrumentation, and he sought out the CD. He listened to it on the Sony, meaning to play through the bass notes in his mind. But the lyrics captured him. Not only the words, the combination of words and music with that voice made him happy, and made him sad. He couldn't remember when last music had made him feel this way, such a yearning for unknown things. And when Bella van Breda asked him if he liked Lize Beekman, it was the first time he could express this to someone. That's why it came out: 'Very much.' With feeling.

Bella said, 'I wish I could sing like that,' and surprisingly, he understood what she meant. He had felt the same yearning, to sing of all the facets of life with the same depth of wisdom and insight and . . . acceptance. To sing of the good and the bad, in such lovely melodies. He had never felt that kind of acceptance. Disgust, yes, that had been with him all his life. He could never explain why he felt this constant, low-grade disgust for everything and, above all, for himself.

He said: 'Me too,' and after a long silence, the conversation blossomed. They talked of many things. She told him the story of her life. He talked about his work, the reliable old stories of peculiar arrests, preposterous witnesses and eccentric colleagues. Bella said she would like to open her own business one day and the light of passion, enthusiasm, shone in her eyes. He listened with admiration. She had a dream. He had nothing. Just a fantasy or two. The kind you kept to yourself, the kind he dreamed up while strumming his guitar in the evenings. Like handcuffing Theuns Jordaan to a microphone and telling him 'Now you sing "*Hex-vallei*", and not a part or a medley, sing the whole fucking song.' With Anton L'Amour on lead guitar and Benny himself on bass, and they were gonna rock 'n' roll, really kick butt. Or to be able to ask Schalk Joubert just once: 'How the fuck do you play bass guitar like that, like it was plugged into your brain?'

Or maybe to have his own four-piece band again. Singing the old blues, Robert Johnson and John Lee Hooker, or the real old rock 'n' roll – Berry, Domino, Ricky Nelson, early Elvis . . .

But he said none of this, just listened to her. Round about ten o'clock she got up to go to the bathroom and when she came back he was on his way back from the sink to the sofa and he said: 'More coffee?'

They were so close and her eyes looked away and her mouth had a small, furtive smile that showed she had an idea what was going to happen next, and she didn't mind.

So he kissed her.

And as Benny sat in the bright summer sun in the Tuesday morning traffic, he remembered that it had been without lust at first, more an extension of their conversation. It was full of consolation, longing, a gentle coming together, just like Lize Beekman's music. Two people who needed to be touched.

They kissed for a long time and then they stood and held each other tight. He was again aware that her body was slimmer than he had expected. She stepped back and sat down on the sofa. He thought she was saying it was enough. But she took off her glasses and carefully put them on the floor to one side. Her eyes looked suddenly deep brown, and defenceless. He sat down next to her and kissed her again and the next thing he could remember she was sitting up, taking off her bra and offering him her lovely breasts with shy pride. He sat in the police car remembering how her body felt – soft, warm and welcoming. He remembered the slow intensity. How he was in her, there on the sofa and lifting himself up to look at her and seeing in her eyes the same immense gratitude that he felt in his own heart. Gratitude that she was there, that this had happened, and it was all lovely and gentle and slow.

Fuck it, he thought, how could that be wrong?

His cell phone rang and brought him back to the present: it must be Dekker asking where he was. But the screen read ANNA and his heart lurched.

It was the fall that saved her.

Instinctively, she had sprinted up the steep row of steps that led up out of the street, up the slope of the mountain between two high ivy-covered walls, and then up a narrow twisting footpath. Table Mountain was suddenly a colossus looming over her, steep slopes of rock and *fynbos* and open stretches. She felt sure she had made a mistake. They would spot her and catch her on the slope. They would grab her and hold her to the ground and slit her throat, like Erin's.

She drove herself up the mountain. She did not look back. The gradient sapped the strength from her thighs, her knees, a slow poison that would paralyse her. Above, to the right, she saw the cable car station, sun glinting off car windscreens, tiny, tiny figures of people, so close, yet so terribly far. If only she could reach them. No, it was too steep, too far, she would never make it.

She saw the fork in the footpath, chose the left one and ran. Forty paces and then a sudden drop, the path unexpectedly falling to a rocky gully that sliced down from high up the mountain. She wasn't prepared for it, her foot landed badly on round pebbles and she fell to the left, downhill. Trying to brake herself with her hands, she banged her shoulder hard and was winded. She rolled over once and lay still, aware that her hands were grazed, that something had struck her chin, but her greatest need was for air, she needed to force it back into her lungs with great, ragged breaths. Her first attempt was a bellowing croak like an animal and she needed to be quiet, they must not hear her. Twice she inhaled hoarsely, then in smaller, quieter breaths. The bank of the stream came into focus and she saw the crevice carved out under the giant rock by centuries of water. Just big enough for her to creep into.

She moved like a snake, over the round river rocks, her bleeding hands held out in front of her, towards the opening. She heard the urgent running steps of her pursuers. How close were they? She realised her rucksack would not fit in. She was running out of time; they would see her. She rose to her knees to tear the rucksack off, but had to stop to loosen the buckle around her belly. She pulled the right then left shoulder straps off, wriggled her body into the hollow and dragged the rucksack after her. Three of them jumped over the dry stream bed three metres away from her, agile, athletic and silent, and she held her burning breath, saw how the blood from her chin dripped on the stones. She lay still, and shut her eyes, as if that would make her invisible to them.

He sat in the traffic with his phone to his ear and said: 'Hello, Anna.' His heart beating in his throat as he thought of last night.

'Benny, we need to talk.'

It was fucking impossible. There was no way his wife could have found out.

'About what?'

'Everything, Benny. I wondered if we could talk tonight.'

About everything? He couldn't gauge her tone of voice.

'We could. Do you want me to come home?'

'No, I thought we could rather . . . go out to eat somewhere.'

Jissis. What did that mean?

'That's fine. Where?'

'I don't know. Canal Walk is sort of halfway. There's a Primi . . .'

'What time would suit you?'

'Seven?'

'Thanks, Anna, that would be nice.'

'Goodbye, Benny.' Just like that, as though he had said the wrong thing.

He sat with the phone in his hand. Behind him a motorist hooted. He realised he should move forward. He released the clutch and closed the gap ahead of him. *About everything, Benny.* What did that mean? Why not at their house? Maybe she felt like going out. Like a kind of date. But when he said: 'That would be nice,' she said goodbye as if she was angry with him.

Could she know about last night? What if she had been there, at his flat, at his door. She would have seen nothing, but she would have been able to hear – Bella who had made such soft, contented noises at one stage. God, he had liked that then, but if Anna had heard . . .

But she had never been to his flat. Why would she have come last night? To talk? Not entirely impossible. And she might have heard something and waited and seen Bella leave and . . .

But if she had, would she want to go out to eat with him?

No. Maybe.

If she knew . . . He was fucked. He knew that now. But she couldn't know.

6

Brownlow Street was a surprise to Griessel because Tamboerskloof was supposed to be a rich neighbourhood. But here the old Victorian houses covered the whole spectrum from recently restored to badly dilapidated. Some were semi-detached, others crouched on the slopes as free-standing colossi. Number forty-seven was large and impressive, with two storeys, verandas and balconies with curlicued ironwork railings, cream walls, and windows with green wooden shutters. It had been restored some time in the past ten years, but now it was in need of more attention.

There was no garage. Griessel parked in the street behind a black Mercedes SLK 200 convertible, two police vehicles and a white Nissan with the SAPS emblem on the door and *Social Services* under it in black type. Forensics' minibus was parked across the road. Thick and Thin. They must have come direct from Long Street.

A uniformed policeman stopped him at the big wooden front door. He showed his identification. 'You will have to go around the back, Inspector; the sitting room is a crime scene,' he said. Griessel nodded in satisfaction.

'I think they are still in the kitchen, sir. You can go right here and then around the house.'

'Thank you.'

He walked around. There was not much garden between the wall and the house. The trees and shrubs were old, large and somewhat overgrown. Behind the house there was a view of Lion's Head. Another policeman was on duty at the back door. He took his SAPS ID out of his wallet again and showed it to the Constable.

'The Inspector is expecting you.'

'Thank you,' he said, and went in through a laundry room and opened the inner door. Dekker sat at the kitchen table, a mug of coffee in his hands and a pen and notebook in front of him. He was totally focused on the coloured woman opposite him. She wore a pink and white domestic uniform and held a handkerchief in her hands, her eyes red from crying. She was plump, her age difficult to judge.

'Fransman . . .' said Griessel.

Dekker looked up irritably. 'Benny.' As an afterthought, he said: 'Come in.' He was a tall, athletic, coloured man, broad-shouldered and strong, with a face from a cigarette advert, handsome in a rugged way.

Griessel went up to the table and shook Dekker's hand.

'This is Mrs Sylvia Buys. She's the domestic worker here.'

'Good morning,' said Sylvia Buys solemnly.

'Morning, Mrs Buys.'

Dekker pushed his mug of coffee away as if to distance himself from it, and pulled his notebook closer with a hint of reluctance. 'Mrs Buys arrived at work . . .' he consulted the notebook, '. . . at six forty-five and tidied up and made coffee in the kitchen before moving to inspect the living area at . . . seven o'clock . . .'

'Damage assessment,' said Sylvia Buys spitefully. 'That woman can make a mess.'

'. . .where she discovered the deceased, Mr Adam Barnard, and the suspect, Mrs Sandra Barnard . . .'

'She's really Alexandra . . .' With distaste.

Dekker made a note and said: 'Mrs Alexandra Barnard. Mrs Buys found them in the library on the first floor. At seven o'clock. The firearm was on the carpet next to Mrs Barnard . . .'

'Not to mention the booze. She's an alky, drinking like a fish every night and Mr Adam . . .' Sylvia lifted the handkerchief, and dab-dabbed at her nose. Her voice grew thinner, shriller.

'Was she under the influence last night?' Griessel asked.

'She's as drunk as a lord every night. I went home at half past four and she was well on her way – by that time of the afternoon she's talking to herself already.'

'Mrs Buys says when she left the house yesterday the suspect was alone. She does not know what time the deceased came home.'

'He was a good man. Always a kind word. I don't understand it. Why did she shoot him? What for? He did her no wrong, he took all of her milly, all her drinking, he just took it, every night he would put her in bed and what did she go and shoot him for?' She wept, shaking her head.

'Sister, you're traumatised. We'll get you some counselling.'

'I don't want counselling,' sobbed Sylvia Buys. 'Where will I get another job at my age?'

'It's not as simple as that,' said Dekker as he climbed the yellowwood stairs to the library. 'You'll see.'

Griessel could sense the tension in the man. He knew his colleagues called Dekker 'Fronsman' behind his back, a reference to his frowning lack of humour and consuming ambition. He had heard the stories, because in the corridors of the Provincial Task Force, they liked to gossip about up-and-coming stars. Dekker was the son of a French rugby player. His mother, a coloured woman from the poverty of Atlantis township, was young and buxom in the Seventies when she worked as a cleaner at the Koeberg nuclear power station. Apparently the rugby player was older, long past his glory days, by then a liaison officer for the French consortium that built and maintained Koeberg. There had been just one encounter and shortly afterwards the rugby player returned to France, without knowing of his offspring. Dekker's mother could not remember his name, so she simply christened her son Fransman, the Afrikaans for Frenchman.

How much of this was true, Griessel could not say. But the child had apparently inherited his father's Gallic nose, build and straight black hair – now trimmed in a brush cut – and his mother's coffee-coloured complexion.

He followed Dekker into the library. Thick and Thin were at work in the room. They looked up as the detectives entered. 'We can't go on meeting like this, Benny, people will talk,' said Jimmy.

An old joke, but Benny grinned, then looked at the victim lying on the left side of the room. Black trousers, white shirt with no tie, one shoe missing, and two gunshot wounds to the chest. Adam Barnard had been tall and strong. His black hair was cut in a Seventies style, over the ears and collar, with elegant grey wings at the temples. In death his eyes were open, making him seem mildly surprised.

Dekker folded his arms expectantly. Thick and Thin stood watching him.

Griessel approached carefully, taking in the book shelves, the Persian carpet, the paintings, the liquor bottle and glass beside the chair on the right side of the room. The firearm was in a transparent plastic evidence bag on the ground, where Forensics had circled it with white chalk. 'She was on this side?' he asked Dekker.

'She was.'

'The Oracle at work,' said Thick.

'Fuck off, Arnold,' said Griessel. 'Had the pistol been fired?'

'Quite recently,' said Arnold.

'But not here.'

'Bingo,' said Arnold.

'I told you he would get it straight away,' said Jimmy.

'Yes,' said Dekker. He sounded disappointed. 'It's an automatic pistol, three rounds are missing from the magazine, but there are no casings here. No blood on the floor, no bullet holes in the walls or book shelves and the shoe is missing. I have gone through the whole house. Jimmy and Co have searched the garden. She didn't *klap* him here. We have to search the car in the street . . .'

'Where is she?'

'In the sitting room with Social Services. Tinkie Kellerman.'

'Knock, knock,' said someone from the door. The long-haired photographer.

'Come in,' said Dekker. 'You're late.'

'Because I had to make bloody prints first . . .' He spotted Griessel. His manner quickly changed. 'Vusi has his photos, Benny.'

'Thanks.'

'Jimmy, did you test her for GSR?' asked Dekker.

'Not yet. But I did put her hands in paper. She didn't like that.'

'Can you do it now? I can't talk to her with paper bags over her hands.'

'If she touched the pistol she will have GSR. I don't know if you can do anything with that.'

'Let me worry about that, Jimmy.'

'I'm just saying. Gunshot residue isn't what it used to be. The lawyers are getting too clever.' Jimmy took a box out of his case. It was marked 'SEM Examination'. He went to the stairs with both detectives in tow.

'Fransman, you've done a good job,' said Griessel.

'I know,' said Dekker.

The CCTV control room of the Metro Police was an impressive space. It had twenty flickering TV screens, a whole bank of video recorders and a control panel that looked as though it belonged to the space shuttle. Inspector Vusi Ndabeni stood looking at a screen, watching the grainy image of a small figure running under the street lights of Long Street. Nine seconds of material, now in slow motion: seven shadowy people in a desperate race from left to right across the screen. The girl was in front, only recognisable thanks to the dark hump of the rucksack. Here, between Leeuwen and Pepper Street, she was only three steps ahead of the nearest assailant, her arms and legs pumping high in flight. Another five people were sixteen to seventeen metres behind. In the last frame just before she disappeared off the screen, Ndabeni could see her turn her head as if to see how close they were.

'Is that the best you have?'

The operator was white, a little man, owl-like behind big round Harry Potter spectacles. He shrugged.

'Can you enlarge this?'

'Not really,' he answered in a nasal voice. 'I can fiddle with the brightness and contrast a little, but if you zoom in, you just get grain. You can't increase the pixels.'

'Could you try, please?'

The Owl worked the dials in front of him. 'Don't expect miracles.' On the screen the figures ran backwards slowly and froze. The man pecked at a keyboard and tables and histograms appeared over the image.

'Which one do you want to see better?'

'The people chasing her.'

The operator used a mouse to select two of the last five figures. They suddenly filled the screen. He tapped the keyboard again and the image brightened, the shadows lightened. 'All I can try is a high pass sharpen . . .' he said. The focus sharpened slightly, but neither of the figures was recognisable.

'You can at least see they are men and that the one in front is black,' said the Owl. Vusi stared at the screen. It wasn't going to help him much.

'You can see they are young men.'

'Can you print this?'

'OK.'

'Are they only on one camera?'

'My shift finishes at eight. I'll have a look if there's something else then. They must have come from Greenmarket or Church Street, but it will take time. There are sixteen cameras in that section. But they don't all work any more.'

'Thanks,' said Vusi Ndabeni. One thing he couldn't understand. If one of the pursuers was only three strides behind her in Pepper Street, why hadn't he caught her before the church? It was five hundred metres away, maybe more. Had he slipped? Fallen? Or deliberately waited for a quieter place.

'One more thing, if you don't mind . . .'

'Hey, it's my work.'

'Can you enlarge the two running in front?'

Griessel walked into the sitting room behind Dekker. It was a large room with big couches and chairs and a huge coffee table, tasteful, old and well restored. Small, delicate Tinkie Kellerman of SAPS Social Services sat upright in an easy chair that dwarfed her. She was the one they sent for when the victim or the suspect was a woman, because she had compassion and empathy, but now there was a frown of unease on her face.

'Ma'am, let me take those bags off your hands,' said Jimmy jovially to Alexandra Barnard, a hunched figure in a white dressing gown. She sat on the edge of a large four-seater couch, elbows on her knees, head hung low, and unwashed grey and blonde hair hiding her face. She held out her hands without looking up. Jimmy loosened the brown paper bags.

'I just have to press these discs on your hands. They are sticky, but that's all . . .' He broke the seal on the SEM box and took out the round metal discs. Griessel saw Alexandra Barnard's hands trembling, but her face was still hidden behind her long hair.

He and Dekker each picked a chair. Dekker opened his notebook.

Jimmy worked quickly and surely, first the right hand and then the left. 'There you go, thank you, madam.' He gave the detectives a look that said 'Here's an interesting one', and then he packed away his things.

'Mrs Barnard . . .' said Dekker.

Tinkie Kellerman shook her head slightly, as if to say the suspect was not communicative. Jimmy walked out rolling his eyes.

'Mrs Barnard,' said Dekker, this time louder and more businesslike.

'I didn't do it,' she said without moving, in a surprisingly deep voice.

'Mrs Barnard, you have the right to legal representation. You have the right to remain silent. But if you choose to answer our questions, anything you say may be used in court.'

'I didn't do it.'

'Do you want to contact your lawyer?'

'No,' and slowly she raised her head and pushed the hair back on either side of her face, revealing bloodshot blue eyes and skin an unhealthy hue. Griessel saw the regular features, hints of former beauty under the tracks of abuse. He knew her, he knew a version of this face, but he couldn't quite place it, not yet. She looked at Dekker, then at Griessel. Her only expression was one of total weariness. She stretched out a hand to a small table beside her and picked up a pack of cigarettes and a lighter. She struggled to open the pack and take out a cigarette.

'Mrs Barnard, I am Inspector Fransman Dekker. This is Inspector Benny Griessel. Are you ready to answer some questions?' His voice was louder than necessary, the way you would talk to someone who was a bit deaf.

She nodded slightly, with difficulty, and lit the cigarette. She inhaled the smoke deeply, as if it would give her strength.

'The deceased was your husband, Mr Adam Barnard?'

She nodded.

'What is his full name?'

'Adam Johannes.'

'Age?'

'Fifty-two.'

Dekker wrote. 'And his profession?'

She turned her tired eyes on Dekker. 'AfriSound.'

'Excuse me?'

'AfriSound. It's his.'

'AfriSound?'

'It's a record company.'

'And he owns this record company?'

She nodded.

'Your full name?'

'Alexandra.'

'Age?'

'A hundred and fifty.'

Dekker just looked at her, pen ready.

'Forty-six.'

'Profession?'

She gave an ironic snort and pushed her hair off her face again. Griessel saw confirmation of the maid's statement that she was a drinker – the trembling hands, the eyes, the characteristic colour and weathering of her face. But she reminded him of something else. He knew he had met her somewhere before.

'Excuse me?' said Dekker.

How do I know her, Griessel wondered. Where?

'I don't work.'

'Home-maker,' said Dekker and wrote that down.

She made the same little noise, loaded with meaning.

'Mrs Barnard, can you tell us about last night's events?'

She sank back slowly into her seat, put her elbow on the armrest and leaned her head on her hand. 'No.'

'Excuse me?'

'I don't know how long I can resist the temptation to say "you are excused".'

The muscles in Dekker's jaw worked as though he were grinding his teeth. Alexandra breathed in slowly and deliberately, as if steeling herself for a hard task. 'I am an alcoholic. I drink. From eleven in the morning. By six o'clock usually I am mercifully drunk. From half past eight on I don't remember much.' In that instant, perhaps because the deep, rich voice resonated somewhere in his memory, Benny Griessel remembered who she was. The word sprang to the tip of his tongue, he almost spoke it aloud, but stopped just in time: *Soetwater*. Sweet water.

She was the singer. Xandra. Lord, how old she looked.

Soetwater. The word activated a picture from memory, a television image of a woman in a tight-fitting black dress, just her and the microphone in the bright spotlight of a smoke-framed stage.

> *A small glass of sunlight,*
> *A goblet of rain*
> *A small sip of worship,*
> *A mouthful of pain*
> *Drink sweet water.*

Mid-Eighties, somewhere around there. Griessel remembered her as she was, the incredibly sensual blonde singer with a voice like Dietrich and enough self-confidence not to take herself too seriously. He had only met her through the television screen and the cover of magazines, in the days before he started drinking. She had four or five hits, he remembered *''n Donkiekar net vir twee'*,

'*Tafelbaai se Wye Draai*' and the big one, '*Soetwater*'. Fuck, she had been this huge star and look at her now.

Benny Griessel felt pity for her, also loss, and empathy.

'So you don't remember what happened last night?'

'Not much.'

'Mrs Barnard,' said Dekker stiffly and formally. 'I get the impression that your husband's death hasn't upset you very much.'

He was mistaken, thought Griessel. He was misreading her; he was too tense, too hasty.

'No, Inspector, I am not in mourning. But if you bring me a gin and dry lemon, I will do my best.'

For an instant, Dekker was uncertain, but then he squared his shoulders and said, 'Can you remember anything about last night?'

'Enough to know it wasn't me.'

'Oh.'

'Come back this afternoon. Three o'clock is a good time. My best time of the day.'

'That is not an option.'

She made a gesture as if to say that was not her problem.

'I will have to test your blood for alcohol.'

'Carry on.'

Dekker stood up. 'I'll just get the technician.'

Griessel followed him. In the sitting room Thick and Thin were busy packing up.

'Can you just take a blood sample before you leave?'

'Sure, chief,' said Jimmy.

'Fransman,' said Griessel, aware that he must tread with care. 'You know I am an alcoholic?'

'Ah,' said Arnold, the fat one, 'detectives bonding. How sweet.'

'Fuck off,' said Griessel.

'I was just about to, anyway,' said Arnold.

'You still have to do the Mercedes in the street,' said Dekker.

'That's next on the list,' and Arnold left the room with his arms full of evidence and apparatus.

'So?' Dekker asked once they were alone.

'I know how she feels, Fransman . . .'

'She feels nothing. Her husband is lying there and she feels nothing. She killed him, I'm telling you. The usual story.'

How do you explain to a non-drinker what she was feeling now? Alexandra Barnard's whole being craved alcohol. She was drowning in the terrible flood of that morning; drink was the only lifeline. Griessel knew.

'You're a good detective, Fransman. Your crime scene is perfectly managed, you do everything by the book and ten to one you're right. But if you want a confession . . . give me a chance. One-to-one isn't so intimidating . . .'

Griessel's cell phone rang. He watched Dekker while taking it out. The coloured man didn't look too keen about his suggestion.

'Griessel.'

'Benny, it's Vusi. I'm at the Metro CCTV room. Benny, there are two of them.'

'Two what?'

'Two girls, Benny. I'm standing here, watching five guys chasing two girls up Long Street.'

7

'Oh fuck,' said Benny Griessel. 'They're *chasing* the girls, you say? In Long Street?'

'The time code says it was this morning at a quarter to two. Five men, coming from Wale Street towards the church.'

'That's what, four blocks?'

'Six blocks between Wale and the church. Half a kilometre.'

'*Jissis*, Vusi, you don't do that to steal a tourist's purse.'

'I know. The other thing is, the footage isn't great, but you can see – the guys chasing them are black and white, Benny.'

'Doesn't make sense.' In this country criminals didn't work together across the colour lines.

'I know . . . I thought, maybe they are bouncers, maybe the girls made trouble in a club somewhere, but, you know . . .'

'Bouncers don't cut the throats of foreign tourists.'

'Not yet,' said Vusi, and Griessel knew what he was alluding to. The clubs and bouncers were a hotbed of organised crime, a powder keg. 'In any case, I've put a bulletin out on the other girl.'

'Good work, Vusi.'

'I don't know if it will help much,' said Ndabeni and ended the call. Griessel saw Dekker waiting impatiently for him.

'Sorry about that, Fransman. It's Vusi's case . . .'

'And this is *my* case.' His body language showed he was ready to argue.

Griessel hadn't expected this aggression, but he knew he was on thin ice. The territorial urges of detectives were strong, and he was just here as mentor.

'You're right,' he said and walked towards the door. 'But it might just help.'

Dekker stayed on the spot, frowning.

Just before Benny left the room he said: 'Wait . . .'

Griessel stopped.

'OK,' said Dekker finally. 'Talk to her.'

She could no longer hear them. Only the birdsong and cicadas and the hum of the city below. She lay in the cool shade of the rock overhang, but she was sweating as the temperature in the mountain bowl rose rapidly. She knew she could not stand up.

They would stop somewhere and try to spot her.

She considered staying there, all day, until darkness fell and she would be invisible. She could do it even though she was thirsty, even though she had last eaten the previous evening. If she could rest, if she could sleep a little, she would have new strength tonight with which to seek help.

But they knew she was there, somewhere.

They would fetch the others and they would search for her. They would backtrack on the path and investigate every possibility and if anyone came close enough, they would see her. The hollow wasn't deep enough. She knew most of them, knew their lean bodies, their energy and focus, their skill and self-confidence. She also knew they could not afford to stop looking.

She would have to move.

She looked down the stream, down the narrow stony passage that twisted downhill between *fynbos* and rocks. She must get down there, crawling carefully so as to make no sound. The mountain was a poor choice, too deserted, too open. She must get down to where there were people; she had to get help. Somewhere someone must be prepared to listen and to help.

Reluctantly she lifted her head from the rucksack, pushed it ahead of her and slid carefully after it. She couldn't drag it; it would be too noisy. She rose to a crouch, swung the rucksack slowly onto her back and clipped the buckles. Then she crawled on hands and knees over the round stones. Slowly, disturbing nothing that would make a sound.

★   ★   ★

Griessel walked into the sitting room and whispered in Tinkie Kellerman's ear. Alexandra Barnard dragged on another cigarette; her eyes followed Tinkie as she rose and left the room. Griessel closed the door behind her and without speaking went to a large Victorian cupboard with leaded glass doors on top and dark wooden doors below. He opened a top door, took out a glass and a bottle of gin and took it across to the chair closest to Alexandra.

'My name is Benny Griessel and I am an alcoholic. It's been one hundred and fifty-six days since my last drink,' he said and broke the bottle's seal. Her eyes were fixed on the transparent fluid that he carefully poured into the glass, three thick fingers deep. He held it out to her. She took it, her hands shaking badly. She drank, an intense and thirsty gulp and closed her eyes.

Griessel went back to the liquor cabinet and put the bottle away. When he sat down he said, 'I won't be able to let you have more than that.'

She nodded.

He knew how she felt at this precise moment. He knew the alcohol would flow through her body like a gentle, soothing tide, healing the wounds and quietening the voices, leaving behind a smooth, silver beach of peace. He gave her time; it took four gulps, sometimes more; you had to give your body time to let the heavenly warmth through. He realised he was staring intently at the glass at her lips, smelling the alcohol, feeling his own body straining for it. He leaned back in the chair, took a deep breath, looked at the magazines on the coffee table, *Visi* and *House & Garden*, two years out of date, but unread and just for show, until she said: 'Thank you,' and he heard the voice had lost its edge.

She put the glass down slowly, the tremor almost gone, and offered him the pack of cigarettes.

'No, thank you,' he said.

'An alcoholic who doesn't smoke?'

'I'm trying to cut down.'

She lit one for herself. The ashtray beside her was full.

'My AA sponsor is a doctor,' he said by way of explanation.

'Get another sponsor,' she said in an attempt at humour, but it didn't work; her mouth pulled in the wrong direction and then Alexandra Barnard began to weep silently, just a painful grimace, tears rolling from her eyes. She put the cigarette down and held the palms of her hands over her face. Griessel reached into his pocket and took out a handkerchief. He held it out but she didn't see it. Her shoulders shook, her head drooped and the long hair fell over her face again like a curtain. Griessel saw it was blonde and silver, a rare combination; most women dyed their hair. He wondered why she no longer cared. She had been a star, a major one. What had dragged her down to this?

He waited until her sobs subsided. 'My sponsor's name is Doctor Barkhuizen. He's seventy years old and he's an alcoholic with long hair in a plait. He said his children asked him why he smoked and he had all sorts of reasons – to help him with stress, because he enjoyed it . . .' He kept his tone of voice easy, he knew the story was unimportant, but that didn't matter, he just wanted to get a dialogue going. 'Then his daughter said in that case he wouldn't mind if she started smoking too. Then he knew he was lying to himself about the cigarettes. He stopped. So he's trying to get me to quit. I'm down to about three or four a day . . .'

Eventually she looked up and saw the handkerchief. She took it from him. 'Was it hard?' Her voice was deeper than ever. She wiped her face and blew her nose.

'The drink was. Is. Still. The smoking too.'

'I couldn't.' She crumpled the hanky and picked up the glass again and drank from it. He didn't answer. He had to give her room to talk. He knew she would.

'Your hanky's . . .'

'Keep it.'

'I'll have it washed.' She put the glass down. 'It wasn't me.'

Griessel nodded.

'We didn't talk any more,' she said and looked elsewhere in the room.

Griessel sat still.

'He comes home from the office at half past six. Then he comes to the library and stands and looks at me. To see how drunk I am. If I don't say anything then he goes and eats alone in the kitchen or he goes to his study. Or out again. Every night he puts me in bed. Every night. I have wondered, in the afternoon when I can still think, if that is why I drink. So that he would still do that one thing for me. Isn't that tragic? Doesn't it break your heart?' The tears began to fall again. They interfered with the rhythm of her speech, but she kept on. 'Sometimes, when he comes in, I try to provoke him. I was good at it . . . Last night I . . . I asked him whose turn it was now. You must understand . . . We had . . . it's a long story . . .' and for the first time her sobs were audible, as if the full weight of her history had come to bear on her. Pity welled up in Benny Griessel, because he saw again the ghost of the singer she had once been.

Eventually she stubbed out the cigarette. 'He just said "Fuck you" – that's all he ever said – and he left again. I screamed after him, "Yes, leave me here", I don't think he heard me, I was drunk . . .'

She blew her nose into the hanky again. 'That's all. That's all I know. He didn't put me to bed, he left me there and this morning, he was lying there . . .' She picked up the glass.

'The last words he said to me. "Fuck you".' More tears.

She drained the last bit of alcohol from the glass and looked at Griessel with intense focus. 'Do you think it could have been me that shot him?'

The plump girl behind the reception desk of the Cat & Moose Youth Hostel and Backpackers Inn looked at the photograph the constable was holding out and asked:

'Why does she look so funny?'

'Because she's dead.'

'Oh, my God.' She put two and two together and asked: 'Was she the one this morning at the church here?'

'Yes. Do you recognise her?'

'Oh, my God, yes. They came in yesterday, two American girls. Wait . . .' The plump girl opened the register and ran her finger down the column. 'Here they are, Rachel Anderson and Erin Russel, they are from . . .' she bent down to read the small writing of the addresses. 'West Lafayette, Indiana. Oh, my God. Who killed her?'

'We don't know yet. Is this one Anderson?'

'I don't know.'

'And the other one, do you know where she is?'

'No, I work days, I . . . Let's see, they are in room sixteen.' She shut the register and went ahead down the passage saying: 'Oh, my God.'

Through careful questioning he got information about the firearm from her. It was her husband's.

Adam Barnard kept it locked up in a safe in the room. He kept the key with him, probably afraid she would do something foolish with it in her drunken state. She said she had no idea how it landed up on the floor beside her. Maybe she did shoot him, she said; she had reason enough, enough anger and self-pity and hate. There were times she had wished him dead, but her true fantasy was to kill herself and then watch him. Watch him coming home at half past six, climbing the stairs and finding her dead. Watch him kneeling beside her body and begging forgiveness, weeping and broken. But, she said with irony, the two parts would never gel. You can't watch anything when you're dead.

Then she just sat there. Eventually he whispered '*Soetwater*' but she didn't respond; she hid behind her hair for an eternity until she slowly held out the glass to him and he knew he would have to pour another if he wanted to hear the whole story.

08:13–09:03

8

Benny Griessel listened to Alexandra Barnard's story.

'Alexa. Nobody calls me Alexandra or Xandra.'

Now, just as he was about to open the front door of Number 47 Brownlow Street to go and find Dekker, he felt a peculiar emotion pressing on his heart, a weightlessness in his head, a sort of separation from reality, as though he stood back a few millimetres from everything, a second or two out of step with the world.

So it took him a while to register that outside was chaos. The street, so peaceful when he arrived, was a mass of journalists and the inquisitive: a flock of photographers, a herd of reporters, a camera team from e.tv and the growing crowd of spectators their presence had attracted. The noise washed over Griessel, loud waves of sound that he could feel in his body, along with the knowledge that he had listened so acutely to Alexa's story that he had been oblivious to all this.

On the veranda a tense Dekker was exchanging fiery words with a bald man, both their voices raised in argument.

'Not before I've seen her,' said the man with a superior attitude and aggressive body language. His head was completely shaven, he was tall and sinewy, with large fleshy ears and one round silver earring. Black shirt, black trousers and the black basketball shoes that teenagers wear, although he seemed to be in his late forties. A middle-aged Zorro. His prominent Adam's apple bobbed up and down in time with his words. Dekker spotted Griessel. 'He insists on seeing her,' said Dekker, still tense. The man ignored Griessel. He snapped open a black leather holder at his belt and brought out a small black cell phone. 'I'm calling my lawyer; this behaviour is totally unacceptable.' He began to press keys on the phone. 'She's not a well woman.'

'He's the partner of the deceased. Willie Mouton,' said Dekker.

'Mr Mouton,' said Griessel reasonably. His voice sounded unfamiliar to his own ear.

'Fuck off,' said Mouton, 'I'm on the phone.' His voice had the penetration and tone of an industrial meat saw.

'Mr Mouton, I won't allow you to talk to a police officer like that,' Dekker said on a rising note. 'And if you wish to make personal calls, you will do it in the street . . .'

'It's a free country as far as I know.'

'. . . and not on my crime scene.'

'Your crime scene? Who the fuck do you think you are?' Then, into the phone:

'Sorry. Can I speak to Regardt, please . . . ?'

Dekker advanced in a threatening way, his temper beginning to get the better of him.

'Regardt, this is Willie, I'm standing on Adam's veranda with the Gestapo . . .'

Griessel put a hand on Dekker's arm. 'There are cameras, Fransman.'

'I won't hit him,' said Dekker and jerked Mouton roughly off the veranda and pushed him towards the garden gate. Cameras flashed and clicked.

'They're assaulting me, Regardt,' said Mouton with somewhat less confidence.

'Morning, Nikita,' said Prof Phil Pagel, the state pathologist, from beyond the gate. He was amused.

'Morning, Prof,' said Benny, watching Dekker push Mouton through the gate onto the pavement. He told the uniform: 'Don't let him through here.'

'I'll sue your arse,' said Mouton. 'Regardt, I want you to sue their fucking arses. I want you here with a fucking interdict. Alexa's in there and God knows what these storm troopers are doing with her . . .' His voice was deliberately loud enough for Dekker and the media to hear.

Pagel squeezed past Zorro and went up the stairs with his black case in hand. 'What a piece of work is man,' he said.

'Prof?' queried Griessel, and suddenly the sense of disconnectedness was gone; he was back in the present, head clear.

Pagel shook his hand. 'Hamlet. To Rosencrantz and Guildenstern. Just before he calls man "a quintessence of dust". I was at the show last night. I highly recommend it. Busy morning, Nikita?'

Pagel had been calling him 'Nikita' for the past twelve years. The first time he had met Griessel he had said: 'I am sure that's how the young Khrushchev looked'. Griessel had to think hard who Khrushchev was. Pagel was flamboyantly dressed, as usual – tall, fit and exceptionally handsome for his fifty-something years. There were some who said he looked like the star of one of the television soapies that Griessel had never watched.

'Things are hectic, as usual, Prof.'

'I understand you are mentoring the new generation of law enforcers, Nikita.'

'As you can see, Prof, I'm brilliant at my job,' Griessel grinned. Dekker came back up the veranda steps. 'Have you met Fransman yet?'

'Indeed, I have had the privilege. Inspector Dekker, I admire your forcefulness.'

Dekker had lost none of his tension. 'Morning, Prof.'

'Rumour has it that Adam Barnard is the victim?'

They both nodded, in synch.

'Take arms against a sea of troubles,' said Pagel.

The detectives looked at him without comprehension.

'I am abusing *Hamlet* to say that this means big trouble, gentlemen.'

'Aah,' said the detectives. They understood.

In the library they stood talking while Pagel knelt beside the body and opened his doctor's bag.

'It wasn't her, Fransman,' said Griessel.

'Are you one hundred per cent certain?'

Griessel shrugged. Nobody could be a hundred per cent certain. 'It's not just what she says, Fransman. It's how it fits in with the scene . . .'

'She could have hired someone.'

Griessel had to concede that that argument had merit. Women hiring others to get rid of their husbands was the latest national sport. But he shook his head. 'I doubt it. You don't hire people to make it look like you did it.'

'Anything is possible in this country,' said Dekker.

'Amen,' said Pagel.

'Prof, the "sea of troubles" . . . Did you know Barnard?' Griessel asked.

'A little, Nikita. Mostly hearsay.'

'What's his story?' asked Dekker.

'Music,' said Pagel. 'And women.'

'That's what his wife says too,' said Griessel.

'As if she hasn't suffered enough,' said Pagel.

'What do you mean, Prof?' Dekker asked.

'You know she was a huge star?'

'No, really?' Stunned.

Pagel didn't look up while he spoke. His hands were deftly handling instruments and the body. 'Barnard "discovered" her, though I have never been very comfortable with that expression. But let me confess my ignorance, gentlemen. As you know, my real love is the classics. I know he was a lawyer who became involved with the pop music industry. Xandra was his first star . . .'

'Xandra?'

'That was her stage name,' said Griessel.

'She was a singer?'

'Indeed. A very good one too,' said Pagel.

'How long ago was this, Prof?'

'Fifteen, twenty years?'

'Never heard of her.' Dekker shook his head.

'She disappeared off the scene. Rather suddenly.'

'She caught him with someone else,' said Griessel. 'That's when she started drinking.'

'That was the rumour. Gentlemen, unofficially and unconfirmed: I estimate the time of death at . . .' Pagel checked his watch. '. . . between two and three this morning. As you have surely deduced, the cause of death is two shots by a small-calibre firearm. The position of the wounds and small amount of propellant residue indicates a shooting distance of two to four metres . . . and a reasonably good shot: the wounds are less than three centimetres apart.'

'And he wasn't shot here,' said Dekker.

'Indeed.'

'Only two wounds?' asked Griessel.

The pathologist nodded.

'There were three rounds fired by his pistol . . .'

'Prof,' said Dekker, 'let's say she is an alcoholic. Say she was drunk last night. I had blood drawn, but will it help, eight or ten hours after the fact?'

'Ah, Fransman, nowadays we have ethyl glucuronide. It can track the residue of alcohol levels up to thirty-six hours afterwards. With a urine sample up to five days after intake.'

Dekker nodded, satisfied.

'But I must throw my weight behind Nikita's theory. I don't believe it was her.'

'How so, Prof?'

'Look at him, Fransman. He must be about one point nine metres tall. He's a little overweight; I estimate on the wrong side of a hundred and ten kilograms. You and I would battle to get his body up those stairs – and we are sober.' Pagel began to pack away his apparatus. 'Let's get him to the mortuary; I can't do much more.'

'Somebody went to a lot of trouble to get him here,' said Dekker.

'And therein lies the rub,' said Pagel.

'Women . . .' Dekker speculated.

Pagel stood up. 'Don't write off the Afrikaans music industry as a potential source of conflict, Fransman.'

'Prof?'

'Do you follow the popular press, Fransman?'

Dekker shrugged.

'Ah, the life of the law enforcer – all work and no time to read the Sunday papers. There's money in the Afrikaans music industry, Fransman. Big money. But that's just the ears of the hippo, the tip of the iceberg. The intrigues are legion. Scandals like divorce, sexual harassment, paedophilia . . . More long knives and apparent back-stabbing than in *Julius Caesar*. They fight over everything – back tracks, contracts, artistic credits, royalties, who is permitted to make a musical about which historical personality, who deserves what place in musical history . . .'

'But why, Prof?' Griessel asked, deeply disappointed.

'People are people, Nikita. If there is wealth and fame at stake . . . It's the usual game: cliques and camps, big egos, artistic temperaments, sensitive feelings, hate, jealousy, envy; there are people who haven't spoken to each other for years, new enmities . . . the list is endless. Our Adam was in the thick of things. Would it be enough to inspire murder? As Fransman correctly pointed out, in this country, anything is possible.'

Jimmy and Arnold from Forensics came through the door. 'Oh, there's Prof, morning, Prof,' said Arnold, the fat one.

'Rosencrantz and Guildenstern are here. Morning, gentlemen.'

'Prof, can we ask you something?'

'Of course.'

'Prof, the thing is . . .' said Arnold.

'Women . . .' said Jimmy.

'Why are their breasts so big, Prof?'

'I mean, look at the animals . . .'

'Much smaller, Prof . . .'

'*Jissis*,' said Fransman Dekker.

'I say it's revolution,' said Arnold.

'Evolution, you ape,' said Jimmy.

'Whatever,' said Arnold.

Pagel looked at them with the goodwill of a patient parent. 'Interesting question, colleagues. But we will have to continue this conversation elsewhere. Come and see me in Salt River.'

'We're not mortuary kind of guys, Prof . . .'

Dekker's cell phone rang. He checked the screen. 'It's Cloete,' he said.

'And let the kettle to the trumpet speak,' said Pagel on the way to the door, because Cloete was the SAPS media liaison officer. 'Goodbye, colleagues.'

They said goodbye and listened to Fransman Dekker give Cloete the relevant infamous details.

Griessel shook his head. Something big was brewing. Just a look outside would tell you that. His own phone rang. He answered: 'Griessel.'

'Benny,' said Vusi Ndabeni, 'I think you should come.'

9

Rachel Anderson crept down the gully. It deepened as she progressed, the sides steep, rough, impassable. They hemmed her in, but offered shelter enough for her to stand. They would have difficulty seeing her. The slope became steeper, the terrain more rugged. It was just after eight, and hot. She clambered down rocks clutching the roots of trees, her throat parched, her knees threatening to give in. She had to find water, she had to get something to eat, she had to keep moving.

Then she saw the path leading up to the right, and steps carved out of the rock and earth. She stared. She had no idea what awaited her up there.

Alexa Barnard watched them carry her husband's body past the door and her face twisted with emotion.

Tinkie Kellerman got up and came across to sit on the couch beside her. She put a soft hand on her arm. Alexa felt an overwhelming urge to be held by this slender policewoman. But she just sat there, moving her arms to grip her own shoulders in a desperate self-embrace. She hung her head and watched the tears drip onto the white material of her dressing-gown sleeve, disappearing as if they had never existed.

Rachel Anderson climbed to just short of the top and peered over the edge of the gully with a thudding heart. Only the mountain. And silence. Another step up and, suddenly realising they could see her from behind, she turned in fright, but there was no one. The last two steps, she was careful. To her left were the roofs of houses, the highest row on the mountain. Ahead was a path running along the back of the houses, with trees offering shade and cover. To the right was the steep slope of the mountain, then the mountain itself.

She looked back once, then stepped hastily onto the path, head down.

Griessel drove back to Long Street in much lighter traffic. Vusi had said he should come to the Cat & Moose.

'What's going on?' he had asked.

'I'll tell you when you get here.' He had the tone of someone speaking in the presence of others.

But Griessel wasn't thinking about that. He sat in his police car and thought of Alexa Barnard. About her voice and her story, about the beauty hidden beneath twenty years of alcohol abuse. He mused on how the mind brought up the memory of the younger, lovelier image and projected it onto the fabric of her current face so that the two were seen together – the past and the present, so far removed and so inseparable. He thought of the intensity with which she had drunk the gin and knew it was a dangerous thing to see, *that* healing. It had unravelled his own desire, so that it dangled inside him like a thousand loose wires. The voice in his mind was saying there was a bottle store right here in Kloof Street, where all the wires could be reconnected, the current restored. The electricity of life would flow strongly once again.

'God,' said Benny to himself and turned deliberately into Bree Street, away from temptation.

When the tears stopped, Tinkie Kellerman said, 'Come, you'll feel better when you've had a bath.'

Alexa agreed and got up. She was a bit unsteady on her feet, so the policewoman guided her up the stairs, through the library and down the passage to the bedroom door.

'I think you should wait here.'

'I can't,' said Tinkie in a voice full of compassion.

Alexa stood still for a second. Then the meaning penetrated. They were afraid she would do something. To herself. And she knew the possibility was real. But first she must get to the liquor, the four centimetres of gin in the bottle underneath her underwear.

'I won't do anything.'

Tinkie Kellerman just looked at her with big, sympathetic eyes.

Alexa walked into the bedroom. 'Just stay out of the bathroom.'

She would take the bottle out of the cupboard along with her clothes. Her body would screen it.

'Sit there,' she nodded towards the chair in front of the dressing table.

The knocking wasn't going to stop. Fransman Dekker went to open the door. Willie Mouton, the baldheaded, black-clad Zorro, stood on the veranda along with an alter ego – an equally lean man, but with a full head of dark hair, painstakingly combed into a side parting. He had the appearance of an undertaker, complete with long sombre face, all-seeing eyes, charcoal suit and tie. 'My lawyer is here. I'm ready for you now.'

'You're ready for me?' Dekker's temper flared at the way the white man talked down to him but, out there in the street, lenses were trained on them, spectators and the press scrummed against the fence.

'Regardt Groenewald,' the lawyer said apologetically and put out a cautious hand. It was a peace offering, forcing Dekker to change gear.

He shook the slim, uncertain hand. 'Dekker,' he said, and looked the lawyer up and down. He had expected a Doberman, not this basset hound.

'He just means that we are ready to talk,' said Groenewald.

'Where is Alexa?' Mouton asked and looked past Dekker into the house. Groenewald moved his flaccid hand to Mouton's arm, as though to restrain him.

'She is being looked after.'

'By whom?'

'By an officer of Social Services.'

'I want to see her.' A white man's command, but once again the lawyer defused the situation.

'Steady, Willie.'

'That is not an option now,' said Dekker.

Mouton looked reproachfully at his lawyer. 'He can't do that, Regardt.'

Groenewald sighed. 'I'm sure they explained to Alexa what her rights are, Willie.' He spoke apologetically, slowly and deliberately.

'But she's a sick woman.'

'Mrs Barnard chose to talk without a lawyer present.'

'But she's not compis mentos,' said Mouton.

'Compos mentis,' Groenewald corrected him patiently.

'Mrs Barnard is not a suspect in the case at this stage,' said Dekker.

'That's not what Adam's maid said.'

'As far as I know, the domestic worker is not in police service.'

'You see, Regardt. That's what they're like. Smartass. When I've just lost my friend and colleague . . .'

'Willie, Mr Dekker, let's all keep calm . . .'

'I *am* calm, Regardt.'

'My client has information connected to the case,' said Groenewald.

'What sort of information?'

'Relevant information. But we can't . . .'

'Then it is your duty to pass it on to us.'

'Not if you get smartass with me.'

'Mr Mouton, you have no choice. Withholding evidence . . .'

'Please, gentlemen . . .' Groenewald begged. Then very cautiously: 'Perhaps we could talk inside?'

Dekker hesitated.

'My client has a strong suspicion of who murdered Adam Barnard.'

'But I don't want to slander,' said Mouton.

'Willie, under the circumstances, slander doesn't enter into it.'

'You know who shot Adam Barnard?'

'My client has no proof, but feels it is his civil duty to share the available information with the law.'

Fransman Dekker looked at the crowd, then at Groenewald and Mouton. 'I think you should come in.'

Rachel Anderson walked along the footpath on the contour of the mountain, hurrying more now as it was level ground and she had left the shelter of the pine trees behind. There were only the houses below, large properties with swimming pools, densely grown gardens and high walls. Beyond them lay the city and the long sweep of Table Bay, a postcard of bright blue sea and a cluster of high-rise buildings squatting together, as if seeking solidarity from their closeness.

It was a lie, all this beauty, she thought. A false front. She and Erin had allowed themselves to be misled by it.

Ahead the path curved to the right, skirting a reservoir. The high earthen bank would conceal her for a few hundred metres.

Behind the bathroom door Alexa Barnard took off her dressing gown and night clothes and then she reached for the bottle she had hidden under her clean clothing. She unscrewed the cap with a trembling hand. There wasn't much in the bottle. She brought it to her lips and drank. The movement was echoed in the tall mirror and she watched it involuntarily. The naked body, its femininity so wasted, her long greasy hair in strings around her face, underarm stubble, mouth open, bottle lifted high in a desperate attempt to catch the last drops. She was startled by this demon, the way the mirror image focused so completely on the bottle.

Who was this person standing there?

She turned away, having drained the bottle, but found no relief. She placed it on the floor and leaned against the wall with an outstretched arm.

Was it really her standing there?

'*Soetwater*,' the sympathetic detective with the unusual features and unruly hair had said. 'How did you come to this?' was what he meant. She had told him, but now, in front of this sudden reflection, the explanation was insufficient.

She turned back and looked at the reflected woman again. The tall body looked so defenceless. Legs, hips, belly with a small bulge, the firm breasts, long nipples, the skin of the neck no longer smoothly taut. A face, worn, used, drunk up.

It was her. *Her* body, *her* face.

God.

'How *did* you come to this?' There was genuine curiosity in her own question. She spun away and stepped into the shower. This far, but she would go no further. She could not.

Mechanically she opened the taps.

Adam was dead. What was she going to do? Tonight? Tomorrow?

The fear that welled up inside her was huge, so that she had to press her palms against the tiles to remain standing. She stood like that a while, the water scalding her, but she did not feel it. The pills, that's what she must get, the sleeping pills, so she could drift away, away from that woman in the mirror, away from the destructive process, the thirst, and the darkness ahead.

The pills were in the room with Tinkie Kellerman.

She would have to do it with something else. Here, in the bathroom. She stepped out of the shower with urgency, pulled open the bathroom cabinet with shaking hands. Too hasty, she knocked bottles over, nothing of use. She picked up her razor, looked at its uselessness, threw it away against the door, scratched around in the cabinet. There was nothing, nothing . . .

'Mrs Barnard?' called the voice from the other side of the door.

Alexa turned and locked the door. 'Leave me alone.' It wasn't even her voice.

'Ma'am, please . . .'

She spotted the gin bottle. She grabbed the neck and struck it against the wall. A shard of glass hit her on the forehead. She examined the sharp glass blade that remained in her hand. She lifted her left arm and sliced violently, deep and desperately, from the palm to the elbow. The blood was a fountain. She sliced again.

In the sitting room Mouton and Groenewald sat side by side on the couch. Dekker was opposite them.

'I don't have proof,' said Mouton.

'Just tell him what happened, Willie.'

They were like those two guys in the old black-and-white films, thought Dekker.

What were their names?

'This guy burst into my office and said he was going to kill Adam . . .'

'And who is this guy?'

Mouton referred to his lawyer. 'Are you sure it's not slander, Regardt?'

'I'm sure.'

'But what if I have to give evidence?'

'Willie, slander will not be an issue.'

'It can ruin their career, Regardt. I mean, what if it isn't him?'

'Willie, you have no choice.'

Laurel and Hardy, Dekker recalled. Two white comedians. 'Mr Mouton, who was it?' he asked.

He drew a deep breath, Adam's apple bobbing like a cock's. 'It was Josh Geyser,' he said, and sat back as though he had unleashed the whirlwind.

'Who?'

'The gospel singer,' said Mouton impatiently. 'Josh and Melinda.'

'Never heard of them.'

'Josh and Melinda? Everyone knows them. Sixty thousand of the new CD, four thousand in one day alone, when they were on the featured music stars on radio RSG. They're big.'

'And why would Josh Geyser want to kill Adam Barnard?'

Mouton leaned forward conspiratorially and suddenly he was speaking very quietly:

'Because Adam nailed Melinda in his office.'

'Nailed?'

'You know . . . He had sex with her.'

'In Barnard's office?'

'That's right.'

'And Geyser caught them?'

'No. Melinda confessed.'

'To Josh?'

'No. Higher up. But Josh was with her when she prayed.'

Fransman Dekker snorted between laughter and disbelief. 'Mr Mouton, you can't be serious.'

'I am!' Indignant. 'Do you think I would make jokes at a time like this?'

Dekker shook his head.

'Yesterday afternoon Josh Geyser came rushing in at a hell of a speed past Natasha and just about broke my office door down. He said he was looking for Adam and I said what for and he said he was going to kill him, because he raped Melinda. So I said, "How can you say a thing like that, Josh?" and he said Melinda said so. So I said, "What did she say?", and he said she'd prayed and confessed to the Big Sin in Adam's office, on the desk, she said it was the devil, but he, Josh, knew about Adam's ways. And he was going to beat him to death. He was crazy, he nearly grabbed hold of me, when I said it didn't sound like rape. He's a huge *ou*, he was a Gladiator before he was saved . . .' Mouton dropped his voice again: 'The story is, he can't . . . you know . . . get it up, because of the steroids.'

'That's not relevant, Willie,' said Groenewald.

'It gives him motive,' said Mouton.

'No, no . . .' said the lawyer.

'Beat him to death, you say?' asked Dekker. 'That's what he said?'

'He also said he was going to kill him . . . no, he was going to fucking kill him, he was going to cut off his balls and hang them over the platinum CD in his sitting room.'

'Adam's ways. What "ways" was Geyser referring to?'

'Adam is . . .' Mouton hesitated. 'I can't believe Adam is dead.' He sat back and rubbed his shaven head. 'He was my friend. My partner. We've come a long way together . . . I told him one day someone would . . .'

Silence descended. Mouton wiped the back of his hand over his eyes. 'Sorry,' he said. 'This is hard for me . . .'

The lawyer reached out a long, thin hand to his client. 'That's understandable, Willie . . .'

'He was this great presence . . .'

Dekker heard the high and urgent voice of Tinkie Kellerman calling: 'Fransman!'

He stood up quickly and strode towards the door.

'Fransman!'

'I'm here,' he called. He saw Kellerman at the top of the stairs.

'Come and help,' she said. 'Hurry.'

A hundred metres beyond the reservoir the path turned left, down the mountain, towards the city, in a wide and shallow ravine. Rachel Anderson walked through pine trees, following the path around huge boulders. She saw a stone wall ahead with a gap in the middle and beyond it to the right an almost completed house behind an enormous oak tree. A cool, deep pool of shade, a place of rest, but her first thought was for a tap to quench her raging thirst.

She went past the garage, eyes searching, towards the street. A sawn-up pine tree filled the doorway of the double garage, stacked in tidy piles. She spotted the tap beside the back door of the house, prayed it was connected, walked faster, stooped and turned it. The silvery water gushed out, hot for a few seconds, then suddenly cool. She dropped down on one knee, turned back the tap a bit, and drank, directly from the spout.

Fransman Dekker had forced enough doors to know you don't use your shoulder. He took a step back and kicked. The door splintered, but stayed shut. He kicked again, and again before it broke, swinging open only about forty centimetres. It was enough to see the blood.

'Oh, dear heaven,' said Tinkie Kellerman behind him.

'What?' said Willie Mouton, trying to get past her.

'Sir, you can't . . .'

Dekker was already in the bathroom. He saw Alexa Barnard lying on the floor. He stepped in the blood and turned her naked body over. Her eyes were open, but unfocused.

'Ambulance,' he ordered Tinkie. 'Now.'

He bent to examine the damage. Her left wrist was deeply cut, at least three times.

The blood still flowed from it. He grabbed a garment off the floor and began to bind it around the wounds, as tightly as he could.

Alexa spoke, the words barely audible.

'Ma'am?' he said.

'The other arm,' she whispered.

'I'm sorry?'

'Cut the other arm, please,' and with a weary hand she held out the broken bottle to him.

She quenched her thirst and washed the blood from her hands, arms and face. Then she stood up, closed the tap and took a deep breath. The city was just below her ... She walked around the corner of the house, less anxious now, fear mellowed by the drink of water.

Then she saw them, only twenty paces away down the street. She froze, breath caught in her throat. They were standing with their backs to her, side by side. She knew them. She was turned to stone. Her heart beat thunderously in her ears.

They were looking down the sloping street.

The garage. The logs. She had to get in there. It was five paces behind her. She was too terrified to take her eyes off them. She shuffled backwards, afraid she would step on something. They must not look around. She reached the wall of the garage. One more step. Then one of them began to turn. The one who had started it all. The one who had bent over Erin with the knife.

In the breakfast room of the Cat & Moose Youth Hostel and Backpackers Inn, nineteen-year-old Oliver 'Ollie' Sands sat with his head in his hands. A bit overweight, he had red hair and pale skin that had seen too much sun. His angular black-rimmed glasses lay on the table in front of him. Opposite him, close to the door, sat Inspectors Vusumuzi Ndabeni and Benny Griessel.

'Mr Sands has identified the victim as Miss Erin Russel,' said Vusi, with the photo of the victim and his notebook in front of him.

'Jeez,' said Sands, shaking his head behind his hands.

'He's been travelling through Africa with Miss Russel and her friend, Rachel Anderson. He does not know where Miss Anderson is. The last time he saw them was last night in Van Hunks, the nightclub. In Castle Street.' Vusi looked to Sands for confirmation.

'Jeez,' the young man repeated, lowering his hands and pulling his glasses closer. Griessel could see his eyes were red.

'Mr Sands, you arrived in Cape Town yesterday?'

'Yes, sir. From Namibia.' The accent was unmistakably American, the voice quavering, emotional. Sands placed the glasses on his nose and blinked, as if seeing Vusi for the first time.

'Just the three of you?' Griessel asked.

'No, sir. There were twenty-one of us. Twenty-three actually, when we left Nairobi on the tour. But a guy and a girl from the Netherlands pulled out in Dar. They . . . didn't like it.'

'A tour?' Griessel asked.

'The African Adventure Tour. Overland, by truck.'

'And you and the two girls were together?'

'No, sir, I met them in Nairobi. They're from Indiana; I'm from Phoenix, Arizona.'

'But you were with the girls last night?' Vusi asked.

'A whole bunch of us went to the club.'

'How many?'

'I don't . . . Maybe ten, I'm not sure.'

'But the two girls were part of the group?'

'Yes, sir.'

'What happened at the club?'

'We had a good time. You know . . .' Sands took off his glasses again, and rubbed a hand over his eyes '. . . we had a few drinks, we danced a little . . .' He replaced his glasses.

The gesture made Griessel suspicious.

'At what time did you leave?' Vusi asked.

'I . . . I was a little tired. I came back at about eleven.'

'And the girls?'

'I don't know, sir.'

'They were still at the club when you left?'

'Yes, sir.'

'So, the last time you saw Miss Russel alive was at the club.'

Sands's face twisted. He just nodded, as though not trusting his voice.

'And they were drinking and dancing?'

'Yes, sir.'

'They were still with the group?'

'Yes.'

'Could you give us the names of the people they were with?'

'I guess . . . Jason was there. And Steven, Sven, Kathy . . .'

'Do you know their surnames?' Vusi pulled his notebook closer.

'Not all of them. It's Jason Dicklurk, and Steven Cheatsinger . . .'

'Could you spell that for us?'

'Well Jason, you know. J.A.S.O.N. And . . . I'm not sure about spelling his surname . . . Can I . . .'

'Is it Steven with a P.H. Or a V?' Vusi's pen hovered over his notes.

'I don't know.'

'Steven's surname?'

'Wait . . . Is it OK if I get the list? All the names are there, the guides and everybody.'

'Please do.'

Sands stood up and walked towards the door. He stopped. 'I have pics. Of Rachel and Erin.'

'Photographs?'

'Yes.'

'Could you get them?'

'They're on my camera, but I can show you . . .'

'That would be good.'

Ollie Sands walked out through the door.

'If we can get a photo of the missing girl . . .' said Vusi.

'He's hiding something,' said Griessel. 'Something to do with last night.'

'Do you think so, Benny?'

'Just now, when he took off his glasses . . . he started lying.'

'He was crying before you came. Maybe it was . . .'

'He's hiding something, Vusi. People who wear specs . . . they have a way . . . There is . . .' Griessel hesitated. He had learned with Dekker to put his mentoring boots down carefully. 'Vusi, you learn things over the years, with interrogation . . .'

'You know I want to learn, Benny.'

Griessel got up. 'Come and sit here, Vusi. The person you are interviewing must always have his back to the door.' He shifted the chairs around and sat on one. Vusi sat down next to him. 'You'll notice if they have something to hide . . . Let's say he was sitting here, at an angle, then he'd have his legs pointing towards the door. Then the signs won't be so obvious. But with the door behind him, he feels trapped. The signs become clearer, he will sweat, keep pulling at his collar, a leg or foot will jump, he will put a hand over his eyes or, if he wears glasses, he will take them off. This one did that when he started talking about coming back early last night.'

Ndabeni had hung on every word. 'Thanks, Benny. I'll ask him about that.'

'Is he the only one here, from the group?'

'Yes. Some of them flew home last night. The rest are somewhere else, a wine tour. Or up the mountain.'

'And this one was here?'

'He was still in bed.'

'Now why would that be?'

'Good question.'

'Do you know how to watch his eyes, Vusi?'

The black detective shook his head.

'First you must get him to write something down, so you know whether he is left- or right-handed. Then you look for eye movement when he answers . . .'

Griessel's cell phone rang and he saw the name on the screen. *AFRIKA*. 'It's the Commissioner,' he said before answering. Vusi raised his eyebrows.

He took the call, 'Griessel.'

'Benny, what the hell is going on?' the District Commissioner: Detective Services and Criminal Intelligence asked, so loudly that even Vusi could hear it.

'Sir?'

'Some lawyer is phoning me, Groenewoud or Groenewald or something, lecturing me like a missionary saying you all made a big cock-up with Adrian Barnard's wife . . .'

'Adam Bar—'

'I don't give a damn,' said John Afrika. 'Now the woman has committed suicide because you intimidated her and she has nothing to do with the whole bloody thing . . .'

A hand clenched his heart. 'She's dead?'

'No, she's not bloody dead, but you are there to mentor, Benny, that's why I brought you in. Just imagine what the press are going to make of this, I hear Barnard is a bloody celebrity . . .'

'Sir, nobody—'

'Meet me at the hospital, you and Fransman Dekker. He can't curb his bloody ambition and if I try to cover for him they say it's because he's a fucking *hotnot* just like me, and I only look after my own people, where the fuck are you, anyway?'

'With Vusi, Commissioner. The church murder . . .'

'And now I hear that's an American tourist, *jissis*, Benny, only on a Tuesday. At the hospital, I'll meet you there, five minutes.' The line went dead. Benny considered the fact that he had given Alexa Barnard the alcohol and that the Commissioner had not said which hospital and then Oliver 'Ollie' Sands walked in with the camera, crying as he stared at the screen on the back. He held it up so that the detectives could see. As Benny Griessel looked he felt that ghostly hand squeeze his heart, that familiar oppression. Rachel Anderson and Erin Russel stood laughing, lovely and carefree, with Kilimanjaro in the background. Young and effervescent, just like his daughter Carla, part of the Great Adventure.

Rachel Anderson lay on her belly behind the heap of pine logs in the cool of the garage and tried to control her breathing.

She thought they must have seen her, because she heard footsteps and voices approaching.

'. . . more people,' said one of them.

'Maybe. But if the Big Guy comes through, we'll have more than enough.'

She knew their voices.

They stopped right in front of the garage.

'I just hope to God she's still out there.'

'Fucking mountain. It's huge. But if she moves, Barry will spot her. And our cops will have the streets covered, we'll get the bitch. I'm telling you, sooner or later we'll get her and this whole fuck-up will go away.'

She lay listening to the voices and footsteps that faded away uphill. *And our cops will have the streets covered.* These were the words that echoed in her mind, that killed the last vestige of hope.

Benny Griessel said in Afrikaans: 'He will talk, Vusi. Just give him a fright. Tell him you'll lock him up. Take him down to the cells, even. I have to go.'

'OK, Benny.' So Griessel left and, outside, on the way to his car, he phoned Dekker.

'Is she still alive, Fransman?'

'Yes, she's alive. Tinkie was with her all the time, but she fucked off into the bathroom and locked the door and cut her wrists with a broken gin bottle . . .'

The one he had poured her drinks from? How did she get it into the bathroom?

'Is she going to make it?'

'I think so. We were quick. She lost a lot of blood, but she should be all right.'

'Where are you?'

'City Park. Did the Commissioner call you?'

'He's the *moer in.*'

'Benny, it's nobody's fault. It's that fucking Mouton who made a huge scene. When he saw the blood, he just lost it . . .'

'We can handle it, Fransman. I'll be there now.' He climbed into his car and wondered if he had missed something in his conversation with Alexa Barnard. Had there been a sign?

Inspector Vusi Ndabeni said: 'I'm your friend. You can tell me anything,' and he saw Oliver Sands reach for his glasses and take them off.

'I know.' Sands began cleaning the glasses on his T-shirt, now with his back to the door.

'So what really happened last night?' Vusi watched for the signs Benny had talked about.

'I told you,' the voice was too controlled.

Vusi allowed the silence to stretch out. He stared unblinking at Sands, but the eyes evaded him. He waited until Sands put the glasses back on, then he leaned forward. 'I don't think you've told me everything.'

'I did, honest to God.' Again the hands went to the glasses and adjusted them. Benny had told him to give Sands a fright. He didn't know if he could be convincing. He took a set of handcuffs out of his jacket pocket and put them on the table.

'Police cells are not nice places.'

Sands stared at the handcuffs. 'Please,' he said.

'I want to help you.'

'You can't.'

'Why?'

'Jeez . . .'

'Mr Sands, please stand up and put your hands behind your back.'

'Oh, God,' said Oliver Sands and stood up slowly.

'Are you going to talk to me?'

Sands looked at Vusi and his whole body shivered once and he slowly sat down again.

'Yes.'

09:04–10:09

I I

Griessel drove down Loop Street towards the harbour. He should have taken Bree Street as there was heavy traffic, slow vehicles, and pedestrians just wandering across the road, all the local chancers. And the Gauteng tourists. They were unmistakable. This was the second wave: the first were the December school holiday brigade, smug motherfuckers who thought they were God's gift to Cape Town. They were usually families with moody, cell-phone-obsessed teenagers, Moms fiercely shopping, Dads unfamiliar with the streets, getting in everyone's way. The second wave would arrive in January, the arrogant fat cats who had stayed behind to make their Christmas killing in Sandton and then come here for their annual spending frenzy.

He saw small groups of foreign tourists, Europeans, so painfully law-abiding, only crossing the road at the traffic lights, noses stuck in guidebooks, wanting to photograph everything. He stopped with the lights showing red as far ahead as he could see. Why couldn't the fucking Metro Police get off their backsides and synchronise them?

That reminded him he ought to call the Field Marshal. Oerson. Perhaps they had found something. No, better to remind Vusi. This was Vusi's case. He drummed his fingers impatiently on the steering wheel, realised it was the rhythm of '*Soetwater*' and could no longer ignore his conscience. Alexa Barnard. He should have seen it coming.

She had told him she had a suicide fantasy. 'I wanted Adam to come home at half past six and climb the stairs and find me dead. Then he would kneel down beside me and say, "You're the only one I ever loved." But being dead, of course, I would never see Adam plead with me; those dreams could never be reconciled.'

He shook his head. How the hell could he have missed that? That's what happened when you got up too early, an hour earlier than usual. He still wasn't quite with it today. And he had given her alcohol as well. Benny the great mentor who 'had forgotten more than others had to learn.'

He sought some excuse in the way she had said it, the story she went on to tell. It had distracted him, created a false impression of a woman who was somehow still under control. She had manipulated him. When he whispered '*Soetwater*', and she held her glass out for more, a fee for her story.

He had fixated on her thirst; that was the real problem. He had poured her two tots and she had pushed the hair back from her face and said, 'I was such a terribly insecure little thing.' And then her history had led his thoughts away from suicide; it had fascinated him. He had heard only her words, the heavy irony, the self-mockery, as though the story was some kind of parody, as if it didn't really belong to her.

She was an only child. Her father worked for a bank and her mother was a housewife. Every four or five years the family relocated as her father was transferred or promoted – Parys, Potchefstoom, Port Elizabeth, and eventually Bellville, which had finally broken the P-sequence. She left half-formed friendships behind with every move, had to start over as an outsider at every school, knowing that it would only be temporary. More and more she began to live in her own world, mostly behind the closed door of her bedroom. She kept a painfully personal diary, she read and fantasised – and in her final years at high school she dreamed of becoming a singer, of packed halls and standing ovations, of magazine covers and intimate sundowners with other celebrities, and being courted by princes.

The source of this dream, and the only constant throughout her youth was her paternal grandmother. She spent every Christmas holiday with her in the summer heat of Kirkwood and the Sunday's River Valley. Ouma Hettie was a music teacher all her life, an energetic, disciplined woman with a beautiful garden, a spotless house and a baby grand in the sitting room. It was a house of scent and sound: marmalade and apricot jam simmering on the stove, rusks or leg of mutton in the oven, her grandma's voice singing or talking, and at night the sweet notes of the piano issuing from the open windows of the small blue house, across the wide verandas, the dense garden and the neighbouring orange orchards, to the rugged ridges of Addo and the changing hue of the horizon.

At first Alexa would sit beside her grandmother and just listen. Later she learned the words and melodies by heart and often sang along.

Ouma Hettie loved Schubert and the Beethoven sonatas, but her true joy was the brothers Gershwin. Between songs she would nostalgically relate the stories of Ira and George. 'Rialto Ripples' and 'Swanee' were magically coaxed from the keys, 'Lady Be Good' and 'Oh, Kay!' were sung. She told Alexa how that song was inspired by George Gershwin's great love, the composer Kay Swift, but that hadn't prevented him from also having an affair with the beautiful actress Paulette Goddard.

On a sweltering evening in her fifteenth year, Ouma Hettie suddenly stopped playing and told Alexa, 'Stand there.' Meekly, she took her place beside the piano.

'Now *sing*!'

She did, in full voice for the first time. 'Of Thee I Sing', and the old lady closed her eyes, only a little smile betraying her rapture. As the last note faded in the sultry evening air, Hettie Brink looked at her granddaughter and, after a long silence, she said, 'My dear, you have perfect pitch, and you have an extraordinary voice. You are going to be a star.' She fetched Ella Fitzgerald's *Gershwin Songbook* from her stack of LPs.

That was how the dream began. And Ouma Hettie's offical tuition.

Her parents were not impressed. A career in singing was not what they had had in mind for their only child. They wanted her to train as a teacher, get a qualification, something practical 'to fall back on'. 'What kind of man wants to marry a singer?' Her mother's words echoed ironically.

In her Matric year there was conflict, long and bitter arguments in the sitting room of the bank manager's house in Bellville. With the verbal ammunition provided by her grandma, Alexa fell back to her last line of defence: 'It's *my* life. *Mine.*' A week before her finals she went for an audition with the Dave Burmeister Band.

Stage fright nearly got the better of her that day. It was nothing new. She had already experienced it at eisteddfods and the occasional performance at a wedding or with obscure bands in small clubs. It became a sort of ritual, a demon that began systematically to attack her four days before an appearance, so that, with a wildly beating heart, perspiring palms and an overwhelming conviction that she was about to make a total fool of herself, she could only complete the trip from dressing room to microphone with a supreme effort of will.

But as soon as she began to sing, with the first note uttered from her constricted throat, the demon melted away as though it had never existed.

At her first performance with Burmeister in a Johannesburg club, her grandma had been there to hold her hand and give her courage. 'This is what you were born for, my dear. Go out there and knock them dead.'

And she had. The reviews in *The Star* were still beside Ouma Hettie's bed when she passed away quietly in her sleep two months later. 'Alexandra Brink, in shimmering black, is so easy on the eye – young, blonde and beautiful. But once she starts to sing, her smoky, sensual voice, complete mastery of classical material, and innovative interpretations indicate a rare maturity and an acute musical intelligence. Her range encompasses Gershwin, Nat King Cole, Ma Rainey, Bessie Smith and Bobby Darin, with Dave Burmeister's arrangements fitting her style and personality perfectly.'

Oliver Sands of Phoenix, Arizona, told Inspector Vusi Ndabeni he had fallen in love with Rachel Anderson on Day Eight of the African Overland Adventure. In Zanzibar. Over a plate of seafood that he had been eating with great concentration.

'You are obviously enjoying that,' said Rachel.

He looked up. She stood on the opposite side of the restaurant table with the emerald-green sea as a backdrop, long, dark-brown hair in a plait over her shoulder, a baseball cap on her head and lovely long legs in shorts. Ollie was a bit self-conscious, embarrassed by the way he had been devouring his meal. But when she smiled and pulled out the chair opposite him with a 'May I join you? I'll have to try some too,' he could scarcely believe his luck.

He told Vusi they had had to introduce themselves to each other on the first night of the tour – in a ring of camp stools beneath the African stars. He hadn't even tried to remember Erin and Rachel's names. Pretty, athletic, educated girls like that never noticed him. When she sat at his table in Zanzibar and ate her own plate of seafood with gusto, he struggled to remember her name, with a sense of panic. Because she had talked to him. She asked him where he was from and what his future plans were. She listened to his answers with interest, told him of her dream to become a medical doctor, and that one day she would like to make a difference, here, in Africa.

And so he lost his heart to a nameless woman.

Alexa Brink's stage fright grew worse. The loss of her grandma was a blow, as though a foundation had collapsed, so she learned to smoke to control the fear.

Despite the glowing reviews and the enthusiastic response of the small but loyal audiences in Johannesburg, Durban and Cape Town, the demon of self-doubt clung to her shoulders every night. With a mean voice it whispered that one day she would be unmasked, someone in the audience would see her for what she really was and cry out that she was an impostor, an outsider and a fake. Alone in the dressing room she could not cope. One night she burst in on Dave Burmeister in tears and confessed her fear. That was the beginning of a vicious circle. With fatherly patience, Burmeister explained that all the great names struggled with stage fright. At first his gentle, quiet voice calmed her and got her behind the microphone. But every night it took a little longer, a little more convincing and more praise before she could make the terrifying walk across the stage.

One day, at his wits' end, Burmeister placed a glass of brandy and Coke in front of her and said: 'For God's sake, just drink it.'

Oliver Sands controlled his attraction to Rachel Anderson with an iron hand. Instinctively he knew he must not reveal his burning desire, he must keep his distance. He didn't look for a seat close to her on the truck, he didn't pitch his tent in her vicinity in the evening. He waited for those magical moments when – usually with Erin – she talked to him spontaneously, or asked him to film them with her video camera at some tourist spot. She sometimes saw him with a book in his hand and asked him what he was reading. They began a conversation about literature. In the evening she would come and sit beside him at the campfire and with her dazzling zest for life would say: 'So, Ollie, did we have a good day today or what?'

Day and night he was completely aware of her, he knew where she was every moment, what she was doing, whom she spoke to. He saw that she was friendly with everyone in the group, he kept count of the time she spent with others and realised he was especially privileged – he received more of her attention and conversation than anyone else. The two lean and self-assured chief guides were very popular with the other girls, but she treated them just the same as the men in the tour group, friendly and courteous, while choosing to take her meals with Ollie, talk to him and share many more personal secrets.

It was like that until Lake Kariba. On their second day there, when they boarded the houseboats, she was different, sombre and quiet, the joy and spontaneity gone.

Alexa Barnard learned to have three drinks before a performance. The dose required to keep the demon sufficiently quiet. It was her limit. Four made her slur, the lyrics swimming in her memory, Burmeister's proud paternal smile wiped from his face by a worried frown. But two was not enough.

She understood the risks. That was why she never had a drink during the day or after the show. Just those three glasses – the first one tossed back an hour and a half before the curtain, the other two taken more slowly. The cellist suggested gin since it didn't leave the odour on the breath that brandy did. She tried gin and tonic, but didn't like it. Dry lemon was her ultimate choice of mixer.

In this way, she kept the demon under control for four years, hundreds of appearances and two CD recordings with Burmeister and his band.

Then she met Adam Barnard.

She noticed him one evening in the little Cape theatre – the tall, virile, attractive man with a thick head of black hair who had listened to her spellbound. The following evening he was back again. After the show he came knocking on her dressing-room door with a bunch of flowers in his hand. He was fluent and charming, and his compliments were measured, and therefore seemed more genuine. He invited her out: a business lunch, he made it clear.

She was ready for what he suggested, aware of the limits of her chosen genre. She was known and popular in a small circle, she had a few glowing interviews in the entertainment sections of a few dailies and modest CD sales. She was aware of the limited scope of her career, audience and income. She had reached the highest rung of a short ladder and her prospects were predictable and uninspiring.

Three days later she signed a contract with Adam Barnard. It bound her to his record company and to him, as manager.

He made good on his professional promises. He sought out Afrikaans compositions from Anton Goosen, Koos du Plessis, and Clarabelle van Niekerk, songs to suit her voice and what would become her new style. He hired the best musicians, developed a specific and unique sound for her and introduced her to the media. He courted her with the same quiet professionalism, and married her. He even weaned her off the three pre-appearance gins with his total support, belief in her talent and his silver, silver tongue. For two years her life and career were everything she had dreamed of. One day an open-air photo shoot for *Sarie* magazine was cancelled due to bad weather and she came home unexpectedly. There, in the same sitting room where she and Griessel had sat, she found Adam with his trousers around his ankles and Paula Phillips on her knees in front of him, performing skilful fellatio with her long fingers and her red-painted mouth. Yes, *that* Paula Phillips, the dark-haired singer with long legs and big boobs, who was still dishing up pointless commercial junk to middle-class ears. That was the day Alexa Barnard began to drink in earnest.

Even though Rachel Anderson had changed in her behaviour towards everyone, Oliver Sands knew it must have been something he had said or done. He replayed every interaction, every word he had said to her, but he could not pinpoint the source of her aversion. Had he said something to someone else, or done something to someone else that had upset her so much? He lay awake at nights, on the trips to Victoria Falls, the Chobe Game Reserve, the Okavango, Etosha, and finally, to the Cape, he would stare out of the window in the faint hope of gaining some insight, some idea of how he could make things right.

The previous night in Van Hunks in Cape Town he had cracked under the strain. What he ought to have said was: 'I can see something is bothering you, Rachel. Do you want to talk about it?' But he had already downed too many beers for Dutch courage. He sat down beside her and like a complete idiot said: 'I don't know why you suddenly hate me, but I love you, Rachel.' He had gazed at her with big hungry puppy eyes in the crazy hope that she would say, 'I love you too, Ollie. I've loved you since that magical day in Zanzibar.'

But she hadn't.

He thought she hadn't heard him over the loud music, because she just sat there staring into the middle distance. Then she stood up, turned to him and kissed him on the forehead.

'Dear Ollie,' she said and walked away between the crush of people.

'That's why I came back here,' Sands said to Vusi.

'I'm not following you.'

'Because I knew the dorm would be empty. Because I didn't want anybody to see me cry.' He did not remove his glasses. The tears trickled under the edge of the frame and down his round, red cheeks.

12

Rachel Anderson lay on her stomach behind the stacked pine logs, powerless and gutted.

Something pressed uncomfortably against her belly, but she did not move. She couldn't hold back the self-pity any longer; it overwhelmed and paralysed her. She did not cry; it was as though her tear ducts had dried up. Her breathing fast and shallow, mouth gasping, she stared at the grain of the sawn wood, but saw nothing.

Her thoughts had stalled, trapped by a lack of alternatives, the door to all escape routes slammed shut, except this single option, to lie in this shade, a gasping, helpless fish on dry land.

She couldn't hear the voices any more. They had walked uphill. Maybe they would see her footprints and follow them here. They would look at the unfinished garage and realise it offered a hiding place and then they would look behind the pine logs and one would grab her hair with an iron grip and slash open her throat. She didn't even think she would bleed, there was nothing left. Nothing. Not even the terror of that chunky blade; it did not release the flood of adrenaline in her guts any more.

Oh, to be home.

It was a vague longing that slowly overcame her – a ghostly vision emerging from the haze, the safe haven, her father's voice, far off and faint. 'Don't you worry, honey, just don't you worry.'

Oh, to be held by him, to curl up on his lap with her head under his chin and close her eyes. The safest place in the world.

Her breathing steadied and the image in her mind was clearer.

The idea took shape, instinctive and irrational, to get up and phone her father.

He would save her.

If there was a murder or armed robbery in his area at night, the SAPS members of Caledon Square had instructions to call the station commander at home. But the more mundane affairs of the previous night had to wait until he was at his desk in the morning and could scan the notes in the register from the charge office. The SC was a black Superintendent with twenty-five years' service to his name. He knew there was only one way to tackle this job, slowly and objectively. Otherwise the nature and extent of that list could undo you. So he ran his pen down the list with professional distance, over the domestic violence, public drunkenness, the theft of cell phones and cars, drug sales, disturbance of the peace, burglaries, assault, indecent exposure and various false alarms.

At first his pen slid over the Lion's Head incident on page seven of the register, but it hovered back. He read through it again more carefully. The reluctant woman who had seen a young girl on the mountain. Then he reached for the bulletin that lay to his left on the corner of the scarred wooden surface. A Constable had brought it in only minutes before. He had scanned it quickly. Now he gave it his full attention.

He saw the connection. At the bottom was Inspector Vusumuzi Ndabeni's name and phone number.

He picked up the phone.

Vusi was walking down Long Street towards the harbour, on his way to the Van Hunks nightclub, when his phone rang. He answered without stopping.

'Inspector Ndabeni.'

'Vusi, it's Goodwill,' said the Caledon Square SC in Xhosa. 'I think I have something for you.'

Benny Griessel stood with his colleagues in one of the examination rooms of the City Park Hospital Casualty Department. He had a strong sense of déjà vu.

Space was limited, so they were quite an intimate little group
behind the closed door. While Fransman Dekker talked with his
habitual frown, Griessel observed the people around him: John
Afrika, District Commissioner: Detective Services and Criminal
Intelligence, in full impressive uniform, his epaulettes weighed
down with symbols of rank. Afrika was shorter than Dekker, but
he had presence, an energy that made him the dominant force
in the room. Beside Afrika was the fragile Tinkie Kellerman, her
delicate features overshadowed by her huge eyes revealing how
intimidated she was by this gathering. Then there was the broad-
shouldered Dekker with his crew cut and angular face; serious,
focused, voice deep and intense as he talked. They said he made
women weak at the knees but Griessel couldn't see how. They
said Dekker had a beautiful coloured wife in a senior position at
Sanlam, and that's how he could afford to live in an expensive
house somewhere on the Tygerberg. They also said that he
sometimes played away from home.

And Cloete, beside him, the liaison officer with tobacco stains
on his fingers and permanent shadows under his eyes. Cloete, with
his endless patience and calm, the man in the middle, between the
devil of the media and the deep blue of the police. How many
times had he been through this, Griessel wondered, in this kind of
emergency meeting, the one who had to make sure all the bases
were covered, so that explanations higher up in the SAPS food
chain would be consistent. The difference now was that he, too,
like Cloete, was caught in a no-man's-land, his created by the
mentorship that he didn't think was going to work.

Dekker concluded his explanation and Griessel drew an
unobtrusive breath, preparing for the predictable conclusion.

'Are you sure?' Afrika asked and looked at Griessel.

'Absolutely, Commissioner,' he said. Everyone but Cloete
nodded.

'So why is the *doos* carrying on like this?' The Commissioner
glared guiltily at Tinkie Kellerman after the expletive and said:
'Sorry, but that is what he is.'

Tinkie merely nodded. She had heard everything by now.

'He was trouble from the start,' said Fransman Dekker. 'He gave the Constable trouble at the gate, insisted on coming in. It was a crime scene, sir, and I do things by the book.'

'Fair enough,' said John Afrika and dipped his head thoughtfully with a hand over his mouth. Then he looked up. 'The press . . .' he looked at Cloete enquiringly.

'It's a major story,' said Cloete, on the defensive as usual, as if he was implicated in the blood lust of the media. 'Barnard is a celebrity of sorts . . .'

'That's the problem,' said John Afrika, and thought some more.

When he looked up and focused on Dekker with an apologetic slant to his mouth, Griessel knew what was coming.

'Fransman, you're not going to like this . . .'

'Commissioner, maybe . . .' Griessel said, because he had been the one who had control taken away from him before, and he knew how it felt.

Afrika held up a hand. 'They will tear us apart, Benny, if Mouton puts the blame on us. You see, we were there, in her room . . . You know what the papers are like. Tomorrow they will say it's because we put inexperienced people on the case . . .'

Dekker got it now. 'No, Commissioner . . .' he said.

'Fransman, don't let us misunderstand each other; it happened on *your* watch,' Afrika said sternly. Then more gently: 'I'm not saying it's your fault; I want to protect you.'

'Protect?'

'You have to understand. These are difficult times . . .'

They knew he was referring to the recent investigational failures that the newspapers and politicians had pounced on like predators.

Dekker tried one last time, 'But, sir, if I crack this, tomorrow they will write . . .'

'*Djy wiet dissie sóé maklikie!*' You know it's not that simple.

Griessel wondered why Cape Coloureds only spoke Cape Flats Afrikaans with each other. It always made him feel excluded.

Dekker wanted to say more, his mouth opened, but John Afrika lifted a warning finger. Dekker's mouth closed, his jaw clenched, eyes fierce.

'Benny, you take charge of this one,' the Commissioner said. 'As of now, Fransman, you work closely with Benny. *Lat hy die pressure vat. Lat hy die Moutons van die lewe handle.*' Let him take the pressure, let him handle the Moutons of this world. And then, almost as an afterthought: 'You're a team, if you crack this . . .'

Griessel's phone rang.

'. . . then you can share the honours.'

Benny took the phone out of his pocket and checked the screen. 'It's Vusi,' he said meaningfully.

'*Jissis*,' said Afrika shaking his head. 'It never rains . . .'

Griessel answered with a 'Vusi?'

'Is the Commissioner still there with you, Benny?'

'He's here.'

'Keep him there, please, just keep him there.'

Tafelberg Road is tarred, and follows the contour of the mountain, starting at 360 metres above sea level. It runs past the cable car station with its long queues of tourists, but just beyond Platteklipstroom ravine a concrete barrier keeps cars out, so only cyclists and pedestrians can continue. From there on it rises and falls between 380 and 460 metres for four kilometres or more around Devil's Peak before it becomes an increasingly rough dirt track, eventually connecting with the Kings Battery hiking trail.

The observation point with the best view of the city bowl is a hundred metres below Mount Prospect on the northern flank of Devil's Peak, just before the path turns sharply east.

The young man was sitting just above the path, on a rock in the shade of a now flowerless protea bush. He was in his late twenties, white, lean and tanned. He wore a wide-brimmed hat, a bleached blue shirt with a green collar, long khaki shorts and old worn Rocky sandals with deep tread soles. He held a pair of binoculars to his face and scanned the ground slowly from left to right, west to east. Below him the Cape was breathtaking – from the cable car sliding, seemingly weightless, past Table Mountain's rugged cliffs to the top, past the sensuous curves of Lion's Head and Signal Hill, over the blue bay, a glittering jewel that stretched to the horizon, to below him where the city nestled comfortably, like a contented child in the mountain's embrace. He saw none of this, because his attention was focused only on the city's edge.

Beside him on the flat rock was a map book of Cape Town. It was open at Oranjezicht, the suburb directly below him. The mountain breeze gently flipped the pages so that every now and then he had to put out an absent-minded hand to flatten them.

Rachel Anderson stood up slowly, like a sleepwalker. She walked around the long stack of logs and looked towards the mountain. She could not see anyone. She walked out of the shadow of the garage and turned right in the direction of the city, across the cement slab and stone paving, then across the tar of Bosch Avenue to where it turned into Rugby Road ten metres further on. She was drained, she could no longer run, she would go and phone her father, just walk slowly and go and phone her father.

The young man with the binoculars spotted her instantly, his lenses sliding over her, a tiny, lonely figure. The denim shorts, the powder-blue T-shirt and the small rucksack – it was her.

'Jesus Christ,' he said out loud.

He pulled the binoculars back, focused on her to make absolutely sure, then took out a cell phone from his shirt pocket and searched for a number. He called and brought the binoculars back to his eyes with one hand.

'Yeah?' he heard over the cell phone.

'I see her. She just fuckin' walked out of nowhere.'

'Where is she?'

'Right there, in the road, she's turning right . . .'

'Which road, Barry?'

'For fuck's sake,' said Barry, putting the binoculars down on the rock and picking up the map. The wind had turned the page again. Hurriedly, he turned the page back and ran his finger over the map, looking for the right place.

'It's right there, first road below . . .'

'Barry, what fuckin' street?'

'I'm working on it,' said Barry hoarsely.

'Just relax. Give us a street name.'

'OK, OK . . . It's Rugby Road . . . Hang on . . .' He grabbed the binoculars again.

'Rugby Road runs all along the mountain, you fucking idiot.'

'I know, but she's turning left into . . .' He put the binoculars down again, searched the map feverishly. 'Braemar. That's it . . .' Barry lifted up the binoculars again. 'Braemar . . .' He searched for her, spotted her in the lenses for a moment. She was walking calmly, in no hurry. Then she began to disappear, as though the suburb was swallowing her feet first. 'Shit, she's . . . she's gone, she just fucking disappeared.'

'Not possible.'

'I think she went down an embankment or something.'

'You'll have to do better than that.'

Barry trembled as he searched the map again. 'Stairs. She's taking the stairway to Strathcona Road.' He pointed the binoculars again. '*Ja*. That's it. That's exactly where she is.'

Griessel stood outside on the pavement with Dekker and Cloete. Through the glass doors they watched John Afrika pacify Willie Mouton and his soberly dressed lawyer. 'Sorry, Fransman,' said Griessel.

Dekker didn't reply; he just stared at the three men inside.

'It happens,' said Cloete philosophically. He drew deeply on a cigarette and looked at his cell phone, which was receiving complaining texts from the press, one after another. He sighed. 'It's not Benny's fault.'

'I know,' said Dekker. 'But we're wasting time. Josh Geyser could be in fucking Timbuktu by now.'

'*The* Josh Geyser?' asked Cloete.

'Who?' asked Griessel.

'The gospel guy. Barnard pumped his wife yesterday in his office and she went and confessed the whole thing.'

'Barnard's wife?' asked Griessel.

'No. Geyser's.'

'Melinda?' asked Cloete urgently.

'That's right.'

'No!' Cloete was shocked.

'Hang on . . .' said Griessel.

'I've got all their CDs,' said Cloete. 'I can't fucking believe it. Is that what Mouton is going around saying?'

'Are you a gospel fan?' Dekker asked.

Cloete nodded only fleetingly and flicked his cigarette butt in an arc down the street. 'He's lying, I'm telling you. Melinda is a sweet thing. And besides, she and Josh are born-again – she would never do a thing like that.'

'Born-again or not, that's what Mouton says.'

'Fransman, wait. Explain this to me,' said Griessel.

'Apparently, yesterday Barnard fucked Melinda Geyser in his office. So her husband, Josh, pitches up yesterday afternoon saying he knows all about it and he's going to beat Barnard to death, but Barnard wasn't there.'

'Can't be,' said Cloete, but as a policeman he knew people were capable of anything and he was already considering whether it might be true. Then his face fell. 'Oh man, the press . . .'

'*Ja*,' said Griessel.

'Benny!' All three turned when they heard Vusi Ndabeni's voice. The black detective came jogging down the pavement and reached them, out of breath. 'Where is the Commissioner?'

As one, all three pointed accusing fingers through the glass doors where a doctor had now joined the Mouton conference.

'The other girl – she's still alive, Benny. But they're hunting her down, somewhere in this city. The Commissioner will have to organise more people.'

Without haste, she walked down Marmion Road in the direction of the city. There was an absence in her, an acceptance of her fate. Ahead she saw a car reversing out of a driveway, a small black Peugeot. The driver was a woman. Rachel did not increase her pace, continued to walk towards her, unthreatening. The woman drove to the edge of the street and stopped. She looked left for traffic, then right. She saw Rachel and for an instant made eye contact, then looked away.

'Hi,' said Rachel calmly, but the woman didn't hear her. She stepped forward and softly knocked on the window with the knuckle of her middle finger. The woman turned her head, irritably. Her mouth had a peculiar shape, the corners pulled down strongly. She turned the window down a few centimetres.

'May I use your telephone, please,' said Rachel, without emotion, as though she knew what the answer would be.

The woman looked her up and down, saw the dirty clothes, the grazed chin, hands and knees. 'There's a public telephone at Carlucci's. On Montrose.'

'I'm in real trouble.'

'It's just around the corner,' and the woman looked again for traffic in Marmion Road. 'Just turn right at the next street, and walk two blocks.'

She wound up the window and reversed. As she turned left to drive away she looked once more at Rachel, suspicion and aversion in her face.

Barry studied the map on the hood of the vehicle and said over his phone: 'Look, she could have gone left into Chesterfield, or she could have taken Marmion, but I can't see her. The angle's not good from here.'

'Which one goes down into the city?' The voice was out of breath.

'Marmion.'

'Then keep your focus on Marmion. We're two minutes from the Landy, but you will have to tell us where she is. It's going to take ten minutes to get the cops there. And by then she could be anywhere . . .'

Barry took the binoculars and held them to his eyes again. 'Hang on . . .'

He followed Strathcona to where it led into Marmion, which was thickly lined with trees. The binoculars stripped the image of perspective, there were too many double storeys and it was too overgrown; only here and there could he see the western pavement and parts of the street surface. He followed the trajectory north towards the city, glanced swiftly at the map. Marmion ended in . . . Montrose. She ought to turn left there, if she wanted to reach the city.

Binoculars again. He found Montrose, broad and more visible from here. He followed it west. Nothing. Would she have turned right? East?

'Barry?'

'Yeah?'

'We're at the Landy. We're going to Marmion.'

'OK,' he said, still looking through the binoculars.

He saw her, far and tiny in the lenses, but unmistakable. She crossed the intersection.

'I have her. She's in Montrose . . .' He looked down at the map. 'She just crossed Forest, heading east.'

'OK. We're in Glencoe. Now just don't lose her.'

13

John Afrika walked out of the glass doors of casualty alone. Apparently, Willie Mouton and the sombre lawyer, Regardt Groenewald, had gone into the hospital. 'Good news, *kêrels*,' said John Afrika as he took his place in the circle. 'Alexa Barnard is out of danger. The damage is not so bad, she's just lost a lot of blood, they're keeping her . . . Oh, Vusi, morning, what are you doing here?'

'I'm sorry, sir, I know you're busy, but I thought I should come and ask for help . . .'

'Don't apologise, Vusi. What can I do?'

'The American girl at the church . . . there were two of them, we know that now . . .' Vusi Ndabeni took out his notebook from the pocket of his neat jacket, stood up straight and said, 'The victim is Miss Erin Russel. Her friend is Miss Rachel Anderson. They came in with a tour group yesterday. Miss Anderson was seen on Signal Hill at approximately six o'clock this morning, pursued by assailants. Sir, she's an eyewitness, and she's in great danger. We need to find her.'

'Damn,' said John Afrika, but the English expletive seemed ineffective in his mouth.

'Pursued by assailants? What assailants?'

'Apparently five or six young men, some white, some black, the witness says.'

'And who is this witness?'

'A lady by the name of . . . Sybil Gravett. She was walking her dog along Signal Hill when Miss Anderson came up to her and asked her for help. She then ran in the direction of Camps Bay after she asked Mrs Gravett to call the police. A few minutes later the young men came running past.'

The Commissioner checked his watch. 'Fuck it, Vusi, that was more than three hours ago . . .'

'I know. That's why I need more people, sir.'

'*Bliksem.*' Afrika rubbed a hand over his jaw. 'I don't have more people. We'll have to get the stations involved.'

'I've already asked the stations, sir. But Caledon Square has to police a union march to Parliament, and Camps Bay has only two vehicles in operation. The SC says they lost one patrol van to theft on New Year's Eve and the other one was crashed . . .'

'*Nee, o bliksem,*' Afrika swore before Vusi could finish.

'I've put out another bulletin, sir, but I thought if we could get the chopper, and put some pressure on the SCs . . .'

Afrika took out his cell phone. 'Let me see what I can do . . . Who the hell is chasing her?'

'I don't know, sir. But they were at a nightclub last night. Van Hunks . . .'

'*Jissis,*' said John Afrika and called a number. 'When are we going to clean out those dens?'

Rachel Anderson walked in through the front door of Carlucci's Quality Food Store, straight up to the counter where a young man in a white apron was busy taking change out of small plastic bags.

'Is there a telephone I can use?' Her voice was expressionless.

'Over there, next to the ATM,' he said and then he looked up. He saw the stains on her clothes, the dried blood on her face and knees. 'Hi . . . Are you OK?'

'No, I'm not. I need to make an urgent call, please.'

'It's not a card phone. Would you like some change?'

Rachel took the rucksack off her back. 'I've got some.' She went in the direction he had indicated.

He noticed her beauty, despite the state she was in. 'Can I help you with something?' She didn't answer. He watched her with concern.

'Jesus Christ,' Barry said over the cell phone. 'She's just gone into a fucking restaurant or something.'

'Shit. Which one?'

'It's on the corner of Montrose and . . . I think it's Upper Orange . . . Yes that's it.'

'We'll be there in two minutes. Just keep looking . . .'

'I'm not taking my eyes off the place.'

The ringing of the phone woke Bill Anderson in his house in West Lafayette, Indiana. With his first attempt he knocked off the receiver, so he had to sit up and swing his feet off the bed to reach it.

'What is it?' his wife asked beside him, confused.

'Daddy?' he heard as he picked up the receiver. He lifted it to his ear.

'Baby?'

'Daddy!' said his daughter, Rachel, thirty thousand kilometres away, and she began to cry.

Bill Anderson's guts contracted; suddenly he was wide awake. 'Honey, what's wrong?'

'Erin is dead, Daddy.'

'Oh, my God, baby, what happened?'

'Daddy, you have to help me. They want to kill me too.'

To her left was a large window looking out on Montrose Avenue; in front of her was the deli counter, where three coloured people exchanged looks when they heard her words.

'Honey, are you sure?' her father asked, his voice so terribly near.

'They cut her throat last night, Daddy. I saw it . . .' Her voice caught.

'Oh, my God,' said Bill Anderson. 'Where are you?'

'I don't have much time, Daddy. I'm in Cape Town . . . the police, I can't even go to the police . . .' She heard the screech of tyres on the road outside. She looked up and out. A new white Land Rover Defender stopped outside. She knew the occupants.

'They're here, Daddy, please help me . . .'

'Who's there? Who killed Erin?' her father asked urgently, but she had seen the two men leap out of the Land Rover and run to the main door of the shop. She threw the receiver down and fled through the shop, past the dumbstruck women behind the deli counter, to a white wooden door at the back. She shoved it violently open. As she ran out she heard the man in the apron shout: 'Hey!' She was in a long narrow passage between the building and a high white wall. Along the top of the wall was a long row of broken glass. The only way out was at the end of the passage to the right – another wooden door. She sprinted, the awful terror upon her again.

If that door was locked . . .

The soles of her running shoes slapped loudly in the narrow space. She pulled at the door. It wouldn't open. Behind her she heard the deli door open. She looked back. They saw her. She focused on the door in front of her. There was a Yale lock. She turned it. A small, anxious sound exploded from her lips. She jerked the door open. They were too close. She went out and slammed it shut behind her. She saw the street before her, realised the door had a bolt on this side, turned and her fingers worked in haste, it wouldn't budge, she heard them at the lock on the other side. She banged the bolt with the palm of her hand; pain shot up her arm. The bolt slid and the door was barred. They jerked at it from the other side.

'Bitch!' one of them shouted.

She raced down four concrete steps. She was in the street, kept running, left, down the long slope of Upper Orange Street, her eyes searching for a way out, because they were too close, even if they went back through the shop, they were as close as they had been last night, just before they caught Erin.

Bill Anderson rushed down the stairs of his house to his study, with his wife, Jess, at his heels.

'They killed Erin?' she asked. Her voice heavy with fear and worry.

'Honey, we have to stay calm.'

'I am calm, but you have to tell me what's going on.'

Anderson stopped at the bottom where the stairs led into the hallway. He turned and put his hands on his wife's shoulders. 'I don't know what's going on,' he said slowly and calmly. 'Rachel says Erin was killed. She says she's still in Cape Town . . . and that she's in danger . . .'

'Oh, my God . . .'

'If we want to help her at all, we have to stay calm.'

'But what can we do?'

The young man in the apron saw the two men who had chased the girl coming back through Carlucci's Quality Food Store. He shouted again: 'Hey!' and blocked the way to the front door. 'Stop!'

The one in front – white, taut and focused – scarcely looked at him as he raised both hands and shoved the young man in the chest, making him stagger and fall with his back against the counter near the door. Then they were past him, out in the street. He scrambled to his feet, saw them hesitate for a moment on the pavement.

'I'm calling the police,' he shouted, rubbing his back with his hand. They didn't respond, but looked down Upper Orange Street, said something to each other, ran to the Land Rover and jumped in.

The aproned young man turned to the counter, reached for the phone and dialled 10111. The Land Rover turned the corner of Belmont and Upper Orange with squealing tyres, forcing an old green Volkswagen Golf to brake sharply. He realised he should get the registration number. He slammed the phone down, ran outside and a short way down the street. He could see it was a CA number – he thought it was 412 and another four figures, but then the vehicle was too far off. He turned and hurried back to the shop.

On the slope of Devil's Peak, Barry's cell phone rang and he grabbed it. 'Yes!'

'Where did she go, Barry?'

'She went down Upper Orange. What happened?'

'Where is she now, for fuck's sake?'

'I don't know, I thought you could see her.'

'Aren't you fucking watching?'

'Of course I'm fucking watching, but I can't see the whole goddamn street from here . . .'

'Jesus! She went down Upper Orange?'

'I saw her, for about . . . sixty metres, then she went behind some trees . . .'

'Fuck! Keep looking. Don't take your fucking eyes off this street.'

Bill Anderson sat in his study with his elbows on the old desk and the telephone to his ear. It was ringing in the home of his lawyer. His wife, Jess, stood behind him, crying softly, her arms wrapped around herself.

'Is he answering?' she asked.

'It's two o'clock in the morning. Even lawyers are asleep.'

A familiar voice answered at the other end, clearly befuddled with sleep. 'Connelly.'

'Mike, this is Bill. I am truly sorry to call you at this hour, but it's about Rachel. And Erin.'

'Then you don't have to be sorry at all.'

There were four uniformed members of the SAPS on duty at the charge office of the Caledon Square police station – a Captain, a Sergeant and two Constables. The Constable taking the call from Carlucci's Quality Food Store was unaware of Vusi Ndabeni's bulletin and the incident on Lion's Head.

He made notes while the young man described the incident in his shop, then he went over to the Sergeant in the radio control room and they contacted the station patrol vehicles. The Sergeant knew they were all near Parliament where a march was taking place that morning. He gave cursory details of the incident and asked one of the vehicles to investigate. He received a chorus of volunteers. The march was small, peaceful and boring. He chose the vehicle closest to Upper Orange Street. The Constable went back to the charge office desk.

He made sure all the paperwork relating to the call was in order.

14

They sat outside a coffee shop on the corner of Shortmarket and Bree Street, five policemen around a table for four. Cloete sat a little apart, beyond the shade of the red umbrella, cigarette between his fingers, talking quietly on his cell phone, pleading for patience from some determined journalist. The rest had their elbows on the table and their heads together.

John Afrika's deep frown showed that his burden of responsibility was weighing heavily on him. 'Benny, it's your show,' he said.

Griessel had known that was coming, it always did. The men at the top wanted to do everything except make the decisions.

'Commissioner, it's important that we utilise the available manpower as efficiently as possible.' He listened to his own words. Why was he always so pompous when he spoke to important people?

Afrika nodded solemnly.

'Our main problem is that we don't know where the Barnard murder took place. We need forensics from the scene. There were exit wounds, there would have to be blood, bullets . . . and then we need to place Greyling at the scene . . .'

'Geyser,' said Fransman Dekker, still sullen.

He ought to have remembered that, Griessel thought. What was the matter with him today? 'Geyser', he burned it into his memory. 'I'll have them brought in to the station, the man and his wife. We need to talk to them separately. Meanwhile Fransman can go to AfriSound . . .' He glanced at Dekker, uncertain whether he had the company name right. Dekker did not react. '. . . the record company. We need to know about Barnard's day. Where was he last night, and with whom? How late? Why? We have to build this case from the ground up.'

'Amen,' said Afrika. 'I want a rock-solid case.'

'We need a formal statement from Willie Mouton. Fransman?'

'I'll handle it.'

'Did anyone else see or hear Geyser yesterday? Who saw Geyser's wife when she went to Barnard's office?'

'The Big Bang,' said Cloete in disgust, his conversation over. Then his phone rang again. He sighed and turned away.

'As far as Vusi's case is concerned – he needs help, sir, someone to coordinate the stations, someone with authority, someone who can bring more people in from the southern suburbs, Milnerton or Table View . . .'

'Table View?' said Dekker. 'That lot couldn't find their own arses with a hand mirror.'

'The chopper can help us in an hour's time. Benny, you'll have to coordinate. Who else is there?' said John Afrika, feeling uncomfortable.

Griessel's voice became quiet and serious. 'Commissioner, this is someone's child out there. They have been hunting her from the early hours of the morning . . .'

Afrika avoided the intensity of Griessel's gaze. He knew where this was coming from, he knew the story of Benny's daughter and her abduction, six months ago.

'True,' he said.

'We need feet on the ground. Vehicles, patrols. Vusi, the photo the American boy took – the one of the missing girl – we need prints. Every policeman in the Peninsula . . . the Metro people . . .' and Griessel wondered what had come of the Field Marshal and his street search.

'The Metro people?' said Dekker. 'Fucking glorified traffic cops . . .'

John Afrika gave Dekker a stern look. Dekker gazed out at the street.

'It makes no difference,' said Griessel. 'We need all the eyes we can get. I thought we should bring Mat Joubert in to coordinate, sir. He's fairly free at the PT . . .'

'No,' said Afrika firmly. He raised his eyebrows. 'You don't know about Joubert yet?'

'What about him?' Griessel's phone rang. He looked at the screen. The number was unfamiliar. 'Excuse me,' he said as he answered, 'Benny Griessel.'

'This is Willie Mouton.' The voice was self-important.

'Mr Mouton,' Griessel said deliberately, so the others would know.

John Afrika nodded. 'I gave him your number,' he said quietly.

Mouton said: 'I phoned Josh Geyser and told him to come to the office, I have something important to say to him. He will be here in ten minutes, if you want to arrest him.'

'Mr Mouton, we would have preferred to bring him in ourselves.' Griessel did his best to disguise his frustration.

'First you complain that I won't cooperate,' said Mouton, touchy now.

Griessel sighed. 'Where is your office?'

'Sixteen Buiten Street. Go through the ground-floor building – our entrance is through the garden at the back. There's a big sign on the wall. Ask for me at reception on the ground floor.'

'We'll be there now.' He ended the call. 'Mouton asked Geyser to come to his office. He'll be there in ten minutes.'

'*Jissis*,' said Dekker, 'what an idiot.'

'Fransman, I will talk to Geyser, but you have to find the wife . . .'

'Melinda?' Cloete still had trouble believing it. 'Pretty Melinda?'

'I'll get their home address from Mouton, then I'll call you. Commissioner, none of this helps Vusi. Is there no one who can help him?'

'Well, it sounds as though the Barnard affair is sorted out. If the case against Geyser is strong enough, lock him up and go and help Vusi. We can tie up the loose ends tomorrow.'

Afrika saw the look on Benny's face and he knew it wasn't the solution he had hoped for.

'OK. We can bring in Mbali Kaleni temporarily until you are free.'

'Mbali Kaleni?' Dekker was taken aback.

'Shit,' said Vusi Ndabeni. Immediately he added: 'I'm sorry . . .'

'*Nee, o fok*,' said Dekker.

'She's clever. And thorough,' said the Commissioner, on the back foot for the first time.

'She's a Zulu,' said Vusi.

'She's a pain in the *gat*,' said Dekker. 'And she's at Bellville, her SC won't release her.'

'He will,' said John Afrika, in control again. 'She's all I have available, and she's on Benny's mentor list. She can coordinate from Caledon Square – I'll ask them to arrange something for her.'

He saw no relief on Vusi and Fransman Dekker's faces.

'Besides,' said Afrika with finality, 'it's only temporary, until Benny can take over.' As an afterthought he added reproachfully: 'And you should be supporting our efforts to develop more women in the Service.'

Easy and athletic, the young black man jogged through the trees of De Waal Park, from the Molteno Reservoir end to the waiting Land Rover Defender in Upper Orange Street.

'Nothing,' he said as he got in.

'Fuck,' said the young white driver. He pulled away before the door was even properly shut. 'We have to get out of here. He would have called the cops. And he saw the Landy.'

'Well, then we'll have to get our own cops here too.'

The white man took his cell phone out of his breast pocket and passed it to the black man. 'Call them. Make sure they know exactly where she disappeared. And get Barry down here as well. He's no use up the fucking mountain any more. Tell him to go to the restaurant.'

Griessel and Dekker walked to Loop Street together. 'What have you got against Inspector Kaleni?' Griessel asked.

'She's the fat one,' said Dekker, as if that explained everything. Griessel remembered her from last Thursday: short, very fat, with an unattractive face, severe as the sphinx, in a black trouser suit that sat too tight.

'And . . . ?'

'We were at Bellville together and she irritates the living shit out of everyone. Fucking bra-burning feminist, she thinks she knows everything, sucks up to the SC like you won't believe . . .' Dekker stopped. 'I'm this way.' He pointed down the street.

'Come to AfriSound when you're finished.'

Dekker wasn't finished yet: 'She has this *moerse* irritating habit of appearing out of nowhere, like a fucking bad omen. She sneaks up, quiet as a wet dream, on those little feet and all of a sudden there she is, always smelling of KFC, though you never see her eating the fucking stuff.'

'Does your wife know?'

'Know what?'

'That you have the horny hots for Kaleni?'

Dekker growled something indiscernible and irascible. Then he threw back his head and laughed, a deep bark that echoed off the building across the road.

Griessel thought about fat policemen as he walked to his car, of the late Inspector Tony O'Grady. Fat Englishman, smartass know-it-all, always chewing nougat with his mouth half open. Didn't bath quite as often as he should. Could drink with the best of them, one of the guys, never unpopular. It was because Kaleni was a woman; the detectives weren't ready for that.

Where were the days of Nougat O'Grady?

Then Griessel had been sober, keen and fearless. Always sharp, he could make a parade room of detectives roar with laughter, every fucking Monday morning. The days of Murder and Robbery, of the ascetic Colonel Willie Theal, already three months in his grave now from cancer, of Captain Gerbrand Vos, later Superintendent, with his bright blue eyes, shot dead in front of his house by a Cape Flats syndicate. And Mat Joubert . . . which reminded Griessel of what the Commissioner had said. He took out his phone and called.

'Mat Joubert,' said the familiar voice.

'I suggested to the Commissioner that we bring the Senior Superintendent in, because we need help and he says: "Don't you know about Joubert yet?" . . .'

'Benny . . .' Apologetic.

'What don't I know yet?'

'Where are you?'

'In Loop Street, on my way to arrest a gospel singer for murder.'

'I have to come to the city. I'll buy you coffee when you're finished.'

'To tell me what?'

'Benny . . . I'll tell you when I see you. I don't want to do it over the phone.'

Then Griessel knew what it was. His heart sank.

'*Jissis*, Mat,' he said.

'Benny, I wanted to tell you in person. Call me when you're done.'

Griessel climbed into his car and slammed the door hard. He turned the ignition.

Nothing ever stayed the same.

Everyone went away. Sooner or later.

His daughter. Gone to London. He had stood beside Anna at the airport watching Carla walk away through the guarded door to Boarding. Dragging her suitcase on wheels in one hand and holding her ticket and passport in the other, hurrying off on the Great Adventure, leaving him, leaving them. His emotions threatened to get the better of him, there next to his estranged wife. He wanted to take Anna by the hand and say: 'It's only you and Fritz left, because Carla is gone now, into the grown-up world.' But he didn't dare.

His daughter looked back once just before she disappeared around the corner. She was far away, but he could see the excitement on her face, the expectation, dreaming of what lay in store for her.

And he always stayed behind.

Would he stay behind again tonight? If Anna didn't want him any more? Would he cope with that?

What if she said: 'OK, Benny, you're sober, you can come home again'? What the fuck would he do then? Over the past few weeks he had started wondering more and more about that. Maybe it was a kind of rationalisation, a way of protecting himself from her rejection, but he wasn't sure that it would work – Anna and him together again.

His feelings about it were complicated, he knew that. He still loved Anna. But he suspected he had been able to stop drinking precisely because he was alone, because he no longer took the violence and death home to his family every night, because he didn't walk in the front door and see his wife and children and be stalked by the fear that they too would be found like that, bodies broken, hands rigid in the terrible fear of death.

But that wasn't the whole story.

They had been happy, he and Anna. Once upon a time. Before he began drinking. They had their little family world, just the two of them at first; then came Carla and Fritz and he had played on the carpet with his children and at night he had snuggled up to his wife and they had talked and laughed and made love with heartbreaking ease, carefree, because the future was a predictable utopia, even though they were poor, even though they owed money on every stick of furniture, and on the car and the house. Then he was promoted to Murder and Robbery, and the future slipped between his fingers, from his grasp, little by little, day by day, so slowly he didn't realise it, so subtly that he got up from a drunken stupor thirteen years later and realised it was all gone.

You could never get it back. That was the fuck-up. You could never go back, that life, those people and those circumstances were gone, just as dead as O'Grady, Theal and Vos. You had to start over, but this time without the naivety, innocence and optimism of before, without the haze of being in love. You were different, you were stuck with the way you were now, with all the knowledge and experience and realism and disillusionment.

He didn't know if he could do it. He didn't know if he had the energy – to go back to where every day was judgement day. Eagle-eyed Anna watching him when he came home at night, where had he been? Did he smell of drink? He would come through the door knowing this, and he would try too hard to prove his sobriety, he would play up to her, he would see her anxiety until she was sure he was sober and then she would relax. It all felt too much for him, a burden he wasn't ready to bear.

Then there was the fact that in the past two or three months, he had begun to enjoy his life in the spartan flat, the visits of his children before his daughter went overseas, when Fritz and Carla sat and chatted with him in his sitting room or a restaurant like three adults, three . . . friends, not hamstrung by the rules and regulations of the conventional family. He had begun to enjoy the silence of his home when he opened the door, nobody watching and judging him. He could open the fridge and drink directly, long and deeply, out of the two-litre bottle of orange juice. He could lie on the couch with his shoes on and close his eyes and snooze till seven or eight o'clock and then stroll down to the Engen garage on Annandale and buy a Woollies Food sandwich and a small bottle of ginger beer. Or his favourite, a Dagwood burger at Steers, then home to type an email to Carla with two fingers, a bite and a swallow in between. He could play on his bass guitar and dream impossible dreams. Or he could return the dish to seventy-something Charmaine Watson-Smith at Number 106. 'Oh, Benny, you don't have to thank me, you're my charity. My policeman.' Despite her years her eyes were full of life and her food was so delicious, every time.

Charmaine Watson-Smith who had sent Bella around. And he had taken advantage of Bella and, fuck it, he was an adulterer, but it had been incredible, so terribly good. Everything has a price.

Perhaps Anna knew about Bella. Perhaps Anna was going to tell him tonight that he might well be sober, but he was an unfaithful bastard and she didn't want him any more. He wanted Anna to want him. He needed her approval, he needed her love and her embrace and the safe haven of their home. But he didn't know if that was the right thing for him now.

Jissis, why did life have to be so complicated?

He was in Buiten Street and there was no parking and the present, the reality of it all, felt to him as though someone had switched on a powerful light. He blinked his eyes against its brightness.

10:10–11:02

15

'No,' said Inspector Mbali Kaleni with absolute finality.

Superintendent Cliffie Mketsu, station commander of Bellville, did not react. He knew he must wait until she had fired her salvo, his outspoken, principle-driven, stubborn female detective.

'What about the other women who have disappeared?' she asked, her round face registering displeasure. 'What about the Somali woman nobody wants to help me with? Why don't we call in the whole Service to work on *her* case?'

'What Somali woman, Mbali?'

'The one whose body has been lying at Salt River mortuary for the last two weeks, but the pathologists say it's not high priority, it could just be natural causes. Natural causes? Because it was a wound that went septic, because she died in a little shack of cardboard and planks, with nothing? Nobody is prepared to help, not Home Affairs, not Missing Persons, not even the stations, even after I sent them each a photo asking them to put it up on the board. When I get there they all just shrug – they don't even know what happened to the bulletin. But let an American disappear, everyone is suddenly jumping through burning hoops.' She folded her arms across her chest. 'Not me.'

'You're right,' Cliffie Mketsu said patiently. His theory was that Kaleni was her father's child. In a country where most fathers were absent, she had grown up with two strong parents – her mother was a nurse and her learned father was a school headmaster in KwaZulu, a leader in the community, who had equipped his only child carefully and deliberately with her own perspective, with good judgement, and the self-confidence to express it, loud and clear. So he had to give her the opportunity. 'I know.'

'The Commissioner specifically asked for you.'

She gave an angry snort.

'It's in the national interest.'

'National interest?'

'Tourism, Mbali. It's our lifeblood. Foreign exchange. Job opportunities. It's our biggest industry and our greatest leverage for upliftment.'

He knew she was melting; her arms dropped from her chest. 'They need you, Mbali, to take charge of the case.'

'But what about all the other women?'

'It's an imperfect world,' he said gently.

'It doesn't have to be,' she said and stood up.

At ten past three in the morning, Bill Anderson sat on the old two-seater leather couch in his study, his right arm around his sobbing wife and a coffee mug in his left hand. Despite his apparent calm, he could hear his own heart beating in the quiet of North Salisbury Street. His thoughts were sometimes with his daughter – and the parents of her friend, Erin Russel. Who would pass on the dreadful news? Should he call them? Or wait for official confirmation? And what could he do? Because he wanted to, he had to do something to help his daughter, to protect her; but where did he begin, he didn't even know where she was right now.

'They should never have gone,' said his wife. 'How many times did I tell them? Why couldn't they have gone to Europe?'

Anderson had no answer for her. He hugged her tighter.

The phone rang, shrill in the early hours. Anderson spilled some of the coffee from his mug in his haste to get up. He answered.

'Bill, it's Mike. I'm sorry, it took a while to track down the Congressman, he's up in Monticello with his family. I just got off the phone with him, and he's going to get things moving right away. First off, he says his thoughts are with you and your family . . .'

'Thanks, Mike, thank him for us.'

'I will. I gave him your number, and he will call us as soon as he's got more information. He's going to call both the US

Ambassador in Pretoria and the Consul General in Cape Town to get confirmation and whatever facts are available. He also knows a staffer with Condi Rice, and he will ask the State Department for all the help they can give. Now, I know you're a Democrat, but the Congressman is a former military man, Bill, he gave up his law practice on three days' notice to serve in the first Gulf War. He gets things done. So don't you worry now, we are going to bring Rachel home.'

'Mike, I don't know how to thank you.'

'You know you don't have to.'

'Erin's parents . . .'

'I'm thinking the same things here, but we need it to be official, Bill, before we say anything.'

'That might be best. I'm thinking of taking Chief Dombkowski with me. I don't think I can do it alone.'

'I'll call the Chief as soon as we have more information. Then we'll both go with you.'

The Sergeant walked out of Carlucci's Quality Food Store to his patrol vehicle, opened the door and picked up the handset of the radio. He called the Caledon Square charge office and spoke to the same Constable who had sent him here. He reported that they had taken a statement, that a young woman had been pursued by a white and a black man, but that there currently was no sign of any of them.

'See if you can find something on the system, a white Land Rover Discovery, registration number CA and the numbers four, one, six, that's all he could see, but he isn't dead certain. We'll look around a bit,' he said, and then he saw the second Metro Police car in minutes driving down Upper Orange. He recalled the two foot patrols in Metro uniform that he had seen on the way here. Why didn't they help with the march instead, he thought. Here they were wandering around looking for traffic offenders. Or buyers for fake drivers' licences.

His shift partner came out of the shop and said: 'If you ask me, it's drugs.'

★　　★　　★

Vusi Ndabeni met the police photographer at the Cat & Moose Youth Hostel and Backpackers Inn and asked them to fetch Oliver Sands and his camera again.

When Sands walked into the entrance hall, he still looked broken.

'I want to use that photograph of Erin and Rachel, please,' said Vusi.

'Sure,' said Sands.

'Can we borrow your camera for a few hours?'

'I can just take the memory card,' said the photographer.

'OK. I need . . . fifty prints. But quickly. Mr Sands, please show our photographer which one is Rachel Anderson.'

'I'll get it back?' asked Sands.

'I can't get the prints to you today,' said the photographer.

Vusi stared at the man with his long hair and unhelpful attitude.

You have to be tough, Benny Griessel had said.

But he wasn't like that. And he didn't know if he could be. He would have to make another plan.

Vusi muffled a sigh. 'Tomorrow? Is tomorrow OK?'

'Tomorrow is better,' the photographer nodded.

Vusi took his phone out of his pocket. 'Just a minute,' he said, and pressed a number in and held the phone to his ear.

'When you hear the signal,' said a monotonous woman's voice on the phone, 'it will be ten . . . seven . . . and forty seconds.'

'May I speak to Commissioner Afrika, please?' said Vusi. He whispered to the photographer. 'I just want to hear if the Commissioner will be angry if the girl is dead tomorrow.'

'When you hear the signal it will be . . .'

'What girl?' asked the photographer.

Oliver Sands looked from one to the other, bewildered.

'Ten seven . . . and fifty seconds.'

'The one in the photo. She is out there somewhere, around Camps Bay, and there are people who want to kill her. If we only get the photographs tomorrow . . .'

'When you hear the signal . . .'

'Hang on . . .' said the photographer.

'I will hold for the Commissioner,' Vusi said into the phone while the woman's voice said, 'Ten eight exactly.'

'I didn't know,' said the photographer.

Vusi raised his eyebrows expectantly.

The photographer looked at his watch. 'Twelve o'clock, that's the best I can do.'

Vusi looked at his phone and ended the call. 'OK. Take the prints to Caledon Square and give them to Mbali Kaleni . . .' and right then his phone rang.

'Detective Inspector Vusi Ndabeni.'

'*Sawubona*, Vusi,' said Mbali Kaleni in Zulu.

'*Molo*, Mbali,' said Vusi in Xhosa.

'*Unjani?*' she asked in Zulu.

'*Ntwengephi*,' he said in Xhosa to make his point and then switched to English.

'Where are you?'

'On the N1, coming from Bellville. Where are you?'

'I'm in Long Street, but I need you to go to Caledon Square.'

'No, brother, I must come to you. I can't take over the case if I don't know what's going on.'

'What?'

'The commissioner said I must take over the case.'

Vusi closed his eyes slowly. 'Can I call you back?'

'I'm waiting.'

Griessel walked into the arcade entrance at 16 Buiten Street. The building was built around an inner garden with paved pathways between flower beds, a fishpond and a birdbath. On the wall of the south wing was the huge logo of AfriSound, the word drawn in stalky letters that were probably meant to look African. The logo was a boastful bird with a black breast, yellow throat and eyebrows, singing with a gaping beak against an orange sun. Griessel had no idea what sort of bird it was. He crossed to the double glass doors. His cell phone rang. He knew this number by now.

'Vusi?' he said as he answered.

'Benny, I think we have a misunderstanding.'

The Metro patrol vehicle stopped beside the two young men in the Land Rover Defender on the corner of Prince and Breda Streets. Jeremy Oerson sat in the passenger seat of the Metro car. He wound the window down and asked the young white man behind the steering wheel of the Land Rover. 'Do you know what she's wearing, Jay?'

The young man nodded. 'Blue denim shorts, light-blue T-shirt. And a backpack.'

'OK,' said Jeremy Oerson and reached for his radio. He nodded to the driver. 'Let's go,' he said.

'Thank you, sir,' said Benny Griessel over the cell phone, turned it off and stood shaking his head for a second in front of the glass doors of AfriSound.

He wasn't a mentor, he was a fucking fireman, all he did was beat out fires.

Griessel sighed, opened the door and walked inside.

There were framed gold and platinum CDs and posters of artists' performances on the blood-red and sky-blue walls. Griessel recognised some of the names. Behind a modern desk of light wood sat a middle-aged black woman, who looked up when he came in. Her eyes were red, as though she had been crying, but her smile was brave.

'May I help you?'

'I'm here for Willie Mouton.'

'You must be Inspector Griessel.' Her pronunciation of his surname was perfect.

'I am.'

'Such a terrible thing, Mr Barnard . . .' She nodded in the direction of the stairs.

'They're waiting for you on the first floor.'

'Thank you.'

Griessel climbed the wooden stairs. The railing was chrome and there were more framed CDs on the wall, with the name of the artist or band on a bronze plaque underneath each one.

The first floor opened up before him. The colour scheme was bright and multicoloured, but the atmosphere was sombre. No music, just the quiet whisper of the air conditioning and the hushed voices of five or six people sitting around a big, flat, chrome coffee table on couches and chairs in brightly coloured ostrich leather – blue, green, red.

They became aware of him and stopped talking, turning to look at him. Griessel saw an older woman crying; everyone looked distressed, but there was no sign of Mouton. Some of the faces studying him were familiar – he guessed they were singers or musicians. Was Josh Geyser one of them? For a second he hoped Lize Beekman or Theuns Jordaan was there, or Schalk Joubert. But what would he say to them, here, under these circumstances?

There was no shame in hoping.

To his left, near the window, a coloured woman stood up from a desk. She was young and beautiful with high cheekbones, a full mouth and long black hair. She walked around the desk. Elegant close-fitting clothes, high-heeled shoes, a slim figure. 'Inspector?' The same subdued friendliness as the receptionist below.

'Benny Griessel,' he said, putting out a hand.

'Natasha Abader.' Her hand was small. 'I am Mr Mouton's PA. Please come with me.'

'Thank you,' said Griessel and followed her down the corridor. He looked at Natasha Abader's pert, perfect bottom and he couldn't help wondering if Adam Barnard had fucked her in his office too. He looked away deliberately, at the framed CD covers on the wall, more posters. There were plaques beside the doors. *AfriSound Promo. Production. Finance & Administration. Recording Studio. AfriSound On-line.* And almost at the back, to the right, *Willie Mouton. Director.*

To the left, another closed door. *Adam Barnard. Managing Director.*

Natasha knocked on Mouton's door and opened it. She put her head in. 'Inspector Griessel is here.' She stood back so that Griessel could enter.

'Thanks,' said Griessel. She nodded and walked back to her desk. Griessel went in. Mouton and his lawyer, Groenewald, sat stretched out like two magnates on either side of a large desk.

'Come in,' said Mouton.

The lawyer, still seated, put out a half-hearted hand to Griessel. 'Regardt Groenewald.'

'Benny Griessel. Is that Geyser out front?'

'No, they are in the conference room.' Mouton gestured with his head towards the far end of the corridor. There was a solemn air about him; the aggression had disappeared.

'They?'

'He brought Melinda along.'

Griessel could not mask his annoyance. Mouton saw it. 'I couldn't help it – I didn't tell him to bring her,' as if speaking to an inferior.

He knew Mouton's kind, self-important in their own little world, used to calling the shots. Now that he had had the ear of the Regional Commissioner, he would think he could keep on interfering. 'We want to question them separately,' Griessel said and took out his cell phone. 'My colleague thought she would be at home. I have to call him.'

He found Dekker's number and called.

'How much does Geyser know?' he asked while it rang.

'Nothing yet. Natasha just told him to wait in the conference room, but you can see he's guilty. Sweating like a pig.'

'Benny,' said Dekker over the phone.

'Things have changed,' said Griessel.

16

Vusi Ndabeni was walking quickly down Long Street when John Afrika phoned him back.

'It's sorted out, Vusi. Inspector Kaleni's commanding officer misunderstood me.'

'Thank you, sir.'

'She's gone to Caledon Square, she will talk to the stations in the meantime.'

'Thank you, sir.'

'She will be a great help to you, Vusi. She's a smart woman.'

'Thank you, sir.'

More than 1,300 kilometres to the north, in the Wachthuis building, part of the Thibault Arcade in Pretorius Street, Pretoria, the telephone of the Acting National Police Commissioner made a single growling noise. He picked it up. 'The Deputy Minister wants to talk to you,' said his secretary.

'Thank you.' He hesitated for a second before pushing the white 'Line 1' button. He knew it would not be good news. The Deputy Minister only phoned when there was bad news about the currently-on-long-leave National Commissioner and his approaching corruption trial.

'Good morning, Minister,' he said.

'Morning, Commissioner,' she said, and he could hear she wasn't overjoyed. 'I just had a call from the US Consul General in Cape Town.'

The front door of Van Hunks was in Castle Street. There was a neon sign with the name and motto: *Smokin'*. Inspector

Vusumuzi Ndabeni pushed and tugged on the handle but it was locked.

'Ai,' he said, and walked around the corner to the entrance of the shop next door, a company that sold lights. He found a coloured woman at the checkout and asked if she knew whether there would be anyone at the club.

'Try the back door,' she said, and went to show him the service alley at the back. He thanked her and walked past men unloading crates of beer from a lorry and carrying them into the club, into the kitchen of Van Hunks. A white man with a short black ponytail and small eyes was supervising the unloading. He spotted Vusi.

'Hey!' he said. 'What do you want?' Aggressive, with a slight accent.

Vusi took out his SAPS identity card. He held it out for the man to read. 'I would like to speak to the manager,' he said politely.

Ponytail, a head taller than Vusi, pulled up his nose at the card and the detective.

'Why?'

'Are you the manager?' asked Vusi, still civil.

'No.'

'I would prefer to speak to him.'

'Her. She is busy.' With a faint accent. Foreign.

'Could you take me to her, please?'

'Have you got the warrant?'

'I don't need a warrant,' he explained patiently. 'I am investigating a murder, and the victim was in this club last night. I just need information.'

While Ponytail weighed him up, Vusi noticed that his eyes were too close together. He had heard that in white people it was a sign of stupidity. That would explain the man's behaviour.

'You wait, because they steal my beer.' Ponytail pointed at the black labourers carrying the beer crates. 'What will the police do about this?'

'Did you report it?'

'Why?'

'So the police can investigate,' said Vusi slowly and clearly. 'You have to go to the charge office and report the crime.'

Ponytail rolled his eyes. Vusi didn't know what he meant by that; surely he could not have put it more plainly? 'Look, my investigation is very urgent. I need to speak to the manager immediately.'

More hesitation. Then the man said: 'Down the passage. Third door right.'

'Thank you,' said Vusi, and walked out of the room.

Willie Mouton held the door to the conference room open for Griessel. The Geysers were seated at the long oval table. They were holding hands. Benny had imagined two young bubbly angelic faces, with that exaggerated joy of the newly converted. But the Geysers were on the wrong side of forty, she maybe older than him. They were tense and grim. Josh was a big man with white-blonde hair and a styled crew cut. There were deep etched lines on his face, a droopy blonde moustache trimmed carefully to his chin. Wide shoulders, big arms, a sheen of perspiration on his forehead. Beside him Melinda looked tiny, like a doll, with her round face and red-blonde hair in a cascade of tight curls, a milky-white skin and long lashes. She had a heavy hand with the make-up, the beauty of another era. There was something about her mouth and eyes that would have marked her as an 'easy girl' in the Parow of Griessel's youth.

'Willie,' said Josh Geyser getting to his feet. 'What's going on?'

'This is Sergeant Benny Griessel of the police, Josh. We would like to talk to you.'

Griessel put out a hand. 'Inspector,' he said.

Geyser ignored Griessel's hand. 'Why?' he demanded with an authoritarian scowl.

'Adam is dead, Josh.'

An invisible hand wiped the scowl from Geyser's face. Griessel watched him pale.

Silence dominated the room.

In her seat, Melinda made a little noise, but Griessel kept his attention on Josh. The big man's shock seemed genuine.

'How?' asked Geyser.

'He was shot yesterday at his house,' said Mouton.

'Oh heavens!' Melinda cried out.

'I would like to talk to you alone, Mr Geyser,' said Griessel quickly, worried that the impetuous Mouton would say too much.

'Melinda, won't you wait in my office?' asked Mouton.

She didn't move.

'You're making a mistake,' Geyser said to Griessel.

'Would you sit down, please, Mr Geyser?'

'Come, Melinda,' said Mouton.

'I'm staying with Josh.'

'Mrs Geyser, I am afraid that I must speak with him alone.'

'She stays,' said Geyser.

Vusi found the manager in a small, untidy office with files and sheaves of accounts strewn across the table and shelves. She was typing figures into a large adding machine, painted nails pecking at the keys with lightning speed. He knocked on the frame of the open door and asked whether she was the manager.

'Yes.' She looked up. Forty, maybe, short black hair, strong features, but hard.

Vusi held out his identification and introduced himself.

'Galina Federova.' She shook Vusi's hand with a self-assured grip. 'Why are you here?' in the same accented English as Ponytail's.

Vusi gave her a quick outline of the case.

'Please sit down.' Somewhere between an order and an invitation, the *please* was a short, powerful *plis*. She began to pick up invoices from the table, looking for something. She found a pack of cigarettes and a lighter, flipped open the packet's lid and offered it to Vusi.

'No, thanks.'

She took one out for herself, lit it and spoke, the smoke trickling from her mouth.

'You know how many people last night?'

No, he said, he didn't know.

'Maybe two hundred, maybe more. We are very poplar.'

The mispronunciation distracted him momentarily. 'I understand that. But something must have happened, Mrs Federova.'

'Call me Galia. It is the Russian way for Galina.'

'Are you the owner?'

'That is Gennady Demidov. I just manage.'

Vusi took his notebook from his inside pocket and scribbled a note.

'Why you write this down?'

He shrugged. 'Till what time are you open?'

'The door close at twelve on a Monday night.'

'And then everybody leaves?'

'No. Nobody can come in, but those inside, they can stay. We close the bar when everybody go home.'

'This morning, at two-fifteen, did you still have people?'

'I must ask the night manager. Petr.'

'Can you call him?'

'He sleeps.'

'You will have to wake him up.'

She wasn't keen. She drew on the cigarette and blew the smoke out through her nose like a bull in a cartoon. Then she began to rifle through invoices again, searching for the phone. He wondered how on earth untidy people managed to function.

Benny Griessel walked closer to Josh Geyser. He looked up at the colossus who was now jutting his jaw out in determination. 'Mr Geyser, let me explain your choices: we can sit here, just the two of us, and talk quietly . . .'

'Regardt and I will be here too, Josh, don't worry . . .' Willie Mouton said behind him.

'No,' said Griessel, taken aback. 'It doesn't work like that . . .'

'Of course it does. He has the right . . .'

Griessel turned around slowly, his patience wearing thin. 'Mr Mouton, I understand this is a difficult time for everyone. I understand that the victim was your partner and you want this case solved. But it is *my* job. So would you please leave so I can get on with it.'

Willie Mouton coloured. The Adam's apple bobbed faster, the voice rose to the frequency of the meat saw. 'He has the right to a lawyer and yesterday he was in *my* office. Regardt and I have to be present.' The lawyer, Groenewald, came down the passage behind Mouton, seeming to know he needed to help.

Benny looked for patience and found a fraction. 'Mr Geyser, this is an interview, not an arrest. Do you want Groenewald to be present?'

Geyser looked to Melinda for help. She shook her head. 'He's Willie's lawyer . . .'

'I am available,' Groenewald said primly.

'I insist on it,' said Mouton. 'Both of us . . .'

Benny Griessel knew it was time to tackle Mouton. There was only one way. He walked purposefully up to the shaven-headed man, the official words ready on his tongue, but the prim lawyer was surprisingly quick. Groenewald jumped in between the two men.

'Willie, if he locks you up for obstruction, there is nothing I can do for you.' He took Mouton firmly by the arm. 'Come, let's go and wait in your office. Josh, you know where to find me.'

Mouton got to his feet; his mouth moved, but no sound came out. Then he turned away slowly, but his eyes stayed on Griessel, challenging. Groenewald tugged at him and Mouton walked to the door, where he stopped to call over his shoulder: 'You have rights, Josh.' Then they were gone.

Griessel took a deep breath and turned his attention to the duo. 'Mr Geyser . . .'

'We were in church last night,' said Melinda.

He nodded slowly, asked: 'Mr Geyser, do you want legal representation?'

He looked to his wife. She shook her head slightly. Griessel saw the dynamic. She was the one with the final say.

'I don't want anybody,' said Josh. 'Let's get this over with. I know what you think.'

'Ma'am, please, would you wait in Mouton's office?'

'I'll be in the front. In the lounge.' She went over to Josh, touched his big arm, gave him a weighted look. '*Beertjie* . . .' she said. *My little bear*. Beside her husband she looked small, but she was taller than Griessel had thought. She was wearing jeans and a sea-green blouse that echoed the colour of her eyes. Ten kilograms ago her body must have been sensational.

'It's all right, *Pokkel*,' said Josh, but there was tension between them, Griessel could sense it.

She looked back once, and closed the door softly behind her.

Griessel took out his cell phone and switched it off. He looked up at Geyser, who stood beside the oval table with his feet planted wide apart.

'Mr Geyser, sit, please.' He gestured to one of the chairs closest to the door.

Josh didn't move. 'Tell me first: are you a child of God?'

17

On the fourth floor of an unobtrusive building at 24 Alfred Street in Green Point, the shoes of the Provincial Commissioner SAPS: Western Cape clicked rapidly down the long corridor.

He was a Xhosa, short, dressed in full uniform, but without his jacket, the sleeves of his blue shirt rolled up to his elbows. He came to a standstill at the open office door of John Afrika, Regional Commissioner: Detective Services and Criminal Intelligence. Afrika was on the phone, but he heard his boss knock and beckoned him to come in.

'I'll call you back,' he said and put the phone down.

'John, the National Commissioner has just phoned. Do we know about an American girl who died last night?'

'We know,' said John Afrika, resigned. 'I was wondering when the trouble would start.'

The Provincial Commissioner sat down opposite Afrika. 'The girl's friend phoned her father in America half an hour ago and said someone is trying to kill her too.'

'Did she phone from here?'

'From here.'

'*Bliksem*. Did she say where she was?'

'Apparently not. The father said it sounded as though she had to run away before she had finished talking.'

'I'll have to let Benny and Vusi know. And Mbali,' said John Afrika as he picked up his phone.

Galia Federova, manager of Van Hunks, spoke over the phone in Russian and then held it out for Vusi. 'Petr. You can talk with him.'

The detective took the phone. 'Good morning, my name is Vusi. I just want to know if something happened in the club this morning, between two o'clock and two fifteen. Two American girls, and some young men. We have them on video, running up Long Street, and we have people who say they were in the club.'

'There were many people,' said Petr, his accent much lighter than the woman's.

'I know, but did anybody notice anything unusual?'

'What is unusual?'

'An argument. A fight.'

'I don't know. I was in the office.'

'Who would know?'

'The barmen and the waiters.'

'Where do I find them?'

'They are sleeping, I think.'

'I need you to call them, sir. I need all of them to come to the club.'

'That is not possible.'

'Yes, sir, it *is* possible. This is a murder investigation.'

Petr sighed deeply on the other end to emphasise his annoyance. 'It will take a lot of time.'

'We don't have time, sir. One of the girls is still alive and if we don't find her, she will be dead too.'

Vusi's mobile began to ring.

'One hour,' said Petr.

'Ask them to come to the club,' said Vusi, and passed the receiver back to Federova. He answered his cell phone. 'This is Vusi.'

'She's still alive, Vusi,' said John Afrika. 'She phoned her father in America, half an hour ago. But I can't get hold of Benny.'

Rachel Anderson sprinted down Upper Orange Street. Her eyes searched desperately back and forth for an escape route, but the houses on both sides were impregnable – high walls, electrified fences, security railing and gates. She knew she had no time, they would come back through the shop, she had maybe a hundred-metre start on them. Her father's voice had given her new urgency, a desire to live, to see her parents again. How horribly worried her mother must be now, her dear, scatterbrained mother.

She saw one house just a block from the shop on the corner to the left, a single-storey Victorian dwelling with a low white picket fence and a pretty garden. She knew it was her only chance. She hurdled the hip-height fence but the tip of her shoe hooked and sent her sprawling into the flower bed beyond, her hands trying in vain to break her fall, her belly skidding across the slippery surface, winding her, the damp garden soil leaving a wide muddy stripe on her blue T-shirt.

She scrambled up quickly, meaning to run around the house, across the front to the back, away from the street before they saw her. Over the grass, a paved path, more flower beds in cheerful white, yellow and blue. Her mouth was gaping to get enough air. Past the furthest corner of the house there were bougainvilleas, big and dense, the purple flowers tumbling over an arbour. A hiding place. She hesitated for only an instant to estimate the size of the bushes, not realising they had thorns. She dived inside, to the deepest shadow at the back. The sharp points pierced her, scratched long bloody tracks on her arms and legs. She cried out softly at the pain, and lay gasping on her stomach behind the screen of leaves. 'Please, God,' she murmured and turned her face to the street. She could see nothing, only the thick curtain of green, and the tiny white flowers in each purple cup.

If they hadn't seen her, she was safe. For now. She shifted her hand down her limbs, to try and pull the thorns out.

'Let me go and phone the American Consul,' the Provincial Commissioner said to John Afrika as he rose. 'I'm going to tell him we are doing everything in our power to track her down. John, you must make sure that that is true. Get Benny Griessel to take full control.'

'Right. But the stations are reluctant to allocate people . . .'

'Leave that to me,' said the Provincial Commissioner. He walked to the door and stopped.

'Isn't Griessel up for promotion?'

'It's been approved; I think he'll be notified today.'

'Tell him. Tell the whole team.'

'Good idea.' Afrika's phone rang. The Provincial Commissioner waited, in the hope that there would be news.

'John Afrika.'

'Commissioner, this is Inspector Mbali Kaleni. I am at Caledon Square, but they say they don't have a place for me.'

'Mbali, I want you to go to the station commander's office, because he is going to get a call right now.'

'Yes, sir,' she said.

'The missing girl . . . She's alive. She called home half an hour ago.'

'Where is she?'

'She did not have enough time to say. We need to find her. Quickly.'

'I will find her, Commissioner.' So self-assured.

John Afrika put down the phone. 'Caledon Square,' he told the Provincial Commissioner. 'They don't want to cooperate.'

'Wait,' said the little Xhosa in his impeccable uniform. 'Let me call him too.'

'Would you like to tell me what happened yesterday?' Griessel sat down on the other side of the oval table, with his face towards the door. The big man was sitting down now, elbows on the table, one hand nervously touching the drooping blonde moustache.

'It wasn't me.' He didn't look at Griessel.

'Mr Geyser, let's start at the beginning. Apparently there was an incident yesterday . . .'

'What would you do if a son of Satan messed with your woman? What would you do?'

'Mr Geyser, how did you find out that Adam Barnard and your wife . . .'

'We're all sinners. But he had no remorse. Never. He never stopped. Idols. Mammon. Whoring.' He gave Griessel an ominous look and said: 'He believed in evolution.'

'Mr Geyser . . .'

'He's a son of Satan. Today he burns in hell . . .'

'Mr Geyser, how did you find out?' With infinite patience.

He shrugged as though he needed to steel himself. 'Yesterday when she came home, she didn't look well, so I asked what was wrong . . .' He leaned his forehead on his hand and looked down at the table. 'First she said "nothing". But I knew something was . . . So I said: "*Pokkel*, you're not okay, what is it?" Then she sat down and she couldn't look me in the eye. That's when I knew something was very wrong . . .' He went quiet, clearly unwilling to relive the events.

'What time was that?'

'Three o'clock, round about.'

'And then?'

'Then I sat next to her and held her hands. And she started crying. Then she said: "*Beertjie*, let us pray, *Beertjie*." And she held my hands tight and prayed and she said: "Lord, forgive me because Satan . . ."' Geyser opened and closed his fists, his face contorted with feeling. ' ". . . because Satan got into my life today." So I said: "*Pokkel*, what happened?" But she just kept her eyes shut . . .' The big man shielded his face with his hands.

'Mr Geyser, I know this is hard.'

Geyser shook his head, still hiding his face. 'My Melinda . . .' he said and his voice cracked. 'My *Pokkel*.'

Griessel waited.

'Then she asked God to forgive her, because she was weak, so I asked her if she had stolen something, but she said, Lord, One John One verse eight, she said it over and over until I said stop, what did she do? Then she opened her eyes and said she had sinned in Adam Barnard's office, because she wasn't as strong as I think, she couldn't stop the devil, and I said what kind of sin, and she said: "of the flesh, *Beertjie*, the big sin of the flesh . . ."' Geyser's voice broke down and he stopped, with both hands over his face.

Benny Griessel sat there suppressing the urge to get up and put his hand on the massive shoulder, to console, to say something. In twenty-five years he had learned to be sceptical, not to believe anything until all the evidence was in. He had learned that when the sword of righteousness hung over your head, you were capable of anything – heart-rending, tearful denial, the pained indignation at being falsely accused, strong protest, deep remorse or pathetic self-pity. People could lie with astonishing skill; sometimes it led to total self-deception, so that they clung with absolute conviction to an imaginary innocence.

So he did nothing. He just waited for Josh Geyser to finish crying.

Galia Federova pressed a switch and neon lights flickered on near the roof of the club, just enough to cloak the large space in twilight.

'You can wait here,' she said to Vusi and pointed at the table and chairs around the dance floor. 'Would you like something to drink?'

'Do you have tea?'

He fancied she smiled before she said: 'I will tell them.' Then she was gone.

He walked between the tables that hadn't yet been set out since the previous night.

He stopped at one, took down the chairs and sat down. He put his notebook, pen and cell phone on the table and looked around in amazement. On the right against the wall was the long bar counter made from rough, thick wooden beams. On the walls were artificial shipwreck ornaments from the era of sailing ships, between modern neon curlicues in piratical designs. On the left, right at the back, was a bank of turntables and electronic equipment, with a dance floor in front. Four dance towers stood metres above the dance floor. High up against the ceiling hung bunches of lasers and spotlights, all dark now. Giant speakers were mounted on every wall.

He tried to imagine how it had been last night. Hundreds of people, loud music, dancing bodies, flickering lights. And now it was quiet, empty and spooky.

He felt uneasy in this place.

In this city too. It was the people, he thought. Khayelitsha had often broken his heart with its pointless murders, the domestic violence, the terrible poverty, the shacks, the daily struggle. But he had been welcome there, the source of law and order, simple people, his people, they respected him, stood by him, supported him.

Ninety per cent of those cases were straightforward. In this city the possibilities were complicated and legion, the agendas inscrutable. It was all antagonism and suspicion. As if he were some intruder.

'No respect,' his mother would say. 'That's the problem with the new world.' His mother carved elephants out of wood in Knysna, sanding and polishing them until they came alive, but she refused to sell them in the roadside stall next to the lagoon, 'Because people don't have respect any more.' To her, the 'new world' was anything across the brown waters of the Fish and Mzimvubu Rivers, but there were no jobs in Gwiligwili, 'at home'. Now she was an exile, cast out on this 'new world'. Even though she only went shopping once a week. The rest of the time she sat in front of the corrugated iron shack in Khayalethu South with her elephants, waiting for her son to phone on the cell phone he had bought for her. Or for Zukisa, to hear how many artworks they had sold to the disrespectful tourists.

Vusi thought of Tiffany October, the slim young pathologist. She had the same soft eyes as his mother, the same gentle voice that seemed to be hiding great wisdom.

He thought of phoning her, but his guts contracted.

Would she go out with a Xhosa?

'Ask her,' Griessel had said. 'It can't do any harm.' He looked for the mortuary number in his notebook.

He phoned. It rang for a long time before the switchboard answered. He took a deep breath to say: 'May I speak to Dr October?' But his courage failed him; the fear that she would say 'no' lurked in the pit of his stomach like a disease. He cancelled the call in panic.

He cursed himself, in angry Xhosa, and immediately phoned Vaughn Cupido, the only member of the SAPS Organised Crime Task Force in Bellville South that he knew. He had to hold for a long time before Cupido answered with his usual, self-assured mantra: 'Talk to me.'

Vusi said hullo and then asked if they knew anything about Gennady Demidov. Cupido whistled through his teeth, as demonstrative as ever. 'Genna. We call him Semi-dof, like in semi-stupid, if you get my drift. Brother, the city belongs to him, pretty much – prostitution, drugs, blackmail, money laundering, cigarettes . . .'

'He owns the Van Hunks club . . .'

'*Ja*. And he's got another club, in Bree, the Moscow Redd; he's got a guest house in Oranjezicht that's really just a brothel and the word is that the Cranky Croc in Longmarket is his in all but name.'

'The Cranky Croc?'

'The Internet café and bar at Greenmarket Square. Easiest place in Cape Town to buy weed.'

'I have an American tourist, about nineteen, whose throat was cut last night up in Long Street. But earlier they had been in Van Hunks . . .'

'It's drugs, Vusi. Sounds to me like a deal that went wrong. They do that, the Russians. Show your network you don't take shit.'

'A deal gone wrong?'

'Semi-dof is an importer, Vusi. The dealers buy from him, a hundred thousand rands' worth at a time.'

'So why don't you arrest him?'

'It's not that easy, brother. He's clever.'

'But the girl only arrived here yesterday, first time in Cape Town. She's no dealer.'

'She must be a mule.'

'A mule?'

'They bring the drugs in. On planes, fishing trawlers, any way they can.'

'Ah,' said Vusi.

'So she probably didn't deliver what she was meant to. Something like that. I can't say what happened, but it's drugs . . .'

*　　*　　*

The station commander of Caledon Square walked down the passage behind Inspector Mbali Kaleni, unable to hide his displeasure.

Ten minutes ago everything had been under control; his efficient police station had been functioning normally and effectively. Then she waddles in, without knocking, orders everyone around, demanding an office that he didn't have, refusing to share with the social worker. Next minute he was being *kakked* on by the Provincial Commissioner, accusing him of bringing the Service into disrepute. Now he had Social Services sharing his office so that this domineering woman could move in.

They walked into the charge office. She looked like an overstuffed pigeon – short, with a big bulge in front and a big bulge behind in her tight black trouser suit. Large handbag over her shoulder, service pistol in a thick black belt around her hips and her SAPS ID card hanging from a cord around her neck, probably because no one would believe she was a policewoman.

She stopped in the middle of the room, feet planted wide apart, and clapped sharply, twice.

'Listen up, people,' she said loudly. *Pee-pol*, in her Zulu accent.

Here and there a head turned.

'Silence!' Sharp and loud.

Silence descended, everyone paid attention: complainants, their companions, uniforms.

'Thank you. My name is Inspector Mbali Kaleni. We have a situation and we need to be sharp. There is an American tourist missing in the city, a nineteen-year-old girl, maybe in Camps Bay, maybe Clifton or Bantry Bay. There are people trying to kill her. We must find her. I am in control of the operation. So I want you to get every vehicle out there, and make sure they get the message. They must come and collect a photo of the girl after twelve o'clock. The Provincial Commissioner has personally called your station commander, and he will not tolerate any problems . . .'

'Inspector . . .' said the Constable who had taken the Carlucci's call.

'I am not finished,' she said.

'I know where she is,' he said, not intimidated, making his commanding officer proud.

'You know?' Kaleni asked, some of the wind taken out of her sails.

'She's not in Camps Bay, she's in Oranjezicht,' he said.

Vusi Ndabeni sat in the twilight of the nightclub and phoned Benny Griessel, but the detective's cell phone was on voice mail.

'Benny, it's Vusi. I think the girls brought drugs in and I think they were supposed to deliver it to Van Hunks. I'm waiting for the barmen and waiter, but I know they're not going to talk. I think we must bring Organised Crime in. Call me, please.'

He looked at his notes again. What else could he do?

The video cameras.

He phoned the Metro Police video control room, and was eventually put through to The Owl.

'I can tell you they came from the lower end of Long Street. The camera on the corner of Longmarket and Long shows the two girls walking past at 01:39. The angle isn't great, but I compared it with the other material. It's the same girls.'

'*Walking* past?'

'They were walking fast, but definitely not running. But at time code 01:39:42 you can see the men coming past. The angle is a bit better, I can see five of them running in the same direction, north to south.'

'After the girls.'

'That's right. I'm still looking for something before that, but there was a camera out of operation on the other side of Shortmarket. So don't hold your breath.'

'Thanks a lot,' said Vusi.

So, here, two hundred metres from the club, they were still walking, unaware of the men chasing them.

What did it all mean?

He made a note in his book. What else?

He must call Thick and Thin. They must search Rachel Anderson's luggage for any sign of drugs.

He looked for their number on his cell phone, found it, but hesitated. Would it help?

The laboratory was six months behind, understaffed, overworked.

Later. First they must find Rachel Anderson.

Fransman Dekker hesitated in AfriSound's large reception room until the beautiful coloured woman got up and approached him.

'Can I help you?' she asked with the same subdued manner as the black woman on the ground floor, but with more interest.

'Inspector Fransman Dekker.' He held out his hand. 'I am sorry for your loss.'

She lowered her eyes. 'Natasha Abader. Thank you.' Her hand felt small and cool in his.

'I'm looking for Inspector Benny Griessel.'

'He's in the conference room.' Her inspection of his fingers for a ring was smooth and practised. She gave nothing away when she saw the thin gold band, but looked him in the eye.

'There is a journalist downstairs at your front door. Please don't let them come up.'

'I will tell Naomi. Can I offer you some coffee? Tea? Anything.' The last was said with a measured smile, perfect white teeth.

'No, thank you,' he replied and looked away. He didn't want to start something now. Under no circumstances.

18

'I'm sorry,' said Josh Geyser.

'No need to be sorry.'

'It's just . . . she's everything to me.'

'I understand,' said Griessel.

'I was finished,' said Geyser. 'I was nothing. Then she took me . . .'

Josh Geyser started at the beginning. Griessel let him talk.

Geyser had his feelings under control now, elbows on the table. Staring at the wall behind Griessel. He had been on the wrong road, he said. He had been a Gladiator on TV – women, drink, cocaine and steroids. A celebrity, with big money and fame. Then the SABC cancelled the show. Overnight. Everything changed. Not immediately; there was still appearance money at the Gauteng casinos for a while, still something in the bank. But seven months later he could no longer afford the rent of the double-storey house in Sandton. They evicted him and the Sheriff took his furniture and the bank took back the BMW and his friends weren't his friends any more.

Three months of bewilderment, of sleeping on other people's couches and asking for a few rand from people who were tired of him and his troubles. Then he found Jesus. In the House of Faith, the big charismatic church in Bryanston, Johannesburg, and his whole life changed. Because it was genuine. Everything. The friendships, the love, the compassion, the concern, the forgiveness for what he had been.

Then one day the pastor said they needed baritones for the Praise Singers, the huge church choir. Josh could always sing, since he was a boy. He had the voice, the instinctive feel for harmony, he was born with it, but his life had taken other directions and he had drifted away from that. So he became a Praise Singer – and on the first day he saw Melinda, this pretty woman with the angel face smiling over the heads of the tenors at him.

After practice she came to him and said: 'I know you, you're White Lightning.'

He said not any more, and then her eyes went all soft and said: 'Come . . .' and took his hand.

In the church coffee bar they exchanged stories. She was a divorcee from Bloemfontein, a former singer in her ex-husband's band, with a life full of sin. After the divorce she had been rudderless and moved to Johannesburg in the hope of finding work. The House of Faith was her salvation, her lifebuoy in the stormy seas of life. They both knew it straight away that night . . . But when you've been so down, so destroyed, you are careful, you talk first, long hours in the safety of the church social spot. Night after night. One day, three weeks later, they were there after choir practice when she asked: 'Do you know "Down to the River to Pray", the Negro spiritual?' He said he didn't and she began to sing the simple melody in her lovely voice, until he had it too and began to sing along in harmony. They sang quietly, just the two of them looking into each other's eyes, because they knew these two voices were perfectly matched. 'It was magic,' said Josh, still staring at the wall, 'like a shaft of light from heaven.' They sang louder, still the same song, and the coffee bar went quiet, dead quiet, until they had finished.

'That's where it all began,' he said.

'I see.'

'She's my everything . . .'

'Mr Geyser . . .'

'Just call me Josh.'

'Josh, I need to know what happened yesterday.'

He looked at Griessel and lifted his hands helplessly. 'It was too much for me.' Griessel just nodded.

'We knew nothing about Adam Barnard. Our first CD came out on the Chorus label. It's a small gospel studio in Centurion.

Adam came to talk to us, said we were too good to be hidden away – we had a wonderful message that the world needed to hear. Ever so holy, called himself a child of God, he just wanted to help . . . so we signed and came to Cape Town. I only heard about his ways then.'

'What ways?'

'You know . . .'

There was a quiet knock on the door. Griessel said 'Come in.'

The door opened. Fransman Dekker put a head inside. 'Benny . . .'

Griessel stood up. 'Excuse me just a moment.' He went to the door and pulled it shut behind him.

'Your cell phone is off,' Dekker whispered.

'I know.' He didn't want interruptions like this now.

'I just wanted to tell you I'm here. They're looking for a place where I can talk to her.'

'I'll come when I'm finished.'

Natasha, the beautiful personal assistant, came walking down the passage. 'Fransman . . .' she called.

Griessel raised his eyebrows.

'What?' asked Dekker.

'First-name terms already . . .' murmured Griessel.

Dekker shrugged 'Story of my life.'

'Fransman, you can sit in the studio,' said Natasha. 'Give us ten minutes.'

Ponytail brought in a tray with a teapot and the necessary tea things. He put it down three tables away from Vusi and walked out again.

Vusi stood up and went over to the tray.

They would all be like this. The Van Hunks employees. Aggressive and unhelpful. He would get nothing out of them, he realised. It was a waste of time, because the theory of drug mules made sense.

He poured tea into a cup, added milk and sugar, then carried the whole tray over to his table.

Oliver Sands had said that Anderson had suddenly changed. He sat down, put the cup aside and paged through his notebook until he found the reference. At Lake Kariba. She had become morose. That must have been when they got the drugs. Or realised they had gone? That might be it.

She and Erin were to bring the drugs like this, because tourists were Africa's new gold, waved easily through the border posts. Maybe they had brought the drugs from America, maybe from Malawi or Zambia. He didn't know how these things worked. It might not be their first time.

And then something happened, or they sold it somewhere else, and then they came and told Demidov here at the club, or Galia Federova or the night manager, Petr. Then they walked back to the Youth Hostel and a minute or two later Demidov sent his thugs to make an example of them, the chase that began somewhere beyond Longmarket Street. They caught Erin up at the church and cut her throat.

'They do that, the Russians. Show their network they don't take shit,' Vaughn Cupido had said.

Was Erin Russel the team leader? Or was Rachel Anderson just lucky to escape?

It was Demidov's people hunting Anderson now. The question was, how did he prove it? How did he stop them?

He reached for the teacup. He must try Griessel again. He picked up his phone and punched in the number. Voice mail again.

Josh Geyser told Griessel he had just let go of Pokkel's hands, right there in the sitting room, because from then on he was like a man possessed. He got into his BMW M3 and drove here from Milnerton Ridge and he could remember nothing of that trip, that's how bad it was. He pulled up halfway onto the pavement because there was never any parking here and he rushed in, ready to break Adam Barnard's neck, he couldn't deny it. If he had found Adam here he would have done something the Lord would have punished him for.

'You admit that you went into Willie Mouton's office and threatened to kill Adam Barnard?'

'I had already told Natasha that out front. I was cursing. I apologised to her, just now. She understands. She knows about the devil.'

'And you went to Mouton?'

'I went into Adam's office first. I thought they were lying to me. But he wasn't there. Then I went to Willie's.'

'And then?'

'I asked him if he knew and he said "no" and then I told him I was going to kill Adam. But Adam wasn't there. What could I do?'

'What *did* you do?'

'I went looking for him.'

'Where?'

'Café Zanne and the Bizerca Bistro.'

'Why there?'

'That's where he hangs out. Lunchtimes.'

'Did you find him?'

'No, thank the Lord.'

'And then?'

'Then the devil left me.'

Griessel raised his brows.

'It was the traffic,' said Josh Geyser. 'When I wanted to go home, I got stuck in the traffic. An hour and a half. That's when the devil left me.' He looked at the wall again and said: 'I sat at the robots in Paardeneiland and cried, because the devil had tested me and I let the Lord down. And Melinda, Melinda . . .'

'Josh, did you go straight home?'

Geyser just nodded.

'Do you own a firearm?'

He shook his head. No.

'We will have to search your house, Josh. We have instruments that can tell if there were guns or ammunition, even if they are not there any more.'

'I don't have a gun.'

'Where were you from midnight last night?'

'With Melinda.'

'Where were you?'

'We went to church last night.'

'Which church?'

'The Tabernacle, in Parklands.'

'Until what time?'

'I don't know . . . I suppose, half past ten.'

'At church?'

'After the service we went to see the pastor. For counselling.'

'Until half past ten?'

'Thereabouts.'

'And then?'

'Then we went home.' He looked at Griessel and saw it was not enough. He interlaced his thick fingers on the table and stared at them with great concentration. 'It was . . . hard. She . . . Melinda . . . She wanted me to hold her . . . I . . .' He went quiet again.

'Josh, did you leave the house last night?'

'No.'

'Not at all?'

'I only went out again this morning. When Willie phoned.'

Griessel looked at Geyser intently. He recognised the simplicity of this giant, the childish honesty. He thought of the tears, his absolute brokenness over his wife's unfaithfulness. He didn't know if he could believe him. Then he thought of the damage Adam Barnard had done, to Alexa, to Josh, to how many others. Then he remembered his own infidelity last night and he got up in a hurry and said: 'You will have to wait here, Josh, if you don't mind.'

Fransman Dekker asked Melinda Geyser to sit on one of the chairs at the big sound desk in the recording studio, but when he closed the soundproof door and turned around she was still standing, like someone who had something pressing to say. 'Sit, please,' he said.

'I can't . . .' Uneasy, tense.

'Ma'am, this will take a while. It's better if you sit.'

'You don't understand . . .'

'What don't I understand?' He sat down in an office chair on wheels.

'I . . . You must forgive me . . . I'm still old fashioned . . .' She gestured with her hand to try to explain.

Dekker looked at her in query.

'I don't . . . I can't talk to you about yesterday . . .'

The way she said it made him suspicious.

'To me?' His voice cut like a knife.

She couldn't look at him, confirming his suspicion.

'Is it because I'm coloured?'

'No, no, I can't talk . . . to a man.'

Dekker heard the way she said it, like someone who had been caught out. He saw the flicker in her eyes. 'You're lying,' the anger flaring quickly in him, like a switch turned on.

'Please, this is hard enough.'

He rose from the chair, startling her into a backwards step.

'Your kind . . .' he said, losing control for a moment, other words welling up behind the rage, his fists opening and closing, but somehow he found control. He made a noise somewhere between disbelief and disgust.

'Please . . .' she said.

He despised her. He walked out of the door, trying to slam it. Outside, Benny Griessel was in the passage with his phone to his ear saying: 'Vusi, I trust the guys from Organised Crime as far as I can throw them.'

Barry sat on the veranda of Carlucci's and listened to the sirens approaching through the city below. He saw a young man in an apron who heard them too, and came outside.

The patrol vehicles raced up Upper Orange, blue lights revolving. Four of them stopped in front of the restaurant with a screech of tyres, doors flung open, blue uniforms tumbling out. From one passenger door, a short, fat, black woman got out with a large handbag over her shoulder and a pistol on her hip.

She came quickly across the street, with the horde of blue uniforms following in her wake.

Around him at the other tables, the restaurant clientele watched the procession with astonishment.

The young man in the apron waited for them on the veranda.

'Are you the man who called in about the girl?' Barry heard the black woman ask with authority.

'I am.'

'Then tell me everything.' She heard shuffling behind her and turned around to see the amused grins on the policemen's faces. Their smiles disappeared under her angry glare.

'You can't all stand in here. Go wait outside.'

19

At seventeen minutes to four, American Eastern Standard Time – five hours behind Greenwich Mean Time and seven hours behind Cape Town, Bill Anderson sat at the laptop on his desk reading Internet articles about South Africa. His wife, Jess, sat on the leather couch behind him, her legs drawn up and covered with a blanket. She jumped when the phone rang shrilly.

He grabbed it. 'Bill Anderson,' he said, the concern discernible in his voice.

'Mr Anderson, my name is Dan Burton. I am the US Consul General in Cape Town.' The voice rang as clear as crystal despite the great distance. 'I know what a difficult time this must be for you.'

'Thank you, sir.'

'Who is it?' Jess Anderson asked, coming to stand close to her husband. He held a hand over the receiver and whispered: 'The Consul General in Cape Town.' Then he held the phone so she could also hear.

'I can tell you that I've just got off the phone with both the National and Provincial Commissioners of the South African Police Services, and although they have not found Rachel yet . . .'

Jess Anderson made a small noise and her husband put his arm around her shoulders while they listened.

'. . . they have assured me they will leave no stone unturned until they have done so. They are allocating every available resource to the search as we speak, and they think it is only a matter of time . . .'

'Thank you, sir . . .'

'Now, the only reason why the Ambassador himself is not calling you, is because he is away on official matters up north in Limpopo Province, but it is my job to coordinate all functions of the US Government in the Cape Town consular district, where I maintain contact with senior South African officials, both provincial and national . . .'

'Mr Burton . . .'

'Please call me Dan . . .'

'Our biggest concern is that Rachel said something about the police when she called.'

'Oh?'

'She said that she could not even go to the police.'

The Consul General was quiet for a moment. 'Did she say why?'

'No, she did not have time. She was very distressed, she said "they're here", and then I just heard noises . . .'

'She said the police were there?'

'No . . . I don't know . . . She said "they're here, please help me" . . . But the way she spoke about the police . . . I don't know, it was my impression that she could not trust them. And I've been doing some reading on the Internet. It says here the man in charge of the whole police force over there is being charged with corruption and defeating the ends of justice. . . .'

'Oh, my God,' said Jess, looking at the computer screen.

'Well . . .' the Consul General seemed to need time to digest this information. 'I know how it looks, Mr Anderson, but I have every reason to believe the law enforcement people in Cape Town are highly competent and trustworthy. I will certainly call the Commissioner right away to get some answers . . . In the meantime, I've taken the liberty of giving your phone number to the authorities. The Commissioner has assured me the officer in charge of the investigation will call you as soon as he can, and he will keep you updated on all developments. His name is . . . Ghreezil, an Inspector Benny Ghreezil . . .'

'Ask about Erin,' whispered Jess Anderson.

'Mr Burton, Erin Russel . . . Is there any news about Erin?'

'It is with great sadness that I have to tell you that Miss Russel was killed last night, Mr Anderson . . .' His wife let the blanket slip from her shoulders, put her hands on her husband's shoulders, pressed her face into his neck and wept.

Inspector Mbali Kaleni told the uniformed policemen that Carlucci's Restaurant was to be treated as a crime scene. She had the whole area cordoned off with yellow tape. Then she cleared the restaurant and had the employees and clients wait at the patio tables while two Constables took their names, addresses and statements.

She ordered a Sergeant to call Forensics to test the back and outside doors for fingerprints. She asked the young man in the apron, the one that had seen everything happen, to go with a Constable in a SAPS vehicle to the Caledon Square police station to help compile an Identikit image of the attackers. The young man said he couldn't; he was in charge of the shop. She asked him if there was someone he could call to replace him. He said he would try.

'Hurry up,' she said in her commanding way. 'We don't have time.'

'Did you check the number?' he asked her.

'What number?'

'The Land Rover's registration number. I got part of it. I gave it to the guys who were here.'

'I will check.'

Before the young man could walk away, she asked him to confirm in what direction the girl and her assailants had run. He pointed, but she held up a chubby hand and said, 'No, come show me.'

She put on her sporty Adidas dark glasses and led the way out of the restaurant, to the corner of Upper Orange and Belmont. The young man pointed towards the city centre. 'I want to make sure. You saw her run that way?'

'No, I told you, I didn't see her run in any other direction, so she must have gone down Upper Orange. The guys came back through the shop, shoved me, ran down to the corner, and the next thing, they came back for the Land Rover. Then they went that way too.'

'They were young?'

'Yes.'

'What is young?'

'I dunno, early twenties . . .'

'Fit and strong?'

'Yes.'

She nodded and gestured that he could go. She called the Sergeant who had come to take the statement. He confirmed that he had radioed in the Land Rover's number.

'Call them. Ask them what they have found.'

He nodded and went over to a patrol car.

She looked at the street again.

Why would they come back for the Land Rover? Two young men, chasing a girl from two o'clock that morning. She must be exhausted, but they didn't run after her, they came back for a vehicle? Made no sense.

She wiped perspiration from her forehead, adjusted the strap of the big black handbag over her shoulder and put her hands on her hips. She was oblivious to the uniformed men watching her, sniggering and whispering behind their cupped hands.

She turned around slowly, looking down every street. She wiped her forehead again. They couldn't see her any more; that was the thing. The two attackers would have pursued her on foot if they could see her. She had disappeared; that was why they fetched the vehicle.

Kaleni called two young Constables who were leaning against a police van. 'You, and you,' she pointed, 'come here.'

They came, laughing self-consciously. She told them to go out the back of the restaurant as far as the wooden door, which was still bolted shut.

'But don't touch anything.'

'Yes, Inspector.'

'And when I say "go", you run back through the shop, out

through the front door, until you get to me. Ask that guy with the apron exactly where they ran, then you follow the same route. You understand?'

'Yes, Inspector.'

'OK. *Ngokushesha!*'

Kaleni walked around the outside to the wooden door. She waited until she could hear the Constables' footsteps in the alleyway on the other side of the door.

'Are you right next to the door?'

'Yes.'

'Don't touch anything.' She checked her watch, waited until the second hand was close to the twelve o'clock mark.

'Are you ready?'

'Yes.'

'When I say go . . .' She counted down from five to one, then barked 'Go!' She heard them take off, feet echoing off the restaurant wall. She watched the second hand travel five, ten, fifteen, twenty, then the two Constables came around the corner. Twenty-four seconds to reach her.

'OK. Now, I want you to start from this door, and run down the street, as fast as you can.'

They looked at her, out of breath, but willing. They took off.

'No, wait!'

They stopped and turned back. They weren't smiling now.

'I will say "go" again,' she said, her eyes on the watch. She waited for the twelve mark again, counting down, and shouted 'Go!' They sprinted away and she kept an eye on them and the watch. The young man had said the attackers had pushed him over. Add one second for that, maybe two. They might have run outside and, not knowing in which direction she had gone, stopped and looked up Upper Orange and to the right down Belmont. Another two or three seconds.

She marked the Constables' progress at twenty-four and thirty seconds, then yelled at them, 'OK!', but they were out of earshot and kept on running, two blue uniforms in full flight down the long hill.

'Hey!' she tried again, to no avail.

'_Isidomu_,' she muttered and began to walk down the street herself, keeping her eyes on the thirty-second mark.

Rachel Anderson heard the sirens racing up the street only twenty metres from where she lay in the bougainvillea bush. She knew they were for her because the man in the restaurant would surely have called the police. And she could hear how the wailing stopped nearby, just up on the corner.

She lay still. All the thorns were out now, only the stinging of her wounds remained, Her breathing was normal, the sweat dried in the deep cool shade. They wouldn't be able to see her, even if they walked past down the street, even if they came into the garden.

She would wait until they stopped looking. Until they went away. Then she would decide what to do.

Mbali Kaleni walked to the corner of Upper Orange and Alexandra Avenue – more or less the twenty-four second mark. She walked slowly across the road to the opposite pavement.

The girl must have turned left here into Alexandra. That was why the men couldn't see her.

Something wasn't right.

She stared up Alexandra Avenue. The slope. A very tired girl. This morning early, before six, someone saw her high up on Lion's Head. Just after ten she was down here in Oranjezicht. She had come a long way, but she was on her way down, to the city. So would she get here and choose a street that led away from her destination? It was uphill, steep; it would be hell on tired legs.

But if you are afraid and your pursuers right behind . . .

Deep in thought, Kaleni rested her hand on the white picket fence of the single-storey Victorian house on her left. She looked for the two running uniformed idiots. Yes, there they were, walking back, chatting happily.

A block further on was the Molteno Reservoir. But that was

more than forty seconds from Carlucci's, even if Rachel Anderson could run as fast as two fresh, fit constables. No, she had to have turned this corner. Or . . .

Kaleni considered the Victorian house, looked at the fence. It was the only house in this part of the street without high walls or fences – the only alternative.

That's when she saw the damage to the flower bed. The ground cover was scraped away in a broad swathe. She took off her dark glasses. The palm prints were there, the footprints beyond, three of them before the edge of the lawn. She judged by sight the distance between the fence and the damage. Could someone climb over here? And land *there*?

She walked on, looking for the garden gate, and found it. She jogged over to it, an odd, hurried figure with a handbag over her shoulder, pistol on her hip and dark glasses in her hand.

'I'm not white enough for her,' Fransman Dekker said when Griessel concluded his call with Vusi.

'What?' said Griessel, his attention still on the phone. 'Sorry, Fransman, I have four more messages . . .' He put it to his ear again. 'Melinda?' he asked.

'I can't talk to a man . . .' Dekker said, in falsetto sarcasm.

'I'll be finished soon . . .' Griessel listened. 'It's John Afrika . . .'

Dekker took two steps down the passage and turned. 'But it's because I'm a *hotnot*. Fucking hypocritical gospel singers . . .' he said and shook his head.

'John Afrika again . . .' Griessel shook his head.

'Such a great Christian,' said Dekker.

'I have to phone the Commissioner back,' Griessel said apologetically. 'The girl . . . She phoned her father. In America . . . Commissioner, it's Benny . . .'

Dekker stopped at the studio door, pressed a palm against it, leaned on it and bent his head.

Griessel said 'yes, sir' and 'no, sir' over the phone, until at last: 'I'm on my way, I'll be there now.' He switched off the phone again.

'She won't talk to you because you're coloured?' he asked Dekker.

'That's not what she says, but it's what she means.'

'Fuck that. She can get a lawyer, and she can ask for a woman to be present, those are her choices . . .'

'You tell her.'

'That's exactly what I'm going to do,' said Griessel.

And then the lights went out.

20

Ndabeni was restless. He drank the last of the tea, put the cup on the tray and pushed it away. How long would it be before the people arrived, before Petr had his staff awake and on the go? What was Mbali Kaleni doing with his case up at the restaurant? That was where the action was; there was nothing going on here. Perhaps he would wait another ten minutes. If no one had arrived by then . . .

Then the big room went dark, everything eerily quiet, even the air conditioning off. Another power cut. Yesterday it had lasted for three hours.

Pitch black, he could see nothing.

He had to get out. He felt for his cell phone, pressed a key to light up the screen and turned it so the light shone over the table, picked up his notebook and pen and got up. He walked carefully between the tables and chairs, down the passage. A faint yellow band of light shone out of Galina Federova's office. He walked over to it, saw she had lit a candle and was busy pushing another into the neck of an empty beer bottle.

'Hi,' he said.

She jumped, said something that sounded like 'Bogh' and nearly dropped the beer bottle.

'I'm sorry . . .'

'Eskom,' she shrugged.

'What can you do?' he asked, rhetorically.

She lit the second candle as well, sat down behind her desk and took out a cigarette.

'I can do nothing.' She lit the cigarette from the candle.

Perhaps Russians were not into rhetorical questions. 'I'm sorry, but I will have to go.'

'I can bring you a candle.'

'No. The girl . . . she was seen.'

'Oh?' The pencil-drawn eyebrows were raised high. He didn't know how to read that. Vusi took a business card out of his pocket and put it down in front of her. 'Please, would you call me when the people from last night arrive?'

Federova picked up the card in her long nails. 'OK.'

'Thank you,' said Vusi. Using his cell phone as a torch, he walked back the way he had come in, through the kitchen, where Ponytail was counting booze bottles by the light coming in from the back door.

'What you do about the power? What the police do?'

He considered explaining carefully to the man that the police had nothing to do with the electricity supply. But he just said: 'We call Eskom.'

Vusi walked out of the back door into the alley, where the sunlight was blinding. He heard Ponytail call: 'Funny. I love funny cop,' but he was in a hurry and his car was up in Long Street, more than ten minutes' walk. He wanted to talk to Kaleni at the restaurant, he wanted . . . Vusi stopped just where the alley opened into Strand Street. There was something he could do, even if Benny Griessel said he didn't want Organised Crime involved. He chose Vaughn Cupido's number and called him.

'Speak to me,' Cupido answered immediately.

'Do you have photos of Demidov's people?'

Cupido didn't answer.

'Vaughn, are you there?'

'Why do you ask?' suspiciously.

'Do you, Vaughn?'

'I cannot confirm or deny.'

'What does that mean?'

'It means I'm just an Inspector. You will have to ask higher up.'

'Ask who?'

'The Senior Sup.'

'Vaughn, we have a man who saw two of the attackers in Oranjezicht just now. If he can ID Demidov's people . . . It could save the girl's life.'

It was quiet again.

'Vaughn?'

'Let me get back to you . . .'

Rachel Anderson heard the click-click of a woman's shoes on the garden path just metres away from her, and another sound, the rhythmic whisper of fabric on fabric. The noise stopped abruptly, then she heard a sigh and someone knocking loudly. Rachel kept her breathing shallow; she turned her head slowly so she could see her feet. Was she deep enough into the bushes?

Again someone hammered on the door. 'Hello, anybody home?' in an African accent, a woman, urgent.

What did it mean?

'Hey, guys!' the same voice barked, authoritarian. 'I called you back, but you did not hear.'

A man's voice answered from the street, then the same African woman: 'No, stay on the pavement, this might be a crime scene. Just go and tell them at the restaurant I need Forensics. Shoe imprints, I want them cast and identified.'

There was the sound of a door opening and a man's voice: 'Can I help you?'

'How are you?'

'That is not an appropriate question. Why are you hammering on my door?' The man's voice answered calm, timid.

'Because your doorbell is broken.'

'It's not broken. There is a power failure.'

'What? Again?'

'Yes. Can I help you?'

'I am Inspector Mbali Kaleni of the SAPS. We are looking for a girl who is running away from assailants, and I think she was in your garden. I want to know if you saw her.'

'I didn't see her . . .'

'Over there. Can you come and take a look?'

'Is that your police ID?'

'Yes.'

'When did this happen?'

'About forty minutes ago. Can you please come and look at your garden? You did not see her?'

'No. But I heard her . . .'

Rachel Anderson's heart went cold.

'You did?'

'Yes,' said the man. 'I heard footsteps, around the corner of the house . . .'

'Here?'

'Yes, just here. But I heard her run to the wall there, I think she jumped over, to the next house. By the time I looked through the window, she was gone.'

'Take a look at the tracks,' said the policewoman.

There was a moment of relief as the voices faded, but her pulse accelerated again because she didn't know where her tracks led. Then she remembered falling in the flower bed when she jumped over the wall. Was that all? Did the tracks lead here? She had stepped in damp ground; mud might have stuck to the grass or the slate of the path.

She heard the woman's footsteps on the path again. She kept dead still and closed her eyes.

Benny Griessel opened the big door of the AfriSound recording studio angrily. John Afrika had told him to hurry; they were waiting for him. The room was pitch dark, as it had no windows. The shaft of light from the open door illuminated Melinda; she stood with big, frightened eyes, hands folded across her breast, Bambi In Danger. He said, 'The power is off,' and she dropped her hands. Had she thought the darkened room was a police ploy?

He went up to her and said with all the patience he could muster: 'Madam, you will have to talk to Inspector Dekker. With or without your lawyer. That is your choice. You can request that a female officer be present, but you are not a victim; it's his discretion.'

'A female officer?' she was confused.

'A female member of the police.'

She thought for a moment. Then she said: 'He misunderstood me.'

'Oh?'

'After yesterday's events, I only meant it would be easier to talk to a woman about it.'

A meek little lamb without guile.

'So what do you want to do?'

'I just want to be sure it's confidential.'

He explained to her that if she or Josh were charged, nothing could be confidential.

'But we didn't do anything.'

'Then it will all be confidential.' So she agreed and he had to ask bloody Mouton where Fransman could question Melinda, because the studio was too dark. Natasha brought in a gas lamp and put it near Melinda in the recording studio.

Griessel and Dekker watched Natasha walk away. When she disappeared around the corner, Benny pulled his colleague by the arm as far as Adam Barnard's empty office. He had received a message from the Commissioner that he needed to pass on to Dekker. He knew what his reaction would be. There was only one way to do it: 'John Afrika says I must bring Mbali Kaleni in to help you.'

Fransman Dekker exploded. Not straight away, as if the implications mounted up in him first. Then he stood up straight, his eyes wild, his mouth opening and closing once, then the jaw muscles clamped shut, twitching as it all burst out and he hammered his fist against Adam Barnard's door: '*Jirre-jissis!*' He spun around, aimed for the door again, but Griessel had him, gripped his arm.

'Fransman!'

Dekker struggled to hold the arm. 'It stays *your* case.'

The coloured detective stopped, eyes staring, arms still up in the air. Griessel felt the strength in the shoulders as he pulled against them.

'I've got a son in Matric,' said Griessel. 'He's always telling me "Pa you must chill" and I think that is what you must do now, Fransman.'

Dekker's jaw began to work again. He jerked his arm out of Griessel's grasp and glared angrily at the door.

'You let everything wind you up, Fransman. It doesn't help shit.'

'You would never understand.'

'Try me.'

'How can I? You're white.'

'What is that supposed to mean?'

'It means you're not coloured,' he said, an angry finger pointed at Griessel's face.

'Fransman, I have no fucking idea . . .'

'Did you see, Benny? Last week, with the Commissioner? How many coloureds were there?'

'You were the only one.'

'Yes, just me. Because they push the darkies. That's why they are sending Kaleni. They must be pushed in everywhere. I'm just a fucking statistic, Benny, I'm just there to fill their fucking quota. Did you watch the Commissioner on Thursday? He only had eyes for the bloody Xhosas, he didn't even see me. Eight per cent Coloureds. Eight fucking per cent. That's how many of us they want. Who decided that? How? Do you know how many brown people that has ruined. Thousands, I'm telling you. Not black enough, sorry, brother, off you go, get a job with Coin Security, go and drive a fucking cash van. But not me, Benny, I'm not going anywhere.' Fransman Dekker's zeal drove him to the words and rhythms of his Atlantis childhood. 'It's my *fokken* life. I was just *so* big, I said to my ma I'm gonna be a policeman. She skivvied her *gat af* so I could get Matric and go to the *polieste*. Not drive a *fokken* cash van . . .'

He wiped spit from his lips. Griessel said: 'I do understand, Fransman, but . . .'

'You think so? Have you been marginalised all your life? Now that you whiteys have affirmative action at your backs, now you think you understand? You understand *fokkol*, I'm telling you. You were either Baas or Klaas, we were *fokkol*, always, we weren't white enough then, we're not black enough now; it never ends, stuck in the fucking middle of the colour palette. Now this white Christian lady says no, she's not talking to a man, but she doesn't know I can read her like I can read all the whiteys.'

'Can you read *me*, Fransman?' Griessel was growing angry too.

Dekker didn't reply, but turned away breathing heavily.

Griessel walked around him, so he could talk to his face. 'They say you've got ambition. Now listen to me, I threw my *fokken* career away because I didn't have control, because I let the shit get to me. That's why I'm standing here now. I didn't have any more options. Do you want options, Fransman? Or do you want to still be an Inspector at forty-four, with a job description that says "mentor" because they don't know what the fuck to do with you? Do you know how that feels? They look you up and down and think, what *kak* did you get up to that you're just a fucking Inspector with all that grey hair? Is that what you want? Do you want to be more than a bloody race statistic in the Service? Do you want to be the best policeman you can be? Then drop the shit and take the case and solve it, never mind what they say or how they talk to you or who John Afrika sends to help you. You have rights, just like Melinda Geyser. There are rules. Use them. In any case, you can do what you want, it won't change. I have been a policeman for over twenty-five years, Fransman, and I'm telling you now, they will always treat you like a dog, the people, the press, the bosses, politicians, regardless of whether you are black, white or brown. Unless they're phoning you in the middle of the night saying "there's someone at the window" – then you're the fucking hero. But tomorrow when the sun shines, you're nothing again. The question is: can you take it? Ask yourself that. If you can't, drop it, get another job. Or put up with it, Fransman, because it's never going to stop.'

Dekker stood still, breathing heavily.

Griessel wanted to say more, but he decided against it. He stepped away from Dekker, his brain at work, shifting his focus.

'I don't believe it was Josh Geyser. If he's lying, he deserves a fucking Oscar. Melinda is the only alibi he has, and there's something about her . . . she doesn't know what he said, let her talk, get her to give you more detail about yesterday, exactly what happened, then phone me and we can compare their stories. I have to go and see the Commissioner.'

Dekker didn't look at him. Griessel walked away down the passage.

'Benny,' said Dekker when he was almost in the reception area. Griessel turned.

'Thank you,' with reluctant frankness.

Griessel gestured with his hand and left.

One of the men in the lounge got up from an ostrich leather couch and tried to intercept him. Benny tried to avoid eye contact, but the man was too quick for him. 'Are you from the police?' He was tall, just over thirty, with a face that seemed very familiar to Griessel.

In a hurry and bothered, he said: 'Yes, but I can't talk to you now.' He would have liked to add 'because they are fucking me around', but he didn't. 'My colleague is still inside. Talk to him when he comes out,' and he jogged down the stairs, across the grass to where his car was parked.

There was a parking ticket stuck to the windscreen, right in the middle of the driver's window.

'Fuck,' he said, frustration surging over his dam wall of self-control. More paperwork that he didn't need. Metro Police had time to write fucking parking tickets, but don't ask them to help with anything else. He left the ticket right where it was, climbed in, started the engine and reversed out, grinding the gears as he drove away. He was going to ask the Commissioner for a clear job description.

Benny Griessel, Great Mentor, just didn't work for him. He had asked John Afrika last Thursday exactly what this job entailed. The answer: 'Benny, you're my safety net, my supervisor. Just keep an eye, check the crime scene management, don't let them miss suspects. *Bliksem*, Benny, we train them until it's coming out of everybody's ears, but the minute they stand on the scene, either it's stage fright or just plain sloppiness, I don't know. Maybe we're pushing them too fast, but I have to meet my targets, what else can I do? Look at the *bliksemse* Van der Vyver case; he's suing the Minister for millions; we just can't let that happen. Look over shoulders, Benny, give a gentle nudge where necessary.'

A fucking gentle nudge?

He had to brake suddenly for the traffic jam up ahead, two rows of cars, ten deep. The power cut meant all the traffic lights were down. Chaos.

'*Jissis*,' he said aloud. At least Eskom was one state institution that was worse than the SAPS.

He leaned back against the seat. It wouldn't help to get angry.

But, fuck it, what were you supposed to do?

From one case to the next. First here, then there. That was a recipe for a disaster.

If Josh Geyser wasn't the one who shot Barnard . . .

That guy inside, he remembered now who he was. Iván Nell, the star, he'd heard all his stuff on RSG; good, modulated rock, although he was stingy with the bass. He was sorry he hadn't talked to him quickly, he could have written to Carla about it tonight, but that's how it went, time for fuck all except sitting in the traffic, cursing.

He was hungry too. Only coffee since last night, he would have to do something about his blood sugar and suddenly he had a desire to smoke. He opened the cubbyhole, scratched around and found a half-pack of Chesterfield and a box of Lion matches. He lit one, wound the window down and felt the heat rising up from the street surface and flowing into the window.

He drew on the cigarette, slowly blowing out the smoke. It dammed up against the windscreen, then wafted out the window.

This morning Alexa Barnard had offered him a cigarette and he had said no thank you. 'An alcoholic that doesn't smoke?' she had asked. He had said he was trying to cut down because his AA sponsor was a doctor.

Then she said get another sponsor.

He liked her.

He should never have given her the alcohol.

And then he remembered that he wanted to atone for his mistake. He felt in his pocket while moving one car-length forward, found the phone and pressed the keys with his thumb.

It rang for a long time, as usual.

'Benny!' said Doc Barkhuizen, always bloody upbeat. 'Are you persevering?'

'Doc, you ever heard of the famous singer, Xandra Barnard?'

'They're taking a lot of interest in a house here,' said Barry over the cell phone. He drove slowly down Upper Orange in his beat-up red Toyota single-cab.

'What sort of interest?'

'There's a thousand uniformed Constables on the pavement, and this fat woman detective standing in the garden with a geriatric guy.'

'So find out what it's about.'

Barry looked at the houses in the street. On the right, a hundred metres down and opposite the Victorian house was a possibility. A long tar driveway to a single garage. 'Yeah . . .' He saw the uniforms watching him. 'Maybe. But not right now, there are too many eyes. Let me give it ten minutes or so . . .'

11:03–12:00

21

The hissing gas lamp that stood on the mixer bench threw an absurd shadow of Melinda Geyser onto the opposite wall. She stood with her face only centimetres from the glass, the recording booths behind her shaded in gloom. Dekker leaned forward in a leather chair on wheels, his elbows on his knees, because the leather back creaked loudly when he leaned back. He was perspiring. Without air conditioning it was getting hotter.

'Sorry about the misunderstanding,' she said, folding her arms under her breasts. Her figure was not without its attractions – the green blouse, jeans with white leather belt and big silver buckle, white pumps with wedge cork heels. But it bothered him, it wasn't what he expected from a gospel artist, the clothes were just that little bit too tight. They made him think of the kind of women who were most blatantly interested in him – late thirties, early forties, looks just starting to fade, and wanting to make the most of the last years of their sensual prime.

Maybe that was just how musicians were. 'Maybe I overreacted,' he said, and the sincerity in his voice was a surprise to him.

'Do you know what the difference is between life and making a CD?' she asked. She kept staring at the glass. He wondered if she was watching her own reflection.

'No,' said Dekker.

'The difference is that in life there is only one take.'

Was she about to lecture him?

'Adam had never asked me to come on my own before. Yesterday morning he phoned to say he *had* to see me. Those were his words, as though he had no choice. As though I was in trouble. "I have to see you. Just you." Like a headmaster sending for a naughty child.'

Then she moved, unfolding her arms, and turning to face Dekker. She took two steps and sat down on a two-seater leather couch opposite him, with her right arm on the armrest and the left on the cushions. She looked him in the eye and said: 'If you have done things in your life that might catch up with you, then you don't argue. You lie to your beloved husband, Mr Dekker, and you go to Adam Barnard's office and ask him what is going on.'

Mister. Now I'm a Mister.

The usually jovial Adam Barnard was serious, she said. Melinda sat dead still while she talked, not moving her hands or body, as if she was on thin ice, over deep waters. There was a determination in her voice.

Barnard had pushed a slim DVD case across his desk to her, the rewritable kind with the manufacturer's logo visible through the transparent plastic. She had looked at him, questioning. He had said nothing. She'd opened it. Inside someone had written on the white surface of the DVD in permanent ink, *Melinda 1987*. She had known right away what it was.

She took a deep breath, looked to the right at the glass, as if to see herself one last time.

'You need to know about my background, Mr Dekker. We live in a strange world, in a society that has to label things to accommodate them.' Her use of language surprised him, more sophisticated than he had expected.

'But the process is neither logical nor fair. If you are a person who by nature struggles to conform, you're called a rebel when you're young. Later you're called other things. I was a so-called rebel. At school I was ... disobedient. I wanted to do everything my way. I was inquisitive. About everything. I had a craving for excitement, for the things a good little Afrikaans girl was not supposed to do. For many years I picked men who represented a certain amount of risk. It was instinctive, not conscious. Sometimes I wonder if it would have turned out differently if *that* had been my only weakness. But it isn't. From an early age I had a need for recognition. An affirmation that I am not ordinary. I wanted to stand out from the crowd. It's not necessarily a search for fame, just a need for attention, I think. In the end it is this combination that makes me who I am.'

She was not stupid, he thought. She was a woman who could easily deceive people. 'I was never terribly pretty. Not that I'm ugly, I'm grateful for that. If I use what I have I can attract attention, but I don't take men's breath away. I knew I was smart enough to study, but there is no degree in what I wanted to do. All I had left to me was my voice. And a stage personality, but that I only discovered later. Then I crossed paths with Danny Vlok. He can play anything from a violin to a trumpet. He had a music shop in the city, in Bloemfontein, and a four-piece band for weddings and parties. I saw his ad for a singer in the *Volksblad*'s Classifieds. Danny dreamed of being a rock star. He tried to look like one. I thought it was cool then, and he was ten years older than me. Worldly wise. He tried to live like a rocker too. Drink and dagga. The problem was that Danny could only sing other people's music. His own was . . . not good. I went for an audition with his band and afterwards we went to his flat in Park Road and had a *zol* and then sex. Two months later we got married in the magistrate's court. Four years later we were divorced.'

She was using the story to punish herself, thought Dekker. It was her penance, this exposure. But she stopped and looked around. 'There's usually some water here. It's hot . . .'

'I'll ask Natasha,' he said and got to his feet. When he went out of the door he saw Josh down the passage, looking restless and worried.

'Are you finished?'

'Not yet, Mr Geyser.'

The big man nodded and went back into the conference room.

Rachel Anderson heard the voices further off, but not the words. They went on for so long that she grew increasingly convinced that there were no tracks leading to her. The tension dissipated slowly from her body; her heartbeat steadied.

Until she heard the click-clack of a woman's shoes, right up close to her, just two or three steps away.

'OK. Thank you,' said the same black woman as earlier.

'I hope you find her,' said the man's voice.

'She can't be far. We will go and search the park.'

'Good luck.'

'OK.' She heard the woman walk away. Moments later the door closed and then she knew she would be safe.

Melinda Geyser gulped down half a glass of water and kept it in the hand that was resting on the arm of the couch.

'We went to play for a wedding in Bethlehem in the Eastern Free State. After the reception we stayed over in the chalets at Lake Athlone. The place was empty. We made a fire outside and sat in the dark, drinking and chatting. Danny said he was going to sleep, he was tired and drunk and doped. By then we had been married for three years and things weren't going so well. But we stayed outside, the other three and myself. They were young, in their twenties, like me. The bass guitarist had a video camera, he'd got it the previous week. He was filming us. At first it was innocent fun, we were playing the fool, pretending we were famous and were being interviewed by the SABC. We kept on drinking. Too much. I think it happened because of the dynamics of our group – Danny was the leader, we were the four employees, the underlings. We started saying things to the video camera about Danny. We mimicked and mocked him. We knew if he got to see the video it would make him furious – he had a terrible temper, especially the morning after a night of drinking. But it was precisely that risk that made it such fun; he was right there, asleep, while we were taunting him on video, there was . . . proof of what we were doing, kind of forever, on video.'

'The guitarist kissed me first. He said he knew what would make Danny totally crazy. He came over and kissed me on the mouth. It wasn't a big leap from there. Not in the state we were in. I don't have to give you the detail. The video shows how they undressed me, with my help, how they each licked a nipple. It shows how two of them had sex with me, one from the front and the other behind. It shows how I enjoyed it. There is a close-up

of my face and you can clearly see . . . You can hear me too . . .'
She looked at Dekker, there was an energy in her. She said: 'I will
always wonder how much the presence of the camera contributed
to the experience.' She was quiet for a while and then her eyes
dropped. 'I never regretted it. Until yesterday. Until I realised my
sins could catch up with Josh. It would hurt him so much to know
all that. He needs another kind of me.'

When she fell silent, Dekker asked: 'Was that on the DVD?'

She nodded.

'Barnard wanted to blackmail you.' He spoke with certainty.

'No. He was the one being blackmailed. When I passed the
DVD back to him and said I knew what it was, he said he had
to pay sixty thousand for it. He said it arrived a week ago by
registered post, with a note saying: *Watch this when you are alone.
Or Melinda's career is over.* The call came three days later, from a
man wanting fifty thousand or he would put it on the Internet. I
asked Adam why he had paid sixty then. He told me the other ten
thousand was to make sure it was the only copy.'

'How did he manage that?'

'I asked him that too. He said this wasn't the first time he had
had to protect one of his artist's interests. He had people who
help with that, an agency. They followed the trail of the money
transfers, until they found the man.'

'Was it the bass guitarist?'

'No. Danny Vlok.'

'Your ex?'

'You have to admit there is some kind of justice in it.'

'How did they make sure it was the only copy?'

'I don't know. I tried to phone Danny when I left here. Someone
at his shop said he was in hospital. He was assaulted in his flat on
Sunday night.'

Dekker digested this information. This thing was getting big.
And complex. 'But why did Barnard tell you this, if it was sorted
out?'

'I think the video aroused Adam.'

'So he blackmailed you?'

'No, he simply spotted an opportunity.'

'Oh?'

'He told me there was nothing to worry about. I was grateful. Then he smiled and put the DVD in the player. I could have walked out. But I wanted to see it again. One last time. We watched it together. When it was over he asked if he could kiss me. I said yes.'

She saw Dekker's expression and she said: 'I was very grateful to Adam. He was discreet. He went to a lot of trouble and expense. Seeing that video again . . . yourself. Young . . . so . . . randy . . .'

Dekker continued to frown.

'You must be wondering how a born-again woman could do something like that. You see, Mr Dekker, I don't believe in a condemning God. I think it was Bishop Tutu who said "God has a soft spot for sinners. His standards are quite low." He's not sitting up there with clenched fists ready to punish us. I believe he's a God of love. He knows we are what we are, just as he made us, with our weaknesses and all. He understands. He knows it brings us ultimately closer to him, knowing how weak we are. He just wants us to confess.'

Dekker was speechless. They sat there in silence, listening to the hiss of the gas lamp. For the first time she clasped her hands on her lap. 'You want to know why I told Josh. That's the thing I can't really explain. I walked out of here with the DVD in my handbag. I knew they knew, Willie, Wouter . . .'

'Wouter?'

'The financial director. Wouter Steenkamp. His office is next to Adam's. I knew they would have heard me because I'm loud when it comes to sex. Adam had his . . . talents. The sound of Natasha's voice when I passed her . . . Maybe she was in the corridor when it was going on. She suspected something. But I was out of there and went and sat in my car. I had the DVD and I wanted to break it. I never knew how hard that is. It bends, but it doesn't easily break, just like the human spirit. I took a pair of tweezers out of my handbag and scratched it with that. That was the best I could do. I scratched it until I was sure it would never work again. I phoned Danny at his shop then drove home and threw the DVD in the rubbish bin. When I went into the house there on the couch was dear, sweet Josh who loves me so unconditionally. He put his arms around me like he always does, but all I could think of was that he would smell the sex on me. Josh must have felt the tension, he's a sensitive man, always wondering if he's good enough for me. It was his caring that caught me, that absolute, honest caring. At that moment I was faced with the difference between his image of me and who I really was. It was devastating, if you will excuse the theatrical language. I believed he had the right to know the truth, but the words wouldn't come out. Old habits, we protect ourselves to the bitter end. I would prefer to believe that I wanted to protect him, because as hard as it is to live with myself, Josh would find it impossible to recover from the whole truth.'

22

When Vusi Ndabeni parked opposite Carlucci's the police helicopter was overhead, the wap-wap of its rotor blades deafening. He spotted Mbali Kaleni standing next to a patrol vehicle with a radio microphone in her hand, the wire looping through the open window. She had a map book of Cape Town open on the car's bonnet and her other hand keeping the pages open.

Vusi crossed the street to her and heard her saying loudly: 'This is the centre point, where I am standing. You must search from here. First, look at all the houses on this block. She wants to stay away from the street, so she must be in a back yard somewhere. Then you look at the parks, De Waal Park just down the road, there is also Leeuwenhof . . . two, three, four blocks away, east. No, wait . . . west, can you see it?'

Vusi stopped beside her. She glanced at him, trying to hear what the helicopter pilot was saying.

'I can't hear you,' she said into the microphone.

'Where do you want us to go after we check the parks?'

'Search the area between this point and the city.'

'Roger.' The helicopter swung north towards De Waal Park. Kaleni stretched through the window to replace the microphone. She couldn't quite reach, she was too short and too wide. Vusi opened the door for her. She handed him the microphone, as though he was to blame. He replaced it, closed the door, the helicopter's racket fading.

'We will find her,' said Kaleni.

Forensics' white bus pulled up. Thick and Thin got out and walked over, carrying their cases.

'Where have you been?' Kaleni scolded them.

★　　★　　★

He was two hundred metres away from the corner of Riebeeck Street when Benny Griessel realised he would have to leave the car somewhere here in Bree Street and walk to Alfred Street. To get across Buitengracht in this traffic chaos would take at least forty minutes.

He found a parking space opposite a cycle shop, which made him wonder whether he ought to put his bike in the car every morning. The power cuts were as regular as the cannon on Signal Hill nowadays. A parking attendant approached with an air of official purpose, her card machine in hand.

'Police,' said Griessel and showed her his ID card, in a hurry to get away, John Afrika's urgent voice ringing in his mind.

'Makes no difference,' the woman said. 'How long do you want to stop?'

Perhaps he should just go. 'How much for two hours?'

'Fourteen rand.'

'*Jissis*,' said Griessel. He dug out his wallet, searched for change, passed it over, locked his car and jogged through the motionless traffic. It was only four blocks on foot; he could take Prestwich and get there faster. Meanwhile he could find out what was going on. On the way he took out his cell phone and phoned Vusi.

'Hello, Benny.' There was the sound of a helicopter in the background.

'Vusi, I'm on my way to the Commissioner; I just want to know what's happening. Where are you?'

'At Carlucci's.'

'Any news?'

'She's missing, Benny, but the helicopter is searching and we have nine vehicles now, another on the way, but the traffic jam . . .'

'I know. Have you talked to Metro?'

'I haven't had time.'

'Leave it to me. We'll have to draw up a timetable, or we'll just be duplicating each other, but I'll call you as soon as I am finished with the Commissioner. Let me know if anything happens.'

'Benny, Organised Crime has photos of Demidov's people. I want the guy at the restaurant here to have a look at them.'

Griessel hesitated. Six months ago he had uncovered a nest of corruption at Organised Crime. They were not on good terms with him, even though there was a whole new team of people and they shared a building in Bellville South. But Vusi's plan did make sense.

'If you can manage it, Vusi. It can't do any harm.'

John Afrika's office, on the fourth floor of 24 Alfred Street in Green Point, was hot without the air conditioning. He was opening a window, when he heard the Provincial Commissioner's urgent steps approaching.

Afrika sighed. More trouble. He remained standing and waited for his boss to arrive. This time the little Xhosa did not knock; he was in too much of a hurry and too worried. 'They say she's afraid of the police,' he said, barely through the door. He walked up to the desk and pressed his hands on its edge like a man suddenly in need of support.

'Commissioner?' Afrika enquired, because he had no idea what he was talking about.

'The Consul General says Rachel Anderson told her father that she could not go to the police.'

'Not go to the police?'

'Her father said it sounded as though she didn't trust the police.'

'*Bliksem*,' said John Afrika and sat down behind his desk.

'My sentiments exactly,' said the Provincial Commissioner.

Buitengracht was a nightmare. The traffic was gridlocked in all five lanes. Griessel darted between the cars, grateful to be on foot. His phone rang. Probably the Commissioner wanting to know where the hell he was. But the screen showed Dekker.

'Fransman?'

'Benny, this is a soap opera,' said Dekker and outlined Melinda's story for Griessel all the way to the corner of Prestwich and Alfred.

'Fuck,' said Griessel eventually. 'What did she say about where they were last night?'

'At the church until eleven. The Tabernacle in Parklands.

Then they went home. Melinda slept on the couch, Josh in the bedroom, but they were at home until this morning. Nor do they own a gun.'

'That's what he said too . . .' Geyser might be lying about the firearm but he had had since last night to get rid of one. 'Fransman, tell Josh you want to search his house . . .'

'I asked that they check the national register. There is no firearm . . .'

'No, I'm not saying we must search it. Just gauge their reactions. Use the usual search warrant story . . .'

'What search warrant story?'

'The one "we can get a search warrant, but if you give us permission that won't be necessary".'

'OK. But the ex, Benny, it might have been him, this thing is a fucking circus. I'm going to phone Bloemfontein, see if they can find something. I'm going to let Josh and Melinda go . . .'

'You can do that. Or you can let them wait in the conference room. Let them sweat a little until you hear from Bloemfontein. And talk to your sexy girlfriend at reception. Where was Barnard last night? Look at his diary, search his office, check his email . . .'

At first Dekker did not respond, then he said: 'OK.' But he wasn't happy.

'Sorry, Fransman, I'm taking over again.'

'I'm trying to chill, Benny. Trying to chill.'

Over the phone, Vusi Ndabeni said to Vaughn Cupido: 'Let me get their email address,' and he went over to the young man in the apron sitting on the veranda with his staff.

'Do you have email here? Our Organised Crime Unit will mail photos of people I want you to look at.'

'We do. The address is info at Carlucci's dot co-za. But it won't help much.'

'Why?'

'There's no electricity. The PC doesn't work.'

Vusi's shoulders sagged, but he told Cupido: 'Send it anyway, Vaughn, here's the address . . .'

Fat Inspector Mbali Kaleni came to stand next to Vusi and asked the young man: 'Are you sure about the Land Rover's registration number?'

'I'm pretty sure it was CA and there was a four, a one, and a six.'

'They say there is no Land Rover Discovery with a CA, a four, one . . .'

'It wasn't a Discovery.'

'It wasn't?'

'I told the guy it was a Defender. Long wheelbase. And new.'

'Men,' said Kaleni shaking her head.

'What do you mean?' asked the young man in the apron.

'Not you,' said Kaleni and took out her cell phone. 'The fools I have to work with.' She called the Caledon Square charge office and listened to it ring for a long time before someone picked up. She asked to talk to the Constable who had done the initial registration number search.

'It wasn't a Land Rover Discovery, it was a Defender. You will have to search again.'

'I can't,' said the Constable.

'Why not?'

'The power is down.'

Benny Griessel was panting and perspiring when he walked into John Afrika's office – from the heat of the day, from the four sets of stairs because the lifts wouldn't work without power and from the sense of urgency building inside him.

The Provincial Commissioner was seated opposite John Afrika. Both looked severe. 'Afternoon, Commissioner.' Griessel checked his watch, saw it was still twenty-five minutes to twelve; it felt like three o'clock already. 'Morning, Commissioner,' he corrected himself.

The little Xhosa stood up, very serious, and put out a hand to Griessel: 'Congratulations, Captain Griessel.'

That caught him off guard. Griessel shook his hand and in confusion looked at John Afrika who winked at him and said: 'Congratulations, Benny.'

'Uh . . .' Griessel said and wiped the sweat from his brow. 'Uh . . .' And then: 'Fuck it, Commissioner.' The Xhosa laughed and put a hand on Benny's shoulder. 'You had better sit down, Captain. I suspect you are going to earn your promotion today.'

In the garden of the Victorian house, beside the three prints of running shoes in the soft earth, tall, skinny Jimmy from Forensics held open the plastic bag of dental cement and watched as fat Arnold poured in a measured amount of water.

'She's so fat, when she weighs herself, the scale says "to be continued" . . .' said Arnold.

'Hee hee,' chortled Jimmy.

'She's so fat, she's got her own postal code,' said Arnold. 'There you go, shake it up.'

'If only she wasn't so bloody bossy,' said Jimmy, zipping up the bag and shaking it. 'I mean, you're not exactly thin yourself, but at least you're not a bitch.'

'Is that supposed to make me feel good?'

'I'm just saying,' said Jimmy, and shook the bag with great concentration. 'All I want to know is what the heck she wants to do with these casts. They know they are the girl's footprints. This is just pissing in the wind.'

'That stuff is ready. Knead it.'

Jimmy kneaded the plastic bag of green goo between his hands.

'I'm not nearly as fat as she is.'

'You're just taller, that's the difference,' said Jimmy. 'Get the mould ready.'

Arnold took a long mould, adjusted it to fit over the footprint and carefully pressed it into the soil. He picked up a bottle of talcum powder and sprinkled it over the print. 'Pour,' he said.

Jimmy opened the bag and held it over the centre of the mould. The paste dribbled out.

'I've got a slow metabolism, that's my problem,' said Arnold. 'But she's quite the eater – I hear it's KFC, morning, noon and night . . .'

★　　★　　★

Inside the Victorian house, behind his net curtains and only ten metres from where Thick and Thin knelt, the old man could not hear their conversation. But he could see them. Just as he had seen the girl jump over the fence, the Land Rover driving past soon afterwards, those young men, searching. And the Constables who had run down Upper Orange Street with such purpose, and the black lady detective who had stopped in thought at the picket fence, and then investigated the flower bed.

He knew who they were looking for. And he knew where she was hiding.

23

Captain Benny fucking Griessel. Could you believe that?

He sat there savouring the glow of his promotion, wishing he could go home to his flat and type an email: *My dear Carla, your father is a captain today.* Tonight he would walk into Primi Piatti where Anna would be seated at a candlelit table and he would bend down to kiss her on the cheek and say: 'Captain Benny Griessel, pleased to meet you,' and she would look up at him in surprise and say 'Benny!' and kiss him on the mouth.

'How did Dekker take the news of Kaleni?' John Afrika broke through his reverie.

'I told him it was still his case, Commissioner,' said Griessel. 'He accepted it.'

Afrika looked sceptical, but merely nodded. 'Have you told her yet?'

He had forgotten. Totally. He would have to move his backside. 'I haven't had the chance yet.'

'Do you know what Mbali means?' the Provincial Commissioner asked. 'Flower. It means a flower in Zulu.'

Afrika grinned. 'She speaks five languages and has an IQ of a hundred and thirty-seven. Not bad for a flower.'

'She'll be sitting in my chair one day,' said the little Xhosa.

'She thinks she's sitting there already,' said Afrika, and the two officers laughed congenially. Griessel grinned, not sure whether it was proper for a Captain to laugh with them.

The Regional Commissioner suddenly went serious. 'Benny, there's a new development. Rachel Anderson's father said she can't go to the police. He thinks she means she can't trust us.'

'Can't trust us?' queried Griessel. The two senior officers

nodded in unison and waited for him to come up with the solution for them.

'That's what she told them over the telephone?'

They nodded again.

'Wait a bit,' he said, leaning forward on the grey cushion of the steel-framed government chair. 'We are looking at this from the wrong angle, Commissioner. Vusi has a theory that she is a drugs mule, both she and the deceased. It would fit with a lot of things – the way they came into the country, the nightclub, the Russians, the rucksack that was cut away, the whole chase. It's not that she can't trust the police – it's because she's a criminal. She can't walk into a police station and say: "Help me, I've brought in a half a million worth of drugs and then cheated Demidov".'

He saw relief flood the faces of the two senior men. But then John Afrika frowned.

'We can hardly say that to the Consul General or her father. Not without proof.'

'We promised her father we would call him,' said the Provincial Commissioner, and when Benny didn't look very enthusiastic he added 'Captain' expressly.

'Immediately,' said John Afrika.

'To reassure him,' said the slight Xhosa.

'It would relieve a lot of pressure.'

'If he knew a senior officer was in control.'

'But we mustn't be too hasty with the drugs idea.'

'I'll get you the number,' said the Provincial Commissioner and rose to his feet.

'Use Director Arendse's office,' said John Afrika. 'He's on leave.' Afrika stood up as well. 'Come, I'll show you where to go.'

Then the power came on with a shudder that travelled through the entire building.

'Aren't you going to arrest him?' Willie Mouton asked in disbelief as the fluorescent light above his bald pate began to flicker, then reflected brightly off it.

'At the moment there are no grounds for arrest,' said Dekker, standing at the door. 'Could I ask you a few questions?'

'What, me?'

Dekker crossed to a chair near the lawyer. 'Please. About Adam Barnard. And the Geysers.'

'Oh. Of course. Please, take a seat . . .' said Mouton without much sincerity.

Dekker sat. 'This morning, at Barnard's house. You spoke about Adam's "ways" just before Mrs Barnard . . .'

He saw Mouton glance at Groenewald for approval.

'The newspapers have written about some of this already, Willie . . .' the lawyer said slowly.

Mouton cleared his throat and rubbed his hand quickly over his shaven head. 'Sexual harassment,' he said warily.

Dekker waited.

'I don't believe that has anything to do with his death.'

'Let them decide on that, Willie.'

'Yes, Regardt, but fifteen years ago a guy could still have a go and the woman could say "no" and it wasn't an issue. Now all of a sudden it's sexual harassment.' Again the hand on the head, a gesture of uncertainty. He fiddled with the silver earring and then leaned forward quickly, a decision made. 'Everyone knows Adam had a thing for women. And they loved him for it, I'm telling you. Fifteen years ago I was promoting and managing tours for pop bands and I heard the stories way back then: Adam had Xandra at home, but that wasn't enough, he wanted more. He came and asked me to join AfriSound, as full partner, to do production and promotion. He told me: "Willie, just so you know – I like women." He wasn't ashamed of it. But harassment? That's a load of crap. Of course he had a go. But he never told a woman he would offer her a contract if she slept with him. Never. He would listen to demo CDs, or go to a show, and then he would say yes or no. "You've got potential, we want to sign you" or "no, you're not a fit for us." I'm telling you, there were singers who tried it on with him, who just walked into his office, all tits and legs and make-up and fluttering eyelashes and he would say straight out: "I'll nail you, but I won't sign you."'

'I'll nail you,' Dekker savoured the term and thought the whiteys really had their own language.

'You know what I mean.'

'What about the harassment?'

'A year ago, Nerina Stahl had a huge offer from Centre Stage and all of a sudden the papers were full of how Adam had harassed her . . .'

'I'm not sure I understand.'

'Nerina Stahl . . . the star.'

Dekker shook his head. Never heard of her.

'You probably listen to Kfm – they are missing the Afrikaans boat altogether.'

'Five-FM,' said Dekker.

Mouton nodded as if that explained it. 'Adam *made* her. Four years ago she was singing . . .'

'You're talking about Nerina Stahl?'

'Yes, she sang for McCully in an Abba tribute, a month in the Liberty in Johannesburg, a month at the Pavilion, one of those shows that come and go. Adam went one evening. Pretty girl, cute voice – young, she was twenty-four then, comes from Danielskuil originally, or Kuruman . . . If we hadn't made her she would have been selling houses for Pam Golding in Plattekloof, I'm telling you. Adam took her out to lunch and told her she could have a solo career. She signed that very afternoon. We got her a boob job and Adam translated a bunch of German pop songs and we spent a bit on a music video. That CD went to twenty-five thousand and two years later she was on that huge show, *Huisgenoot Skouspel*. She still had a year to go on her contract with us when Centre Stage offered her more and she went to the papers with the fucking sexual harassment story, because that was the only way she could get out of her contract. Then there were three others who jumped on the bandwagon, two has-beens . . .'

'Mr Mouton . . .' Dekker made a gesture indicating he should slow down. 'Centre Stage?'

'It's a rival label. They only had English acts before the Afrikaans wave and then they tried to steal people from other labels. Nikki Kruger went over to them, and the Bloedrivier Blues Band. And Ministry of Music. But Nerina came up with this harassment suit.'

'And so there were other women who came forward?'

'It was just for the fucking publicity. Tanya Botha and Largo, they both bombed and so . . .'

He saw Dekker's frown. 'You know, bombed, sales took a nose dive. Tanya went all deep suddenly, her first two CDs had been covers, we developed a nice sound for her, but suddenly she wanted to sing her own stuff, all pain and suffering, and nobody wanted to listen to that. And Largo . . . I don't know, I suppose her sell-by date had arrived.'

'And did they also accuse Adam Barnard of sexual harassment?'

'Front page of *Rapport*. "*Sangeresse span saam teen seks*", Singers Speak Up Against Sexual Harassment, or something.'

'What was the nature of Nerina Stahl's complaint?'

'A load of rubbish, I'm telling you. All about how Adam could never leave her alone, couldn't keep his hands off her in his office, wanted to take her home with him all the time, but everyone knew Xandra was sick at home and that wasn't the way Adam operated.'

'And then?'

'We told Nerina she could go and the storm was over. Tanya Botha and her lawyer sat down with us, we offered her thirty thousand and she was happy with that. I see she's launching a gospel CD now for some or other new label. Everyone's singing Afrikaans gospel now, the market is hot.'

'When last was there any talk of this?'

'I'm not sure . . . only every time the newspapers have nothing to write about. Regardt?'

'It's been quiet for the last five or six months. But now that Adam is dead . . .'

'Can you imagine what a circus it's going to be? And no one will remember that he saved the Afrikaans music industry.'

'How so?' asked Dekker.

'Nobody has done more for the *luisterliedjie* than Adam Barnard. Anton Goosen maybe . . .'

'What is the *luisterliedjie*?'

'It was before your time, early Eighties. But you have to understand the scene in those years. In the Seventies Afrikaners just listened to fluff . . . Jim Reeves, G Korsten, Min Shaw, Groep Twee, Herbie and Spence . . . pop, like "I love, you, I love you" lyrics. It was the golden era of Apartheid and people didn't want to think, they just wanted to hum along. Then along came Anton Goosen and Koos du Plessis and they wrote original stuff, great lyrics . . . In any case, they talked about the Music and Lyrics Movement, don't ask me why. Or just the *luisterliedjie*, because you had to listen to the words, you couldn't just hum it. In any case, Adam was in his twenties, working for De Vries & Kotz , one of those gigantic legal firms, but he wasn't happy and he was crazy about music. He listened to everything, the pubs, the small clubs, and he noticed there was all this raw talent, but the big record labels were not interested; they only wanted the big stars. Then he discovered Xandra. Did you know Alexa Barnard was a major star?'

'I heard . . .'

'He resigned his job and started AfriSound, signed Xandra and a few others. He got hold of the best songs and he marketed them cleverly, because he knew that was the future. They did OK. Not great, but they did more than survive and then came *Voëlvry*, and he played both sides of the fence . . .'

'*Voëlvry*? Like in "free as a bird"?'

Mouton sighed. 'Have you ever heard of Johannes Kerkorrel and Koos Kombuis?'

'Yes.'

'They were part of it. That's where I began, touring with one of those guys. We slept in kombis and we didn't have a studio or a label. We sold tapes out of the back of a minibus in the late Eighties. I did everything from driving the van to trying keeping the guys sober, buying food, building sets, fixing the amplifiers, putting up posters, collecting the ticket money . . . Those were wild days, it was great. *Voëlvry* was protest music in Afrikaans, you know, against Apartheid. The students bought into that like you wouldn't believe, in their thousands, while mom and dad in the suburbs were listening to Bles Bridges' love ballads. This new wave happened right under their noses. It was then that Adam came to see me – that's when we began to work together. We were the men who made *Voëlvry* legit. We gave them a label that took them mainstream, with management and marketing and promotion. It just got bigger and bigger and just look at Afrikaans music now. In the last five or six years it has exploded because the language is under threat, and all the papers can write about is harassment, I fucking ask you, or about that "De la Rey" hit, but few people listen to the whole CD. Do you know most of the songs are about sex and booze?'

'What songs?'

'On the "De la Rey" CD.'

Dekker shook his head, thinking before he replied: 'Did Adam Barnard say anything during the past week about a DVD?'

'What DVD?' There was genuine surprise.

'Any DVD.'

'We are busy with a couple of DVDs. Josh and Melinda's is scheduled for the KKNK, a live recording . . .'

Dekker shook his head again. 'Did Barnard say anything about a DVD that he received in the post?'

'Why would anyone send him a DVD? Production and promotion is my department. If he did receive anything he would have passed it on to me.'

'There is a possibility that he did receive a parcel containing a DVD. Last week. Did he mention anything?'

'Not to me. What kind of DVD was it? Who said he received one?'

'Did he open his own post?'

'Adam? Yes, who else would do it?'

'Didn't he have a secretary?'

'Natasha is PA to both of us, but she wouldn't open our post. We do almost everything electronically. If there were a DVD, she would have brought it to me. What was on this DVD?'

'I can't divulge details at this stage, Mr Mouton. Who can I speak to about payments that Mr Barnard would have made during the past week or so?'

'Payments? Why would you want to know *that*?'

'Willie . . .' Groenewald cautioned.

'It's my company, Regardt, I have a right to know. What are the Geysers going around saying?'

'Willie, his investigation is *sub judice*. That means he doesn't have to—'

'I know what it means, Regardt, but it's my company now that Adam is no longer with us.'

'Mr Mouton, unfortunately you are obliged to answer my questions.'

The Adam's apple bobbed; the hand fiddled with the silver earring. 'What was your question?'

'Who can I talk to about payments that Mr Barnard made in the past week?'

'To whom?'

'To anyone.'

'Adam was in charge of finance and admin. He signed the cheques. But Wouter would know. He's the accountant.'

'Where would I find Wouter?'

'Next door down.'

'Thank you,' said Dekker and rose. 'I will also have to search Mr Barnard's office. Has anyone been in his office since yesterday night?'

'Ask Natasha, I don't know.'

Dekker went to the door.

'They're lying,' said Mouton. 'The Geysers are lying to save their own butts. Payments? What payments?'

'Willie . . .' said Groenewald.

Griessel sat in the absent director's office. The big chair was comfortable and the desk very broad and clean. He studied the sheet of white paper the Provincial Commissioner had given him. *Bill Anderson* was written on it. Plus a number with overseas codes.

He was reluctant to make the call. He wasn't good at this sort of thing. He would try too hard to reassure and that would spark false hope, and he knew how the man felt. If Carla were to phone him from London and say there were people trying to kill her, people who had killed already, he would go out of his mind. He would climb on the first fucking plane.

But that wasn't all that was worrying him.

Ever since John Afrika had walked out of here and shut the door behind him, Griessel had been worrying about the other alternative. What if Rachel Anderson were not a mule?

Gennady Demidov was notorious, with an extensive web of activities. Rumour had it that there were city councillors in his pocket. SAPS members as well. At least a few uniforms. There had been a complaint of assault, something about people being beaten with baseball bats because they didn't want to sell property to Demidov – property that the city council needed to buy to build the World Cup soccer stadium. The docket disappeared from the Sea Point station and witnesses stopped talking. Six months ago the Organised Crime Unit had been cleaned up with great fanfare.

There was a new commanding officer, new detectives, quite a few from Gauteng and KwaZulu, but six months was a long time. The Russian had deep pockets.

He would not be very popular with the Commissioners for that theory.

Griessel sighed, lifted the receiver and heard the dialling tone.

He would say: 'This is Captain Benny Griessel.'

At least that would feel bloody good.

24

Vusi Ndabeni, Mbali Kaleni and the young man in the apron stood at the computer in the small cubicle of an office at Carlucci's. They watched the email download.

'Don't you have ADSL?' asked Kaleni, as though it were a crime not to.

'We don't need it,' said the young man.

Vusi wondered if he was supposed to know what ADSL was, but he was saved by a cell phone ringing. Kaleni's.

'Yes,' she answered sharply, irritable. She listened for a long time. 'Hold on.' She took her big black handbag off her shoulder, plunged a hand into its depths and brought out a black bound notebook and pen set. She opened it solemnly, put it on the table, clicked the pen in readiness and said: 'OK. Shoot.'

Then: 'I mean, give it to me.'

She made a note, said, 'I've got it,' and ended the call. 'Vusi, I am going to Parklands. They have a hit on the registration number.'

'The Land Rover?'

'Yes. A Mr J. M. de Klerk of Twenty-four Atlantic Breeze in Parklands registered a Two thousand and seven Land Rover Defender One-ten Hard Top in September. Registration number CA four-one-six, seven-eight-eight-nine. And he was born in Nineteen eighty-five. A young guy.'

'Not a Russian,' Vusi said in disappointment.

'Must have a rich dad,' said the young man in the apron as he opened an email.

'Those Landies cost three hundred grand.'

'Where does he work?' Vusi asked hopefully.
'Same address. He works from home.'

Griessel heard the phone ring on another continent. It was crystal clear and he wondered what time it was in West Lafayette, Indiana.

'Anderson,' said the voice on the other end.

'Mr Anderson, my name is Benny Griessel . . .' Griessel was aware of his Afrikaans accent, and for a fraction of a second the logical next sentence lay on the tip of his tongue, '. . . and I'm an alcoholic.' He bit it back and said, 'I am a Captain in the South African Police Services and I'm in charge of the search for your daughter. I am very sorry for the circumstances, but I can tell you we are doing our absolute best to find her and protect her.'

'Thank you, Captain, first of all, for taking the time to call. Is there any news?' The voice was polite and American, making the situation feel unreal to Griessel, like a TV drama.

'We have a police helicopter searching the area where she was last seen, and we have more than ten patrol units looking for her in the streets, with more coming. But so far, we have not located her.'

There was a silence over the phone, not just the usual static of a local call.

'Captain, this is a difficult thing for me to ask, but when Rachel spoke to me over the telephone, she said that she could not go to the police . . . I hope you understand, as a parent, I am very concerned. Do you know why she said this?'

Griessel took a deep breath. It was the question he had been afraid of. 'Mr Anderson, we have been thinking about this . . . matter . . .' Those were not the right words. '. . . this question, I mean. It could mean different things, and I am investigating all the possibilities.' It didn't seem enough. 'I want to tell you, I have a daughter the same age as Rachel. My daughter is in London at the moment. I know how you feel, Mr Anderson. I know this must be very . . . difficult for you. Our children are all we have.' He knew it sounded odd, not quite right.

'Yes, Captain, that is exactly what I have been thinking these past few hours . . . That is why I am so concerned. Tell me, Captain – can I trust you?'

'Yes, Mr Anderson. You can trust me.'

'Then I will do that. I will trust you with my daughter's life.'

Don't say that, thought Griessel. He had to find her first. 'I will do everything I possibly can,' he said.

'Is there anything we can do from here. I . . . anything . . .?'

'I am going to give you my cell phone number, Mr Anderson. You can call me any time you like. If Rachel calls you again, please give her my number, and tell her I will come to her, just me, if she is worried . . . And I promise you, I will call you if there is any news.'

'We were thinking . . . We want to fly out there . . .'

He didn't know how to respond to that. 'I . . . You can, of course . . . Let me find her, Mr Anderson. Let me find her first.'

'Will you, Captain?' There was a desperate note in his voice, grabbing at a lifeline.

'I will not rest until I have.'

Bill Anderson put the phone down carefully and sank back into his chair. He put his hands over his face. His wife stood beside him, her hand on his shoulder.

'It's all right to cry,' she said to him in a barely audible whisper.

He didn't reply.

'I will be strong now, so you can cry.'

He slowly dropped his hands. He looked at the long rows of books on the shelves. So much knowledge, he thought. And so useless now.

He dropped his head. His shoulders shook.

'I heard him,' said Jess Anderson. 'He will find her. I could hear that in his voice.'

Captain Benny Griessel sat with his elbows on the director's desk and his chin in his hand.

He shouldn't have said it. He didn't want to make promises. He should have stuck to: 'I will do everything I possibly can.' Or he should have said: 'In the circumstances I don't want to make predictions.' But Rachel Anderson's father had pleaded with him.

'Will you, Captain?'

And he had said he would not rest until he found her.

Where the fuck did he begin?

He dropped his arms and tried to concentrate. There were too many things happening at once.

The helicopter and patrols were not going to find her. She was hiding, afraid of the police. And he didn't know why.

The solution was to find out who was hunting her. Vusi's plan looked better and better. He must check on their progress.

Griessel stood up and reached for his cell phone. But then it rang loudly in the silent office, startling him.

'Griessel.'

'This is Inspector Mbali Kaleni of the South African Police Service, Benny.' Her Zulu accent was strong, but every Afrikaans word was enunciated with care. 'We traced a Land Rover Defender that fits the number. It belongs to a man in Parklands, a Mr J. M. de Klerk. I am on my way.'

'Very good work, but the Commissioner asked if you would help with another case. Fransman Dekker's investigation . . .'

'Fransman Dekker?'

Griessel ignored the disdain in her voice. 'Can I give you his number? He's in the city . . .'

'I have his number.'

'Call him, please.'

'I don't like it,' said The Flower, 'but I will call him.'

'On the eleventh of January we electronically transferred an amount of fifty thousand rand into an ABSA account, on Adam's instructions,' said the accountant of AfriSound, Wouter Steenkamp, with modulated precision.

He was comfortably ensconced behind a large flat-screen computer monitor, elbows on the desk and fingers steepled in front of his chest. He was a short man in his early thirties with an angular face and heavy eyebrows. He clearly took trouble with his appearance – the thick-rimmed glasses and short hair were equally fashionable, there was a careful, deliberate two-day growth of black stubble on his chin, and dark chest hair was just visible at the open collar of his light-blue sports shirt with narrow white stripes. Chunky sports watch, tanned arms. No lack of self-confidence.

'Who was it paid to?' Dekker asked from his chair opposite.

Steenkamp consulted his screen without untwining his fingers. 'According to Adam's note the account holder was "Bluegrass". The bank branch code was an ABSA branch in the Bloemfontein city centre. The transaction was successful.'

'Did Mr Barnard say what the payment was for?'

'In his email he asked me to put it under "sundry expenses".'

'That's all?'

'That's all.'

'Was there also a payment of ten thousand?'

'Exactly?' Steenkamp's eyes scanned the spreadsheet on his screen.

'I believe so.'

'In the past week?'

'Yes.'

'Not on my records.'

Dekker leaned forward. 'Mr Steenkamp . . .'

'Wouter, please.'

'According to my information, Adam Barnard used an agency to determine who was behind the Bluegrass account. At a fee of ten thousand rand.'

'Aah . . .' said Steenkamp, sitting up straight and reaching for his neat in-tray. He lifted documents and pulled one out. 'Ten thousand exactly,' he said and offered it to Dekker. 'Jack Fischer and Associates.'

Dekker knew the company – former senior white police officers who had taken fat retirement packages five or six years ago and set up their own private investigation business. He took the document and examined it. It was an invoice. *Client: AfriSound. Client contact person: Mr A. Barnard.*

Under *Item* and *Cost* was printed: *Administrative enquiries, R4, 500. Personal interview, R5,500.*

'Personal interview?' he read aloud.

Steenkamp just shrugged.

'Is this Adam Barnard's signature here?'

'It is. I only pay if either he or Willie has signed it.'

'So you don't know what the account was for?'

'No. Adam didn't discuss it with me. He put it in his out-tray and Natasha put it in here. If it was signed by him—'

'Do you often use Jack Fischer?'

'Now and then.'

'You know they are private investigators?'

'Inspector, the music industry is not all moonlight and roses . . . But Adam usually handled that sort of case.'

'Would Willie Mouton know?'

'You will have to ask him.'

'I will have to keep this account.'

'May I make a copy first?'

'Please.'

Inspector Vusi Ndabeni had never flown in a helicopter before.

The pilot passed a headset to him over his shoulder, someone closed the door, the engine made a mighty roar, the rotors turned and they lifted off. His stomach churned. He put on the earphones with trembling hands and watched De Waal Drive shrink below him.

Sometimes these machines dropped out of the sky, he thought. One shouldn't look down, someone once told him, but the city was below them now, Parliament, the Castle, the railway tracks leading to the station in tidy ranks; the harbour, sea, blinding as the sun reflected off it. Vusi took his dark glasses from his jacket pocket and put them on: 'Does Table View know we're on our way?' he said, looking down at Robben Island in wonder.

'Turn the microphone – it's too far from your mouth,' said the co-pilot and demonstrated what he should do.

Vusi bent the microphone around to the front of his mouth. 'Do Table View know we're coming?'

'Do you want to talk to them?' asked the pilot.

'Yes, please. We're going to need patrol vehicles.'

'Let me get them for you.'

With glittering Table Bay to the left and the industries of Paarden Island stretching away to his right, Inspector Vusumuzi Ndabeni spoke to the SC of Table View over a helicopter radio. When he had finished, he wondered what his mother would say if she could see him now.

25

Benny Griessel jogged down Buitengracht again. The traffic jam had cleared as though it had never existed. His mind was on the fugitive Rachel Anderson. Where was she heading? The only possibility was the Cat & Moose Youth Hostel; that was where her luggage was, and her friend Oliver Sands. Where else could she go?

He phoned Caledon Square and asked the radio operator to send a unit to Long Street. 'But they must not park in front of the Cat & Moose. Tell them to wait inside. If she does come, she mustn't see them.'

That was all he could do. According to Vusi, the eyewitness at Carlucci's had looked at the covert photos of Demidov's troops, shaken his head and said no, it was none of them.

That really meant fuck all, because Organised Crime might not have sent all the pictures. Or the pictures could be out of date. Or they didn't have photos of all of Demidov's people.

Either he or Vusi would have to go back to Van Hunks again. But first he would see what the house in Table View produced. He had to give the whole search some direction. He would use Caledon Square as the base; it was central, that was where the radio connection with the patrol cars was.

He ran the last two hundred metres to his car, aware of the heat now smothering the city like a blanket.

'I don't know what it was for,' said Willie Mouton, and passed the Jack Fischer invoice back across the desk to Dekker. 'I don't think they will tell you.'

'Oh?'

'It's sensitive. Client privilege.'

'What is?'

'No, Willie,' said Groenewald, the lawyer.

'Of course it is. They guarantee confidentiality. That's why we use them.'

'Privilege only counts for doctors, psychologists and legal practitioners, Willie. If the police have a warrant, they can get the information.'

'What is the use of their guarantee then?' The Adam's apple bobbed.

'Is there anyone specific that you deal with at Jack Fischer?' Dekker asked.

'We work with Jack himself. But you're barking up the wrong tree, I'm telling you.'

Rachel Anderson could no longer hear the helicopter.

At first the silence was eerie, but gradually it became reassuring. In spite of her tracks in the flower bed, even though a black policewoman had been only two steps from her hiding place, she had evaded them.

She made up her mind. She would stay here until dark.

She checked her watch. It was eleven minutes to twelve. Another eight hours before the sun went down. A long time. But let them look for her in other places; let them forget about this garden.

The pain from the scratches and bruises was a dull constant in her body. She would have to make herself comfortable if she were going to lie here that long.

Slowly she sat upright and pressed the thick, thorny branches to one side. She didn't want to make any noise, or show movement. She didn't know whether there were eyes trained on these plants.

The rucksack would have to come off. She could use it as a pillow.

She loosened the clips, pulled the straps off her shoulders and lowered the rucksack. It snagged on the branches and thorns, awkward, behind her. With care she untangled it and put it on the ground. She turned on her back slowly and let her head rest on the bag.

The ground underneath her was not too uncomfortable. The dense shade would protect her from dehydration. She knew her blood sugar was low, but she would survive until night fell. She would have to find a telephone; somewhere someone would allow her to phone, they must, she would beg. She had to tell her father where she was.

She drew a deep breath and looked up through the dense leaf cover to where patches of sky shone through. Her eyes closed.

Then she heard the front door of the house open.

Barry drove up in his Toyota bakkie from the city side. Upper Orange was quiet now, the police vehicles and uniforms gone. Only a white microbus with a SAPS emblem still remained up on the corner.

He wondered if it would be worthwhile to watch the Victorian house.

He looked for the driveway that he had noted earlier, turned up it and drove to the back against the garage door. He picked up the binoculars that lay beside him on the worn seat cover. He realised he couldn't see the house from here. The wall on the left was too high.

He climbed onto the load bed of the Toyota and leaned back against the cab with the binoculars to his eyes. It was barely a hundred metres to the Victorian house. He let the binocular lenses sweep across the house.

It was dead still.

He checked the garden. Back to the house.

A waste of time.

Then the front door opened. A man appeared. Barry focused on him and waited. An old man stood in the front door. Dead still.

Josh and Melinda Geyser were sitting close together at the big oval table in the conference room when Dekker opened the door. They looked at him expectantly, but said nothing until he was seated – one chair away from Josh.

'Inspector Griessel and I don't believe you are suspects in the case at this stage . . .'

'At this stage?'

'Madam, the investigation has only just begun. We—'

'We didn't do it,' Josh said emphatically.

'Then help us to take you off our list.'

'Who else is on the list?' asked Melinda.

Dekker wanted to shut her up. 'We are trying to trace a parcel.' He saw the fright on her face.

'What parcel?' asked Josh.

'I am not at liberty to tell you, Mr Geyser, but I am asking you again: help us.'

'How?'

'Give us permission to search your house, so we can make sure there is nothing that connects you with Barnard's death.'

'Such as?'

'A firearm. You can refuse, and we would have to obtain a search warrant. But if you give permission . . .'

Josh looked at Melinda. She nodded. 'Go ahead. There isn't anything.'

Dekker looked at her intently. He saw only the decisiveness. 'Wait here, please. I will be back as soon as possible.'

When Mbali Kaleni walked through the double ground-floor doors of AfriSound there were four white people standing in front of the black receptionist, in animated conversation.

'Excuse me,' said Kaleni and held up her identity card. 'Police.'

All four turned to her. One had a camera slung around the neck.

'Are you here about the Barnard case?' a young woman with very short blonde hair asked.

'Are you from the newspapers?' asked Kaleni.

'*Die Burger*,' the woman said. 'Is it true that Josh and Melinda Geyser are being questioned in there?'

'I don't talk to the media,' she said and directed herself towards the receptionist.

'Inspector Dekker. *Ngaphakathi*?'

'Yes, he's inside.'

'Please,' another journalist called out, 'are the Geysers here?'

Kaleni just shook her head as she climbed the stairs. '*Izidingidwane.*'

Rachel Anderson lay stock still, but she couldn't hear anything.

Had he just opened and closed the front door?

She barely breathed.

There were footsteps, scarcely audible: one, two, three, four.

Then silence.

'The policewoman told me you are an American girl,' said the same voice she had heard earlier. She was startled by the abruptness and then she tensed as she realised he was speaking to *her*.

'I saw you when you jumped over the fence. I saw how scared you were. And then, the men in the Land Rover . . .' There was great compassion in the voice, but the fear that he knew she was there paralysed her.

'The policewoman told me those men are hunting you, that they want to hurt you.'

She breathed through her mouth, silently.

'You must be very frightened, and very tired. I suppose you don't know who to trust. I will leave the door unlocked. If you want to come inside, you are most welcome. I am alone. My wife died last year. There is food and drink inside, and you have my word that no one will ever know you were here.'

Emotion welled up in her. Self-pity, gratitude, the impulse to leap up.

No!

'I can help you.'

She heard feet shuffling.

'I will be inside and the door is unlocked.'

It was quiet for a moment before she heard his footsteps moving away again. The door opened and shut.

Then there was the roar of a cannon and her whole body jerked in alarm.

12:00–12:56

26

Fransman Dekker stopped for a second in the passage of AfriSound, deep in thought, one arm folded and the other on his cheek, staring at the simple patterns of the long woven dhurrie on the floor. All the doors around him were closed: the Geysers behind him in the conference room, Mouton and his lawyer in the office on the left, the accountant Wouter Steenkamp on the right.

He should phone Bloemfontein and find out what they had, he must go to Jack Fischer and Associates, he must search Barnard's office, he must talk to Natasha about Barnard's schedule yesterday. He didn't know which of these to do next and he was not keen on Jack Fischer or Natasha Abader. The detective agency was full of whites, all ex-policemen who loved to sing to the press if they could show the SAPS in a bad light. Natasha was a temptation he did not need. The story of Adam Barnard, womaniser, was a mirror held up to him. He didn't want to be like that; he had a good, pretty and clever wife who trusted him with her life.

The cannon roared the noonday shot from Signal Hill, breaking his train of thought. He glanced up and saw fat Inspector Mbali Kaleni's stormy face approaching through the reception area, or lounge, or whatever these music people called it.

'Fuck,' he said softly to himself.

Benny Griessel heard the cannon as he crossed the threshold of the Caledon Square police station and thought how it startled him every time; he would never get used to it. Was it really only twelve o'clock? He saw the long-haired photographer trotting across to him from inside, eyes searching, with a pack of photos in his hand.

'Are you looking for Vusi?'

'Yes,' said the photographer. 'He's just missing.'

'He's gone to Table View. You're fucking late.'

'We had a power cut, how am I supposed to make copies without electricity?' the photographer asked and angrily held out the prints to Benny.

He took them. 'Thanks.'

The photographer walked off without a word. Indignant.

Griessel looked at the print on top. Rachel Anderson and Erin Russel, laughing and alive. Light and dark, blonde and brunette. Russel had the face of a nymph, with blonde hair cut short, a small pretty nose, big green eyes. Rachel Anderson was sultry, her beauty more complex, dark plait over her shoulder, long, straight nose, wide mouth, the line of her jaw enchanting and determined. But both still children, with carefree exuberance, eyes bright with excitement.

Behind them, brooding, was the only other African iconic mountain landmark, Kilimanjaro.

Drug mules?

He knew anything was possible, he had seen it all before. Greed, recklessness, stupidity. Crime had no face; it was a question of tendency, background and opportunity. But his heart said no, not these two.

She was torn between her fear of trusting anyone, and the decency in the man's voice. She couldn't stay here, because someone knew where she was; she couldn't go back to the streets, it would start all over again. The knowledge that the door was open just a few steps away, offering a safe haven, food and drink, overcame her and won every argument.

She got up slowly, heart racing, aware of the risk. She picked up the rucksack and crawled on her knees, avoiding the thick, scratchy branches higher up, to the edge of the leaf curtain.

There was a small stretch of paved garden path, a single step, a low veranda, a brown doormat saying *WELCOME* and the wooden door, its varnish faded with age.

She hesitated there, considering the consequences one last time. Then she crept the last few centimetres, blinking in the bright sunlight. She stood erect, straightening legs stiff from lying so long. She walked fast with long strides over the path, the step, the shaded part of the veranda. She put her hand on the door handle of oxidised copper, cool under her palm, breathed in and opened the door.

Barry wasn't looking through the binoculars. They were too heavy to hold up permanently without a prop.

His head was turned a few degrees away, looking up the street towards Carlucci's. He saw movement in the periphery, more than a hundred metres away at the house. His head turned and he screwed up his eyes. He saw the figure for an instant, small at this distance; the blue of a garment was the shade he was looking for. He lifted up the binoculars, looked through them and adjusted the focus.

Nothing. 'Shit,' he said out loud.

He kept the lenses trained on the front door. He could only see part of it behind the baroque detail of the veranda, but there was no one there.

Was he imagining things? No, he had seen it. He blinked, concentrating. Small figure, blue . . .

'Shit,' he said again, because it might have been imagination. Up on the mountain he had thought he had seen her a few times; it had pumped adrenaline in his veins, but when he adjusted the focus it was usually a false alarm, optical illusions caused by hope and expectation.

He lowered the binoculars and looked at the house with his naked eyes. He wanted to reconstruct the dimensions of that moment.

She had been moving there. Just there, right hand on the doorknob? Left hand stretched back, holding something. The rucksack?

Binoculars up again. Where had she come from? For the first time he recognised the potential of the bougainvilleas, the old overgrown arbour. He studied the depth of it. 'Fuck me,' he said, the possibility slowly dawning in his mind, the way she could have run, the fat policewoman inspecting the flower bed on the left . . .

He reached for his cell phone in the pocket of his denims, took it out without taking his eyes off the house.

It had to be her. It explained how she disappeared without trace. He was almost certain.

Almost. Ninety per cent. Eighty.

If he made a mistake . . .

'Shit!'

The house was quiet and cool.

She stood in the hallway and listened to her own breathing. A classic piece of wooden furniture stood against the wall, with a large oval mirror above it. Alongside were dark wood-framed portraits of bearded faces in black and white.

One step forward. The floorboard creaked and she stopped. To the left a large room opened up between two plain pillars; she leaned forward to look inside. A lovely large table with a laptop almost lost between piles of books and papers. Shelves against the walls crammed with books, three big windows, one looking out on the street and the fence she had jumped over. An old, worn Persian carpet on the floor in red, blue and beige.

'I'm in the kitchen.' The man's voice directly ahead was soothing, but she felt frightened anyway.

Books. So like her parents' house. She must be safe with a book person.

She walked in the direction of the voice. One of the rucksack's straps dragged whispering across the wooden floor.

Through a white-painted door frame was the kitchen. He stood with his back to her. White shirt, brown trousers, white sports shoes; he looked like an aged monk with his thinning grey hair around the bald spot that shone in the fluorescent light. He turned slowly from his work at the table, wooden spoon in hand.

'I'm making an omelette. Would you like some?'

He was older than she had thought at first, with a slight stoop, a kind face between deep wrinkles, loose skin above the red cravat around his neck, liver spots on his head and hands. His eyes were watery, faded blue, mischievous behind the over-large gold-rimmed spectacles. He put the spoon down beside a mixing bowl, wiped his hands on a white dishcloth and held one out towards her. 'My name is Piet van der Lingen,' he said, his smile revealing white false teeth.

'Pleased to meet you,' she said automatically, a reflex, and shook his hand.

'Omelette? Perhaps some toast?' He picked up the spoon again.

'That would be wonderful.'

'You are most welcome to hang the rucksack on the pegs at the door,' and he pointed with the spoon to the hall. Then he turned back to his mixing bowl.

She stood there, unwilling to accept the relief, the anticlimax, the relaxation.

'And the bathroom is down the passage, second door on the left.'

'I saw her,' said Barry over the phone, sounding more certain than he felt.

'Where?'

'She went into a house just a block from the restaurant.'

'Jesus. When?'

'A few minutes ago.'

'You saw her?'

'I was lucky, I just caught a glimpse, but it was her. No doubt.'

'A glimpse? What the fuck does that mean?'

They sat in the recording studio. Fransman Dekker wanted to tell her about the Barnard case. Inspector Mbali Kaleni said: 'Just a minute,' and shut her eyes. She wanted the American girl's case out of her thoughts; she had been so sure she would track her down. Now she cleared her head and opened her eyes. 'Go ahead,' she said. Dekker talked, gave her the details in a businesslike way, cursorily, the scowling execution of forced labour.

Mbali was not surprised by his attitude.

She knew her male colleagues did not like her. The one who liked her least of all was Fransman Dekker. But that didn't disturb her because she knew why. Generally the men felt threatened by her talent and they were intimidated by her ethics and her integrity. She didn't drink, smoke, or curse. She didn't hold her tongue either. The SAPS was not a place for sweet talking; the task was too big and the circumstances too difficult for that. She said what she thought. About their egos, too often the axis around which everything turned. About their incessant sexism and racism. About their lack of focus. Too much 'Let's throw a chop on the grill', or 'Let's get a quick beer', like boys that hadn't yet grown up. Too much talk in the office about sport, politics and sex. She told them straight out it was inappropriate. They hated her for that. But Dekker had an extra reason to hate her. She'd caught him out a few weeks ago. He was in the corridor where he thought nobody could hear him. Cell phone to his ear, whispering words of lust to a Tamaryn, when his wife's name was Crystal. When he slunk back into the office she had gone and stood at his desk and said: 'A man should be faithful to his wife.' He just stared at her. So she said: 'Fraud comes in many different guises,' and left. Since then she had seen the hatred in his eyes. Because she knew, and despised him for it.

But there was work to be done here. So she listened attentively. She answered him only in English, although he spoke Afrikaans. Because she knew he hated that too.

Rachel Anderson closed the bathroom door behind her, feeling an urgent need to pee. She unzipped her denim shorts, pulled the garments down to her knees and sat down. The relief was so great and the sound so loud that she wondered if he could hear her from the kitchen. Rachel looked around the bathroom. The walls were a light pastel blue, the porcelain fittings snow white. The old restored claw-foot bath was suddenly tempting, hot foamy water to draw out the dreadful fatigue and dull aching of her body. But she suppressed the thought, a surrender she wasn't yet ready for. And the old man was cooking in the kitchen.

When she was finished she bent over the basin, opened the taps, picked up the soap and washed the dried blood and mud off her hands, all the dirt from touching rocks and plants, walls and earth. She watched it rinse away. She mixed hot and cold water in cupped hands and splashed her face. Then she took the cake of soap, lathered it over her cheeks and forehead, mouth and chin, and rinsed again.

The dark-blue towel was fresh and rough. She rubbed it slowly over her face and hung it up neatly again. Only then did she look in the mirror. In a habitual motion her hands reached for her hair and brushed it back from her face.

She looked haggard. Dreadful. Her hair was a mess, strands had escaped from the plait and framed her face, her eyes were bloodshot and there were lines of fatigue around her mouth. There was a cut on her chin, surrounded by a light purple bruise and another small graze across her forehead; she didn't know where she had got that. Her neck was grimy, like her powder-blue T-shirt.

But you are *alive*.

She was filled with enormous gratitude. Then came the guilt, because Erin was dead, dear Erin. The emotion washed over her like a tidal wave, sudden and overwhelming, the awful shame that she could be glad at being alive while Erin was dead. It broke down her defences and let her relive it fully for the first time: the two of them fleeing in terror, Erin putting a hand on the church wall and jumping over the sharp cast-iron railings. A fatal error.

'No!' she had screamed, yet followed blindly, jumping over so effortlessly. Erin had stopped on a narrow path in the churchyard, in the deep, dark shadows between huge trees. Rachel realised they were trapped; she had run on desperately looking for a way out. She intended to take the lead, show the way around the church and thought Erin was following. She was already behind the building, out of sight and away from the streetlights, when she realised she couldn't hear Erin's footsteps. She turned around, feeling deadly fear like a weight she was dragging along with her. Where was Erin? Reluctant and afraid, she had run back to the corner of the church building.

Erin was on the ground and all five were around her, bending over, kneeling, yowling like animals. The knife had flashed. Erin's desperate scream, abruptly cut off. Black blood in the dark.

That moment was petrified in the synapses of her brain, surreal, overwhelming. As heavy as lead.

She had run for her life. Around the back of the church. Over the fence again. She had a bigger lead this time.

Relief. Gratitude. She was alive.

In front of the bathroom mirror it was all too much for her. She could not look at herself. She let her head hang in shame, grasping the sides of the basin in despair. The emotion was physical, a nausea rising from her stomach that made her guts spasm and made her want to vomit, a wave of dry retching. She bellowed once, and shuddered. Then she began to cry.

Vusi Ndabeni sat in the front seat of one of the patrol vehicles between a Constable and an Inspector, both in uniform. Behind them on the West Coast Road was another police van.

They had wanted to put the sirens and lights on but he had said: 'No, please don't.' He wanted to arrive at J. M. de Klerk's house without fanfare, surround it quietly and then knock on the door. The Inspector said he knew where the address was, one of the crescents in Parklands, a new residential area where the white and up-and-coming black middle classes lived shoulder to shoulder in apparent harmony; the new South Africa successfully practised.

At a set of traffic lights they turned right into Park Road. Shopping centres, townhouse complexes, then left again down Ravenscourt, right in Humewood. These were not the linear street blocks of Mandela Park and Harare in Khayelitsha, but a maze of crescents and dead ends. Vusi looked at the Inspector.

'It's just up front here, first left, second right.'

Houses, townhouses, flats, all neat and new, gardens in development, with small trees or none at all.

'We mustn't park in front of the house,' said Vusi. 'I don't want to scare him.'

'OK,' said the Inspector, and showed the Constable which way to drive. Eventually a road sign said 'Atlantic Breeze'.

Townhouses. The numbers on this side were in the forties, big complexes behind high walls. 'Are they all townhouses?' asked Vusi.

'I don't think so.'

But Number 24 was. They stopped some way off. 'Let me get out,' said Vusi. The Inspector opened the door and slid out.

There was a high white wall with spiky metal deterrent on top and large painted numbers, a two and a four. In the centre was a large motorised iron gate and townhouses behind in a countrified style, blue and green shutters alongside plain-coloured window frames, and an A-frame roof. Yet another quick property speculation that would become stale and uninspiring in five years' time.

'Ai,' said Vusi. This was not the way he had visualised it. He beckoned to the vehicle with the two other uniforms. They got out and everyone came over to stand with him. 'The jackets,' he said. The Inspector opened the back of the police van. The bulletproof vests were no longer in the tidy pile they had been earlier. Vusi took one, pulled it over his head and began to buckle it up. 'You too. Wait here while I have a look, and have the gate opened.' They nodded enthusiastically. He crossed the street and walked alongside the wall. There was a panel at the closed gate with a grid for a speaker, call buttons, some with names alongside. He scanned them and saw no de Klerk. On the top left was one labelled *Administrator*. He pressed it. An electronic beep sounded. Then nothing.

He pressed again. No answer.

He looked through the railings of the gate. The drive ran straight in – then turned ninety degrees to the left and disappeared behind a block of townhouses. He could see no sign of life. He pressed the button, without hope.

The speaker crackled and whistled briefly. A monotone woman's voice said: 'What do you want?'

★   ★   ★

Sixteen storeys above the bustling crowds of Adderley Street, the man stood at the window with his back to the luxury of the apartment behind him. He looked out over the city. In front of him was the Golden Acre, to the left the Cape Sun Hotel, behind that the tower blocks of the Foreshore area, a miscellany of architectural styles against the horizon. The blue sea was visible, though spoiled by the harbour cranes, two drilling rigs and the masts of ships.

The man's hair and full beard were trimmed short, sandy and prematurely greying – he didn't look fifty yet. He was fit and lean in denim shirt and khaki chino trousers with blue boat shoes. In the reflection of the high wide window the tanned face was expressionless.

He had one hand in his pocket; the other was holding a slim cell phone. He shifted his gaze from the view to the keyboard of his phone. From memory he typed in a number and held the instrument millimetres from his ear. He heard it ring once before Barry answered. 'Mr B.'

The man nodded slightly in satisfaction at the quick reaction time and the calm in Barry's voice.

'I'm taking control,' he said, his tone measured.

'Right.' Relief.

'Describe the house to me.'

Barry did his best, describing the single storey, the corner site and the position of the front door.

'Does the house have a back door?'

'I don't know.'

'If it has, it should be towards Belmont Avenue?'

'That's right.'

'OK. I'm going to send Eben and Robert to cover that angle. I am also working on the assumption that she has no need to leave through the back door, because she does not know that we saw her. Is that a fair assumption, Barry?'

'Yes, sir.'

'And she also does not know that we are watching the house.'

'Yes, sir.'

'Good. Let's keep it that way. I hear you saw only one occupant, an old man.'

'Right.'

'No evidence of others?'

'No, sir.'

'Good. Now listen carefully, Barry. You, Eben and Robert will have to be ready to move in case of an emergency. If you get the call, go in and get her, no matter what it takes. Do you understand me?'

'Yes, sir.'

'But that would be second prize, and only if she calls the cops. We don't know why she hasn't called them yet, but it can happen at any moment, and we will have maybe five minutes' warning. Which means you will have to be very quick.'

'Right.' Anxiety broke through his voice.

'And whatever you do, get the bag.'

'OK.'

'And we don't need witnesses.'

'I don't have a gun.'

'Barry, Barry, what did I teach you?'

'Adapt, improvise and overcome.'

'Exactly. But it might not be necessary, because we are working on first prize. It will take twenty or thirty minutes to put together, to make sure it's quick, quiet and clean. In the meantime, you are my main man, Barry. If we call, go in. If she leaves, get her. No mistakes. We can't afford any more mistakes. Do you understand that?'

'Yes, sir.'

'Are you sure? Have you thought of all the implications?'

'I have.'

'Good.'

As he put the cell phone in his pocket he saw the police helicopter flying across Table Bay directly towards him. He kept his eyes on it until it flew past, low over the city.

27

The uniforms stood outside with machine pistols and bulletproof vests. Vusi alone was inside with the complex administrator. She reminded him of bread dough, pale and shapeless; even her voice had no character.

'De Klerk is in A-six. He is not a renter; he owns. I don't see him often. He pays his levy with a debit order.'

She had fitted out one room of her townhouse as an office. She sat at a small cheap melamine desk. There was a computer screen and keyboard in front of white melamine shelves for files, one of which was open beside the keyboard. Vusi stood at the door.

'Is he here now?'

'I don't know.' A bald statement of an uninteresting fact.

'When last did you see him?'

'I think it was in November.'

'So he was last home in November?'

'I don't know. I don't get out much.'

'Are there phone numbers?'

She checked. 'No.'

'Can you describe him?'

'He's young.' She put a podgy index finger on the document. 'Twenty-six.' She looked up at Vusi and saw the question on his face. 'Tallish. Brownish hair.'

'Where does he work?'

The index finger moved across the printed document in the file. 'It just says "consultant" here.'

'May I have a look, please?'

She shifted the file. He took out his notebook and pen, put them down on the file and studied the form. Initials and surname *J. M. de Klerk*. An identity number.

Unit: Two-Bedroom Duplex.
Status: Owner and occupant.
Sub-let: No.
Levy: R800 p.m.
Occupation Date: 1 April 2007
Occupation: Consultant
Postal Address: Unit A6, Atlantic Breeze 24, Parklands 7441
Business Address: N/A
Telephone Home: N/A
Telephone Business: N/A
Cellular: N/A
Address and contact details: Next of kin: N/A

There was a hurried signature underneath a declaration that he accepted the rules and regulations of the complex.

'Does he drive a Land Rover Defender?'

'I don't know.'

Vusi pushed the file back towards her. 'Thank you very much,' he said and then hopefully: 'Do you have a key to his place?'

'I do.'

'Could you open up for us, please?'

'The regulations state I must have a search warrant on file.'

Benny Griessel sat in the radio room of the Caledon Square station with a map of the city on the table, his notebook and pen on top. He listened to the young sergeant talk to every patrol vehicle about the streets they had covered. He made hurried notes, trying to form an image of where she might be, where she might be going, what they ought to do. He struggled to get his head around it all – too many permutations and uncertainties.

His phone rang. He motioned the sergeant to keep the radio quiet for a moment, quickly checked the screen and answered.

'Vusi?'

'Benny, we need a warrant to get into the house.'

'Isn't he there?'

'I don't think so. We are going to knock, but the caretaker has a key . . .' A woman's voice spoke in the background. 'The administrator,' said Vusi. 'She has a key.'

'We don't have enough for a warrant, Vusi. Three numbers of a registration . . .'

'I thought so. OK. I'll call again . . .'

Griessel put down the phone, picked up his pen and motioned the sergeant to carry on. He studied the map, moving the tip of the pen towards the Company Gardens. That was where she was.

His instinct told him she was there, because he knew De Waal Park, he knew Upper Orange, it was his home, his territory, his cycling route. Upper Orange Street, Government Avenue, the Gardens. If he were in her shoes, if he had to run from there, afraid and unsure, roughly aiming for Long Street, he would run that way.

'I want two teams in the Gardens,' he told the sergeant. 'But first they must come and collect photos.'

Piet van der Lingen heard sobbing inside. He stood slightly stooped outside the bathroom door with his hand lifted to knock softly. He didn't want to frighten her.

'Rachel,' he said softly.

The sobs stopped abruptly.

'Rachel?'

'How do you know my name?'

'The policewoman told me. You are Rachel Anderson, from Lafayette in Indiana.' There was a long silence before the door slowly opened and he saw her with tears on her cheeks.

'West Lafayette, actually,' she said.

He smiled with great kindness. 'Come, my dear. The food is almost ready.'

Fransman Dekker told fat Inspector Mbali Kaleni about the money that had been paid to Jack Fischer and Associates, to the sum of ten thousand rand. At that moment he realised with brilliant clarity and insight how he could solve a whole number of problems. He planned his strategy while he briefed her. He must be careful how he held out the carrot. She was known for her ability to smell a rat.

'The Bloemfontein affair is the key,' he said, careful to keep his voice neutral. 'But Fischer and Co. are clever. Are you up to it?' He had chosen the words with great care.

She made a derisive noise in her throat. 'Clever?' She rose to her feet. 'They're just men,' she said, already heading for the door.

He felt relieved but gave nothing away. 'They're old hands,' he said.

She opened the door. 'Just leave Bloemfontein to me.'

After Vusi had tried knocking on the front door and the back door, he sent the uniformed police to ask the neighbours if anyone knew de Klerk. He stayed behind on the back patio, trying, from beside the large barbecue drum on wheels, to peer through the only gap in the curtains.

He saw an open-plan room with a small kitchen right at the back and an empty beer bottle on a cupboard. There was a sofa of dark material and, right ahead of him, the corner of a huge flat-screen TV.

No carpet on the tile floor. The beer bottle might have been there for weeks. There was ash in the *braai*, equally uninformative.

He stood in the shade of the small balcony, looking at the scrap of lawn, and waited for the policemen to return.

The 'administrator of the body corporate' told him these townhouses, with two bedrooms and a bathroom upstairs, a large living area, open-plan kitchen and guest toilet downstairs, cost a fraction under a million rand apiece last year. A new Land Rover was more than three hundred thousand. Big new TV. How could a twenty-six year old afford all this?

Drugs, thought Vusi.

He saw the policemen returning. He could tell from the way they walked they had nothing to report. Suddenly he was in a hurry and went to meet them. He wanted to get back to the city, to Van Hunks, because that was where the key to this puzzle lay.

It felt surreal, the old man in his impeccably white shirt pulling out a chair for her. The delicious aroma of fried bacon made her hunger flare up, an awakening animal. The table was neatly laid for two. The drops of condensation running down the big glass jug of orange juice made her crave its sweet, cold taste.

He walked over to the stove, asked whether she would like cheese and bacon on her omelette. 'Yes, please,' she said. He encouraged her to have some orange juice. She poured with a slightly trembling hand and brought the glass to her lips, trying to control the raging thirst.

Could he make her two slices of toast?

'Please.'

He busied himself, greasing a pan, adding the whisked egg yolks to the white he had already beaten stiff, pouring the mixture into the pan. There were fried bacon bits on a plate with grated cheese. He put the frying pan on the gas plate.

He always set for two, he said, ever since his wife died. He had started the habit even before then, actually, when she was sick. It made him feel less alone. It was a great privilege to have someone at the table, now. She must excuse him, he was going to talk far too much, as he didn't get much company. Just the books; they were his companions now. When had she last eaten?

She had to think about it. 'Yesterday,' she said, and remembered the big burgers they had had around four in a place with an American Sixties atmosphere, almost. 'A hole in the wall,' Erin had said, and then she shut down her memory bank, because she didn't want to remember.

He sprinkled bacon and cheese on the omelette and opened the oven. Took the pan off the gas flame, put it in the stove and closed the oven door. He turned to face her. It fell flat so easily, he said, if you weren't careful. He saw her glass was empty. He came to the table and refilled it. She thanked him with a small, genuine smile. There was silence, but a comfortable one.

'The books,' she said, half a question, to make conversation, to be polite, to say thank you.

'I used to be a historian,' he said. 'Now I'm just an old man with too much time on my hands and a doctor son in Canada who emails me and tells me to keep busy, as I still have a lot to give.'

He bent at the oven and had a look. 'Nearly ready,' he said. 'I'm writing a book. I promised myself it is my last. It's about the rebuilding of South Africa after the Boer War. I'm writing it for my people, the Afrikaners, so they can see they have been through the same thing as the black people are going through now. They were also oppressed, they were also very poor, landless, beaten down. But through affirmative action they got up again. Also economic empowerment. There are very great parallels. The English also complained about service delivery at the municipalities which was suddenly not as good any more, because incompetent Afrikaners had taken over . . .' He picked up pot-holders and opened the oven. The omelette had risen high in the pan, melted the cheese and the aroma wafted her way, making the saliva gush in her mouth. He picked up a spatula and slid the omelette out onto a snow-white plate, adeptly folded it and brought it to her.

'Catsup?' he asked, a mischievous twinkle in the eyes behind the big gold-rimmed spectacles. 'I believe that's what you call it.'

'No thanks, this looks lovely.'

He shifted the salt and pepper closer and said he had learned not to use salt, doctor's orders from his son, and anyway his capacity to taste wasn't what it used to be. Consequently the omelette might need some more salt.

'The trouble with omelettes is that I can only make one at a time. Go ahead and eat yours while I do mine.'

He went back to the stove again. She picked up her knife and fork, cut through the puffed egg and brought it to her mouth. She was incredibly hungry and the flavour was heavenly.

'But the book is also for our black people,' he said. 'The Afrikaners rose up again, an amazing achievement. Then their power corrupted them. The signs are there that the black government is going the same way. I am afraid they will make the same mistakes. It would be such a pity. We are a country of potential, of wonderful, good people who all want only one thing: a future for our children. Here. Not in Canada.' He put the pan in the oven again. He said he was a cheese fanatic and his son said dairy was not good for him. At seventy-nine he reckoned it didn't matter so much any more and he smiled again, showing those even white false teeth. The toast! He clean forgot . . . He clicked his tongue and took two slices of bread out of a plastic bag and put them in the toaster.

'This is delicious,' she said, because it was. Already she had eaten half the omelette. 'Can I brew us some good coffee? There is an exceptional beanery in the Bo-Kaap. They do their own roasting, but I grind it myself.'

'That would be wonderful,' She felt like getting up and hugging him. The grief was huge and heavy inside her, held at bay by his enthusiasm and hospitality.

He opened the kitchen cupboard and took out a big silver tin. He said he mustn't forget about his omelette in the oven; that was the trouble with age: the forgetfulness. He really could multi-task in his young days, but now that was all he remembered – his young days. He measured coffee beans into a grinder and pressed the button. The blades made a sharp noise as they chopped up the beans. He murmured something; she could just see his lips moving. He finished the grinding, opened the filter of the coffee machine and poured the coffee into it. He picked up his pot-holders and opened the oven.

'A mixture of cheddar and Gruyère, it always smells better than it tastes. That is one thing about old age. Your sense of smell lasts longer than taste.'

The toaster popped the two slices up. He took a small plate, put the toast on it and brought it to her. 'Some green fig preserve? I have a really good Camembert to go with it, rich and creamy, made by a small cheesery near Stellenbosch.' He opened the fridge and took it out anyway before she could reply.

He was back at the stove, sliding the omelette onto his plate. He brought it to the table, sat down and took a mouthful. 'I often add feta as well, to this particular mixture, but it might be too salty for a young woman . . . the coffee!' He jumped up again with surprising energy, to put water in the coffee-maker. He spilled some on the counter and wiped it up with the white dishcloth before turning on the machine and sitting down again.

'West Lafayette. You're a long way from home, my dear.'

28

On the sixteenth floor of the apartment block, the man with the trimmed grey beard stood etched against the bright city panorama, his hands behind his back.

In front of him were the six young men. They looked at him, not intimidated, expectant. Three black, three white, united by their youth, leanness and fearlessness.

'Mistakes have been made,' the man said in English, but with a distinctive accent.

'Learn from them. I am taking charge now. This is not a vote of no confidence. See it as an opportunity to learn.'

One or two nodded slightly; they knew he didn't like emotional display.

'Time is our enemy. So I shall keep it short. Our friend in Metro will provide a suitable vehicle, a panel van that has been unclaimed in the pound in Green Point for four months. Go and get it; Oerson is waiting at the gate. Leave the bus in the parkade of the Victoria Junction Hotel.'

He picked up a shiny metal case from the floor and put it on the table in front of him.

He looked at one of the young men. 'The Taurus?'

'Underwater in the harbour.'

'Good.' The greybeard unclipped the case and swivelled it around for all to see. 'Four Stechkin APSs, the APB model. The B stands for *Bes-shumniy*, the Russian word for "quiet", because the barrel is bored out for low velocity and, as you can see, they come with a silencer. These weapons are thirty-five years old, but they are the most reliable automatic pistols on the planet. Nine millimetre, twenty in the magazine; the ammunition is less than six months old. The silencers don't mean that the weapon is completely silent. It makes a sound equal to an unsilenced point-two-two pistol; enough to attract attention, which we do not want. Only use it in an emergency. Is that clear?'

Everyone nodded this time, greedy eyes on the guns.

'Much more stopping power than the Taurus. Remember that. The numbers have been filed off; they cannot be traced to us. Make sure you wear gloves, and get rid of them if necessary.'

He waited another second to make sure there were no questions.

'Very well. This is how we're going to do it.'

Inspector Fransman Dekker was on his way over to where Natasha was sitting when the tall white man intercepted him.

'Are you from the police?'

'I am,' said Dekker. The face seemed familiar.

'I'm Iván Nell,' he said with an inflection of the powerful voice that said the name meant something.

'Weren't you on that TV show?'

'I was one of the mentors on *Superstars* . . .'

'You sing . . .'

'That's right.'

'My wife watched *Superstars*. Pleased to meet you. You must excuse me – we're a little busy here this morning,' said Dekker and began moving again.

'That's why I'm here,' said Nell. 'Because of Adam.'

Dekker stopped reluctantly. 'Yes?'

'I think I was the last person to see him alive.'

'Last night?' The singer had his full attention now.

Nell nodded. 'We were eating at Bizerca Bistro down near Pier Place until ten o'clock.'

'And then?'

'Then I went home.'

'I see.' Dekker thought for a while. 'And Barnard?'

'I don't know where Adam went. But this morning when I heard on the radio . . .' Nell looked around at the people who were sitting too close for his liking, at Natasha who had got up and come closer. 'Is there somewhere we could talk?'

'What about?'

Nell came up close and spoke quietly: 'I think his death has something to do with our conversation last night, I don't know . . .'

'What did you talk about, Mr Nell?'

He looked uneasy. 'Can we talk somewhere else?' It was an urgent whisper.

Dekker suppressed the impulse to sigh. 'Can you just give me two minutes, please?'

'Of course. I just don't want you to think, you know . . .'

'No, Mr Nell, I don't know,' said Fransman Dekker. He looked at Natasha who was waiting patiently only steps away from them, then back at Nell. 'Just give me a moment.'

'Of course.'

Benny Griessel was not good at sitting and waiting. So he left the radio room, walked through the busy charge office and the security doors out onto Buitenkant Street. His brain was busy and his courage was low. They were not going to find her. He had fourteen patrol vehicles driving in a grid pattern, and one was parked in Long Street with the men waiting at the Cat & Moose. He had ten foot patrols, two of them searching the Company Gardens. The helicopter had returned from Table View and covered the entire bloody city. There was no sign of her.

Where could she be?

He walked to his car, unlocked it and took out the Chesterfields from the cubbyhole, locked the door again and stood on the pavement, holding the pack of cigarettes. What was he missing?

Was there something in the chaos of the morning that he had missed? It was a familiar feeling. On the day a crime took place, there was so much information, his head would be overflowing, the pieces unconnected and crowding each other out. It took time, a night's sleep sometimes, for the subconscious to sort and file, like a slow secretary working at her own unhurried tempo.

He took out a cigarette and put it between his lips.

He was missing something . . .

He slid the box of matches open.

The Field Marshal. Jeremy Oerson and the search for the rucksack.

He began to walk hastily back along the pavement, putting the matches in his trouser pocket, and the cigarettes back in the pack. He went into the police station. Was that the only item knocking at the door of his consciousness?

In the radio room he asked a uniformed policeman where he could get a telephone directory.

'Charge office.'

Griessel fetched one, paging through it as he walked back. The local government numbers were all right at the back. He found Metro and put the book on the old government-issue table of dark wood, next to his maps, notebook, pen and cell phone. He kept a finger on the number and phoned. Two rings and a woman's voice said: 'Cape Town Metropolitan Police, good afternoon, *goeimiddag.*'

'Jeremy Oerson, please.'

'Please hold,' she said and put him through. It rang for a long time. A man answered.

'Metro.'

'Jeremy Oerson?'

'Jeremy is not here.'

'This is Insp . . . Captain Benny Griessel, SAPS. Where can I get hold of him, it's quite urgent?'

'Hold on . . .' A hand was held over the receiver and muffled words exchanged. 'He should be back soon. Do you want his cell phone number?'

'Please.' Griessel reached for his pen and book.

The man recited the number and Griessel wrote it down. He rang off and phoned it. Oerson answered instantly.

'Jeremy.'

'Benny Griessel, SAPS. We talked this morning in Long Street.'

'Yes.' A total lack of enthusiasm.

'Did you find anything?'

'Where?'

'In the city. The girl's rucksack. You were supposed to be looking . . .'

'Oh. Yes. No, there was nothing.'

Griessel was not impressed by his attitude. 'Can you tell me exactly where you searched?'

'I'll have to check. I didn't do it myself. We *do* have work, you know . . .'

'I thought that *was* your work, fighting crime?'

'Your case isn't the only one we are working on.'

No, indeed, they had parking tickets to write, but he limited himself to the subject at hand: 'And you are absolutely sure you found nothing?'

'Nothing that belonged to the girl.'

'So you did find something?'

'The streets are full of stuff. There's a bag of junk in my office, but there is no passport or a purse or anything that would belong to an American woman.'

'How do you know?'

'Do you think I'm stupid?'

Jissis. Griessel breathed deeply and slowly. 'No, I don't think you're stupid. Where is the bag?'

Oerson waited before he answered. 'Where are you now?'

'No, tell me where your office is and I'll have it fetched.'

Natasha Abader unlocked Adam Barnard's office and said: 'I will have to give you the password if you want to check his laptop.'

She went in and Dekker followed. There were large framed photographs on the walls, Barnard and stars, one after the other, the men with an arm around Barnard's shoulder, the women with an arm around Barnard's waist. Every photo had a signature and a message in thick black marker. 'Thank you, Adam!' 'Adam for president!!!' 'With love and thanks.' 'The star in my heaven.' 'You are my darling.' Hearts, crosses to represent kisses, music notes.

He looked at the desk on which, according to her personal testimony, Melinda Geyser had been screwed. Apart from the laptop there was nothing else on it. His imagination ran riot, Melinda lying on her back on the wide wooden surface, stark naked, legs hooked over the shoulders of the standing Barnard, her mouth open in ecstasy as Adam fucked her, the sounds audible through the thin walls.

Dekker looked at Natasha guiltily. Her attention was on the laptop, eyebrows raised in query.

'What?'

'Adam left his laptop on.'

Dekker walked around the desk and stood beside her. He could smell her perfume. Subtle. Sexy. 'So?'

'He wouldn't usually do that. I switch it on when I come in, so he . . .'

The screensaver was on, the AfriSound logo like a small flag fluttering. She moved the mouse, the screensaver disappeared, replaced by a request for a password. Natasha bent down to type it in, her long nails clicking on the keys and her neckline gaping. Dekker's view was good; he could not look away. Her breasts were small, firm and perfect.

She stood up suddenly. His eyes slid away to the screen. There were no programs open.

'I will have to look at his emails.'

She nodded and bent down again to work the mouse. Why couldn't she sit down? Did she know he was looking?

'Where is his diary?'

'He used Outlook. Let me show you,' and she shifted the mouse, clicking here and there. 'You can use Alt and Tab to change between email and calendar,' she said, and then she moved away so he could sit down in the large comfortable chair.

'Thanks,' he said. 'Can I ask you a few questions?'

She went over to the door. At first he thought she was ignoring him, but she shut the door, came back and sat down opposite him. She looked him full in the eyes.

'I know what you want to ask.'

'What?'

'You want to know whether Adam and I . . . you know . . .'

'Why would I want to ask that?'

She shrugged dismissively. It was a sensual gesture, but he suspected she was unconscious of that. She had a subdued air about her, sad. 'You're going to interview everyone,' she said.

Now he did want to know, but for another reason. 'Did you?' His head was screaming, Fransman what are you doing? But he knew what he was doing – looking for trouble and he could not stop himself.

'Yes.' She dropped her eyes.

'Here?' He gestured at the desk.

'Yes.'

Why had she given herself to a white man, a middle-aged white man, when she was lovely enough for the cover of a magazine? He wanted to know if that meant she was easy, accessible. To him.

'This morning I'm glad that I did,' she said.

'Because he's dead?'

'Yes.'

'There are stories about him . . . and women.'

She did not respond.

'Did he force women?'

'No.' With an attitude that said she objected to the question.

'Did you hear, yesterday? When Melinda was here?'

'Yes, I did.' Without blushing or averting her eyes.

'Do you know why he sent for her?'

'No. I only saw in the diary that she was coming.'

'But usually Josh is with her.'

Again the shrug.

'This is what I don't understand: there are three of you who heard him . . . "nailing her",' his fingers made quotation marks around the words, 'a gospel artist in his office, and nobody thought it was strange. What kind of place is this?'

That made her angry; he could read her body language, the way she pulled her mouth, suddenly tight and sour.

'Come on, sister, think how it looks.'

'Don't "sister" me.'

He waited for an explanation, but she just sat there.

'Did Adam say anything about a DVD last week? Something that came in his post?'

'No.'

'Do you know who shot him?'

It took a while for the answer to come, reluctantly, more of a question: 'Josh Geyser?'

'Maybe not.'

She looked surprised, brushing long hair back over her shoulder in a practised motion.

'Why do you think it was Josh?'

'I saw him yesterday. He was angry enough. And he's . . . weird.'

'Weird?'

The shrug again, which conspired to make her breasts move oddly under the tight, thin material. 'Gladiator turned gospel singer. Don't you think that's weird? Look at him . . .'

'I can't lock him up because of the way he looks. Who else was angry with Adam Barnard?'

She made a wry noise. 'This is the music business.'

'And that means . . .'

'Everyone is angry with everyone sometimes.'

'And everyone screws everyone else.'

She was indignant again.

'Who else was angry enough to shoot him?'

'I really don't know.'

He asked the question that fascinated him: 'Why were . . . the women so crazy about him? He was over fifty . . .'

She stood up, crossed her arms over her breasts, cold and angry. 'He would have been fifty-two. In February.'

He waited for an answer but none was forthcoming. He egged her on: 'Why?'

'It's not about age, it's about aura.'

'Aura?'

'Yes.'

'What aura?'

'There's more than one kind.'

'What was his aura?'

'You wouldn't understand.'

'Educate me.'

'He had an aura of power. Very strong.' Then she looked into his eyes with a challenge and said: 'Women like the power of money, and he had that. And for many women he was the gateway to the stars. He could introduce them to the celebrities with money. But there is another power that is totally irresistible – the power to empower.'

'Now you've lost me.'

'Second prize is to have a powerful man in your life. First prize is to have the power yourself so you don't need a man. That was the kind of power Adam Barnard could give.'

'To the artists? He could give them fame and fortune?'

'Yes.'

He nodded slowly. She hesitated, then turned and walked to the door.

'But you're not a singer,' he said.

With one hand on the doorknob, without looking around, she said: 'Second prize is not so bad.'

She opened the door and went out.

'Send the Nell *ou* in, please,' he called after her, but he couldn't tell if she had heard him.

29

Alexa Barnard became aware of someone beside her bed.

She opened heavy eyelids and felt the dull ache in her forearm, the weight of her body and the peculiar odour of the hospital ward. On the right of her bed she saw large eyes behind thick spectacles. She tried to focus, but closed her eyes again.

'My name is Victor Barkhuizen, and I am an alcoholic,' said a voice very quietly and sympathetically.

She opened her eyes again. He was an old guy.

'Benny Griessel asked me to look in on you. The detective. I am his AA sponsor. I just want you to know you are not alone.'

Her mouth was very dry. She wondered if it was the medication, the stuff that made her sleep.

'The doctor?' she asked, but her tongue stuck to her palate, her lips were stiff and the words wouldn't form.

'You don't have to speak. I'm just going to sit here with you a while and I will leave my number with the ward sister. I will come again tonight.'

She turned her head towards him with effort and managed to open her eyes. He was short and stooped, bald and bespectacled, and the hair that he still had around his head hung down his back in a long plait. She slowly put out her right hand. He took it and held it tight.

'You're the doctor,' she tried to say.

'For my sins.'

'I smoke,' she said.

'And you don't even have a fever.'

She didn't know if the smile registered on her face. 'Thank you,' she said and closed her eyes again.

'No problem.'

Then she remembered, somewhere through the haze she had had a thought, a message. Without opening her eyes she said: 'The detective . . .'

'Benny Griessel.'

'Yes. I need to tell him something.'

'I can send him a message.'

'Tell him to come. About Adam . . .'

'I'll tell him.'

She wanted to add something, something that evaded her now, like silver fish slipping from her grasp into dark water. She sighed and felt Victor Barkhuizen's hand and pressed it slowly to make sure it was still there.

'I'd like to call my dad. I'll pay, of course,' said Rachel Anderson as she helped him carry the plates to the sink, in spite of his protests.

'No need for that,' he said. 'The phone is on the table, where I work.'

Then he laughed. 'If you can find it. Go, I will clear the dishes.'

'No,' she said. 'The least I can do is to wash up.'

'Under no circumstances.'

'Please, I insist. I love washing up.'

'You lie with such grace, my dear.'

'It's true! At home I do it all the time.'

'Then we'll do it together,' he said as he squirted dish-washing liquid over the plates and opened the taps. 'You do the washing, I'll dry and put them away. Do you still live with your parents?'

'Oh, yes, I just finished high school last year. This is supposed to be a gap year, before I go to college.'

'Here, you can wear these gloves . . . And where would you go for your studies?'

'Purdue. My parents work there.'

'They're academics?'

'My dad has tenure at English Lit. My mom's at the School of Aeronautics and Astronautics, on the Astrodynamics and Space Applications research team.'

'Good grief.'

'She's a real scientist, the most scatterbrained person I know. I love her to death, she's brilliant, she does spacecraft dynamics, orbit mechanics, it's about satellite control, how their orbits decay, how they re-enter the earth's atmosphere, and it's like a rhyme, I can say it, but I don't understand anything she does, I think I take after my dad, and I'm talking too much, right now.'

He put a hand on her upper arm. 'And I'm enjoying every minute, so talk all you like.'

'I miss them very much.'

'I'm sure you do.'

'No, it's more like . . . I left home almost two months ago, I've been away from them for so long, it makes you . . . I didn't know how dreadful I was, such a teenager . . .'

'We all were. It's the way life works.'

'I know, but it took a really bad thing . . .' Her hands stopped moving, her head drooped onto her chest and she stood still.

He said nothing at first, just watched her with immense compassion. He saw the tears rolling silently down her face. 'Would you like to talk about it?'

She shook her head, fighting for control. It came slowly. 'I can't. I shouldn't . . .'

'You're almost done. Go and call your father.'

'Thank you.' She hesitated. 'You've been so very kind . . . I . . .'

'I have done very little.'

'Would it be rude if I . . .?'

'I don't think you have a rude bone in your body, my dear. Please, just ask.'

'I'm dying for a bath, I don't think I've ever been this dirty, I'll be quick, I promise . . .'

'Good heavens, of course, and take all the time you need. Would you like a bubble bath? The grandchildren gave me some for my birthday, but I never use it . . .'

There was no parking in Castle Street. Griessel had to park a block away from the Van Hunks club in Long Street, and the parking attendant descended on him like a vulture. He paid for two hours and walked hastily towards the nightclub, surprised to find Vusi waiting at the front door.

'I thought you were still on your way?'

'Those Table View guys are crazy. Sirens all the way. This door is locked. We have to go round the back.'

'I sent for the eyewitness from Carlucci's, Vusi. And Oliver Sands from the hostel,' Griessel said as they walked side by side.

'OK, Benny.'

They turned into the service alley. Griessel's cell phone rang: the screen said MAT JOUBERT.

'Hey,' said Benny, answering.

'Is that *Captain* Benny Griessel?' Joubert asked.

'Can you fucking believe it?'

'Congratulations, Benny. It's high time. Where are you?'

'Nightclub in Castle Street. Van Hunks.'

'I'm just around the corner. Would you like some Steers?'

'*Jissis*, that would be great.' He had last eaten the previous night. 'A Dagwood burger, chips and Coke; I'll pay you back.' His belly rumbled in expectation. 'Wait, let me ask Vusi if he wants something too . . .'

On the third floor of a recently restored office building in St George's Mall, the lift doors opened to release the fat woman.

She hitched the handbag over her shoulder, shifted the pistol on her belt and walked purposefully across the thick, light brown carpet to where a middle-aged coloured receptionist sat behind a dark wood desk. She took the SAPS identity card hanging around her neck between her thumb and forefinger and aimed it at the receptionist, looking up at the words *Jack Fischer and Associates*, which were displayed on a dark wooden panel, every letter cut from gleaming copper and individually mounted.

'Inspector Mbali Kaleni, SAPS. I need to talk to Jack Fischer.'

The coloured woman was unimpressed. 'I doubt he is available,' she said, putting a reluctant hand out to the telephone.

'Is he here?'

The receptionist ignored her. She typed in a four-figure number and said in an undertone: 'Marli, there is a woman from the police who wants to talk to Jack . . .'

'Is Jack here?' Kaleni asked again.

'I see,' said the coloured woman into the telephone with an air of satisfaction. 'Thank you, Marli.' She replaced the phone and sniff-sniffed with a slight frown. 'What *is* that smell?'

'I asked you if Jack Fischer is here.'

'Mr Fischer's diary is full. He can only see you after six.'

'But he is here?'

The woman nodded unenthusiastically.

'Tell him it is in connection with the murder of his client, Adam Barnard. I want to talk to him within the next fifteen minutes.'

The receptionist opened her mouth to respond, but she saw Kaleni turn and waddle to one of the large easy chairs against the wall. She sat down and made herself comfortable, placed her handbag on her lap and took out a white plastic bag with the letters KFC and the logo of an old bearded, bespectacled man on it.

The receptionist's frown deepened as Kaleni put her chubby hand into the plastic bag and took out a little red and white carton and a tin of Fanta Grape. She watched the policewoman put her handbag on the ground and the Fanta on the table beside her, opening the carton with absolute concentration.

'You can't sit there and eat,' she said with more astonishment than authority.

Mbali Kaleni lifted a chicken drumstick out of the packet. 'I can,' she said, and took a bite.

The receptionist shook her head and made a little noise of disbelief and despair. She picked up the phone, without taking her eyes off the munching policewoman.

Galina Federova walked down the passage with Vusi and Griessel behind her. Benny smelled the alcohol even before they entered the big nightclub – that familiar, musty old smell of drinking holes where alcohol has been poured, drunk and spilt, the smell that for more than ten years had offered him a refuge. His stomach contracted in fear and anticipation. As he went through the door and the club opened out before him, his eyes sought out the shelves of bottles against the wall, long rows glinting like jewels side by side in the bright lights.

He heard the Russian woman say: 'This is the night shift,' but he continued staring at the liquor, his head full of memories. He felt a powerful wave of nostalgia for days and nights of drinking with forgotten booze buddies. And for the atmosphere of these twilight places, that feeling of total submission, clasping a glass with the knowledge that a refill was only a nod away.

The taste in his mouth now was not the brandy or Jack Daniels that he used to drink, but the gin that he had poured that morning for Alexa Barnard. He recalled her relief with disturbing clarity; he could see the effect of the alcohol on her so clearly, how it drove out all the demons. That was what he desired now: not the smell or the taste, but the calm, the equilibrium that had evaded him all day. He craved the effect of alcohol. He heard Vusi say his name once, twice, and then he dragged his face away from the bottles and concentrated fiercely on his colleague.

'These are the night-shift staff,' Vusi said.

'OK.' Griessel looked around the room, aware that his heart was beating too quickly, his palms sweating, knowing he must squeeze the longing out of himself by force. He looked at all the people. Some of the staff were seated at tables, others were busy arranging chairs and wiping down tables. For the first time he heard the music in the background, unfamiliar rock.

'Can you ask them to sit, please?' he said to Federova, thinking he must pull himself together pretty smartly; he had a young, lost and frightened girl to find.

The woman nodded and clapped her hands to get everyone's attention. 'Come. Sit.' Griessel noted that they were all young and good looking – mostly men, nine or ten of them; four women. None of them looked particularly impressed to be here.

'Can someone turn off the music?' Griessel asked, his patience worn thin by the general lack of interest, the liquor and the urgency inside him.

A young man got up and walked over to the sound system, pressed or turned something and it went suddenly quiet.

'They are from the police,' said Galina Federova in a businesslike voice, but her irritation came through. 'They want to ask questions about last night.' She looked at Griessel.

'Good afternoon,' he said. 'Last night, two American girls visited this club, young tourists. This morning, the body of one of them was found at the top of Long Street. Her throat was cut.'

He ignored the subdued sounds of dismay; at least he had their attention now. 'I'm going to pass around a photograph of the victim and her friend. We need your help urgently. If you remember them at all, put up your hand. We believe the other girl is still alive, and we have to find her.'

'Before it is too late,' said Vusi Ndabeni softly beside him.

'Yes,' said Griessel, and gave half of the photographs to Vusi, walked to the back table and began to hand them out, watching how they looked at the picture with the usual macabre interest.

He went and stood in front again, waiting for Vusi to give out the last photos.

Federova sat down at the bar and lit a cigarette. In front of him the young workers' heads were lowered, busy studying the photos.

Then two or three slowly looked up, warily, with that tentative expression that said they recognised the girls, but they didn't want to be first to raise a hand.

30

Mbali Kaleni was aware of the disapproval of the coloured receptionist, but didn't understand it. A person had to eat. It was lunchtime and here was a table and chairs. That was the problem with this country, she thought, all these little cultural differences. A Zulu eats when she must eat; it was normal, natural, and no big deal. She wasn't bothering anyone; she had no issue with how and what and when brown people or white people ate. If they wanted to eat their tasteless white sandwiches behind closed office doors or somewhere in a claustrophobic little kitchen, that was their problem. She didn't judge them.

She shook her head, took out the tub of mashed potatoes and gravy, lifted the transparent lid, picked up the white plastic teaspoon and made sure she took a small, well-mannered portion. This was part of her ritual: first she ate all the chicken, then the potato, leaving half of the cold drink for last. And, as usual, she thought while she ate. Not about the murder of the music man; it was the American girl who haunted her. She had been so sure she would find her. Her colleagues had been running around in a panic; in the crisis they had acted like headless chickens, but that was the way men were. In an emergency they had to *do* something; they couldn't suppress the impulse. This situation called for calm, for logic and causal thought. That was how she had found the trail in the flower bed.

And then, nothing. That was what she found perplexing.

The girl would not have jumped the picket fence only to clamber over the next wall and run down the street again.

But the old man had said he had heard her go up to the wall.

Why didn't Rachel Anderson knock on his door and ask for shelter? Too little time.

And if time was so short, she would have hidden from the street some other way. Why hadn't the helicopter spotted her? The way it seemed to Kaleni as she thought the situation through was that there were only two options for a fugitive woman trying to stay off the streets: get inside a house, or hide somewhere in a garden where nobody could see her. If she hadn't gone into the old man's house, she must have climbed over the northern wall to the next house. But Kaleni had had a policeman, a tall, skinny Xhosa, look over the wall for her, because she was too short. He said there was nothing there, just a little herb garden and a plastic table and chairs.

Had she climbed over the next wall as well and gone through the next yard? The helicopter would have spotted her sooner or later.

And if she had travelled so far, why did Mbali Kaleni have such a strong feeling that she was close by?

She scraped out the last of the potato, put the lid back on the tub, and the tub back in the little carton.

When she was finished here she would go back to Upper Orange. Have another look. She owed that to the girl: a woman's calm, logical and causal thought.

Iván Nell sat opposite Fransman Dekker in Adam Barnard's office and said in his deep voice: 'I wanted to see Adam, because I believe they are cheating me. Of my money.'

'How's that?'

'It's a long story . . .'

Dekker pulled his notebook and pen nearer. 'Can you give me the main points?'

Nell leaned forward in his chair, put his elbows on his knees and said with a serious expression: 'I think they are cooking their books. Last night I told Adam I wanted to bring in an auditor, because things didn't look right. And when I heard over the radio this morning that he was dead . . .'

'What made you think things were not right?'

'Well, to get sales figures had become like pulling teeth; it's very difficult to get something out of them. Then, last year, the money I

received for some songs in compilations by independent labels . . .
It was a heck of a lot more than I expected. Then I started doing
my own sums . . .'

'So AfriSound is not your label?'

'No, they were, until February last year.'

'They made your CDs?'

'My contract was for three original albums and the option of a
Greatest Hits. That came out last year, all with Adam.'

'And then you went to someone else?'

'No, I started my own label.'

'Because AfriSound cheated you?'

'No, no, I was not aware then that they were robbing me.'

Dekker leaned back in the comfortable chair. 'Mr Nell, can you
start at the beginning, please?'

'I . . . please call me Iván.'

Dekker nodded, impressed, but he didn't show it. He had
expected an attitude: the man was famous, white and successful.
But there was no ego, no talking down to a coloured policeman,
just a genuine desire to help.

'At varsity I started playing in pubs, for pocket money mostly,
around Nineteen ninety-six. I did English covers, Kristofferson,
Cohen, Diamond, Dylan, that sort of thing, just me and my
guitar. When I graduated in ninety-eight, I started going door
to door to get gigs in Pretoria. I started singing in Café Amics,
McGinty's, Maloney's, some places without pay. Nobody
knew about me. I used to do two sets of English covers and
the last set in Afrikaans with a couple of my own songs thrown
in just to test the audience. Then it started happening, when
the time came for the last set, the place would suddenly be full.
The people would sing along. And the audiences grew bigger,
like there was a hunger for Afrikaans stuff, like they wanted to
belong somewhere, the students, the younger people. In any
case, the gigs increased. Eventually I was playing six nights a
week, making more money than I did at work, so I went full time
in Two thousand. In Two thousand and one I made my own CD
and I sold it at the shows . . .'

'For which label?'

'No, I didn't have a label.'

'How can you make a CD if you don't have a label?'

'You just have to have money. There was this guy at Hartebeespoort who had a studio in an outside room. I recorded it with him. He charged about sixty thousand then. I had to borrow the money . . .'

'So why would you need a label?'

'For just about everything, but mostly for capital. If you want to make a decent album, a solid recording with good musicians and enough studio time, you need about two hundred thousand. I couldn't afford that. That first CD of mine was quite primitive, you can hear that. But you sit in the pub at night and sing, and then you tell people there's a CD, and they have had a couple of drinks and so they buy it, let's say ten per night, then you get your money back. But you can't play it on the radio; it's just not good enough. If you're with a label they pay for a band, a producer, sound engineer; they market the thing, distribute it – it's a whole different ball game.'

'So how did you end up with AfriSound?'

'Adam heard what was happening up there, about the audiences growing and so on. So he came up to listen and said he wanted to sign me. I mean, Adam Barnard, it's what a guy dreams about, he's this legend, Mr Afrikaans music. He gave me my big break; he put me on the map. I will always be grateful to him for that . . . Anyway, we signed for three albums and the option of a *Greatest Hits*. He said for the first one I must record my first album again with the best musicians. Adam produced it himself; it was a dream team. They paid RSG Radio to play the CD; the album went double platinum. It took more than three years, but we did well. So did the next two albums, and the *Greatest Hits*, all platinum already.'

'So why don't you want to sing with AfriSound any more?'

'Many reasons. Look, the big labels are going to squeeze every cent out of you. They make big promises, but they don't always keep them . . . but in the end it's about margins. From a record company you get twelve per cent, sometimes less. But on your own you get everything less input costs, eighty, eighty-five per cent once you've recouped your studio expenses. That is one heck of a difference. And now I have the capital to rent a decent studio long enough to make the best possible product.'

'What do you mean when you say you "did well"? What amounts are we talking about?'

'Look, it depends . . .' Uncomfortable, as though he didn't really want to talk about it.

'Plus minus.'

'*Jonkmanskas* was my first album with Adam. It only did fifteen thousand in the first year, but you have to build your brand, because if people like your second album they will go back and buy your first. So, *Jonkmanskas* started reasonably, but now it's on a hundred and fifty thousand . . .'

'And what is your share of that?'

'That also depends on whether I sold it myself at a concert or if you bought it in a shop.'

Dekker sighed. 'Iván, I'm trying to get my head around the music business. Give me a ball-park figure of what you earn with a CD. Nowadays.'

Nell sat up slowly, still uncomfortable with the subject. 'Let's say about seven hundred and fifty, over three to four years.'

'Seven hundred and fifty thousand?'

'Yes.'

'Fuck,' said Dekker and made a note in his book. 'Now how did they cheat you?'

'It may sound like a lot of money, Inspector, but that is before tax, and there are a lot of expenses . . .'

'How did they cheat you?'

'I don't know. That's why I want to bring in an auditor.'

'Surely you must have a theory?'

'Well, last year, I did three songs for compilation albums – one for Sean Else's rugby CD and two for Jeremy Taylor, a country album and Christmas album. Sean and Jeremy are independents, and when I got the rugby CD money, I started wondering, because it was a shitload of money, proportionately much more than I was getting from Adam and them. When the country CD payment came, it was the same story. So I looked carefully at the statements, at the deductions and sales and royalties, and the more I looked, the less sense it made. You must remember, on a compilation album you are one of ten or more artists; so you would be getting roughly ten per cent, say, of the royalties you would usually receive. I wasn't expecting much. In the end it was good money. Then I started getting suspicious.'

'And you spoke to Adam Barnard?'

'I phoned him about a week ago, and said I wanted to come and see him. I didn't say why; I just said I wanted to talk about my contract. He said let's go and have a relaxed dinner.'

'And that was last night?'

'That's right.'

'What was his reaction?'

'He said that as far as he knew, they had nothing to hide. When I said I wanted to bring my own auditor, he said "no problem".'

'And then?'

'He offered me a new contract. I said "no thank you". And that was that. So we talked about other things. Adam . . . He was great company, as always. His stories . . . The thing is, usually Adam will party to twelve or one o'clock, he never tires. But last night, at about half past nine, he said he had to make a quick phone call, and he went and stood outside to phone, and when he came in he said he had to leave. We got the bill and we left about ten o'clock.'

Dekker looked at Barnard's diary. Alongside 19:00 was written *Iván Nell – Bizerca* but there were no further entries for later that night. He made a note in his notebook: *Cell phone 21:30??* and wondered what had happened to Adam Barnard's cell phone, because it wasn't on the scene that morning.

'You have no idea who he called?'

'No. But he wasn't the sort of guy who would leave the table to phone. He would just sit with you and talk, never mind who it was. When I heard this morning he had been shot, once I was over the worst shock, I started to wonder.'

★　　★　　★

She stood with one foot in the hot foam bath and considered surrendering herself to the luxury, longing to wash her hair and scrub her body, then just lying back and letting the pain and the fatigue melt away.

She couldn't. She had to phone her father; they would be insane with worry. But she wanted to bath quickly first. In the kitchen just now, she had seen a way out for the first time since last night, a prospect of safety. If she phoned her father, he could get someone to fetch her, someone from the embassy, maybe, and they could question her and she would tell them everything. It would be a long process, long discussions over everything that had happened. That meant it would be hours before she could wash off the blood and sweat and dust. She must take the opportunity to clean herself quickly now.

She got into the bath and sat down. The hot water stung the scratches and cuts, but the satisfaction was immense. She slowly lay back until her breasts slipped under the foam.

Hurry.

She sat up fast, with great self-discipline, stood up, picked up the soap and washcloth and began to scrub her youthful body.

12:57–14:01

31

A waitress, two waiters and a barman remembered Erin Russel and Rachel Anderson. Griessel had them sit at a separate table with Vusi. He took a seat with his back to the bar so he couldn't see the bloody bottles, but there was nothing he could do about the smell.

'The rest can go home,' Galina Federova ordered.

'No, I still need them.' The Carlucci's man still had to see if he recognised any of them.

'For what?'

She was starting to get on Griessel's nerves. He wanted to tell her it was none of her fucking business, he didn't like her attitude, but his urgency to gain any available information made him hold back. 'Let them wait ten minutes,' he said, curtly, so she'd get the message, stop messing them around.

She said something in Russian, shook her head and walked out. Griessel watched her leave. Then he slowly turned back, trying to clear his head as he asked the young people around the table. 'Who would like to start?'

'They were sitting right here,' said one of the waiters, pointing at a table close by and fiddling self-consciously with a necklace of wooden beads around his neck. And then all the waiters suddenly looked up at the door behind Griessel. He turned as well. Mat Joubert stood there, a bag of takeaways in each hand.

'Carry on,' said Joubert, 'I'm with Captain Griessel.' He approached the table, put down the bags, took out boxes and pushed them towards Vusi and Benny. The aroma of chips made Griessel's belly stir.

'Thanks, Mat.'

'Thanks, Sup,' said Ndabeni.

Joubert just nodded in acknowledgement, pulled up a chair and joined them at the table.

'This is Senior Superintendent Mat Joubert of the Provincial Task Force,' Griessel told the waiters, as he saw they were intimidated by the size of his colleague. 'He's not a patient man,' he lied, for good measure. He looked at the waiter who had spoken first. 'Where were we?'

The waiter looked at Griessel and then respectfully at Joubert, his voice suddenly sincere. 'Those two in the photo were sitting alone at first. I served them. They were drinking Brutal Fruit. This one, the blondie, she was partying hard. The other one only had four or five, the whole evening. A bit strange.'

'Why?' asked Griessel. He tore open the sachet of Steers salt and sprinkled it over his chips.

'The backpackers . . . usually they booze it up.'

Griessel suppressed the impulse to look at the rows of bottles behind the bar. 'How did you know they were backpackers?' he asked, using the plastic fork to spear a few chips and pop them into his salivating mouth.

The waiter's face gained a sincere frown. 'I have been working here for two years now . . .'

With his mouth full of potato, Griessel could only nod, motioning with his fork for the young man to elaborate.

'You get to know them. The tan, the clothes, the accents . . . and they don't tip much.'

'When did they arrive?'

'Um, let's see . . . before my first smoke break, about nine, say.'

Griessel speared more chips. 'And they were sitting on their own at first?'

'For a while. Then the place filled up. I do eight tables – I can't say precisely. They were dancing; lots of guys asked them. At one time there were five at the table – friends, it seemed.'

'Boys or girls?'

'Ah . . . both . . . Listen, you have to understand . . .' He looked specifically at Mat Joubert, '. . . it's chaos here when the place is full. I remember the girls, because they were pretty, but that's about all.'

'So you don't remember the men who sat with them?'

'No.'

'Would you recognise them if you saw them again?'

'Maybe.'

Griessel popped open the tab on the can of cold drink. 'And you?' he addressed the rest.

'I just saw them dancing,' said the waitress. 'My tables are over there. They were dancing together a lot, which isn't that strange, but they looked as though they were arguing, you know, they were standing there arguing and dancing. But that's all I can tell you.'

With a mouth full of Dagwood burger, Griessel nodded in the direction of the barman. 'This one . . .' he said, identifying Erin Russel with a finger tapping on the photo, 'she . . . My post is the top end of the bar. Two guys were standing there drinking, and she came up there at one stage and talked to them. I remember her because I thought that's the ten ass of the evening, she talked to these two . . .'

'The ten what?'

'It's a game we barmen have. We give points for the best legs and ass and . . . so on. Out of ten. And . . .'

'You're sick,' said the waitress.

'What about you girls? The other day when that guy from *Idols* . . .'

Mat Joubert leaned his arms slowly on the table, making his broad shoulders appear even broader. The barman bit off his words and looked guiltily at Joubert. 'In any case, she had a ten ass. The rest wasn't bad either. Definitely nine legs and I reckon an eight . . .'

'Tell me about the men,' Griessel said impatiently.

'The one . . . I sort of remember his face, he's been here before . . . the other one, I don't know . . . Two friends, I think, they were drinking together, not dancing, just standing at the bar and chatting.'

'And then?'

'I told the other barmen we had a ten butt at the bend. There, where the bar counter turns to the wall. But when I looked back, she was gone. And the men left suddenly too.'

'Wait, wait, wait. She stood and talked with them? What about? Could you hear?'

'No, I wasn't . . . paying attention.'

'You were looking at her bum,' said the waitress crossly.

The barman ignored her.

'And then she left?'

'I didn't actually see her leave.'

'How long was she with them?'

He thought about that. 'Look, I didn't see her arrive, we're always on the go, there are never enough barmen here. All I know is that I saw her standing there. I had a quick look, and then I went to get more drinks, and when I had a chance to have a decent look, I noticed her butt. I went to tell Andy and them, but when I wanted to show them, she was gone. She might have been there for five minutes. Or ten . . .'

'When they left, were they in a hurry?'

'Absolutely.'

'What time was that?'

'Round about . . . Well, it was late, I can't say exactly, sometime after one o'clock?'

Griessel and Vusi looked at each other. This was getting interesting. 'You have seen one of them here before?'

'I think so. He seemed slightly familiar.'

'Describe him to me.'

'Tallish guy . . .' His words dried up.

'Old? Young? Black? White?'

'No, a white guy about my age, early twenties, short darkish hair, very tanned . . .'

'And the other one?'

'Black guy, also early twenties . . .'

The waiter with the wooden beads suddenly pointed a finger at the door behind Griessel's back and said excitedly: 'That *oke* was at their table last night.'

The detectives turned quickly. Against the wall, waiting patiently, were three SAPS men in blue uniforms. One had a large, transparent rubbish bag on the floor beside him. Between them stood Oliver Sands and a young man Griessel hadn't seen before. 'Yes, we know,' said Griessel.

'The other man is the guy from Carlucci's,' said Vusi, and stood up. Griessel followed him.

'Is that the bag for me from Metro?' Griessel asked one of the uniforms.

'Yes, Inspector.'

'It's Captain now,' said Mat Joubert from the table.

'Genuine, Benny?' asked Vusi, and there was real happiness in his voice.

Before leaving Adam Barnard's office, Fransman Dekker phoned Forensics.

'Jimmy here,' said the thin one.

'Jimmy, it's Fransman Dekker. I just wanted to know – about the Barnard case – have you found his cell phone anywhere?'

It took Jimmy a while to put two and two together. 'Just hold on . . .'

Dekker heard him say faintly: 'Arnie, that music *ou* who was shot, did we find a cell phone?' and then to Dekker: 'No, Fransman, we found *fokkol*.'

'Not in his car either?'

'*Fokkol*.'

'Thanks, Jimmy.' Dekker stood still for a second in thought, opened the office door and walked over to Natasha Abader's desk. She was on the phone, but when he approached she held a hand over the receiver and raised her eyebrows at him. 'Adam Barnard's cell phone number?'

She kept her hand over the phone as she recited the number. He keyed it in. 'Thanks.' He walked away while it rang. He walked down the passage – perhaps Barnard's phone was in his office, in which case he would hear it. But the only ringing was in his ear. It went on and on. Just when he expected it to go over to voice mail, a familiar voice said: 'Hello?'

'Who is this?' Fransman Dekker asked in surprise.

'This is Captain Benny Griessel of the SAPS,' said the voice.

'Captain?' said Dekker, completely bewildered.

Griessel and Vusi were hoping that the young man from Carlucci's would identify one of the Van Hunks personnel, when a cell phone began ringing shrilly, with the triiing-triiing of an antique farm telephone. A lot of people checked their phones, until a policeman said: 'It's in the bag.'

Griessel ripped open the refuse bag and began scratching around frantically. He grabbed something, fished the phone out of it. He stared at it in disbelief for a second before answering. The conversation was surreal – talking to someone who apparently knew him – until the puzzle was solved. 'Benny, it's Fransman Dekker talking. I have just dialled Adam Barnard's number.'

'You're joking.'

'No.'

'You will never fucking believe where this phone was. Inside a black shoe, in a bag of stuff Metro picked up this morning in the streets around the churchyard murder scene.'

'A shoe? Did you see what size it was?'

Griessel picked up the shoe, looked inside but saw nothing. He turned it over. The numbers were worn down. 'It's a ten and a half.'

'Fucking unbelievable.'

'Where did they find it?'

'I don't know; you'll have to ask Jeremy Oerson at Metro. He's a Field Marshal or something there.'

'What's a Field Marshal?'

'I mean he's some or other fucking fancy rank. Wait, I'll give you his number . . .' He began looking it up on his own cell phone.

'And you're a Captain now?' Griessel heard how Dekker tried to keep the envy out of his voice. Then he said: 'Can you look up his call history for me?'

'Hold on.' It took a while because he wasn't familiar with the make of phone.

'I think he called someone last night, just before ten,' said Dekker.

Eventually Griessel found the right icon. NO RECORDS, read the screen.

'There's nothing here,' he told Dekker.

While Barry answered his phone, his eyes were on the delivery vehicle parked on the corner in front of Carlucci's.

'Barry here.'

'Why haven't they gone in yet?' said the man with the grey beard.

'They can't. There's a delivery truck at the shop up the street, parked in Upper Orange, and the driver is looking right down the street.'

'How long?'

'Well, they've been unloading for a while now, so it shouldn't be long . . .'

A moment of silence on the line. 'We're running out of time.'

It was the first time Barry had heard a tinge of concern in the man's voice. But then he was back in control: 'Call me when it's clear. I want to know exactly when they go in.'

'OK, Mr B.'

32

His moustache was as big as his ego, thought Mbali Kaleni.

She was sitting with Jack Fischer at a round table in his luxurious office. On one side was the expansive dark wood desk, on the other a bookshelf covering the whole wall with what looked like legal reference books. On each of the two remaining walls was a single large oil painting, landscapes of the Bushveld and the Boland respectively. Behind the desk, deep red, heavy curtains hung at the window. On the floor was a Persian carpet, new and beautiful.

Fischer was approaching sixty with a full head of hair painstakingly combed into a side parting. Greying temples framed the weathered hawkish face, with the fine wrinkles of a lifelong smoker. And that wide, extravagant moustache. She suspected the dark-blue suit was tailor-made, the fit was too good.

She did not like him. His heartiness was false and slightly condescending, the kind of attitude towards black people that was typical of many Afrikaner men of a certain age. He had risen from his desk with a blue folder in one hand and asked her to take a seat at the round table. He opened the conversation with 'How can we help you?' *We*. And when she explained, he smiled beneath his moustache. 'I see.' And: 'I would offer you refreshments but I understand you brought your own.'

She did not react.

'You realise I am not obliged to release the information without a warrant.'

She settled herself in the expensive chair and nodded.

'Nonetheless, we *are* former members of the Force.'

It was the 'nonetheless' that spurred her to show him a thing or two about language.

'Nowadays we prefer to refer to the SAPS as "the Service",' she told him. 'I was relying on the fact that former members would appreciate the significance and urgency of a murder investigation.'

Once more he deployed that superior smile under his moustache. 'We understand only too well. You will have my full cooperation.'

He opened the file. On the inside cover was the word 'AfriSound' and a code number. She wondered whether the record company's accountant had phoned him to let him know the police were on their way. That in itself would be interesting.

'We simply tracked the AfriSound payment of fifty thousand rand to the account of one Mr Daniel Lodewikus Vlok, and subsequently contacted a subcontractor in Bloemfontein to go and talk to Mr Vlok. The purpose of that conversation was merely to make sure Mr Vlok was aware of the payment and the circumstances leading thereto. We did not want to point out an innocent man to our client.'

'So the subcontractor assaulted him.'

'Absolutely not.' Indignant.

She looked at him with an expression that said, she might be a woman in a man's world, but that didn't mean he should think she was stupid.

'Inspector Kaleni,' he said with that fake courtesy, 'we are the private investigation company with the fastest-growing turnover in the country – because we are ethical and effective. Why would I put our future in jeopardy by illegal activities?'

That was the moment she made the link between the ego and moustache. 'The name and contact details of the subcontractor?'

He was reluctant to supply them. At first he just gazed at one of his paintings, his body language expressing an inaudible sigh. Then slowly he stood up to take the address book out of one of the drawers of his giant desk.

Mat Joubert said he had to get going, because he could see they were busy. Griessel walked with him to the door. Once they were out of earshot of the others, the big detective said: 'Benny, I'm going to join Jack Fischer's company.'

'*Jissis*, Mat,' said Griessel.

Joubert shrugged his massive shoulders. 'I've thought about it for a long time, Benny. It was a difficult decision. You know: I'm a policeman.'

'Then why are you buggering off? For the money?' He was angry with Joubert, now he was practically the last white man left in the SAPS, and they had come a long way together.

'You know I wouldn't leave just for the money.'

Griessel looked away to where Vusi was sitting with Oliver Sands. He knew Joubert was telling the truth, because Mat's wife Margaret was financially very comfortable after a big inheritance. 'Why leave then?'

'Because I'm not enjoying it any more, Benny. With SVC I could contribute, but now . . .'

Joubert had been commanding officer of the former Serious and Violent Crimes Unit and he was good, the best boss Griessel had ever worked for. So he nodded now with some understanding.

'I've been with the Provincial Task Force for four months now, and I still don't have a portfolio,' said Joubert. 'No people, no job description. They don't know what to do with me. John Afrika has told me I have to accept that I will not be promoted – that is simply the way it is now. That wouldn't bother me so much, but just sitting around . . . I'm also getting too old for all the shit, Benny, the National Commissioner's monkey business, the disbanding of the Scorpions, the racial quotas that change every year; everything is politicised. And if Zuma becomes President, the Xhosas will be out and the Zulus will be in and everything will change again – a new hierarchy, new agenda, new troubles.'

And where does that leave me, Griessel wanted to ask, with growing apprehension, but he just kept looking at Joubert.

'I've done my bit, Benny. Everything I could for the new country. What are my options at this age? I'll be fifty in July. There's a man recruiting police for Australia, he came to see me, but why would I want to go there? This is my country, I love this place . . .'

'OK,' said Benny Griessel, because he could see how serious Joubert was. He suppressed his own frustrations.

'I just wanted to let you know.'

'Thanks, Mat . . . When are you leaving?'

'End of the month.'

'Isn't Jack Fischer a bastard?'

Joubert smiled. Only Benny would say it like that. 'How many bastards have we worked for, Benny?'

Griessel grinned back. 'A lot.'

'Jack and I were together in the old Murder and Robbery. He was a good detective, honest, even though he stopped at every available mirror to comb his hair and moustache.'

Bill Anderson hurried down the stairs at nine minutes past six in the West Lafayette morning. His lawyer, Connelly, and the city Police Chief, Dombowski, were waiting in the hallway with his wife.

'Sorry to keep you waiting, Chief,' said Anderson. 'I had to get dressed.'

The Police Chief, a big, middle-aged man with the nose of an old boxer, put out his hand. 'I'm really sorry for the situation, Bill.'

'Thanks, Chief.'

'Shall we go?' asked Connelly.

The other two men nodded. Anderson took his wife's hands in his. 'Jess, if she calls, just stay calm and find out as much as you can.'

'I will.'

'And give her the number of the Captain. Ghree-zil, she *must* call him . . .'

'Would you rather stay, Bill?' asked Connelly.

'No, Mike, I have to be there. I owe it to Erin and her folks.' He opened the front door. The cold seeped in and his wife pulled her dressing gown more tightly around her body. 'I've got my cell. You'll call,' he said to her.

'Right away.'

They walked out on the porch. Anderson closed the door behind him. Deep in thought, Jess returned slowly to the study.

The phone rang.

She started, with her hand to her heart in fright and an audible intake of breath. Then she ran back to the front door, pulled it open and saw the men getting into the police car.

'Bill!' she shouted, her voice shrill and frightened.

He came running and she hurried to the phone.

Rachel Anderson sat at the table where Piet van der Lingen's laptop and a myriad reference books and papers were strewn across the table. In her ear the phone kept ringing on another continent – far too long, she thought, what was her father doing?

'Rachel?' Her mother said suddenly, anxious and out of breath.

'Mom!' Rachel was caught off guard, expecting her father's calm.

'Oh, my God, Rachel, where are you, are you all right?' She could hear the underlying hysteria and fear.

'Mom, I'm fine, I'm with a very kind man, I'm safe for now . . .'

'Oh, thank God, thank God. We've spoken to the police over there, we've spoken to the Ambassador and the Congressman, it's going to be all right, Rachel. Everything's going to be . . . Bill, she's safe, she's with somebody, a kind man, Rachel, this is such wonderful news, I love you honey, do you hear me, I love you so very much.'

'I love you too, Mom . . .'

'Now, I'm going to put your father on, listen very carefully, he's going to give you a number to call. Promise me you will do exactly what he says, Rachel, please.'

'I promise, Mom. I'm OK, I know this must have been really tough for you . . .'

'Don't you worry about us, we are going to take care of all this, honey, it's so great to hear your voice, I can't believe it, here's your father, I love you, you hear, I love you very much.'

'Love you too,' said Rachel Anderson, and smiled through the sudden tears of longing and gratitude. Her father came on the line: 'Honey? You're OK?'

'Yes, Dad, I'm OK, I'm with a very kind gentleman, I'm sitting in his house, I'm perfectly safe.'

'I can't begin to tell you what a great relief that is, honey, that's really great news.' Her father's voice was calm. 'We've been pretty busy on this side, trying to get you help, I've spoken to the Consul General in Cape Town, they are standing by, I'm going to give you their number, but first, I'm going to give you the number of a police Captain. Now, I know you said something about the police when you last called, but this man was recommended by their top structure, and I spoke to him personally. He's in charge of your case, and he gave me his word that he'll make sure you are safe, OK?'

'Are you sure?'

'Absolutely, even their Secretary of ... their Police Minister knows about you, the Consul General is talking to them, so this is very high level, nothing can happen to you. So can you take down the numbers?'

She looked across the desk and spotted the end of a yellow pencil under a printed document, pulled it out and turned over one of the typed sheets.

'I'm ready,' she said with determination and inexpressible relief. The nightmare was nearly over.

Mbali Kaleni parked on the Parade. In bright sunlight she walked down the alley of flower sellers, past the old post office, between stalls selling anything from shoes to packets of nuts. For a second she contemplated buying some candy-coated cashews, but reconsidered, she wanted to get to Upper Orange quickly. She just wanted to go back to that house . . .

She walked faster, swinging her big, black handbag with every stride.

'Just explain one thing to me,' said Griessel to Oliver Sands. He was standing: Oliver sat at the table wide-eyed, as though the attention was too much for him to handle.

'Why did the girls bring backpacks with them to the club?'

'Those bags . . .' Sands said. 'They never went anywhere without them. It's a girl thing, I think. You know, make-up and stuff . . .'

Griessel considered the bag that Oerson had brought. Small and compact. That made sense. He would have to sort through the plastic refuse bag, but not here. He would have to go back to Caledon Square.

'Jeremy speaking,' Oerson answered his phone and Fransman Dekker could tell he was a coloured man, and he was probably in a car.

'Bro', my name Fransman Dekker, I'm SAPS, howzit that side?' he said, because Griessel had warned him the Metro officer was a 'difficult character'.

'No, things going with springs, and you?'

'Just so, bro', listen, there was a helluva surprise in that bag of stuff your people found, a shoe, number ten and a half, if I can just find out where it was picked up.'

'No idea, bro', but I'll get the men to come in and tell me.'

'Many thanks, it's a murder case, I have to run, you know how it goes.'

'I know. Give me ten minutes, I'm sort of tied up at the moment.'

'Will you call me?'

'*Daatlik*, bro'.'

Dekker rang off and knocked on the door of the accountant, Wouter Steenkamp. There was no answer so he opened the door. Steenkamp was on the phone, saying: '. . . fucking police will have to help, or I'll have to make another plan.' He saw Dekker and said over the phone 'Hold on,' then to Dekker: 'The press are blocking reception. You'll have to help control them.'

'OK.'

'They'll help,' he said into the phone. 'Right, bye.' He looked at Dekker expectantly.

'I will go and tell them to wait outside. It would be best to lock the front door.'

'What a mess,' said Steenkamp.

'Just wait here, we need to talk some more,' said Dekker.

'Now what?'

'New information,' said Dekker before leaving to go and manage the media. 'There are some who say you are cheating them.'

★　　★　　★

'Your people can go,' Vusi said to Galina Federova.

'So, you will not arrest anybody.' She was sarcastic, cigarette between her fingers.

'No. They've been a big help.'

Griessel thought Vusi was too polite; he should tell the fucking foreigner he would throw her ass in jail if she wanted to be funny. He realised his patience was worn thin. He had to get out of here, away from the smell of alcohol and the sight of bottles. The fucking thirst was just below the surface. He had absolutely no idea what he was going to do next. They knew the girls had been here, they knew there had been discussions and arguments. They knew two men had left shortly after the girls and they knew there had been a chase down Long Street, but all of that helped fuck all, because it could not tell them where she was. And then his cell phone rang and he plucked it out angrily and said: 'Benny Griessel.'

'I've been to see Alexa Barnard, Benny,' Doc Barkhuizen said.

'Is she OK, Doc?'

'She's pumped full of medication, but you know what lies ahead for her. She's a strong woman, Benny. Beautiful too. I can see why you're so concerned about her.'

'Fuck off, Doc.' As Doc Barkhuizen chuckled on the other end, he heard the beep of another incoming call.

'She said when you have a chance, she would like to talk to you. Something to do with her husband.'

'Doc, I've got another call, it's a bit crazy right now, thanks for going to see her. We'll talk later,' he said and accepted the other call.

Griessel said his name and a woman with an American accent asked: 'Is that Captain Benny Ghree-zil?' He thought, wasn't that what I just fucking said, but he answered civilly: 'Yes.'

'My name is Rachel Anderson. My dad said I should call you.'

The name burned right through him, through the disappointment over Mat Joubert, through the frustrations of the day and the desire to drink, jolting his body as he said: '*Jissis.*' Then 'Yes, yes, are you safe, where are you?' Adrenaline and relief washed through him, he took two steps to Vusi's shoulder and put an urgent hand on it. His black colleague looked around and he said: 'Rachel Anderson,' and pointed at the phone. Vusi's whole face lit up.

'Yes, I'm with a Mr Pete van der Liengen, the address is . . .' Griessel heard a man speaking in the background. Then Rachel's voice again: '. . . Number six Upper Orange Street . . . In Orainisiegh?'

'Yes, yes, Oranjezicht, Six Upper Orange, just stay there, I'm on my way, don't open the door for anybody, I will call when I get there, please, Miss Anderson,' he pleaded. Dear God, this was good news. Griessel gestured to Vusi that they must go, jogged out the door and headed for the alley, faster and faster, hearing Vusi's shoes on the floor behind him.

'I'm not going anywhere,' said Rachel Anderson, and her voice sounded cheerful, as if she was looking forward to his arrival and Benny was out the back door, into the alley and running as fast as he could.

Barry stood on the back of his bakkie and watched the driver of the delivery vehicle get in and start the engine. He looked to the right where the upright, bold silver Peugeot Boxer panel van stood waiting. His phone was ready in his sweaty hand. He pressed the call button and held it up to his ear.

'Yes?' said the man with the grey beard.

'The truck is leaving.'

'Good. Can you see the panel van?'

Barry looked at the dirty, dusty Peugeot. 'Yes, they're moving.'

'Jay is going to call Eben, they will cover the back door. Then he'll turn the van around and come back to the front gate in Upper Orange, so the nose is pointing towards the city. When they get out and go through the front gate, you tell me.'

'Right. Stand by.'

33

Piet van der Lingen stood next to his big work table. 'The police are on their way,' she said, 'Captain Benny Ghree-zil.' The old man witnessed a transformation – her eyes brightened and the tension melted away. He smiled at her with his white false teeth and said: 'We will have to teach you proper Afrikaans pronunciation – it's Griessel.' 'Gggg . . .' she tried it, sounding as though she was clearing phlegm from her throat.

'That's it,' he said. 'And roll the "r" as well. G-riessel.'

'Ghe-riessel.'

'Almost. Ggg-rrriessel.'

'Griessel.'

'Very good.' They laughed together. She said: 'How will I ever be able to thank you?'

'For what? For brightening an old man's day?'

'For saving my life,' she said.

'Well, when you put it that way . . . I demand that you come and have lunch again, before you go home.'

'I would love to . . .'

She saw him look up and away, at the window, with sudden concern shadowing his face. Her eyes followed his and she saw them, four men coming up the garden path. 'Oh, my God.' she said because she knew them. She got up from the chair. 'Don't open the door!' The fear was back in her voice. 'They want to kill me – they killed my friend last night!' She ran a few steps down the passage, a dead end. She heard someone wrenching at the front door and spun around in panic.

Then the leaded glass of the front door shattered. She sprinted back across the hall on the way to the kitchen, the back door. A hand came through the gap to unlock the front door from inside. 'Come on!' she shouted at van der Lingen. The old man stood frozen to the spot, as though he planned to stop them.

'No!' she screamed.

The door opened. She had to get away and ran through the kitchen, hearing a shot in the hall. She whimpered in fear, reached the back door and spotted the long carving knife in the drying rack. She grabbed it, tugged open the back door, and stepped outside in sudden dazzling sunlight. There were two more between her and the little gate in the corner, charging at her, black and white, with determined faces. Urgent footfalls behind her, she had only one choice. She ran at the one in front of her, the white man whose arms were spread wide to seize her. She whipped up the knife, stabbing at his chest with hatred and loathing and shrill terror. He tried to pull away, too late, the knife piercing his throat. His eyes filled with astonishment.

'Bitch!' the black man yelled and hit her with his fist. The blow landed above her eye and a cascade of light exploded in her head. She fell to the right, onto the grass, hearing their shouts. She struggled to get up, but they were on her, one, two, three of them, more. Another fist slammed into her face, arms pinned her down. She heard their short, brute grunts, saw an arm lifted high, something chunky and metallic swinging at her face, and then the darkness.

Griessel raced. He had taken the blue revolving light out of the boot and plugged it into the cigarette lighter. It was propped on the dashboard, but the fucking thing wouldn't work. So he just drove with the Opel's hazard lights flashing, but that didn't help much. He pressed long and hard on the hooter, saying to Vusi: 'I should have taken a car with a fucking siren.' They sped up Long Street through one red traffic light after another. Every time he had to slow down, stick his arm out of the window and wave frantically at the crossing traffic. Vusi did the same from his window.

'At least she should be safe,' said Vusi warily, ever the bloody diplomat. Griessel knew that what he really meant was: 'We needn't drive so madly – she said she was with a good man.'

'She should be,' Griessel said and waved wildly, hooting continuously, 'but I can't afford a fuck-up.' He put his foot down, and the Opel's tyres squealed.

Mbali Kaleni was driving serenely down Annandale in dense traffic near the turn into Upper Orange. She put on her indicator light to change lanes, waiting patiently, but no one would give her a gap. She shook her head, Cape Town drivers; in Durban this sort of thing would never happen. Eventually the stream in the right-hand lane thinned and she swung over, keeping the indicator on.

The traffic lights were red.

It looked like a hornet's nest, Fransman Dekker thought, the crowd abuzz, with microphones poised to sting you.

He stood on the stairs, and shouted loudly: 'Attention, everyone.'

They swarmed on him, there must have been twenty people, all talking, the stingers aimed at him in desperate hands. He could only hear snatches of the questions '. . . Iván Nell shot him?' '. . . the Geysers praying for?' '. . . tried to murder Alexa Barnard?' 'Is Josh Geyser under arrest?' '. . . Xandra dead?'

He held up his right hand, palm forward, dropped his head to avoid eye contact and just stood there. He knew they would quieten down eventually.

Kaleni saw them.

She spotted the panel van in front of the house, thinking at first it was those clowns from Forensics. She couldn't stand them, and wondered irritably what they were still doing here.

There was movement on the other side, the Belmont Avenue side, as she approached.

People were carrying something.

What was going on?

Closer still she saw there were four men in a hurry, each holding onto a piece of something. They moved crab-like along the pavement, but the picket fence hid their burden. She saw they were heading for the panel van parked in Upper Orange. Strange.

They were carrying a person, she saw as they came around
the corner and out from behind the obscuring fence. She kept
her eyes on them: it was the girl, lifeless, they were gripping her
arms and legs. Mbali accelerated and her hand reached for her
hip, pressed the leather loop off her service pistol, swung across
the road and aimed for the front of the panel van. She was going
too fast and could not stop in time, braked hard. In front of her
one man jumped out of the van from the driver's side, holding a
pistol fitted with a silencer. The small tyres of the Corsa squealed,
the car skidded sideways, on a collision course for the kerb. She
wrestled with the steering wheel and came to a standstill just a
metre from the Peugeot, at right angles to it. Instinctively, she
noted the registration number, CA 4 . . .

She saw a pistol aimed at her, the windscreen starred and the
bullet slammed against metal behind her. She wanted to dive
down, but the safety belt held her.

'*uJesu,*' she said quietly and reached a hand to unclip it.

He shot her. She felt the dreadful blow to her body, but the
safety belt was loose, she flattened herself, right hand reaching for
her pistol. She lifted it and fired off three blind shots through the
windscreen. The pain was an earthquake that rippled through her,
slowly, unstoppable. She checked the wound. A hole below her
left breast, blood trickling into a pool on the upholstery. Pity, she
always kept the car spotless. She fired off more shots and sat up
quickly. The pain ripped through her torso. Quickly she scanned
for him through the windscreen. He wasn't there. Movement, here
he was, just beside the door, pistol in both hands, long deadly
silencer aimed at her eye. She saw a kind of African necklace
around his neck, the beads spelling out a word. She jerked back
her head, swung her pistol around in the certain knowledge of
death. Fleeting sadness, so short, this life, as she saw his trigger
finger tighten with purpose.

Griessel blasted a path through the traffic with his hooter and
turned from Annandale into Upper Orange. A man in a fucking
yellow Humvee gave him the finger, two cars had to brake sharply

as he raced over the crossing. Vusi clutched the handle above the door, speechless.

Benny sped on, accelerating out of the corner. They were nearly there. A madman in a big silver panel van came racing downhill in the middle of the road. Benny hooted again and swerved out of the way. He caught a glimpse of the driver's face, a young asshole with a fierce expression, then he looked up at the street ahead, which was suddenly empty. He changed down a gear, flattened the accelerator, engine protesting, another gear change, charged up the hill. This was his territory, his flat was only one block away in fucking Vriende Street; stupid bloody name, he still thought so. De Waal Park to the right, then Vusi said, 'It's just up there,' and they crested the rise. They both saw the Corsa at the same time, and neither spoke, because from the angle it had stopped, something was not right.

The single cab bakkie drove right in front of him, reversing out of a driveway from the left side of the street. Griessel slammed on the brakes and the Opel nose-dived, rubber screeched and smoked, and he skidded until the left wheels struck the kerb. 'Fuck,' he said smelling the burning rubber, jerked the Opel back, just missing the Toyota's front fender. He saw the man behind the wheel's big, wild, shocked eyes. Griessel looked at the Corsa, was the window smashed? He swung across the road and stopped behind the small white car, leapt out and heard the Toyota racing away towards the city. He glanced quickly after it, fucking asshole. He noted the street number on the wooden gate. Number 6. Bullet casing, he smelled cordite. Trouble here, bullet holes in the windscreen and the driver's window and there was someone behind the wheel, fuck, fuck.

'It's Mbali,' Vusi shouted as he pulled open the other door.

Griessel saw her head on her chest, blood on the headrest. He pulled open the door. '*Jissis*,' Griessel said, trying to feel her neck for a pulse. His fingers slipped in the blood. He saw the wound below her ear, bits of jaw, white chips and a pulsing vein pumping out thick red fluid.

'Get the ambulance! She's alive!' He shouted louder than he meant to, his heart racing. He gently pulled her by the shoulder, until he had her turned over with her back to him, then he put his hands under her arms and felt more blood lower down. Carefully he pulled her out of the car and laid her on the pavement. Vusi came running around the car with his cell phone in his hand.

Two wounds, but the one in the side of her head was bleeding the most. He got up quickly and felt for his handkerchief, found it, bent beside Mbali Kaleni and pressed the hanky against the hole. He heard Vusi talking urgently over the phone. He swapped the hand holding the handkerchief and got hold of his phone, hearing a car skid around the corner in Belmont at great speed, he couldn't turn in time, just saw the tail, something. He looked at Kaleni, she wasn't going to make it, the ambulance would take too long.

'Help me,' he said to Vusi, 'I'm taking her myself.'

Vusi knelt beside him and said calmly, 'Benny they're on their way.'

'*Jissis*, Vusi, are you sure?' as he searched his phone for the Caledon Square number.

'They know it's a policewoman. They're coming.'

Griessel pressed the hanky harder. Mbali Kaleni moved, a jerk of the head. 'Mbali,' he said in despair.

She opened her eyes. Looked far away, then focused on him. 'The ambulance is coming, Mbali,' he wanted to encourage her: 'You're going to make it.'

She made a noise.

'Take it easy, take it easy, they'll be here soon.'

Vusi picked up Mbali's hand. He talked quietly to her in an African language. Griessel noted the small Xhosa man's calmness and thought Vusi might not be hardass, but he was strong.

Mbali was trying to say something. He felt her jaw moving under his hand, he saw the blood running out of her mouth. 'No, no, don't talk now; the ambulance will be here soon.'

He looked up at the house. 'Vusi, you will have to see what's going on inside there.' The black detective nodded, jumped up and ran. Griessel looked at Mbali. Her eyes were on him, pleading. He held the hanky tight against her neck, realising he still had his phone in the other hand. He phoned the station. They needed more people. Mbali Kaleni's eyes closed.

34

At first she was only aware of the noise, voices shouting, the high revving of an engine. Then she felt the pain in her face and she wanted to put a hand over it, but she couldn't. There was the sensation of movement, a loss of balance, a vehicle turning sharply, accelerating.

Then she remembered everything and she jerked.

'The bitch is waking up,' one of them said. She tried to open her eyes, she wanted to see, but she could not. One eye was swollen shut, the other would not focus, her vision was blurred. Four people were holding her down. The pressure on her arms and legs was too much, too heavy, too painful.

'Please,' she said.

'Fuck you.' The words were spat out with hatred, flecks of saliva spattered her face. A cell phone rang shrilly.

'It's the Big Guy,' said a voice she knew.

'Fuck.' Another familiar voice. 'Tell him.' She flicked her eyes across, but could not see them, only the four holding her. They were all looking forward now.

'Jesus. OK.' Then: 'Mr B, it's Steve. The fucking bitch stabbed Eben . . . No, he was with Robert, on the back door . . . It's bad, chief . . . No, no, he's with Rob in the bakkie, you'll have to call him . . . OK. Yes, it's here . . . No . . . OK, hang on . . . The boss wants to know what's in the bag . . .'

The one holding her leg let go. 'Here, take it,' he said and then she kicked him with all her might, struck him somewhere.

'Fuck!' A heavy blow against her head, her leg clamped fast again, and she screamed, in frustration, pain, fury and fear. She fought wildly, straining her arms and legs to break free, but it was no good.

★　★　★

Vusi came running, Griessel could hear his hasty steps.

'Benny, there's an old man inside. He's been shot, but he's alive.'

'An old man, you say?'

'Yes, wounded in the chest, through the lung, I think.'

'Nobody else?'

'Nobody.'

'Fuck.'

Then suddenly and clearly, the wail of an ambulance.

'You do that again, I'll shoot you in the fucking leg, you hear me?'

The spit-sprayer's face was right up against hers, grimacing, his voice crazed. She closed her eyes and went limp.

'It's not in here,' said Steve up front.

'Jesus,' said Jay.

'Mr B, it's not in the bag . . . Yes, I'm positive.' A long silence, then the sound of the vehicle slowing to a more regular speed, smoother. Then: 'There was no time, and then this fucking fat cop turned up, but Jay shot her, she's a goner . . . No, I'm telling you, there was no time . . . OK . . . OK . . .' The sound of a cell phone snapping shut. 'The Big Guy says to take her to the warehouse.'

Once he had managed to get the last member of the press out of the door and locked it, Fransman Dekker heard a voice behind him: 'Fuck this, you'll have to do something, it can't go on like this.'

Mouton stood on the stairs, hands on his hips, looking very displeased. 'I'll phone now, our PR people will come and help,' said Dekker.

'PR?'

'Public Relations.'

'But when will you be finished?'

'When I have asked all my questions,' said Dekker, and climbed the stairs, past Mouton, who turned and followed him.

'How many questions do you still want to ask? And you're talking to my employees without a lawyer being present. It can't go on like this – who do you want to talk to now?'

'Steenkamp.'

'But you talked to him already.'

They walked through the spacious seating area. Dekker stopped in his tracks and shoved his face close to Mouton's. 'I want to talk to him again, Willie. And I have the right to talk to every fucking member of your staff without your lawyer sitting in. I'm not doing this little two-step with you again.'

Mouton's skin flooded with crimson from the neck up, his Adam's apple bobbing as though words were dammed up beneath it. 'What did Iván Nell say to you?'

Dekker stalked off down the corridor. Mouton followed him again, two steps behind. 'He's not one of our artists any more; he has no say here.' Dekker ignored him, went to Steenkamp's door and opened it without knocking. He wanted to shut it before Mouton came through, but then he saw that fucking legal undertaker sitting across from the accountant.

'Please, take a seat, Inspector,' Groenewald said in his dispassionate voice.

The paramedics ran from the front door with the stretcher. Griessel held the garden gate open for them, then jogged after them. 'Will she make it?'

'Don't know,' said the front one, holding out the bag of plasma to Griessel. 'Hold that while we load, just keep it high.'

'And the old man?' Griessel took the plastic bag of transparent fluid. Vusi held one ambulance door to prevent the wind blowing it shut.

'I think so,' the paramedic said. They lifted the old man up in the stretcher and pushed him in beside Mbali Kaleni, two figures lying still under light-blue blankets. One paramedic ran around to the driver's door, opened it and jumped in. The other one jumped in the back. 'Close the doors,' he said and Griessel and Ndabeni each took a door and slammed. The ambulance sirens began to wail as it pulled away in Upper Orange, made a U-turn and passed them, just as the first of a convoy of patrol vehicles appeared over the hump of the hill.

'Vusi,' Griessel said, loud enough to be heard over the noise of the sirens, 'get them to seal off the streets and keep everyone away. I don't want to see a uniform closer than the pavement.'

'OK, Benny.'

Griessel took out his cell phone. 'We will have to get Forensics as well.' He stood and surveyed the scene – Mbali's car, the strewn bullet casings, the front door open, its glass shattered. The old man had been shot inside there and somewhere they had grabbed Rachel Anderson . . . It would take hours to process everything. Hours that he did not have. *The hunters have caught their prey. How long would they let her live? Why hadn't they killed her here, like Erin Russel? Why hadn't he and Vusi found her body here? That was the big question.*

One thing he did know, he needed help, he needed to make up time. Between Vusi and himself they didn't have enough manpower.

He called Mat Joubert's number. He knew it would piss off John Afrika. But in the big picture, that was a minor issue.

'Benny,' Joubert recognised his number.

'Mat, I need you.'

'Then I'll come.'

Wouter Steenkamp, the accountant, laughed, and Willie Mouton, leaning his long skinny body against the wall, gave a snort of derision. The lawyer Groenewald shook his head ruefully, as though now he had heard everything.

'Why is that so funny?' Fransman Dekker asked.

Steenkamp leaned back in his throne behind the PC and steepled his fingers. 'Do you really believe Iván Nell is the first artist who believes he is being fleeced?'

Dekker shrugged. How would he know?

'It's the same old story,' said Willie Mouton. 'Every time.'

'Every time,' mused Steenkamp, and laced the tips of his fingers together, turned the palms outward and stretched until his knuckles cracked. He laid his head back on the back of the chair. 'As soon as they start making good money.'

'In the beginning, with the first cheque, they come in here and it's "thanks, guys, *jislaaik*, I've never seen this much money".' Mouton's voice was affected, mimicking Nell. 'Then we're the heroes and they are so pathetically grateful . . .'

'But it doesn't last,' said Steenkamp.

'They're not doing it for aaaart any more.'

'Money talks.'

'The more they get, they more they want.'

'It's a flash car and a big house and everything that opens and shuts. Then it's the beach house and the sound equipment bus with a huge photo of you on it and everything has to be bigger and better than Kurt or Dozi or Patricia's. To sustain all that costs a shitload of money.'

Groenewald nodded slowly in agreement. Steenkamp laughed again: 'Two years, *pappie*, you can set your fucking calendar to it, then they start coming in here saying: "What is that deduction and why is this so little?" and suddenly we've gone from hero to zero, and they have forgotten how poor they were when we signed them.' His hands were on his lap now, his right hand twirling his wedding ring.

'Nell says—' Dekker began.

'Do you know what his name was?' Mouton asked, suddenly pushing himself off the wall and heading for the door. 'Sakkie Nell. Isak, that's where the *I* in Ivan comes from. And please don't forget the accent on the "a".' Mouton opened the door. 'I'm going to get myself a chair.'

'Iván Nell says he compared your figures with the amounts he made from compilations with independents.'

This time even the lawyer sang in the choir of indignation. Steenkamp leaned forward, ready to speak, but Mouton said: 'Wait, Wouter, hold onto your point, I don't want to miss the joke,' and he walked out into the passage.

Benny Griessel stood in the hallway, the urgency hot in him. He didn't want to get too involved with this part of the investigation, he had to focus on Rachel and how to get her back.

He pulled on rubber gloves and looked fleetingly at the blood on the pretty blue and silver carpet where the old man had been shot, the shards of stained glass on the floor. He would have to phone her father.

How the hell had they found her? How did they know she was here? She had phoned from this house. *My name is Rachel Anderson. My dad said I should call you.* She had talked to her father and then with him. How long had it taken him to get here? Ten minutes? Nine, eight? Twelve at the very most. How could they have driven here, shot Mbali and the old man and carried Rachel off in twelve minutes?

How was he going to explain this to Rachel's father? The man who had asked him: *Tell me, Captain: Can I trust you?*

And he had said: 'Yes, Mr Anderson. You can trust me.'

Then I will do that. I will trust you with my daughter's life.

How had they found her? That was the question, the only one that mattered, because the 'how' would supply the 'who', and the 'who' was what he needed to know.

Now. Had she phoned anyone else? That was the place to start. He would have to find out. He took his cell phone out of his pocket to phone Telkom.

No, phone John Afrika first. Fuck. He knew what the Regional Commissioner: Detective Services and Criminal Intelligence was going to say. He could already hear the voice, the consternation. *How, Benny? How?*

Griessel sighed, a shallow, hurried breath. That fucking feeling he had had this morning – that there was trouble brewing . . .

And this day was still far from over.

Mouton pushed his luxury leather desk chair up to Groenewald, sat down and said: 'Let the games begin.'

'Let me explain to you about a compilation first,' said Steenkamp, leaning over the desk, picking up a pencil and twirling it between his fingers. 'Some or other clown decides he wants to make money out of Valentine's Day or Christmas or something. He phones a few people and says: "Have you got a song for me?" There are no studio costs, not a cent, because the recording has already been done. That makes a huge difference, because all he has to do is market the CD a bit, make a few TV ads that he gives to a guy with an Apple and Final Cut to cobble together, so really he's only paying for the airtime and he sticks it in the fifteen-second slots in *Seven de Laan* for three days and all the old biddies snap it up.'

'He does his accounts on the back of a cigarette box,' said Mouton irritably.

'No overheads. We sit here with an admin department and financial department and marketing and promotions department. We carry forty per cent of a distribution wing, because we are a full-service operation – we stand by the artist for the long term. We build a brand, we don't just flog a few CDs,' said Steenkamp.

'Tell him about RISA and NORM,' said Mouton.

Steenkamp pulled a sheet of A4 paper out of the printer beside him and made a start with the pencil, writing RISA alongside. 'Recording Industry of South Africa.'

'Fucking mafia,' said Mouton.

'At least they present the SAMA Awards,' said Groenewald, and Mouton snorted derisively.

'They take twenty-five cents for every CD we sell, because they . . .' he made quotation marks with his fingers, ' "protect us from piracy".'

'Ha!' said Mouton.

'Do you think the independent making the compilation is going to keep score? Is he going to pay on every CD? Not likely, because it's work, it's a schlepp, it's expense and it's profit.' Steenkamp scribbled another star, wrote NORM on the paper.

'NORM are the guys who have to see to it that, if I write a song and you do a cover of it, I get paid. Six point seven per cent. But that's the theory. In practice it's only us big players who pay. If you're an independent, you have to put down your NORM money when the CDs are printed. So you print five thousand here and another five thousand there, but you tell NORM you only had five thousand printed, you show them the slips, and you pay only half. NORM is ripped off and the songwriter is ripped off and the independent is laughing all the way to the bank.'

'We have to pay NORM as the sales come in,' said Mouton, 'audited figures, everything above board. But then the artists complain: "Why is my share so small?"' He mimicked Nell's voice again. 'Let me tell you another thing. Half of the hits in this country are German pop songs that have been translated. Or Dutch or Flemish or whatever. What Adam did – and he was brilliant at it – he had guys in Europe and as soon as there was a pop song that stood out they would email it in MP3 format and Adam would sit down with a pen and write Afrikaans lyrics. Forty minutes, that's all it took, and he would phone Nerina Stahl and—'

'That was before she left . . .'

'All her fucking hits were German pop, who do you think is going to get them for her now? Anyway, we sit with the whole caboodle, we have to administer it all. That money has to go to Germany, the songwriter and the publisher have to get their cut. But here comes this independent and he gets someone to do a cover of Adam's translation of this German song . . . you get it?'

'I think so,' said Dekker, engrossed.

'. . . and now Adam must be paid, the German and his publisher must be paid, but the independent says, no, we only made five thousand, but he's lying, because there's no control over distribution, the independents do their own now and nobody keeps track.'

'That's why the cheques are so big.'

'Then the bastard comes along and says we are bloody cheating him.'

'Let him make his own CDs and we'll see. Let him pay two hundred thousand for a studio out of his own pocket, let him cough up his own four hundred thousand for a TV campaign.'

'Amen,' said Groenewald. 'Tell him about the passwords and the PDFs.'

'Yes,' said Mouton. 'Ask Sakkie Nell if the independent sends him a password-protected PDF.'

Steenkamp drew another star. PDF. 'There are only three or four big CD distributors in South Africa. These are the guys who load up the CDs and distribute them to the music shops around the country, Musica and Look and Listen, Checkers and your Pick 'n Pay Hypermarkets. Adam started a distribution arm, but it's an independent company now, AMD, African Music Distribution, we own forty per cent. What they do is, like all the big players, they keep sales records of every CD and every three months they send a password-protected PDF file of every artist's sales to me. We transfer the money to the artist . . .'

'Before we get the money from the distributors,' said Mouton.

'That's right. We pay it out of our own pockets. The risk is ours. I email him the same PDF statement, just as I received it from the distributor, complete, so he can see everything. Nobody can fiddle with the statement because we don't have the password.'

'So tell me how can we rip them off?' said Mouton.

'Impossible,' said Groenewald.

'Because we're too fucking honest, that's the problem.'

'But let him make his own CDs. Let him feel the overheads. Then we'll talk again.'

'Amen,' his lawyer confirmed.

35

John Afrika had ranted and raved over the telephone: 'You phone the father in America, Benny, you phone him, fuck knows I can't do it, how the hell, I'm on my way, *jissis*, Benny, how the fuck did it happen?' He slammed the phone down and Griessel was left standing with his cell phone in his hand, wondering whether Jack Fischer and Associates had a job for an alcoholic who was stuffing up two cases in a single day. He felt like smashing his phone against the wall. But he had just hung his head and stared at the floor, thinking what was the use of being sober, he might as well get drunk. Then Vusi ran in, breathless, and said, 'Benny, it was the delivery van that nearly hit us – we have an eyewitness.'

So now they were on the pavement with a woman, dark glasses, early thirties, a little pale and shy. At first glance she was quite ordinary, unimpressive, until she began to talk in a soft, melodious voice that seemed to come from the depths of her heart. She said her name was Evelyn Marais and she had seen everything.

She had come out of Carlucci's on the way to her car across the street. She pointed to a red Toyota Tazz, about ten years old. She had heard shots and had stopped in the middle of the street. She spoke calmly and clearly, without haste, but she was obviously not entirely comfortable with all the attention. 'The first shots didn't even sound like gunshots, more like firecrackers; only later did I realise what they were. Then I looked. There were four of them carrying a girl out of there,' she pointed an unvarnished nail at the corner of Belmont. 'They—'

'The girl, how were they carrying her?'

'Two had her by the shoulders, two carried her legs here behind the knee.'

'Could you tell if she was resisting?'

'No, it looked like she was . . . I think there was blood on her hands, I thought maybe she was hurt and they were helping her to the van, an ambulance . . .'

'Was it an ambulance?'

'No. I just assumed. For a moment. Logical, in a way, before the other shots went off. They were much louder. But I couldn't see who was shooting, they were in front of the van. I only saw them when they came running around it. One man, the driver, had a pistol with a silencer in his hand.' This was the moment that Griessel began to suspect she was not just your average eyewitness.

'A pistol with a silencer?'

'Yes.'

'Ma'am, what work do you do?'

'I'm a researcher. For a film company. And it's Miss, actually.'

'Can you describe the men?'

'They were young, in their twenties, I'd say. Handsome boys. That's why I assumed at first that they were helping her. Three were white, one was black. I didn't notice their hair colour, sorry . . . But they . . . three of them were in jeans and T-shirts, no, one was wearing a golf shirt, light green, almost lemon, it looked quite good with the jeans. Oh, and the other one was in brown chinos and a white shirt and collar with some writing over the pocket. It was too far to see . . .' Griessel and Ndabeni looked at her in amazement.

'What?' she said uncomfortably, shifting her dark glasses up onto the top of her head and looking back at Griessel. He saw brilliant blue eyes, the shade of a tropical sea. The sight of them changed her whole face from pale to lovely, from ordinary to extraordinary.

'You are most observant, Miss.'

She shrugged shyly. 'It's just what I saw.'

'The girl, Miss, it's very important, you said she had blood on her hands?'

'Yes, her hand, wait a bit, her right hand and her arm up to here,' she indicated her elbow.

'Nowhere else?'

'No.'

'But she wasn't struggling?'

'No.'

'Did it look as though she was . . . unconscious?'

'I . . . perhaps. No. I don't know. But she wasn't struggling.'

'And the panel van?' Vusi asked. 'You don't know what make it was?'

'A Peugeot. But I must admit, I didn't know that. Only when it drove off did I see the logo. The one with the little lion, you know, rearing up . . .'

Griessel just nodded. Fuck it, he wouldn't have made the lion and the Peugeot connection. He looked at her eyes and thought, this woman is a genius.

'A silver Peugeot, but quite dirty,' she said. 'I will have to check what model it was . . .' Before Griessel could say that wasn't necessary, she added: 'And the registration number if you want it, of course.'

'You got the registration number?' Griessel was astonished.

'CA four-oh-nine, then a little hyphen,' and she drew a line horizontally in the air with her finger, 'and then three-four-one.'

The detectives plucked out their cell phones simultaneously. 'Miss,' said Benny Griessel, 'would you like to come and work for us?'

'In any case,' Willie Mouton said, standing up and starting to wheel his chair back towards the door on its silent wheels. 'Adam phoned me last night, some time after nine, to tell me about Iván Nell's stories.'

'And?' Fransman Dekker asked.

'We laughed about it. Adam said, let him bring his auditor, let him run up some overheads himself.'

'That's it?'

'Adam said he was going home, because Alexandra wasn't well, he was worried about her. And that's where Josh Geyser was waiting for him. I don't care what he's telling you. I'm not a detective or anything, but you can see in that man's eyes he is capable of anything.'

★   ★   ★

'Vusi, we're working against the clock now,' Benny Griessel told him at the garden gate. 'I've sent for Mat Joubert . . .' He noticed Ndabeni's expression. 'I know, but fuck the Commissioner, we have to get the girl. I want you to follow up on the Peugeot. It might be a false number plate, but let's try. I don't care what you have to do, there can't be hundreds of them in Cape Town. Forget about the scene, forget everything, the panel van is your baby.'

Vusi nodded enthusiastically, fired up by Griessel's urgency.

'Mat Joubert can deal with the scene, I'm going to get her, Vusi. All I want to do now is find her. I just want to make a quick pass through the house, see if there is anything significant, then I am going to try and work out how they knew she was here. Some way or another . . . I don't know how, I want to find out who else she phoned . . .'

'Fine, Benny.'

'Thanks, Vusi.' He turned and walked into the house, trying to reconstruct the event quickly. In the hallway they had smashed the leaded glass of the front door, opened it and gained entry. They shot the old man here. On the left was a giant study, once a sitting room perhaps. The large work table was covered with countless documents and a telephone. To one side a chair was overturned. Had she phoned from here?

He walked down the passage, looking into all the bedrooms. Nothing of note. On the way back he went into the guest bathroom. It smelled faintly of recent use. He traced a finger along the bath. It was wet. He sniffed. Soap. That meant nothing. He examined the inside surface of the bath thoroughly. Hair in the plug, two long, dark strands. Rachel's? He went out. She had taken a bath. She had time for that. That meant she trusted the old man a great deal. He must find out his name.

He crossed the hall again and went into the kitchen. Everything was immaculate. He spotted the open back door, ran out, careful to watch where he stepped. He saw blood outside, a long trail over a paved pathway and part of the lawn. Fear gripped his heart. He squatted down reluctantly to examine the splashes.

God, had they cut her throat? The thought was a blade in his guts.

No, not possible. He had asked Evelyn Marais if the blood was only on her hands.

Yes, her hand, her right hand and her arm up to here.

Nowhere else?

No.

But the blood pattern outside told a different story.

Hoping she hadn't left yet, he jumped up and ran out through the back gate, left in Belmont to where the growing crowd stood behind the yellow tape on the corner, under the watchful eyes of policemen. His eyes searched out the Tazz. There it was still, the woman seated inside, looking as though she was about to drive off. 'Sorry, sorry,' he said to get through the crowd. The Tazz pulled away, but he was just in time to slap the side of the car. She looked up in fright, saw him and stopped. 'Miss,' he gasped, out of breath, standing at her door while she wound down the window, lifted her dark glasses and rested her right arm on the door. 'Excuse me,' he said.

'It's OK.' The blue eyes watched expectantly.

'The girl ...' He struggled to catch his breath. '... are you absolutely sure about the blood ... just on her arm?'

She turned off the engine and shut her eyes. She sat like that for about half a minute. Griessel curbed his enormous impatience, wanting her to be sure.

The eyes opened. 'Yes,' she nodded decisively.

'There was no blood anywhere else?'

She shook her head from side to side, absolutely certain. 'No, just the arm.'

'Not on her head or neck?'

'Definitely not.'

'Thank God for that,' said Benny. He picked up the hand resting on the open window frame and kissed the back of it. 'Thank you,' he said. 'Thank you, thank you,' and he turned and began to jog back.

It wasn't Rachel Anderson's blood.

Fransman Dekker's first instinct was to blame Mouton and Steenkamp for his frustration, for the anger that was bottled up inside him. He stood behind the closed door of Adam Barnard's office and looked up at the framed photographs. He felt like grabbing one, throwing it on the ground and jumping on it. It was the way Mouton had said Josh Geyser did it, as though Dekker were an idiot. It was the way Steenkamp leaned back in his chair, smug, *windgat* whitey . . .

He glared at Adam Barnard in one photo. Big man full of confidence. The smile was the same in every photo, the way he looked at the camera, his body angled slightly, hands around the shoulders or waists of the artists. He was the very image of success, Mr Beloved, not an enemy in the world.

Impossible.

And that, Dekker knew, was the source of his frustration: he was in a dead-end street. The whole investigation was slowly but surely sinking into a swamp of, fuck it, improbabilities. Nothing made sense and the whiteys were laughing at him.

And where was Mbali Kaleni?

He walked around the desk, sat down and put his elbows on the desk, head in his hands and rubbed his eyes. He would have to think, he would have to suppress this anger and think it all through from the beginning, because none of the pieces fitted together. Josh and Melinda Geyser. Both were lying. Or neither. The video? The blackmailer? Where *was* Mbali? She had found something and was following it up, she was going to solve the case and he would look like a fool. He took his phone out of his pocket and called her number. It rang and rang and rang.

She would see who was calling, she was ignoring him on purpose. His temper flared up again, like a wildfire.

Wait, wait, wait. Calm down.

He put his head in his hands again and closed his eyes. Fuck knew, he would have to pull finger to crack this one.

Concentrate: Adam Barnard was carried into his house, up the stairs to his drunken wife.

That meant someone who knew his wife passed out, blind drunk, every night. That meant someone who was strong enough to carry the dead weight of Adam Barnard. Someone who knew

Barnard had a pistol in the house – and knew where to find it.
Forget Bloemfontein and the blackmailer, there was no way. The
knowledge of the pistol was key.

Who would know?

Josh Geyser? Perhaps. Maybe Melinda too. Knowledge. Motive.
Strength.

But Benny Griessel had said it wasn't Josh. Griessel was
nobody's fool, even though they said he used to drink like a fish.
Was Griessel mistaken, how much of the new Captain's attention
was on the churchyard murder? He was only human after all . . .
Knowledge of the pistol. How many people would know that?
Alexa Barnard, another one pronounced innocent by Griessel, an
alcoholic woman. Was Benny being objective? As a sister-in-drink,
had she pulled the wool over his eyes? Did she have help? A lover?

Who else? If you took into account that seventy or eighty per cent
of crimes were committed by someone in the immediate family.

Then it struck him – the maid. Whining Sylvia Buys, only
concerned about where she would find another job. Sylvia, who
was so terribly fond of Adam Barnard, so quick to lay the blame
on Alexandra. He must not overlook her. Motive? Anything. Had
Adam caught her stealing? Confronted her?

How well had the Geysers known Barnard? Would they have
visited the house?

Would one of them have known where to find the pistol? He
would have to find out. He would have to phone Griessel first, tell
him he had doubts about Alexandra, about the Geysers. Benny
wouldn't like it.

Where was Mbali?

Someone knocked.

'Yes?'

Natasha Abader put her head around the door. 'There is a
policeman at the door. He says he wants to show you where they
found a shoe.'

He jumped up. 'Thank you,' he said and walked over to her. 'I
want to talk to you again, please.'

She didn't look too ecstatic about that.

14:02–15:10

36

Dekker and the young black Metro policeman had to shoulder their way through the journalists at the front door, over the tiny lawn, pass the koi pond, through the access tunnel for the building to Buiten Street. The press kept throwing questions at him like accusations, until they shook off the last vulture on the corner of Bree Street. When would Cloete come and sort out this chaos?

'Up there, around the corner,' the Metro man said and they walked in silence. Dekker realised the southeaster had picked up and the perfect summer day was gone. He looked up at the mountain. The cloud was beginning to form on its tabletop like an omen. By late afternoon the wind would be gale force; but then it was January, there was nothing you could do about that.

The Metro man led him to a corner, they turned left into New Church Street and crossed the road. Six paces further on he stopped and pointed with his baton.

'Right there.'

'The shoe was lying here?'

'Just there,' the man confirmed. 'Almost in the gutter.'

'You're sure of this?'

'This is where I found it.'

'You didn't look inside it?'

'Inside the shoe?' The man screwed up his face in an expression of suspicion, as if he wasn't completely convinced of Dekker's intelligence.

'I wouldn't have either,' said Dekker. 'Thanks a lot.'

'Can I go now?'

'Wait. I just want to know, did they ask you to pick things up?'

'Yes, Senior Inspector Oerson sent us. We had to pick up anything that might have been in a rucksack. Anything. Then I saw the shoe. I picked it up and put it in the plastic bag. I found a hat too, over there on the corner of Watson Street. But that's all. I took it to Abrams, he had the big rubbish bag. I put it in the big rubbish bag. Abrams took the big rubbish bag to Senior Inspector Oerson, because he said he wanted to see everything.' He was thorough and systematic, as though he still harboured doubts about Dekker being the sharpest pencil in the box.

'Thank you. That's all I wanted to know.'

The man nodded, turned around and strolled away, swinging his baton, one hand on his cap to protect it from the wind.

Dekker considered the spot where the shoe had lain. Then the corner of New Church and Buiten. About two to three hundred metres from AfriSound.

What was the significance of that?

He took out his phone. It was time to call Benny Griessel.

The Metro Police licensing department told Vusi the Peugeot Boxer panel van, CA 409–341, belonged to CapSud Trading . . .

'Spell that for me, please,' Vusi asked.

'Capital letter C, a-p, capital letter S, u-d . . . the contact person is a Mr Frederik Willem de Jager, the address is Unit Twenty-one, Access City, La Belle Street in Stikland.'

'Thank you very much,' said Vusi.

'But there's a tag on it,' the woman said. 'The vehicle is in the pound.'

'Which pound?'

'Our vehicle impound. Just here next to me in Greenpoint.'

'Is it there now?'

'That's what the system says.'

Vusi thought it over. He asked: 'Do you have a phone number for de Jager?'

'Yip.' She gave it to him.

Griessel stood at the big table holding a sheet of paper with two numbers on it. One of them was his cell phone number. The other was a Cape number that he did not recognise. He studied the handwriting, comparing it to the notes in tiny, almost illegible scribbles on the hordes of documents strewn across the table. The numbers were written in larger, rounder and more feminine script.

Rachel Anderson?

He dialled the other Cape number. Three rings and a woman answered with a distinctive accent. 'United States Consul, good afternoon, how may I help you?'

'Oh, sorry, wrong number,' he said and terminated the call.

'Gourmet Foods, good afternoon,' a woman's voice answered.

'Is that not CapSud Trading?'

'This is CapSud, trading as Gourmet Foods.'

'Could I speak to Mr de Jager, please?'

'Who is this speaking?'

'This is Inspector Vusi Ndabeni of the South African Police Service.'

'Mr de Jager is deceased, Inspector.'

'Oh. I'm sorry. When did he pass away?'

'Four months ago.'

'I am calling to enquire about a Peugeot Boxer panel van, registration CA four-oh-nine, three-four-one, that is registered in the name of CapSud Trading.'

'That must be the stolen one.'

'Oh?'

'We bought it early October last year, then we sent it to the sign writers to have our logo applied. It was stolen that very night from the sign writers. And you never caught them.' Accusatory.

'Are you aware that the vehicle was in the Metropolitan Police pound?'

'Yes, they recovered it in Salt River, in a Fire Service parking spot, so they towed it away and impounded it and called us. That was mid-October.'

'Why have you never collected it, ma'am?'

'Because when Frik died everything was frozen. Nobody could draw money or sign a cheque, and the estate will only be wound up in two months' time. This is the New South Africa, you know, you have to wait and see.'

'So, as far as you know, the panel van has been in the pound ever since?'

'Must be, because every week someone phones and says we must come and pay the fine and collect it, and the more I explain about Frik, the less it helps because next week someone else phones.'

'You are Mrs . . .?'

'I am Saartjie de Jager. Frik's wife.'

'May I ask how Mr de Jager died, ma'am?'

'Cholesterol. The doctor warned him, I warned him, but Frik wouldn't listen. He was like that all his life. Now I'm the one trying to clear up the mess.'

Everything happened at once. Griessel waited impatiently at the big table for his contact at Telkom to get back to him, John Afrika walked gingerly past the blood in the hallway, looking at it in horror, saying: '*Nee, o, jirre,*' Griessel's cell phone began to ring and Vusi came through the front door with an excited 'Benny!'

He thought it was the Telkom man, turned away from his colleagues and answered it. 'Griessel.' Through the window he saw Mat Joubert walking up the garden path.

'Benny, it's Fransman.'

Too much at once. 'Fransman, can I call you back?' Behind him the Commissioner said something reproachfully.

'Benny, just a quick one, how sure are we that Barnard's wife and Josh Geyser are not involved?'

He needed to tell Afrika that he had asked Joubert to come, before there were fireworks. 'Don't know,' he said, his mind not on the conversation.

'So I can question them some more? I'll get Mbali to talk to Alexandra . . .'

The female detective's name forced him to focus. 'Don't you know yet?' he asked.

'What are you doing here?' he heard John Afrika say behind him. He turned. Joubert had entered the room. He put his hand over the receiver as Dekker asked, 'Don't I know what yet?'

'Commissioner, I'll explain,' said Griessel and then to Dekker: 'Mbali was shot, Fransman. Here in Upper Orange, the American girl . . .'

Dekker was dumbfounded.

'She's in hospital,' Griessel said.

'The American girl? What was Mbali doing there?'

'That's what I wanted to ask you.'

'How would I know? I sent her to Jack Fischer.'

'Jack Fischer?' he asked in surprise, and then realised it was the wrong thing to say with both Afrika and Joubert nearby.

'They did some work for AfriSound, but I think it's a dead end. Is Mbali OK?'

'Fransman, we don't know, I'm sorry, I have to run. Talk to Geyser again if you think you should. I'll call you later.' He ended the call and said: 'Commissioner, I asked Mat to come and help.' Afrika's face began to screw up in protest but Griessel didn't give him the chance. 'All due respect, Commissioner,' he began, knowing that what he was about to say was not respectful at all, but he didn't give a damn any more, 'you said there's a manpower problem. Mat is . . . underutilised at PT, he's the best detective in the Cape and I have an American girl that I have to find, whatever it takes. You can fire me tomorrow, you can demote me to Inspector or Sergeant if you like, but, fuck knows, there's no time to waste. Vusi is working on the panel van they took Rachel Anderson away in, I am going to find out who the hell knew she was in this house. We don't have time to process the scene and I need someone who knows what he's doing. You said I must phone Rachel's father, and I will do it, but not before I know what is going on. Because he is going to ask me and I want to have answers that will satisfy a girl's father. So, please, let's skip the shit and get the girl.' Then he added a final, hopeful: 'With respect, Commissioner,' and waited for the guillotine to drop.

John Afrika looked at Griessel, at Joubert, at Ndabeni, and back to Griessel again. Conflicting emotions passed like the seasons

across his face. He nodded slightly. 'Get her, Benny,' he said, and
walked out, careful not to step in the pool of blood.

Griessel's phone rang again, he answered it and the man from
Telkom said: 'Benny, between twelve and two there were only two
calls made from that number. The first was to West Lafayette in
Indiana, that's in America, and the second was to you.'

'Dave, what time was the first one made?'

'Hold on ... thirteen thirty-six. It lasted for two minutes,
twenty-two seconds.'

'Thanks, Dave, thanks a lot.' He ended the call and thought. He
tried to piece the thing together, the thousands of loose strands in
his head.

'Benny ...' Vusi said, but he held up a hand, checked his cell
phone screen, looked up the call register for the record of Rachel's
call to him. He received it at thirteen forty-one. Then he had run
out of Van Hunks and they had raced here. If her attackers had
somehow intercepted her first call, they had only had five minutes
more. What if they had been in the area somewhere nearby? They
must have arrived just after he had finished speaking to Rachel.
That was some quick reaction. Too quick ...

A spark lit up in his brain, a flash of insight. 'Vusi, was it here on
the corner that she went into the café?'

'The deli,' Ndabeni nodded.

'And then she ran down here,' Griessel indicated Upper Orange.

'Mbali found footprints in the garden.'

Griessel scratched his head. 'They were waiting somewhere,
Vusi. They must have seen her, but with all the police around ...'

'Benny, the panel van ...'

But Griessel did not hear him. Why hadn't they shot her? Just
the old man. They had cut Erin Russel's throat. But they allowed
Rachel to live when they could easily have killed her. Here in this
house. But they abducted her?

Another revelation.

'The rucksack,' he said. They had cut Erin Russel's rucksack off
her shoulders. He bent and looked under the table. 'See if you can
find a rucksack.' He walked down the passage. 'Vusi, take the left,

the bathroom, that bedroom, I'll take the right.' He stopped. 'Mat, please, can you look in the kitchen and outside?'

'What does the rucksack look like?'

'I have no idea,' said Griessel. But a thought occurred to him and stopped him in his tracks so that Vusi nearly bumped into him. He began to phone feverishly. As the sergeant in Caledon Square answered, he identified himself and asked if there were still uniforms at the Cat & Moose in Long Street.

'Yes, they are still there.'

'Sarge, tell them to ask where the American girls' luggage is. Erin Russel and Rachel Anderson. They must find it, and guard it with their lives.'

'I'll do that.'

Griessel said to Ndabeni: 'They're looking for something, Vusi, the fuckers are looking for something the girls have. That's why Rachel is still alive.' And he dashed off to the bedrooms to look for the rucksack.

37

'What now?' Natasha Abader asked as he closed the late Adam Barnard's door behind her.

'Sit down, please,' said Dekker, leaning against the desk, intimidating her with his proximity.

She didn't like that, her beautiful eyes showed it, but she sat.

'Can I trust you, sister?'

'I told you, I'm not your sister.'

'Why not, sister? Are you too la-di-da working here with the whiteys and I'm just a common *hotnot* from Atlantis? You're *chlora, finish en klaar.*'

'Do you think that's what it's about?' Her eyes flashed. 'You can't stand it that I slept with a white man, can you? No, it's no use shaking your head, I saw how you changed, just like that, when I said he did it here with me too. Let me tell you, he wasn't the first white man and he won't be the last. But I don't discriminate, I sleep with whoever I want, because it's the New South Africa, but you don't want to know about that. You want to "brother" and "sister" us all. You want us to be a separate tribe, us coloureds; you're the kind who goes around complaining how hard it is to be a coloured. Wake up, Inspector, it's useless. If you don't integrate, you won't. That's the trouble with this country, everyone wants to complain, nobody wants to do anything, nobody wants to forget the past. And, just for the record, how many white women have you slept with?'

He looked away, towards the window.

'I thought so,' she said.

'What makes you think I have?'

'What woman can look at you and not think of sex?' she said.

Now he looked her in the eyes, and she looked back, challenging, angry.

'I'll take that as a compliment.' Knowing he had lost the battle, he tried to consolidate his position.

'Why am I here?'

Now he felt uncomfortable to be so close. He stood up and walked around the desk.

'Because I trust you.'

She shook her head, long hair cascading.

'I am going to tell you things you can't repeat,' he said.

She just looked at him.

'The people who shot Adam Barnard knew him very well. They know his wife passes out every night. They know where he keeps his pistol. You are the only one I can trust. Tell me who knows him that well.'

'How can you say that? He was shot in his house . . .'

'No, he was shot somewhere else. Maybe not far from here, in the street. We found his shoe. And his cell phone.' He saw that surprised her and it gave him satisfaction.

'Then they took him to his house and carried him up the stairs and put him down there . . . Who knows about his wife, Natasha? Who knows about the pistol? The Geysers?'

She adjusted her skirt and brushed her hair back over her shoulder before answering. 'No. I don't think so. I don't think they have ever been to his house. Adam was . . . ashamed of Alexa. A few times she'd . . .'

'What?'

'Made a scene when he took people to his house. He lived here. From morning to night. He would go home about seven o'clock, but he would come back, often. Eight o'clock, nine o'clock, then he would work till twelve . . .'

'So who would have known that?'

She considered before she answered. 'I really can't say.'

'Please. Take a guess.'

'A guess?'

'Speculate.'

'I knew about his wife . . .'

'Who else?'

'Willie and Wouter and Michèle . . .'

'Who's Michèle?'

'She's been sitting in there all morning. She does the PR.'

'I thought Willie Mouton did production and promotion?'

'Yes, but she does the *PR*. Promotion is when we pay for something. PR is when the papers write about stuff, or someone is on TV or radio and you don't pay for it.'

'Which one is Michèle?'

'She's the oldish woman who was sitting with Spider and Iván . . .'

He had a vague recollection of an older woman between the younger men. 'And she knows Adam well?'

'They've worked together for years. From the beginning. She went freelance about seven years ago but she still does our PR on contract.'

'She went freelance?'

'You know, she set up her own agency. For artists who don't have a label, or for minor labels.'

'Did she and Adam get on well?'

'They were like brother and sister . . .' There was a hint that this wasn't the whole story.

'What does that mean?'

'They say Adam and Michèle were lovers. Years ago.'

'How many years ago?'

'It's just rumours.'

He gave her a look that said, 'Drop the shit.'

'From when Alexa began drinking, apparently. He went and cried on Michèle's shoulder. She was married herself then . . .'

'Fuck,' said Dekker.

She looked at him with disapproval.

'Damnit, sister,' he said indignantly. 'My list keeps getting longer.'

Mat Joubert walked back through the kitchen to the hall where Griessel and Vusi were watching him expectantly. He shook his head. No rucksack. He watched Benny process the information silently. Joubert waited patiently until he knew he could speak.

'You know about the blood out there?' he asked Griessel, watching him while he said 'yes'. Benny was standing still, head tilted sideways, right hand reaching unconsciously for his head and the fingers scratching in the thick, unruly hair just behind his ear.

A feeling of compassion swept over Joubert for this colleague, this friend, this man he had known for a lifetime. Griessel's frame had always been too small for all his energy, so that sometimes it seemed to vibrate, shock waves of passion pulsing through it like a tsunami. That face – twenty years ago it had an elfish quality, the mischievous cheek of the court jester, with an infectious laugh and a preposterous witticism perpetually crouched behind those bright Slavic eyes and wide mouth, ready to take off in full, unstoppable flight. You could barely see it now – life had eroded it away in a network of tiny furrows. But Joubert knew that in that brain the synapses were firing now. Griessel, sent from pillar to post all morning, was trying to get his head around the puzzle. When he succeeded the sparks would fly. Benny had the brain of a detective, always faster and more creative than his. Joubert had always been slow, methodical and systematic, but Griessel had instinct, natural flair, the sparkling fly half to Joubert's plodding front ranker.

'It might be drugs,' said Griessel, but to himself. 'I think the . . . the rucksack . . .'

'Benny, the panel van was in the Metro pound,' said Vusi.

Griessel stared into nowhere: '. . . the girls . . . no, I don't know. Maybe they stole the drugs. Or took them but didn't pay . . .'

Joubert waited quietly, till he saw Benny focus on him and Vusi. Then he asked: 'Is it the girl's blood?'

'No.' Then Benny focused sharply on Joubert, with sudden insight, and he said: 'It's someone else's blood, not Rachel's, it's the blood of one of those fuckers.' He grabbed his phone.

Joubert said, 'Benny, let me phone the hospitals.'

'No, Mat, let Caledon Square do it,' and he called their number and gave the order to the radio room Sergeant: 'Any young man between the age of, say, eighteen and thirty-five, any colour, any race, any language, Sarge, every young fucker with blood on him, I want to know about.' Then Griessel looked at Vusi and said: 'Metro's pound?'

'That's right. The same Peugeot, same registration. It was stolen, and Metro recovered it in Salt River. It has been parked in the pound since October, because the owner died of a heart attack and the estate is frozen. I'm going, Benny. I'm going to find out what's going on there. How did they get it out of the pound?'

Joubert saw a flicker in Griessel's eyes, a momentary realisation. 'What?' He knew the value of Benny's intuition.

Griessel shook his head. 'Don't know. Something. *Jissis*, I have to sit and think, but there's no time. Vusi, excellent work, go and find out, let's get the van, because that's about all we have . . .' A sudden intake of breath. 'Wait,' he called Ndabeni back. 'Vusi, I want to make absolutely sure, the man from the deli, did he look at the pictures of Demidov's people?'

'He did.'

'Nothing?'

'Nothing.'

'OK. Thanks.'

Vusi jogged away and Griessel hung his head while Mat patiently stood and watched him. For a long time. In silence, so that the tick-tock of the grandfather clock in the study could be heard. The two of them were the dinosaurs of the SAPS, he thought, an endangered, dying breed. Political global warming and racial climate change should have taken their toll long ago, but here they were still, two old carnivores in the jungle, limbs stiff, teeth blunt, but still not completely ineffective.

Griessel scratched audibly at the bushy hair behind his ear. He grunted: 'Hu . . .' turned and went outside. Joubert followed tranquilly across the little doormat and the veranda, past the bougainvilleas and down the slate pathway. Griessel opened the garden gate and went and stood in the street. He turned to face Lion's Head. Joubert stood behind him, looking, seeing the rocky dome rising above the city, feeling the wind, watching how it ruffled Benny's hair even more. This day that had dawned in such perfection, was being overtaken by the southeaster. Tonight it would howl like a demon around the side of Table Mountain.

'Before six this morning, up there,' said Griessel, pointing at Lion's Head, 'she told a woman to call the police. Those young men had been chasing her since two in the morning. At eleven at the deli there, she told her father over the tickey-box that she couldn't talk to the police . . .'

Tickey-box, thought Joubert. A prehistoric word.

Griessel dipped his head again. Then he looked up at Table Mountain. His eyes measured the distance to Lion's Head. He looked at Joubert. 'Five hours after she was on Lion's Head she arrives at the café. And the fucker parks in the street and comes in after her. How did they know, Mat? Where was she in between, why couldn't they find her? Why did she change her mind about the police?' He lifted his hand to his hair again. 'What do you do? A girl, a foreigner, you are desperate to find her, she could be anywhere. How do you watch the whole city?'

They stared at the mountain. As always, Griessel's ability to put himself in someone else's shoes, either victim or the perpetrator, charmed Joubert.

Then he realised what Griessel obviously already had. They had been sitting on the mountain and watching the whole city. 'Could be,' he said.

'*Fokkol* use to us now,' said Griessel, still one step ahead. 'They've got her.'

'But you can't see this house from the mountain,' said Joubert, nodding at the Victorian building beside them.

'That's true . . .' Lost in thought again, Benny's brain was searching, Joubert knew. He knew the frustration, the junkyard of information from a day like today when everything happened at once. You had to sift through the chaos; everything you had heard and seen, everything you knew, had to be sorted. For him it was the labour of the night, when he lay beside Margaret, behind her warm body with his hand on the rounding of her belly. Then his thoughts would travel down slow, systematic pathways. But

Griessel's process was different: impatient, quick, not always faultless, but much faster. Griessel's head jerked, a tumbler had dropped and he looked down the street and began walking in that direction. Joubert had to stretch his long legs to keep up. A hundred metres further on, Griessel stopped in a driveway, looking at the house, the garage. 'He sat here, in a bakkie . . .' Excited. 'He nearly drove us off the road . . .'

Griessel jogged up the drive, turned and looked back at Piet van der Lingen's house and said: 'No . . .' He walked back and forth, jumped up and down and said: 'Mat come and stand here.'

Joubert came and stood there.

'Stand on your toes.'

Joubert stretched.

'What can you see of the house?'

The big man looked. 'Just too low to see everything.'

'He drove out of here, a guy in a bakkie. Toyota four-by-four, faded red, the old model. Little fucker behind the wheel was young, in a hell of a hurry, drove right in front of us and raced off towards the city . . .'

Joubert focused differently, unburdened by memories. 'He could have stood on the bakkie,' he said. 'He would have been able to see everything then.'

'*Jissis*,' said Griessel. 'Young, he was young, just like the others.' He looked at Joubert. 'I will recognise him, Mat, if I see his fucking face again. I will know him.' He was quiet for a heartbeat, then he said: 'An old Toyota . . . that's not a drug dealer's car, Mat . . .'

Griessel's phone rang. He checked the screen before he answered. 'Sarge?' He listened for about forty seconds and began walking. Mat Joubert walked behind him, faster and faster, keeping his eyes on Griessel. Here came the tsunami again.

'Get more people, Sarge,' said Griessel over the phone. 'I'm coming.'

Griessel looked back at Joubert, the familiar, spark-shooting fire in his eyes. 'About ten minutes ago someone dropped off a young white guy at City Park Casualties, and then left. In haste. Victim was stabbed in the throat with a blade; they might be able to save him. I'm off, Mat . . .' Griessel began to run.

'I'll do the scene,' shouted Joubert after him.

'Thanks, Mat.' Benny's words were blown away on the wind.

'Get her, Benny,' shouted Joubert, but he couldn't tell if Benny had heard him. He watched his colleague's running figure, so determined, so urgent, and again he felt that emotion, nostalgia, sadness, as though it were the last time he would see Benny Griessel.

38

It was Jess Anderson who broke the silence in the study and put words to their anxiety. 'Why doesn't he call?'

Bill Anderson did not want to sit, he wanted to walk up and down to vent some of his tension. But he couldn't, because he knew that would upset his wife even more. So he sat beside her on the brown leather couch. His lawyer friend, Connelly, and the Police Chief, Dombkowski, had insisted he stay, so he could be here when the South African policeman phoned. Now he was sorry he hadn't gone along to Erin's parents. It was his duty. But he couldn't leave Jess alone in these circumstances.

'It's almost forty minutes,' she said.

'We don't know how far he had to travel,' said Anderson.

'We could call him . . .'

'Let's give it a little more time.'

They held her down on the concrete floor, four of them. A fifth put a blade under her T-shirt and cut it away, then her shorts, then her underwear. The same knife that had cut Erin's throat, the same hand, stripped her naked, effortlessly. They pulled her up and pushed her against the narrow steel pillar, her arms bent backwards and tied with something around the pole. Then they stood back and all she could do was sink down as far as her bonds allowed, to hide her shame, so that her gaze fixed on her running shoes.

'Where is it?'

She didn't answer. She heard him coming, footfalls on the floor, two steps only. He grabbed her hair and jerked her head up so that it banged against the metal of the pillar. He knelt in front of her.

'Where is it?' the question was repeated.

Her left eye was swollen shut and painful. She focused the other on him. His handsome face was against hers, calm. As ever. His voice carried only authority, control.

Her revulsion for him was greater than her fear of death. This knowledge came in a rush; it liberated her and brought with it the impulse to do something, to kick, to spit, and she began to collect saliva in her mouth. For everything he had done, everything, she wanted to cast scorn and hatred on him, but she reconsidered. She was not powerless. They could not kill her. Not now. Not yet. She could buy time. She was not alone. *I'm on my way, don't open the door for anybody, I will call when I get there, please, Miss Anderson,* the policeman's voice, the caring, the will to make her safe, to rescue her. He was somewhere now, looking for her, he would find her; somehow or other he would find out who was hunting her. It was so obvious, he would find out, he would find her.

She answered the man by shaking her head slowly from side to side.

He took her hair in an iron grip. 'I'm going to hurt you,' he said. In his practical way.

'Go ahead.' She tried to keep her voice as even as his.

He laughed, right in her face. 'You have no idea . . .'

It didn't matter, she thought. Let him laugh.

He let her hair go suddenly and stood up. 'Their luggage is still at the Cat & Moose . . .'

'We should have taken that long ago.'

'We didn't know, Steve. You know what she said in the club . . . Where the fuck is Barry? Call him, go get their stuff.'

'They're not going to just give it to us, Jay.'

She lifted her head and saw them looking at each other. There was tension between them.

Steve, the black guy, eventually nodded, turned and left. Jay spoke to another one, one she didn't know: 'There's a hardware shop one block up, right-hand corner . . .'

She saw his hand dip into his pocket, take out a few notes and hand them over.

'I want pruning shears. We'll cut off her toes. Then her fingers. Then her nipples. Pity though. Great tits.'

It took a while before Fransman Dekker asked Michèle Malherbe if she and Adam had slept together. Her dignity overwhelmed him when she came through the office door, so it was only later that he realised she was smaller than he thought. Her hair was blonde, cut short and her face attractive. Her age hard to pin down until he looked at her hands later and realised she must be in her late fifties or early sixties. She introduced herself, listened attentively to his rank and name and sat down in one of the guest chairs with an aura of controlled loss. Dekker could not sit at Barnard's desk, it felt wrong at that moment. He took the other guest chair.

'It's a great loss, Inspector,' she said with her elbows on the arms of the chair and her hands held together in her lap. He could see she had been crying. He wondered, immediately, how a woman like her could fall for Adam Barnard.

'It is,' he said. 'You knew him well?'

'Nearly twenty-five years.'

'Ah . . . uh . . . madam, I understand you know the industry very well, the circumstances . . .'

She nodded, her face serious and focused.

'Why would someone want to . . .' He searched for a euphemism. '. . . do away with him?'

'I don't think Adam's death has anything to do with the industry, Inspector.'

'Oh?'

She lifted her right hand in a small gesture. There was a single, elegant ring on her middle finger. 'We may be an emotional lot, by definition. Music is emotion, after all, is it not? But in essence there is no great difference between the music industry and any other. We fight, we argue, we compete with each other, we say and do things that were better not said or done, but it's like that everywhere. The only big difference is that the media . . . tends to wash our dirty laundry in public.'

'I'm not sure I understand.'

'I'm trying to say that I can't think of a single reason why anyone in Adam's world would want to murder him. I can't think of anyone who would be capable of that.' He drew in a breath to respond, but she made the same gesture and said: 'I'm not naïve. I have learned that our nature allows for anything. But after a quarter-century working with people, you see all sides, and you pick up a fair amount of wisdom along the way from which you can draw in circumstances like this.'

'Madam, the way this happened . . . points to someone who had information about Adam's domestic situation.'

She didn't look away. Her eyes were light brown. Her sensuality was subtle, he thought, maybe in the blend of what he knew about her and her refinement. 'I'm not sure I know what you are referring to.'

'They knew about his wife, for example . . .'

Her smile was sympathetic. 'Inspector, unfortunately dear Alexandra's situation is general knowledge. Especially in the industry.'

'Did Barnard talk about it?'

Muted indignation. 'Adam would never dream of doing that.'

He waited.

'I can understand if the press makes this seem like an environment where nobody cares, Inspector, but that is a false impression. There are many of us who still have contact with Alexa, who regularly try to communicate in the hope that she will . . . recover. She is a wonderful person.'

'Are you one of them?'

She nodded.

'But I understand you were more than just friends with Adam Barnard?' It was deliberate.

She looked at him in disappointment. 'I will leave my lawyer's number with Natasha,' she said and walked slowly, with dignity, to the door, opened it and closed it quietly behind her.

He sat staring at the closed door, despising himself. Also knowing that he had no idea what to do next.

★   ★   ★

The nurse at Casualties told Griessel he would have to talk to the superintendent and he asked her to phone him. It's not a man, the nurse bridled, and Griessel said he didn't care what it was, she had better phone.

She dialled a number, whispered over the phone, replaced the receiver and said the superintendent was in a meeting. Her attitude intensified a few degrees.

'Miss, I have a female detective in that operating theatre with two gunshot wounds and I don't know if she is going to make it. I have a nineteen-year-old American girl who has been abducted by people who cut her friend's throat in Long Street this morning. That . . .' and he had to suppress the urge to say 'fucker' with huge effort, as he jabbed a thumb over his shoulder at the operating theatre '. . . man in there is my only chance to find her before they kill her. Let me tell you now, if anything happens to her because you are obstructing the law, you will all sleep in the dirtiest, most crowded cell I can find in the Peninsula. I hope you understand me very well.'

She swallowed her indignation and picked up the phone again with wide eyes and redialled the number. 'Julie, I think Dr Marinos should come to ICU immediately,' she said.

At the gate of the Metropolitan Police vehicle pound the young traffic officer in a gleaming uniform opened a fat green file, paged through it fussily, pressed the relevant page flat with his palm and ran his finger down to an entry on an official form.

'Yes, that particular vehicle was booked out at precisely twelve thirty-four with me. And here . . .' he turned the page, and rotated the file so that Vusi could read it from the other side of the desk '. . . is the release form, stamped and signed.'

'Who signed it?'

The traffic officer turned the file back again and studied the signature. 'I can't say.'

'Who can tell me?'

'You would have to ask Administration.'

'Where is Administration?'

'There. In the licensing building. But you have to go upstairs. First floor.'

'Thank you. May I take the form with me?'

The traffic officer shook his head. 'I can't help you there. The form has to stay here.'

Vusi thought the man was joking. But there was not a trace of humour. 'Are you serious?'

'This file is my responsibility. Regulations.'

'Mister . . .'

'It's Inspector.'

'Inspector, we are working on a case of murder and abduction, we are running out of time.'

'Administration has a duplicate of the form. Just give them the case number.'

Vusi wondered why the man had not told him that in the first place. He took out his notebook, opened it and clicked his pen and said, 'Would you give me the number, please?'

Mat Joubert pulled on rubber gloves, bent at the open door of Mbali Kaleni's Corsa and picked up the bullet casings in the footwell and beside the seat. He noted the number in his book. He heard the feet of Thick and Thin of Forensics shuffle on the tar beside him where they were circling the other casings with chalk and placing a small plastic triangle with a number beside every group of casings. They worked in silence.

He stood up, leaned his big torso inside the Corsa, pressing on the headrest and the steering wheel. Kaleni's big black handbag lay on the front passenger seat. On top was an A5 notebook, the pages folded back on the spiral, blood on the top page, fine drops, something written down.

He picked the notebook up carefully, brought it out of the car and stood upright outside. He took his reading glasses out of his breast pocket, flicked them open and placed them on the bridge of his nose. He stared at the three letters written in a shaky hand in capital letters: *JAS*.

He called Jimmy, the tall, skinny forensic technologist. 'I need an evidence bag.'

'I'll bring it, Sup.' Keen. Why did his colleagues complain about Thick and Thin? They never gave him any trouble.

JAS. The Afrikaans for 'coat'. Unfathomable.

Jimmy brought him a transparent ZipLoc bag and held it open. Joubert put the notebook inside so the written letters were visible. Jimmy zipped it up.

'Thanks, Jimmy.'

'Pleasure, Sup.'

Joubert bent again at the open door and peered under the seat. There was a pen, but nothing else.

He took out his own pen from his pocket and used it to scratch the other one closer until he could reach it with his fingers. He held it so he could see it through his reading glasses. Mont Blanc Starwalker. Cool Blue. On the navy-blue shaft of the pen were two faint blood prints.

He turned and walked over to Jimmy while thinking about the pieces of evidence. The blood on the notebook was not necessarily significant. But the bloody fingerprints on the pen were. Mbali Kaleni had written the letters J, A and S after she had been wounded.

JAS?

A perp wearing a coat? Or was it Zulu?

He reached for his phone. He would have to find out.

39

The superintendent of the City Park Hospital, a well-groomed woman in her forties, nodded her head just three times while Griessel was talking. She said: 'Captain, one moment, please,' and walked quickly through the glass doors with the lettering *Operating Theatre. Personnel Only.*

Benny could not stand still. He walked as far as the nurses' desk and back to the theatre doors. Let the fucker live, please, just long enough to get what he needed. He looked at his watch. Nearly twenty-five to three. Too much time had elapsed since they took her. Too many possibilities. But they hadn't shot Rachel Anderson, because there was something they wanted. It was his only chance, his only hope.

At the periphery of his consciousness something flitted past, ghostly visions, fleeting and intangible, leaving only an impression – this morning. He stood still and closed his eyes. What was it? His brain seemed to tell him that, no, the wounded fucker was not his only hope. There was something else. He must go back to the beginning. This morning, what had happened? At the churchyard? What were the important things? The rucksack, cut off Erin Russel . . .

The superintendent burst through the doors and came over to Griessel. She began to speak before she reached him. 'Captain, his carotid artery was cut, relatively high up, I'm afraid, where there is not much protection. He lost an enormous amount of blood, we had a Code Blue in there, but they were able to resuscitate him. His condition is critical, they are still trying to close the wound, under the circumstances a very difficult procedure, especially since his blood pressure is so low and the bleeding could not be entirely halted. But I am afraid there is no chance of you talking to him in the next five or six hours. Even then I doubt whether communication will be meaningful. His vocal chords have been damaged, apparently – to what extent they don't yet know.'

He digested the information, frustration forcing a curse to the surface, but he swallowed it down.

'Doc, his clothes, I want his clothes, anything he had on him.'

'I'm going to call,' said Bill Anderson decisively. He got up abruptly from the leather couch and went to the phone on his desk. He looked at the number he had written down, picked up the receiver and keyed it in. He stood listening to the initial silence on the line and then the crystal clear ring on the southernmost tip of another continent.

Griessel's phone rang and he looked at the screen, saw it was MAT JOUBERT and answered: 'Mat?'

'Benny, I don't know what it means but Mbali Kaleni wrote the word "jas" in her notebook, and I am reasonably sure it was after she was shot. There are bloody fingerprints on the pen and blood spatters on the page. I thought it might be Zulu, but it doesn't seem to be.'

'Jas?' then he heard the soft ring tone of another incoming call. 'Mat, hold for me.' He saw the long number, the unfamiliar code, and knew who it would be.

God.

He couldn't talk to them now, he couldn't, what would he say? What could he say?

Sorry?

They would be terribly worried because he hadn't phoned. This was their child. They had the right to know.

'Mat, I'll call you back.' He switched calls and said: 'Mr Anderson?'

'Oh, thank god, Captain, we were getting very worried. Is Rachel OK?'

Shit.

'Mr Anderson, Rachel was not at the address she gave me. We are still trying to track her down, but we are making good progress.'

'She wasn't there? How is that possible?'

'I don't know, sir. I honestly don't know.'

Two young men full of fire and self-confidence walked into the Cat & Moose Youth Hostel, up to the plump woman at the reception desk.

'Hi,' said the black one and smiled. 'We've come for Rachel's stuff.'

'Who?'

'Rachel Anderson, the American girl. You know, the one who was missing.'

'Are you from the police?'

'No, we're friends.'

'Don't I know you?' asked the generously built girl.

'I don't think so. So where is her luggage?'

'Down there, in their room, with the police. Did they find her?'

'With the police?' The friendliness wavered.

'Yes, they're guarding it. Guns and everything. You'll have to talk to them. Did they find the girl?'

They didn't answer her. They looked at each other. Then they walked out.

'Hey!' the girl shouted, but they didn't even look back. She came around from behind the desk and ran out through the door onto the Long Street pavement. She saw them walking fast. They looked back once and disappeared around the corner.

'I know you,' she said, and hurried off to find the two men who were guarding the luggage.

He wanted to pull off her running shoes. She pressed her feet against the cement floor with all her strength, so that he swore, stood beside her and violently kicked her feet out from under her with his boots.

Her legs shot forward and she fell hard on her bare bottom. She lunged up, trying to struggle upright and hide her feet under her again, but one of the others had grabbed her legs and held them in a ferocious grip.

'Jesus, you're a piece of work,' Jay said to her.

She spat at him, but missed. She tried to jerk her legs free. It was no use. Jay began to untie her laces and pulled the shoe off her foot. He wrinkled his nose at the smell.

'Don't you Yankee bitches ever change your socks?'

She spat again, ineffectually. He had the other laces undone and pulled off the other shoe, threw it aside and pulled off both socks. 'You had better hold one leg,' he said to the third man. 'This is going to drive her nuts.'

He stretched to reach the pruning shears, a big tool with green handles. 'OK, one last time: where is the video?'

'Dead and buried,' she said.

Now there were two of them holding her legs, pressing down with their full weight so that her heels pressed painfully against the concrete floor.

'No,' Jay said to one of them. 'I want her to see what I'm doing. Move a little.'

He grabbed her right foot, his hand around the cushion and the big toe. He brought the shears closer, looked at her, put the blades around her little toe. She jerked with all her might. They were too strong for her. He closed the handles. The pain was immediate and immense. She screamed against her will, a sound she did not know she could make.

The blood made the toe stick to the silver blades. Jay shook them and the bit of flesh and nail fell in the dust.

'This little piggy . . .' said the one who was holding her right leg, and giggled nervously.

She cried hysterically.

'Where's the video?' Jay asked and gripped her foot again.

'Fuck you,' she screamed.

He grinned, held the foot tightly, hooked the blades around the second toe and snipped it off.

'In my big bag,' she shrieked, because the pain, the brutality and the humiliation was too much.

'Good. Where is the bag?'

'At the youth hostel.'

Then Jay's cell phone rang and they all jumped in fright.

                        *   *   *

The superintendent came back through the glass doors with bloodied clothing in a large transparent plastic bag. Griessel told Bill Anderson: 'I am really sorry, but I have to go. If there is any news, I will call you, I promise.'

Silence over the line. 'I don't think your promises mean all that much,' and then the audible click as the American put down the phone. Griessel stood frozen to the spot, torn between the injustice and the knowledge that, as a father, he would have felt the same.

The superintendent held out the bag to him. 'Captain, this is everything, I don't know whether it will help you.'

He came back to the present, replaced his phone in his pocket and took the plastic bag. 'Have you got a pair of rubber gloves around here?'

'Miss, get the captain a pair of surgical gloves,' the doctor ordered. The nurse trotted off down the corridor. 'Will that be all, Captain?'

'Doc, my colleague, Inspector Kaleni?'

'The black woman?'

'Yes. Any news?'

'Her chances are better than the young man's in there. The gunshot trauma to her neck . . . it looks like the jawbone deflected the projectile, so that it only damaged the edge of the carotid artery above the fourth cervical vertebra. Apparently she received treatment on the scene to control the bleeding, which made a great difference.'

'Will she make it?'

'It's too early to say.'

The nurse returned with the gloves. 'Thank you,' he said.

'Let me know if you need anything,' the superintendent said and walked towards the lift.

'Thank you very much, Doc,' he said and put the big plastic bag on the nurses' desk. He pulled on the gloves hastily. It looked like a pair of trousers, shirt, a pair of brown boots . . . He opened the bag and took out the shirt. White T-shirt, dark with blood. That meant no breast pocket. He took out the shoes and put them to one side. Then the trousers, jeans, with a worn leather belt. He felt in the pockets and took out a bunch of keys, studied them. Car keys with Mazda on them, four other keys – two that would open a house door and two smaller ones. For padlocks? No use. He put the keys beside the shoes. Nothing else in that pocket. In the other he found a handkerchief, clean and neatly folded. He turned the trousers over and immediately felt the back pockets were empty. But there was something on the belt, heavy, a pouch of rust-brown leather with a flap folded over some object. He unclipped the flap.

Inside the flap something was written, but he concentrated on the contents of the pouch – a Leatherman, it seemed. He pulled it out. Red handles, printed with *Leatherman* and *Juice Cs4*. The multi-tool was not new and bore the marks of use. Fingerprints, he could get fingerprints off it. He applied himself to the flap, lifting it up again. Three letters were written on it with permanent ink marker: *A.O.A.*

Initials?

What is your name, fucker? Andries? He thought of Joubert, of the word Mbali had scribbled. *Jas.* He would have to phone Mat back, but first he must finish this. He put the Leatherman back in its pouch and went back to the plastic bag. Only a pair of underpants were left, and a pair of socks. He took them out and turned them over in his hands looking for more initials, a laundry label, anything, but there was nothing. *A.O.A.*

Jas?

'Miss,' he said to the nurse, 'do you perhaps have a small plastic bag?' He pulled the brown belt out of the jeans and took off the pouch.

She nodded, penitent, eager to help after the good example set by the superintendent.

She searched under her desk and produced an empty pill packet.

'That's perfect,' said Griessel, 'thanks a lot.' He placed the Leatherman, pouch and all, in the packet. Then he put the packet in his shirt pocket. He pushed the clothing back into the big bag and looked up. The nurse was gazing intently at him, as though any minute he was going to perform a miracle.

He pulled off the rubber gloves, hesitating, where could he dispose of them?

'Give them to me,' she said softly.

He nodded his thanks, passed them to her, took out his cell phone and called Mat Joubert.

'Benny,' the deep voice said.

'Jas?' said Griessel.

'J.A.S. Just the three letters. Did you find anything?'

'Another three letters. A.O.A. With full stops between. I think they are the fucker's initials.'

'Or an abbreviation.'

'Could be.'

'J.A.S. Could also be an abbreviation, I don't know ... Or a suspect wearing a coat, in this weather ...'

A spark lit up in the back of Benny Griessel's mind, two thoughts coming together ... then it collapsed.

'Say that again.'

'I said J.A.S. could be an abbreviation too.'

Nothing, the insight was gone, leaving no trace.

His cell phone rang softly in his ear. Now what? He checked. It was the Caledon Square radio room. 'Mat, I've got another call, we'll talk.' He manipulated the phone's keys, said: 'Griessel.' The Sergeant said: 'Captain, two men just tried to collect the girl's luggage at the Cat & Moose.' Griessel's heart lurched.

'Did you get the bastards?'

'No, Captain, they ran away, but the manager says she knows one of them.'

'*Jissis*,' said Griessel, grabbing the plastic bag and starting to run. 'I'm on my way.'

'Right, Captain.'

'How the hell do you know about the Captain?' Griessel asked as he stormed out through the door into the street, nearly knocking two schoolgirls head over heels.

'Good news travels fast,' said the Sergeant, but Griessel didn't hear. He was too busy apologising to the girls.

40

The woman at Cape Town Metropolitan Police: Administration pulled out the form from a file. She frowned and said: 'That's funny . . .'

Vusi waited for her to explain. Distracted, she laid the form to one side and paged through the file, searching. 'I couldn't have . . .' she said.

'Ma'am, what's the problem?'

'I can't find the receipt.'

'What receipt?'

She put the file aside and began pulling documents out of a basket that was three storeys high. 'The form says the pound and traffic fines were paid . . .'

'Would it help if we knew whose signature that is?'

'These people, they sign like crabs.' She kept on looking through the decks of the in-basket, found nothing, picked up the single sheet, studied it and put a fingernail on the form. 'Look, the boxes are both clearly marked – traffic offence, fine paid, and pound release costs. But there is no receipt . . .'

'Is that the only way someone can get a vehicle out of the pound?'

'No, the other options are "Court Order" and "Successful Representation".' She showed him the relevant blocks. 'But then there would be documentation to confirm that also . . .'

'Ma'am, the signature . . .'

She stared at the scrawl at the bottom of the form. 'Looks like . . . I'm not sure, could be Jerry . . .'

'Who is Jerry?'

'Senior Inspector Jeremy Oerson. But I'm not sure . . . it looks like his.'

'Could we try to find out?'

'*You* can, I'm swamped.'

'Could I have a copy of the form?'

'That will be five rand.'

Vusi reached for his wallet.

'No, you can't pay me, you have to pay the cashier on the ground floor and bring me the receipt.'

Inspector Vusi Ndabeni looked at her, the simmering impatience slowly awoke. 'It might be easier to just ask Oerson,' he said.

'They're on the second floor.'

Fransman Dekker saw Griessel run around the corner of City Park Hospital and called out Benny's name, but the white detective had gone. Probably better that way, Dekker thought, because he wanted to start at the beginning again, go over the ground that Griessel had covered that morning. He wanted to talk to Alexa again; from whatever angle he studied the case, it had to be someone close to Adam Barnard. Inside knowledge.

And not the kind that Michèle Malherbe had been referring to. *Unfortunately dear Alexandra's situation is general knowledge. Especially in the industry.* He knew her kind, the 'see, hear, speak no evil' kind. Sat there full of dignity – see, I'm a decent Afrikaner woman, pillar of the community, grieving deeply – but she fucked Barnard while they were both married. He, Fransman Dekker, knew the type: dressed like a nun, prim, disapproving, they were the wildcats in bed. He'd had one last year, white woman from Welgemoed, neighbour of a car-hijacking victim. He had knocked on the door looking for eyewitnesses. She was scared to open the door, eyes open wide behind her glasses, blouse buttoned up to her chin. Just over forty, housewife, kids at school, husband at work. When he had finished asking his questions, there was something about her, a reluctance to let him go. 'Would you like tea?' She couldn't even look him in the eye. He knew then, because it wasn't the first time it had happened to him. So he said 'thank you', ready for it, curious about what was under the chaste clothing. So he directed the conversation: 'It must be lonely at home,' and before

the cups were emptied, she was talking about her marriage that
was faltering and he knew the right noises to make, to prepare her,
to open her up. Ten minutes later they grabbed each other, and
she was hungry, hungry, hungry; he had to hold her hands – she
was a scratcher. 'I'm married.' He had to prevent her marking his
back. Lovely body. A wildcat.

And the words she had shouted while he fucked her on that big
white sitting-room sofa.

He took out his SAPS identity card, held it up so the woman at
City Park reception could read it and said: 'I want to see Alexandra
Barnard.'

'Oh,' she said, 'just a moment,' and picked up the phone.

For a moment, when he reached his car, Griessel considered
running the six city blocks, but what if he had to race off from
there . . .? He jumped into the car and pulled away. His cell phone
rang. He swore, struggling to get it out of his pocket.

FRITZ. His son. His feelings about tonight descended on him
again, the date with Anna at seven o'clock made him instinctively
look at his watch. A quarter to three; another four hours. Should
he phone and say tonight was going to be difficult?

'Fritz?' he said wondering whether his son knew anything about
Anna's intentions.

'Dad, I'm done with school.'

'What do you mean?'

'Dad, we got this fat gig . . .'

'We?'

'The band, Dad. *Wet en Orde*, that's our name, but you don't spell
the "en", it's just that "and" sign, you know, that looks like an "s", Pa.'

'An ampersand.'

'Whatever. *Wet en Orde*, like your job, Law and Order, it was my
idea, Pa. Don't you think that's cool?'

'And now you're leaving school?'

'Yes. Dad, this gig, we're opening for Gian Groen and Zinkplaat
on a tour, Dad, they are talking about twenty-five thousand for a
month, that's more than six thousand per guy.'

'And?'

'I don't need school any more, Pa.'

The call came through at 14:48 to the office of the Provincial Commissioner: Western Cape. The little Xhosa answered, forewarned by his secretary. It was Dan Burton, the American Consul.

'Mr Burton?'

'Commissioner, could you please tell me what's going on?'

The Commissioner drew himself up behind his desk. 'Yes, sir, I can tell you what is going on. We have every available police officer in Cape Town looking for the girl. We have what we believe is the best detective in the Peninsula leading the task force, and they are doing everything in their power, at this very moment, to try and find the young lady in question.'

'I understand that, sir, but I've just had a call from her parents, and they are very, very worried. Apparently, she was safe, she called this Captain Ghree-zil, but he took his sweet time to get there, only to find her gone.'

'That's not the information I have, sir . . .'

'Do you know what's going on? Do you know who these people are? Why are they hunting her like an animal?'

'No, we don't know that. All I can tell you is that we are doing everything we can to find her.'

'Apparently, sir, that is not enough. I am really sorry, but I will have to call the Minister. Something has to be done.'

The Commissioner stood up from his desk. 'Well, sir, you are most welcome to call the Minister. But I am not sure what else we can do.' He put the phone down and walked out, down the passage to John Afrika's office. On the way he said one word in his mother tongue; the click of the word echoed off the walls.

She did not hear them arguing on the other side of the wooden door. She sat with her naked back against the pillar, dreadful pain in her foot, blood still running from the two stumps and the severed toes lying on the cement floor. Her head drooped and she wept, tears and mucus streaming from her nose, mouth and eyes.

She had nothing left.

Nothing.

They told Vusi Ndabeni that Senior Inspector Jeremy Oerson was out. He could reach him on his cell phone. They had the same sullen, 'it's-not-my-problem' attitude and thinly disguised superiority that he could not fathom. It had been like this the whole day – the ponytail at the club, the Russian woman, the man at the pound, the woman at Administration: nobody cared, he thought. In this city it was everyone for himself. He suppressed his escalating unease, the frustration. He must try to understand these people – that was the only way to deal with it. He took the number but before he could phone they said: 'Here he is now.'

Vusi turned, recognised the man; he was the one who had been at the church this morning – dreadful uniform, not quite so neat now, face shiny with perspiration.

'Inspector Oerson?' he asked.

'What?' Hurried, irritated.

'I am Inspector Vusumuzi Ndabeni of the SAPS. I am here about a vehicle that was booked out of the pound at twelve thirty-four, a Peugeot Boxer panel van, CA four-oh-nine, three-four-one . . .'

'So?' Oerson kept on walking towards his office. Vusi followed, amazed by his attitude.

'They say you signed the form.'

'Do you know how many forms I sign?' Oerson stood at a closed office door.

Vusi took a deep breath. 'Inspector, you were at the scene this morning, the American girl . . .'

'So?'

'The vehicle was used to abduct her friend. It is our only clue. She is in great danger.'

'I can't help you, I just signed the form,' said Oerson, shrugging and placing a hand on the door handle. 'Every day they come running in here, those girls down there, wanting someone to sign. I only check that everything is in order.'

Behind the door a telephone began to ring. 'My phone,' said Oerson and opened the door.

'Was everything in order with that vehicle?'

'I wouldn't have signed it if it wasn't.'

The phone continued to ring.

'But they say there is no receipt or anything.'

'Everything was correct when I signed it,' said Oerson, going into the office and closing the door.

Vusi stood there.

How could people be like that?

He pressed a hand on the closed door's frame. He must ignore them; he had a job to do. What he should do is investigate the whole process from the beginning. Where would you begin if you wanted to retrieve a vehicle from the pound? Who took your particulars; did anyone ask for an ID?

He sighed, ready to turn away, when he heard Oerson's voice say something inside that sounded familiar . . . *Cat and Moose* . . . *Wait, hold on* . . .

Vusi stood spellbound.

The door opened suddenly; Oerson's face accused him. 'What are you still doing here?'

'Nothing,' said Vusi and left. Halfway down the passage he looked back. Oerson was leaning on the door to monitor his progress. Vusi kept on walking. He heard the door shut. He stopped at the stairs.

The Cat & Moose? What did Oerson have to do with that?

Coincidence?

Oerson had been there this morning, very early. A Senior Inspector from Metro.

He was the one who had found the rucksack. He was the one who had walked up with it, full of bravado; he was the one who had rummaged in it before handing it over. In the club, Benny Griessel had talked to Fransman Dekker, he had told Dekker to call Oerson about the bag of stuff they had picked up.

Oerson had signed the form. His attitude, arrogance, the sweat on his brow.

Cat & Moose.

Snake in the grass.

Vusi wondered whether he ought to phone Griessel first. He decided against it. Benny had a thousand things to think of.

He turned and went back to Oerson's closed door.

41

They told Fransman Dekker he could not see Alexandra Barnard now. 'Doctor says she's on medication,' as if the burning bush itself had made the pronouncement. It irritated the living hell out of him. 'You are obsessed with Doctor, fuck Doctor' – that was what someone should tell them sometime, but he did not. Benny Griessel's words today had struck home.

They say you are ambitious, so let me tell you, I threw my fokken *career away because I didn't have control . . .*

It was the first time in his life that someone had spoken to him that way. It was the first time anyone had taken the trouble. He had been crapped out by the best, but that was different, usually no more than disapproval and criticism. With Griessel it was different.

'When will I be able to see her?' he asked the woman, under control now.

'Doctor says sometime after four, the medication should have worn off by then.' He checked his watch. Ten to three. He might just as well get something to eat; he was hollow inside, thirsty too. It would give him a chance to think – and what else could he do, he had let Josh and Melinda go home? 'I want to know if you leave the city,' he threatened and avoided the reproachful eyes. He had gone over to Natasha and said: 'Can you give me the contact details of all the staff?' and she gave him a look that said she knew why he wanted them.

He left the hospital feeling ravenous.

Vusi stood and listened at Oerson's door. He heard English spoken. *But if they don't know what we're looking for, let's wait. Sooner or later they'll move the stuff.* A long silence. *Are we absolutely sure?* A short, barking laugh, scornful. And then the words that stopped Vusumuzi Ndabeni's heart: *Let's make sure, and then kill the bitch. Before she fucks up everything. But wait for me, I want to see . . .*

Vusi's hand dropped to his service pistol, took hold of it and pulled it out. He lifted his left hand to open the door and saw how it was shaking, realised his heart was beating wildly and his breathing was shallow, almost panicky.

No, I'm fine. They have nothing, no proof. Oerson, inside, so smug.

It gave Vusi pause, he froze. Because all he had were suspicions and a conversation overheard. He caught a glimpse of the coming minutes: he would burst in, Oerson would deny everything, he could arrest him and he would refuse to cooperate, demand a lawyer, it could take hours and the girl would die. Oerson's word against his.

I'm coming, Oerson had said in there. *Wait for me.*

Vusi Ndabeni whispered a prayer. What should he do?

He shoved the pistol back in the holster, turned and ran down the passage. He would have to follow Oerson. While he was contacting Benny.

Oh God, he must not let this man slip away.

There was no parking in Long Street. A SAPS patrol vehicle was already double-parked. Griessel pulled two wheels onto the broader pavement in front of the 'Travel Centre – Safari Tour Specialists' building beside the Cat & Moose, leapt out and, seeing the metre maid a hundred metres down the street, knew he was going to get a ticket. He muttered a curse, locked the car and jogged to the entrance of the building with its garish pink and orange colours. He sidestepped a young couple at the door conversing in a foreign language. The plump girl was behind the desk, in animated discussion with two uniformed men, one of the Caledon Square patrols. He ran up to them. She did not recognise him. He had to say: 'Benny Griessel, SAPS, I was here this morning. I hear you recognised one of the men.'

Her face changed in the blink of an eye from insecure receptionist to indignant witness. 'I've just been telling your colleagues, they just waltzed in here and said they were taking the luggage, can you believe it?'

'And you recognised one of them?'

'Tried to bluff their way past me, telling me they were her friends, do they think I am stupid?'

'But you knew one of them?'

'I don't know him, but I've seen him. So I just said: "Why don't you guys go talk to the SWAT team in there?" and they, like, stopped dead, and the next thing . . .'

'A SWAT team?' Griessel asked.

'Yes, those buddies of yours guarding the luggage in there, and the next thing, they just waltzed right out again.'

'Miss, where have you seen this man?'

'Here . . .' She waved her hand. Griessel wasn't sure what it was meant to include.

'In the hostel?'

'Well, he might have been in here, but I've seen him around, you know, he's in the industry, I'm sure.'

'What industry?'

'The tourist industry,' as though it went without saying.

'Look,' said Griessel, desperate that this not turn out to be a disappointment. 'A girl's life depends on the fact that we have to identify this guy, that you remember where you've seen him, so please . . .'

'Really?' The responsibility came to rest on her, the indignation evaporated and enthusiasm took its place. 'Well, OK, look . . . I, I know I've seen him at the café . . .'

'What café?'

'The Long Street Café.'

'Does he work there?'

'No, he was, like, a customer . . .' Deeply thoughtful, eyes squinting, the picture of concentration.

Griessel tried another tack. 'OK, can you describe him?'

'He's black. Tall. Handsome guy, you know, twenty-something . . .' Then her face brightened. 'He's, like, skinny, you know, that look . . . like all the guides, that's most likely where I saw him, in the café with the others . . .'

But Benny Griessel wasn't listening to her because the elusive, slippery thing in his mind was rushing at him, he had to shut her up, he said: 'Wait, wait . . .'

'What?' she said, but he didn't hear her, his hand combed through his hair, and lingered on his neck. He scratched behind his ear, head bent, thoughts jumbled, he must get them in order. This morning . . . Griessel looked to the right where they had talked to Oliver Sands this morning, that's what his head had been trying to tell him all fucking afternoon, it was that conversation. He tried to recall it, groping in the dark. Ollie had talked about the club, the girls in the club . . .

No. Nothing. Wrong track.

He watched the girl behind the reception desk, looking disgruntled after being silenced. She'd said he's, *like, skinny, you know, that look . . . like all the guides,* that was the trigger. The guides. What had Sands said about that? Vusi had asked the questions this morning. He'd wanted to know who was with Sands and the girls at the club. Sands said a whole bunch. A group. And somewhere along the way he had said the guides were there too.

He whispered to himself. '*Jissis.*' Because the thing was almost within his grasp, if he could only see it. He was unaware that he made a gesture of frustration, he was unaware of the two uniforms and the girl staring at him and looking vaguely concerned.

Griessel's phone began to ring. He ignored it. Not now. He tried to dredge up the words of that morning's conversation from his memory. He stood at the desk, put his palms flat on it and dipped his head. The girl stepped back half a pace.

Vusi Ndabeni, cell phone to his ear, listened to Griessel's number ringing while he watched Jeremy Oerson hurry out of the Metro building and go to his car.

'Answer me, Benny,' he said and started to walk quickly towards his own car. Oerson climbed into a Nissan Sentra with the city police badge on the door.

The phone continued to ring.

'Please, Benny,' but the call diverted to Griessel's voice mail just as Vusi got his car unlocked and jumped in.

'Are you all right?' the Cat & Moose girl asked Griessel.

One of the uniforms realised what was going on and hushed her with a finger to his lips.

Benny stood still. He, Vusi and Oliver Sands. At the table. Sands telling them they came on the tour through Africa. They talked about last night. The club. The girls. The drink. Who was with them, Vusi had asked. A whole bunch. Do you know the names? Vusi had his notebook ready and Sands said . . .

The answer came like a hammer blow. It made Griessel's body shudder. 'Fuck,' he said in triumph, loudly, startling the others. Oliver Sands had given them the names, the funny names, the funny pronunciation, that was the spectre that had been running through his head the whole goddamn afternoon, one name, he heard it now in Ollie's voice: Jason Dicklurk. *Dicklurk*. This morning Griessel had thought to himself, what a fucking funny name. Dick Lurk. But the redhead's pronunciation, that had been the problem. *Jissis*, he should have made the connection. Rachel's father calling him *Ghree-zil*, only the Afrikaners could say their own names. And one Zulu. Mbali Kaleni. She had phoned him while he was sitting in that office with the Commissioner. *This is Inspector Mbali Kaleni of the South African Police Service, Benny.* Zulu accent, but her pronunciation was flawless. *We traced a Land Rover Defender that fits the number. It belongs to a man in Parklands, a Mr J. M. de Klerk.*

Dicklurk was de Klerk. J. M. de Klerk. Jason de Klerk. One of the guides.

'The tour company,' he said to the girl. 'Which tour company were the girls with?'

'Tour company?' she asked, intimidated by Griessel's fervour.

'You know, the people who took them through Africa.'

'Oh.' For a second there was a frown, then her face brightened: 'African Overland Adventures. That's where he works, the black guy, that's where I've seen him, they do all their Cape accommodation bookings with us, I sometimes go to see their—'

'Where are they?'

'Just one block down. My God, that's where—'

'Show me,' said Griessel and ran to the door. She came after him, stopped on the pavement, pointed to the right, across the street. 'On the corner.'

'Come, *kêrels*,' said Benny Griessel to the uniforms as another insight lit up his head. A.O.A. *African Overland Adventures*. On the spur of the moment he kissed the plump girl on the cheek before he ran off.

She watched him speechlessly.

42

Fransman Dekker took a bite of the toasted chicken mayonnaise sandwich in his left hand while he scribbled in his notebook with his right.

Alexa Barnard. That attitude this morning.

Inside knowledge.

A woman hiding in her house all day long. Alone. Lonely. Drinking. Lots of time to think about her husband, her life, her lot. A husband who was chronically unfaithful, a man who couldn't keep his hands off anything in a skirt. A man making big bucks while his wife rotted away at home.

Don't expect me to believe that she had never wondered what life would be like without the bastard, Fransman thought. Consider the national sport: hire a coloured to do your shooting. Or the stabbing. Three or four cases in the past year alone. It was a disease, a fucking epidemic.

Come on, Sylvia, come and have a chat with the madam, tell me where I can find someone to knock the master off.

Or: Sylvia, I see you're carrying off the silverware. So before I call the police, let's have a little talk.

Or: the master has a fat life insurance policy, my dear. What sort of share are we looking at if you find us a gunman?

Inside knowledge. Two women with all the inside knowledge in the world.

Only one little problem with that. *You don't hire people to make it look as though you did it*, in the exalted words of Captain Benny Griessel. But, oh Captain, my Captain, what if she read the papers and saw what mistakes those other girls made. And she thought: I won't fall into the same traps, I'm too clever, I'm a former pop star,

I'm not thick. I'll make it look like a frame-up, Captain. Suspicion one step removed. The music business is a war zone, they'll look at them before they look at me. And when they do look at me, hey, I'm an alky, how could I drag this man's big body up the stairs?

What do you say to that, Captain?

In his dash to African Overland Adventures, weaving through pedestrians on the pavement, Griessel thought that was what Mbali Kaleni must have been trying to write.

Jason.

How had she known? What made her go back to Upper Orange Street? What did she see that everyone else missed?

Just before he burst through the doors, his phone started ringing again. He wasn't going to answer it. He was going to get Jason de Klerk and then find Rachel Anderson.

She had to live.

John Afrika sat with the receiver in his hand listening to Griessel's phone ringing.

Opposite him stood the Provincial Commissioner.

'If we are making a mistake . . .'

'Benny is clean,' Afrika said.

'John, we're talking about my career.'

'This is Benny, leave a message,' over the phone. Afrika sighed and replaced the receiver. 'He's not answering.'

'They are going to clean up when Zuma gets in. They will use any excuse. You know how it is. Zulus in, Xhosas out.'

'Commissioner, I understand. But what am I supposed to do?'

'Is there no one else?'

John Afrika shook his head from side to side. 'Even if there were, it's too late now.'

He looked at the phone. 'Benny is clean.' He didn't sound so sure of himself any more.

Jeremy Oerson turned left into Ebenezer. Vusi gave him a gap, then pulled away himself, feeling tense: don't let the man get away.

The Metro Nissan was on the way to the Waterfront under the Western Boulevard Freeway. Vusi drove cautiously, not daring to get too close, or too far. He had to see where he turned off.

Oerson drove into the Harbour Road traffic circle and then out to the right.

He was heading for the N1.

Vusi relaxed fractionally. That would make it easier.

Griessel banged open the double glass doors with the two Constables behind him. The lobby of African Overland Adventures was spacious – a long counter with two young women and a man behind it, a flat-screen TV against the wall, a few coffee tables and easy chairs. Nine young people standing or sitting, some drinking coffee. Everyone looked up, startled. Griessel pulled out his service pistol before he reached the desk. His cell phone was still ringing in his pocket.

'SAPS. *Staan net stil dan het ons nie moeilikheid nie.*'

'What did he say?' a voice asked from an easy chair.

He turned and saw the Constables had their pistols in their hands too. He nodded in approval. 'I said, just keep still and everything will be fine. Nobody's leaving and nobody is going to make a phone call.'

Everyone was quiet. Griessel's phone as well. The sound of the TV drew his attention. The big screen displayed images of an African adventure. On the walls were big posters with scenes of the continent, laughing young people with mountains, animals and lakes in the background. On the long desk were containers of brochures.

'Please turn off the TV.'

'Can we see some ID?' a girl asked from behind the desk, a sultry, stubborn beauty. He pulled out his identity card. Everyone watched TV nowadays, he thought, maybe he should start wearing it around his bloody neck like Kaleni.

The stubborn one inspected it. 'Is that for real?'

'What is your name?'

'Melissa.' It was a challenge.

'Please switch off that television, and then you call the police. Dial one zero triple one, and tell them Captain Benny Griessel needs back-up at African Overland Adventures. Tell them to call the Sergeant at Caledon Square.'

'I'll have to move,' said Melissa. 'The remote is under here . . .'

'Then move,' said Griessel. She stretched and took out the remote control and aimed it at the TV. Griessel saw she had a tattoo of barbed wire on her upper arm. The room went quiet. 'Now call the police,' he said.

'It's OK. I believe you.'

'Call them.'

She walked reluctantly to the telephone and picked it up.

'Which one of you is Jason de Klerk?'

It was a while before the other desk girl answered. 'Jason isn't here.'

'They're not answering,' said Melissa.

'They will. Where is Jason de Klerk?'

'We don't know.'

'All the men, I want you to show us your IDs.' To the Constables he said: 'Check them.'

'Jason hasn't been in since yesterday,' said Melissa.

'So where can he be?'

'Your emergency number sucks. They're still not answering,' she said irritably.

Griessel exploded. He walked up to the counter and stretched over it, his face as close to her as he could reach. 'Now you listen to me, you little shit: Jason and his friends cut the throat of one of your clients last night, and they are going to kill again if I don't stop them. Right now, I'm thinking you don't know anything about it, but that can change very quickly, and you don't want that, take my word for it. So I am going to ask you one more time: where can I find him? And if you get clever with me again, you are going to be very fucking sorry, do you hear me loud and clear?'

She swallowed audibly. 'Yes,' she said. 'He might be at home. He might be at the offices or the warehouse, they are between trips, I just don't know.'

'The offices?'

'Second floor. You use the entrance next door.'

'And the warehouse?'

'Stanley Road in Observatory,' then the emergency number finally answered and she said: 'I've got an urgent message from a ...What was your name again?'

All three came back through the door. Rachel did not even look up.

'Hold her legs,' said Jason de Klerk and picked up the pruning shears from the floor where he had left them. The other two squatted down beside her and took hold of her legs.

'Rachel,' said de Klerk, but she did not respond. 'Rachel!'

'She's fucked, Jay,' one of the others said.

'We have to make sure.' He knelt at her foot. 'Rachel, listen to me. We have to make sure you're telling the truth about the video, OK? This is very important, it really is a matter of life or death, do you understand?'

No reaction.

He put the blade around the base of the middle toe of her right foot. 'So tell me again, where is it?'

'She's not even hearing you.'

'Please,' she said so they could barely hear. 'It's in the big bag.'

He cut the toe off. Her body jerked. 'Jesus,' said one of the men holding her legs.

'Are you sure?' Jason's voice was still calm. 'Are you very sure?'

'Yes, yes, yes, yes, yes, yes ...' loud and hysterical, her body convulsing.

He held another toe. 'Exactly where is the bag?'

A primeval sound erupted from her.

'For fuck's sake, Jay, what more do you need?' the other young man asked, his face misshapen with abhorrence.

Jason, furious, hit him with the back of his hand. 'Do you know what's at stake here, arsehole? You want to spend the rest of your life in prison?'

Vusi Ndabeni followed Jeremy Oerson as he took the right-hand lane on the N1's Eastern Boulevard and then the off-ramp to the N2. He kept his distance, just over four hundred metres, with seven cars between them. He picked up his cell phone and called Benny Griessel again.

The 'offices' of African Overland Adventures on the second floor were behind a steel security door. Griessel pressed the intercom button. A woman's voice said: 'Yes?' He said: 'Police. Open up.'

The locks clicked and the door opened. He immediately looked to see if there was another exit. But he saw none, only three women, desks, computers, filing cabinets. He kept his ID card handy. 'Come with me, please, downstairs.'

'Why?' they were worried about the pistol in his hand.

'I'm looking for a Jason de Klerk?'

'He's not here.'

'I know. Come.' He gestured with his pistol. They walked meekly ahead of him, to the stairs.

His cell phone rang. Who the hell wanted him so badly? He pulled it out. *VUSI.*

'Vusi, this is a bad time.'

'Benny, I'm sorry, but things happened, I think I'm following someone who is on his way to Rachel.'

Griessel froze. There was something about Vusi's rapid-fire voice, the flood of words, desperation. '*Jissis.*'

'Benny, you'll never believe it. Jeremy Oerson. I overheard him. He's involved, how, I don't know.'

Jeremy Oerson? What the fuck?

'Where are you?'

'On the N-two, just before Groote Schuur. He's just taken the off-ramp to Main Road.' Observatory. The warehouse. 'Vusi, I think he's going to Stanley Street, there's a warehouse, African Overland Adventures. Stay with him, Vusi, I'm on my way,' and Griessel's feet clattered down the stairs, making the three middle-aged women look back, fearful.

'Benny!' said Vusi. Afraid he would ring off.

'I'm here.'

'They're going to kill her, Benny. As soon as Oerson gets there.'

15:12–16:14

43

Griessel told the Constables to let no one out of the adventure shop; they didn't know who was involved. Once reinforcements arrived, they were to seal off the offices upstairs, no records were to leave the place, no calls were to be made, to let the phone ring, nobody was to answer it. Anyone who came in must stay.

They nodded keenly.

Out through the door, into the busy normality of Long Street. He pushed the pistol back into his holster, ran fifty metres and stopped suddenly. The traffic. In the police sedan with no siren or lights. He turned back, sidestepping people on the pavement, and banged open the glass doors again. Every eye in the place was on him. Do you have a patrol vehicle with a functioning siren?

Yes, Captain. The Constable rummaged in his trouser pocket, took out his keys and flung them in an arc to Griessel. He missed them. Melissa made a scornful noise but he ignored her, picked up the keys, jerked open the doors and ran.

There was only one vehicle between Vusi Ndabeni and Jeremy Oerson when they stopped at the traffic lights where Browning joined Main Road.

Vusi pulled the sun visor down and sat as high in his seat as he could to hide his face. Oerson's indicator light was on, ready to turn right.

Where was Stanley Street?

African Overland Adventures? And the Metro police? He couldn't see any connection. The light changed to green. Vusi gave him a lead, a hundred metres, then he pulled away intending to turn right as well, but a car approached from the front and he had to wait.

When he did turn into Main Road he couldn't see Oerson's Sentra.

Impossible.

Vusi accelerated, tense again. Where could he have gone? He drove past Polo Road leading off to the left, looked down it and saw nothing. He looked right, there were no options, only the Muslim Graveyard and the hospital. He passed the Scott Road turn-off on the left. He saw the Sentra, in the distance, a long way down Scott.

Vusi braked – too late – he was past the turn. He slammed the car into reverse and looked back. Traffic was coming down Main Road. He had no choice. He reversed quickly. Two minibus taxis rocketed down on him, one leaning hard and continuously on his hooter. It swerved in behind the other and barely missed Vusi. But he had reversed far enough and turned left down Scott, just in time to see Oerson turn right half a kilometre away.

Was it really him?

De Waal Drive would be the quickest. Griessel flipped the switches for the siren and blue lights and pulled away with screeching tyres. The traffic opened up in front of him, past St Martini, the Lutheran Church where everything had begun that morning. It felt like a week ago, what a fucking day. The light was red at the Buitensingel crossing, he drove only marginally slower, the motorists saw him coming. Then he turned left, fighting with the steering wheel, into Upper Orange, more traffic.

The Upper Orange crossroad was also red. It took precious seconds to get across carefully and then he put his foot down, over the bridge at the Gardens Centre. The bends of De Waal lay ahead, he picked up his cell phone from the seat, he must call Vusi, he must get reinforcements. The task force, SWAT, the plump girl had called them. No, that would take too long, even if they mobilised within the theoretical fifteen minutes, it would be too late.

He and Vusi would find out what was going on first.

Vusi answered on the second ring. 'Benny.'

'Where are you?'

His black colleague said something inaudible.

'I can't hear you.'

'Stanley Street, Benny, I don't want to talk too loud. I can see the warehouse. Their trucks are parked there. African Overland Adventures.'

'Tell me how to get there, Vusi, I haven't got a map.'

'It's easy, Benny. Take the Groote Schuur off-ramp, right into Main . . .'

'I'm coming down De Waal, Vusi, that's not going to help me.'

Vusi said something in Xhosa, a cry for help, then he asked: 'Will you find Main Road in Observatory?'

'Yes.'

'Then turn down Scott . . . eastwards. Then all the way down over Lower Main, then first right and you will see them.'

'I'm coming.'

'Oerson has gone in, Benny, hurry.'

Jeremy Oerson pushed the big sliding door only wide enough for him to enter. He took off his dark glasses and put them in his breast pocket and closed the door behind him.

The big warehouse was quiet: tents, sleeping bags, water cans, tools, petrol drums, sand shovels, car jacks all in tidy piles. On one side was a new white Land Rover Defender.

'Halloo,' he said.

To the left and right two men stood up from behind piles of goods, each with a Stechkin APS pistol aimed at him.

'Christ,' he said and lifted his hands high. 'It's me.'

They slowly lowered the weapons. Jason de Klerk came out from behind the Land Rover. 'I tried to call you, Jeremy.'

'I'm a senior fucking police officer, I can't answer my cell when I'm driving.'

'You're a fucking traffic cop.'

He ignored the remark. 'Where is she?'

'Mr B wants to know: can you get to the luggage?'

Oerson walked deeper into the warehouse and looked about. Behind a pile of tents sat another one, sulky, with blood on his upper lip. 'Not now,' he said. 'So what happened to him? Did she get rough?'

'I didn't mean now, Jerry,' said Jason irritably. 'But you can get it, right?'

'Don't worry, as long as they don't know what they're looking for, we're fine. They'll take it to an evidence room, and then it's easy.'

'How easy?'

'I'll grease a few palms, and get some dumb fuck to go in and take it. Little video tape, slip it in your pocket, easy-peasy. Tomorrow, next week, this will be old news, girl's gone, pressure's off. Relax. Where is she?'

'You're absolutely sure?'

'Of course I'm fucking sure. For a thousand bucks they'll be standing in line to do it.'

'OK,' said Jason and took out his cell phone.

'She's alive, isn't she?' Oerson asked. 'Because you guys owe me a favour.'

When the Roodebloem turn-off flashed past, Griessel realised he should have taken it. He cut through to the Eastern Boulevard and the same route as Vusi, but it was too fucking late. The only alternative was Liesbeeck Park, then down Station Road, but it was going to take a minute or two, three, longer.

The van's wheels squealed around the last turn before De Waal joined Hospital corner. Traffic was dense, there was no time to think. What was Jeremy Oerson's connection with the whole affair? He nearly drove into a pharmacy delivery motorcycle and had to swerve out in front of another car. Horns blared, couldn't the idiots hear the siren? Then he was around the bend on the N2 Settlers road and swung over into the left-hand lane. They gave way now and he stomped on the accelerator. Jeremy Oerson? Metro? African Adventures?

What the fuck?

He entered the Liesbeeck off-ramp too fast, the turn much sharper than he remembered, and the red traffic light was totally unexpected. Cars were crossing the road in front of him. Too late to brake. The van began to skid, he was going to hit someone. Then he was through between two cars, wrenching the wheel to get it under control, accelerated again. Out the other side.

He only turned off the siren when he turned onto Lower Main.

Benny was taking too long.

Vusi's car was parked halfway between Scott and Stanley on the pavement. He had his service pistol on his lap, ready cocked. He could see the warehouse through the windscreen – a long building, brick walls, galvanised zinc roof. Large white-painted sliding doors behind four trucks and four trailers, each bearing the legend African Overland Adventures. Big vehicles, the seating deck high with luggage space below. She was in there. Where was Benny? Perhaps he should go inside. But how many were there? Oerson and the person Oerson had spoken to over the phone. How many more?

He sat there, breathing fast, his heart thumping in his chest.

He pulled the car keys out of the ignition, got out, walked around, opened the boot and looked up. They wouldn't be able to see him. There were no windows on this side anyway. He put his pistol down in the boot, took off his jacket and picked up the Kevlar bulletproof vest. He put it on and picked up his pistol. He checked his watch. 15:22. Late.

He would have to do something.

He came to a decision; the girl's life was the main priority. He pulled back the pistol's slide and gently closed the boot.

He was going in.

Then he heard the squeal of rubber on tar behind him and looked back. A SAPS patrol van came around the corner, drove straight towards him and stopped in a cloud of dust on the pavement. A figure jumped out with unkempt hair and gun in his hand.

Benny Griessel had arrived.

★   ★   ★

'Hey!' said Jeremy Oerson, but she didn't look up. She just lay slumped against the pole, stark naked, he could see everything, the tits, the bush between her legs, the bleeding right foot and three toes lying in the dust like fat insect grubs.

He stood with his feet planted wide in black boots, the pistol in both hands aimed at her head.

'Get her to look at me,' he said to one of them.

'Just fucking get it over with.'

'No. I want to see her face. Hey, Yankee, look at me.'

Slowly she lifted her head. Hair hung over her forehead in strings. He saw the eye swollen shut, black and purple, dried blood on her temple. 'You guys really fucked her up,' he said.

Her head was raised, but the eyes were still somewhere else.

'Do it, Jerry.'

'Look at me,' he said to her, saw the eyes rise to meet his. He pressed the safety off with his thumb.

44

'Take the back, Vusi, there must be a door. I'll give you time,' said Griessel as he ran. He saw the black detective swerve off towards the corner of the building.

He reached the big white sliding door and pressed his back against the wall, service pistol in both hands in front of him. His breath was racing. He had to get it under control, he counted, thousand-and-one, thousand-and-two, thousand-and-three, wanting to give Vusi twenty seconds. He prayed. Dear Father, let her be alive.

Thousand-and-seven. When had he prayed last? When Carla was in mortal danger, his prayer had only been partially answered. He would take that, anything, just so that he could please phone Bill Anderson and say: 'She's alive.' Thousand-and-twelve. He heard a shot, jumped, grabbed the door with his left hand, dragged it open, ducked and ran in. He saw a young man, tall and lean, directly in front of him with a silencer aimed at his heart. He knew in that instant that it was all over, his own pistol was degrees too far to the right.

The shot cracked and blew Benny Griessel off his feet. His back slammed into the door and pain exploded in his chest. He was fleetingly aware of the strangeness, of feeling first the bullet and then hearing the shot. He fell to the ground.

That unease he had had all day, that expectation of evil, here it was.

Oerson waited for her eyes. He wanted his to be the last face she would see. He wanted to know what mortal fear looked like, he wanted to see the light of life fade out of her. But above all he wanted to know how it felt, the power, they said the power was indescribable. He had wondered for so long what it felt like to take a life.

She looked into his eyes. He saw no fear. He wondered if they had drugged her. She looked absent.

Then he heard the shot. He looked around, at the door.

Another shot.

'Shit,' he said.

Vusi sprinted around the first corner, along the short side of the warehouse, then the next corner. High windows, two metres off the ground. A single steel door with a big padlock on it. Locked. He did not hesitate. He steadied against the wall, aimed and shot the padlock, one shot. The nine-mm projectile blew it to bits. He tugged the door open. It was gloomy inside, a smallish room, a kitchen, with dirty glasses and coffee mugs in the sink and another closed door.

He heard a shot, not loud, a small calibre, perhaps. Benny! He ran to the inner door and opened it. It was a large open space, equipment in piles. A beam of light shone from the front through the big sliding door. Someone was lying there dead still. Oh God, it was Benny. Movement, a young white man to the left of Vusi, a long weapon in his hand. 'Don't move!' No good, the young man swung around. Vusi fired. The man fell in slow motion. Vusi had never shot anyone before, *uSimakade*, what was this city doing to him? A bullet smacked into the wall beside Vusi. It came from the right. He dived behind drums and rolled to the right, stood up, pulled the trigger, once, twice, three times. The man staggered and fell on a stack of plastic cans. He had had no choice – it was survival. He had killed a man, he realised. He stood up slowly, eyes on the still figure, watching the blood run out of the body and over the white plastic of the cans in long trails. Life blood.

A shadow moved on his right, he came back to reality, too late, the pistol pressed against his head. 'Black cunt,' the voice said.

★　　　★　　　★

Awful pain in his chest, Griessel could not move, could not breathe. He was lying on the cement floor. Death would come, it was all over, he should have waited for the task force. At the periphery there was movement, on the other side, he tried to turn his head. Vusi. A thundering shot, someone fell, further to the right. Everything in slow motion, unreal, vague, detached. This was the beginning, the tumbling away from life, he would hear the scream of fear, the terrifying scream when you fell into the deep dark abyss. Why wasn't he afraid? Why this . . . peace, just an intense longing for his children, his wife, Anna. Now he knew he wanted her, wanted her back, now, too late. Movement. He could see. Not dead yet. Vusi fired again, three times. He watched his colleague. His breath came more easily now. Why? Benny's hand moved slowly to his chest and touched the gaping wound. Dry. No blood. He looked, and felt. A hole in his breast pocket. No blood. Why the pain? He felt the hard object, gripped it.

The Leatherman. The bullet had struck the Leatherman. Relief burned through him, a shooting consciousness. He had made an utter fool of himself, thinking he was going to die. He heard a voice. 'Black cunt.' He looked up. The one who had shot him stood there, with a long-muzzled gun to Vusi's head.

Griessel reached for his pistol on the floor, grasped it, raised it, no time to aim. Pulled the trigger, saw the man's arm jerk, saw Vusi fall, fired again, missed. The man just stood there. His silenced pistol had disappeared. Benny tried to stand, his whole ribcage on fire, pain burning white, Leatherman or not. He crawled first, got to his feet and stumbled closer.

Vusi moved.

Griessel aimed his service pistol at the man. 'Don't move,' he said. He saw the man was holding his arm. The elbow was shattered, lots of blood, a mess of tendons and fragmented bone.

Vusi stood up. 'Benny . . .' His voice was faint, Griessel's ears were deafened by the shots.

'I've got him, Vusi.'

'I thought you were dead.'

'So did I,' said Griessel, almost embarrassed. He jerked the man by the collar. 'Lie down,' he said. The man sank slowly to his knees.

'Where is Rachel?'

The man looked around slowly, at the closed door behind him. 'There.'

'Is she alone?'

'No.'

'Is Jason in there, Jason de Klerk?'

No response. Griessel prodded him again with the pistol. 'Where is Jason?'

A moment of silence. 'I'm Jason.'

Rage swept over Griessel, frustration, relief. He grabbed de Klerk by the hair. 'You fucking rubbish,' he said, and felt a powerful desire to kill him, shoot him in the throat, for Erin Russel, for everything, his finger tightened around the trigger.

'Benny!'

There was a noise behind them, a door closing. Both detectives spun around and aimed.

'Don't shoot!' another young man stood there, hands in the air, looking scared, blood on his upper lip.

'On the floor,' said Vusi.

'Please,' he said and lay down immediately.

'Where is Rachel?' Benny asked.

'She's in there,' said the other one.

They looked at the door. 'Vusi, if he moves,' Griessel said, and strode towards the door.

'Look out,' said the man. 'Oerson is with her.'

She was aware of the gun pointed at her, of the man in his magnificent uniform towering above her. He spoke her name. Did he know her? She raised her eyes, trying to focus, why was the other one still standing here, the young one, one of those who had held her legs?

A shot cracked. Her eyes shut in reflex, she expected to feel it, coming from the weapon pointed at her.

But her eyes opened as the man in uniform swore. He had

turned away from her and pointed his pistol at the door. The other man ducked and crept towards the wall.

Someone shot again in there, a softer bang.

'What the fuck?' the uniformed man whispered.

Another shot, deafening. He moved quickly to beside the door, and again it boomed in there, three times.

Then it struck her: the policeman. Griessel. He had found her. She wanted to sit up. She moved her legs and the pain in her foot was incredible, but she didn't care, she drew her heels back, found a grip. Another shot, one more. He was shooting them, Benny Griessel, he must kill them all. She braced herself against the cold pillar. If only she could stand up. The uniform and the young man were frozen, petrified. Another two shots. Silence.

'I'm going out,' said the young man and opened the door, and shut it immediately.

'Shit,' said the uniform.

Voices inside, indecipherable words. Then only the uniformed man's fast and shallow breathing.

'He's going to kill you,' she said to him, with hatred in her voice.

He moved suddenly, came to her, a boot left and right of her knees and pushed the gun into her cheek. 'Shut the fuck up,' he hissed. 'You're going with me.' Then he looked around at the door, wild-eyed.

She kicked him. She brought up her knee, her sore right foot's knee, and struck him between the legs with everything she had left. 'Now!' she shrieked. Her voice was a desperate command. The uniform shouted something and fell onto her. A booming noise as the door was kicked in, and then a single shot and the man fell away from her. She saw him standing in the doorway, a figure with a pistol in his hand, a hole in his shirt, hair needing a cut and strange Slavic eyes.

'Benny Griessel,' she said, with perfect pronunciation.

He lowered the weapon, moved towards her with deep compassion in his eyes. He grabbed her clothes off the floor and hastily covered her, put his arms around her and held her tight.

'Yes,' he said. 'I have found you.'

45

Just after four, the nurse came out of the hospital room and said
to Fransman Dekker: 'Fifteen minutes.' She held the door open so
he could enter.

Alexa Barnard was sitting up against the cushions. He saw the
bandage on her forearm, then the look of dawning disappointment.

'I was expecting the other detective,' she said slowly, words not
well formed. The medication had not wholly worn off.

'Afternoon, ma'am,' he said neutrally, because he could use her
drowsiness; he must avoid conflict and win her trust. He dragged
a blue chair closer, nearly right up to the bed. He sat down with
his elbows on the thin white bedspread. She stared at him with
vague interest. She looked better than she had this morning – her
hair was brushed and tied back in the nape of her neck, so that her
unobscured face appeared stronger, the faded beauty like a fossil
in a weathered rock bank.

'Captain Griessel is not on the case any more,' he said.

She nodded slowly.

'I understand better now,' he said quietly and sympathetically.

She lifted an eyebrow.

'He was . . . not an easy man.'

She searched his face until she was convinced of his sincerity.
Then she looked past him. He saw the moisture collect gradually
in her eyes, her lower lip's involuntary tremble. With her healthy
right arm she wiped the back of her hand over her cheek in slow
motion.

Better than he'd hoped. 'You loved him very much.'

She looked somewhere beyond Dekker, nodded slightly, and
wiped her cheek again.

'He hurt you so much. All those years. He kept on hurting you over and over.'

'Yes.' Barely a whisper. He wanted *her* to talk. He waited. She said nothing. The sound of a helicopter came through the closed curtains in front of the window, the wap-wap increasingly loud. He waited till it subsided.

'You blamed yourself. You thought it was your fault.'

Her gaze shifted to him. Still silent.

'But it wasn't. There are men like that,' he said. 'It's a disease. An addiction.' She nodded, agreeing, as though she wanted to hear more.

'It's a drug for the soul. I think they have an emptiness inside here, a hole that is never filled, it might help for a little while, then in a day or two it starts all over again. I think there's a reason, I think they don't like themselves, it's a way of . . .' His command of formal language left him stranded.

'Gaining acceptance,' she said. He waited, gave her time. But she gazed steadily at him, expectantly, pleading almost.

'Yes. Acceptance. Maybe more than that. There's something broken in here, they want to make it whole. A hurt that has come a long way, that never completely goes away, it just comes back every time, worse, but the medicine helps less and less, it's a . . .' His wave of the hand sought a word, deliberately now.

'A vicious circle.'

'Yes . . .'

She would not fill the silence that he had created. At first he wavered, then he said: 'He loved you, in his way, I think he loved you a lot, I think the problem was that he didn't want to do it, but every time he did he thought less of himself, because he knew he was hurting you, he knew he was doing damage. Then that became the reason he did it again, like an animal gnawing at itself. That can't stop. If a woman showed she wanted him, it meant he wasn't so bad, then he didn't think any more, he just felt, it was like a fever coming over him, you can't stop it. You want to, but you can't, however much you love your wife . . .' He stopped suddenly, aware of the fundamental shift, and sat back slowly in his chair.

He watched her, wondering if she had caught on. He saw that she was somewhere else. Heard her say: 'I asked him to get help.'

He hoped. She looked at the little table beside her bed. Above the drawer was a slit where a tissue dangled. She pulled it out, wiped her eyes one by one and crumpled the paper in her right hand. 'I think there was a time when I tried to understand, when I thought I could see a little boy in him, a rejected, lonely boy. I don't know, he would never talk about it, I could never work out where it came from. But where does anything come from? Where does my alcoholism come from? My fear, my insecurity. My inferiority? I have looked for it in my childhood, that's the easy way out. Your father and mother's fault. They made mistakes, they weren't perfect, but that's not enough . . . excuse. The problem is, it comes from inside me. It's part of my atoms, the way they vibrate, their frequency, their pitch, the key they sing in . . .'

He had an idea where she was headed.

'Nobody can help . . .' he encouraged her.

'Just yourself.'

'He couldn't change.'

She shook her head. No, Adam Barnard couldn't change. He wanted to prompt her: 'So you did something about it,' but he gave her the chance to say it herself.

She slowly sank back against the cushion, as though she were very tired.

'I don't know . . .' A deep sigh.

'What?' he asked, a whispered invitation.

'Do we have the right? To change people? So that they suit us? So that they can protect us from ourselves? Aren't we shifting the responsibility? My weakness against his. If I were stronger . . . Or he was. Our tragedy lay in the combination, each was the other's catalyst. We were . . . an unfortunate chemical reaction . . .'

His fifteen minutes expired. 'And something had to give,' he said. 'Someone had to do something.'

'No. It was too late to do anything. Our habits with each other were too set, the patterns had become part of us, we couldn't live any other way any more. Past a certain point there is nothing you can do.'

'Nothing?'

She shook her head again.

'There is always something you can do.'

'Such as what?'

'If the pain is bad enough, and the humiliation.' He needed more than this. He took a chance, gave her something to work with: 'When he starts cursing and threatening you. When he assaults you . . .'

She turned her head slowly towards him. At first expressionless, so that he couldn't tell if it was going to work or not. Then the frown began, initially as though she was puzzled, but with increasing comprehension and a certain restrained regret. Eventually she looked down at the tissue in her hand. 'I don't blame you.'

'What do you mean?' but he knew he had failed.

'You're just doing your job.'

He leaned forward, desperate, trying another tack. 'We know enough, Mrs Barnard,' he said still with empathy. 'It was someone with inside knowledge. Someone who knew where he kept his pistol. Someone who knew about your . . . condition. Someone with enough motive. You qualify. You know that.'

She nodded thoughtfully.

'Who helped you?'

'It was Willie Mouton.'

'Willie Mouton?' He couldn't keep the astonishment out of his voice, not sure what she meant, though a light seemed to have gone on for her.

'That's why I asked the other detective . . . Griessel to come.'

'Oh?'

'I must have been thinking like you. About the pistol. Only four of us knew where it was, and only Adam had the key.'

'What key?'

'To the gun safe in the top of his wardrobe. But Willie installed that. Four, five years ago. He's good at that sort of thing, he was always practical. In the old days he did stage work for the bands. Adam couldn't do anything with his hands, but he didn't want to bring outside people in, he didn't want anyone to know about the gun, he was afraid it would be stolen.

This morning . . . Willie was here, he and the lawyer, it was a strange conversation, I only realised once they left . . .' She stopped suddenly, having second thoughts, the hand with the tissue halfway between bed and face.

When she stopped he couldn't stand the suspense. 'What did you realise?'

'Willie always wanted more. A bigger share, more money. Even though Adam was very good to him.'

'Ma'am, what are you trying to tell me?'

'Willie came and stood here at my bed. All he wanted to know was what I could remember. I last saw Willie more than a year ago. And then here he was this morning, as though he actually cared. He made all the right noises, he wanted to know how I was, he said he was so sorry about Adam, but then he wanted to know if I remembered anything. When I said I didn't know, I was confused, I couldn't understand . . . he asked again: "Can you remember anything – anything?" Only when they left a while later . . . I lay here, the medication . . . but I heard his words again. Why was he so keen to know? And why was his lawyer here? That's what I wanted to tell Griessel, that . . . it was strange.'

'Ma'am, you said he helped you.'

She looked at him in surprise. 'No, I never said that.'

'I asked you who helped you. And you said Willie Mouton.'

The door behind Dekker opened.

'No, no,' said Alexandra Barnard, totally confused, and Dekker wondered what was in the pills she had taken.

'Inspector,' said the nurse.

'Another five minutes,' he said.

'I'm sorry, that's not possible.'

'You misunderstood me,' said Alexa Barnard.

'Please,' said Dekker to the nurse.

'Inspector, if the doctor says fifteen minutes, that is all I can give you.'

'Fuck the doctor,' he said involuntarily.

'Out! Or I'll call security.'

He considered his options, knew he was so close, she was confused, he wouldn't get another chance, but the nurse was a witness to this statement.

He stood up. 'We'll talk again,' he said and walked out, down the passage to the lift. He pressed the button, angry, pressed it again and again. So close.

The door whispered open, the big lift was empty. He went in and saw the G-light on, folded his arms. Now she wanted to point at Willie Mouton. He wasn't going to fall for that.

The lift began to descend.

He would go and talk to the maid, Sylvia Buys. He had her address in his notebook. Athlone somewhere. He checked his watch. Nearly twenty past four. To Athlone in this traffic. Maybe she was still in the house in Tamboerskloof.

Willie Mouton? He recalled the chaos this morning in the street, the militant Mouton, the black knight, shaven-headed earring-wearer on his fucking phone. To his lawyer. Mouton, who was desperate for him to arrest Josh and Melinda.

The lift doors slid open. People were waiting to come in. He walked out slowly, thoughtfully. He stopped in the entrance hall.

The lawyer who had been with him all day, the spectre of a man, so grave. Mouton and Groenewald here, with Alexa. 'What can you remember?' Why?

Was the drunk woman lying?

Adam phoned me last night, some time after nine, to tell me about Iván Nell's stories. His cell phone rang. He saw it was Griessel, who believed she was innocent.

'Benny?'

'Fransman, are you still at AfriSound?'

'No, I'm at City Park.'

'Where?'

'At the hospital. In the city.'

'No, I mean where in the hospital?'

'At the entrance. Why?'

'Stay there, I'll be with you in a minute. You're not going to believe this.'

46

With the crooked pliers of the Leatherman that had saved his life, Benny Griessel cut Rachel Anderson's hands free. Then he went and fetched four sleeping bags, asked Vusi to call for backup and medical support, spread two sleeping bags on the floor for her to lie on and covered her shivering body with the other two.

'Don't leave me,' she said.

'I won't,' but he heard Oerson groan and went to find the Metro officer's pistol before sitting down with her, taking out his cell phone and calling John Afrika.

'Benny, where the fuck are you? I've been phoning . . .'

'Commissioner, we got Rachel Anderson. I'm sitting with her now. We're in Observatory, but I just want to ask one thing: send us the chopper, she needs medical assistance, she's not bad, but I'm definitely not taking her to Groote Schuur.' There was a heartbeat of silence before Afrika said: 'Hallelujah! The chopper is on its way, just give me the address.'

'I'm sorry, Mr Burton, but I just don't believe you,' said Bill Anderson over his cell phone. 'There's a warning right here on the US consulate's website, stating that fourteen Americans have been robbed at gunpoint after landing at the OR Tambo International Airport in the past twelve months. I've just read that a South African government Minister has said police must kill criminal bastards, and not worry about regulations. I mean, it's the Wild West out there. Here's another one: "More police were killed in the years since the end of Apartheid than in the previous period in that country's history."

'"Armed robberies at people's homes have increased by thirty per cent." And you are telling me we won't need protection?'

'It sounds worse than it is, I can assure you,' the American Consul reassured him.

'Mr Burton, we are flying out this afternoon. All I want you to do is to recommend someone to protect us.'

Dan Burton's sigh was audible. 'Well, we usually recommend Body Armour, a personal security company. You can call a Ms Jeanette Louw . . .'

'Can you spell that for me?'

Just then the house phone on Anderson's desk began to ring and he said: 'Excuse me for one second,' picked up the receiver and said: 'Bill Anderson.'

'Daddy,' he heard the voice of his daughter.

'Rachel! Oh, God, where are you?'

'I'm with Captain Benny Griessel, Daddy . . .' and then her voice broke.

Griessel sat with his back to the wall, both arms around her. She leaned heavily on him, her head on his shoulder, while she spoke to her father. When she was finished and passed the phone back to him, she looked up at him and said: 'Thank you.'

He didn't know how to answer her. He heard the sirens approaching, wondering how long it would take the helicopter to get here.

'Did you find the video?' she asked.

'What video?'

'The video of the murder. At Kariba.'

'No,' he said.

'That's why they killed Erin.'

'You don't have to tell me now,' he said.

'No, I have to.'

She and Erin had shared a tent the whole tour.

Erin had adjusted easily to the new time zones, slept well, got up with the sun, stretched pleasurably, yawned and said: 'Another perfect day in Africa.'

Initially Rachel struggled to fall asleep at night. After the first week it improved, but every night, somewhere between one and three, her body clock woke her. Later she would vaguely recall moments of consciousness while she reoriented herself and wondered at this astonishing adventure, this special privilege, of lying listening to the noises of this divine continent. And she would sink away, carefree and light as a feather, into cosy sleep.

At Lake Kariba the moonlight had taken her by surprise. Some time after two in the early hours, near wakening, she had become aware of the glow and opened her eyes. She thought someone had switched on a floodlight. Then truth dawned – full moon. She was enchanted by its brightness, its immensity, and was ready to drift back to her dreams. In her imagination she saw the moon over Kariba, the beauty of it. She realised she must capture it for her video journal. It could be the opening shot of the DVD she would make at home on Premiere Pro. Or the background of her title-sequence animation in After Effects, if she ever found enough time to unravel the secrets of that software.

Carefully, so as not to disturb Erin, she crawled out of her sleeping bag, took her Sony video camera and went out into the sultry summer night.

The camp was quiet. She walked between the tents to the edge of the lake. The view was as she had suspected, another breathtaking African show – the moon a jewel of tarnished silver sliding across the carpet of a billion stars, all duplicated in the mirror of the lake. She switched the camera on, folded out the small LCD screen and chose 'Sunset & Moon' on the panel. But the moon was too high. She could film either the reflection or the real thing, but not both in one frame. She looked around and spotted the rocks on the edge of the lake about a hundred metres away. An acacia tree was growing out of them. It would give her height, a reference point and perspective. From the top of the rocks she tried again. She experimented with the branches of the tree, until she heard the sounds, below, scarcely fifteen metres away.

She had turned to look. Two figures in the dark. A muffled argument. She sat down slowly, instinctively, and knew it was Jason de Klerk and Steven Chitsinga at one of the trailers.

She smiled to herself, aimed her camera at them and began to film. Her intention was mischievous. These were the chief teases, the head guides who mocked the European and American tourists about their love of comfort, their bickering, complaining, their inability to deal with Africa. Now she had evidence that they were not perfect either. She smiled, thinking she would reveal it at breakfast. Let them feel embarrassed for once.

Until Steven pulled open one of the large storage drawers under the trailer and bent to get something. He jerked roughly at it and suddenly the shape of another person stood between them, a smaller figure beside the lankiness of the two guides.

A man's voice called out one word. Steven grabbed the smaller figure from behind and put a hand over his mouth. Rachel Anderson looked up from the screen now, dumbstruck, she wanted to be certain the camera was not lying. She saw something shiny in Jason's hand, bright and deadly in the moonlight. She saw him drive it into the small figure's chest and how the man slumped in Steven's grip.

Jason picked up the feet, Steven took the hands and they dragged the figure away into the darkness.

She sat there a long time. At first she denied it, it could not be real, a dream, a complete fantasy. She turned off the sound of the video and played it back. The image quality was not great, the camera was not renowned for its results in the dark, but there was enough, until the truth struck home: she had witnessed a murder, committed by two people to whom she had entrusted her life.

The next day passed in a haze. She realised she was traumatised, but didn't know what to do. She withdrew. Again and again Erin asked her: 'What's wrong?' Later: 'Did I do something?' She just said: 'I'm not feeling well.'

Erin suspected the first symptoms of malaria. She cross-questioned her about symptoms and Rachel answered vaguely and evasively, until her friend gave up. She wanted to report the murder, but to whom? There were so many rumours about the police in Zimbabwe, so many stories of corruption and politics that she hesitated. After a visit to the Victoria Falls, they left the country and passed into Botswana. Then there was no more opportunity. Just the dismay she carried with her and the knowledge that the murder in Zimbabwe by Zimbabweans was not the concern of another country's police. Not on this continent.

In Cape Town they went with a few others to the Van Hunks nightclub, unaware that Jason would turn up later.

They had both been drinking, Erin with great fervour. She began to scold Rachel in an escalating flood of complaints – at the table, on the dance floor. At first just with words like razors, later with tears of drunken melancholy. About friendship, trust and betrayal.

The alcohol had weakened Rachel's resolve. It made her emotional, feel the urge to lighten the burden of her secret and deny the horrible accusations against her. Eventually, with their heads close together at the table, she told Erin everything. Erin calmed down. She said it couldn't be true, it must be a misunderstanding. Not Jason and Steven. Impossible. Rachel said she had watched the video many times over in the early morning hours. There was no mistake.

Let's ask them, let's clear this thing up. This was the reasoning of a fairly intoxicated, naïve arch-optimist who never saw evil in anyone. No, no, no, Rachel had protested, promise me you won't say anything, never, let's go home, my father will know what to do.

Erin had promised. They danced. Erin went off somewhere, came back to the table. She said Jason and Steven were here, she had asked them about it, they said she was dreaming. Rachel looked up across the sea of faces and found Jason's eyes on her. He had a cell phone to his ear, and an expression of chilling determination. She had grabbed her rucksack and told Erin to come, they had to get out of there, now. Erin had argued, she didn't want to leave, what was Rachel's problem? Rachel had grabbed her arms and said, 'You come with me. Now!'

They were a few hundred metres from the club down Long Street when Jason and Steven emerged. They looked left and right,

saw them and began to run. The other three had joined them from
somewhere. Barry, Eben and Bobby.

She knew they were running for their lives.

In the Toyota bakkie, Steven Chitsinga and Barry Smith turned
out of Scott into Speke Street and saw the police vehicles in front
of the African Overland Adventures warehouse, a horde of blue
lights flashing and uniforms everywhere.

Steven said a word in Shona; Barry was silent, braked sharply
so that the big off-road tyres squealed. He jerked the gear lever
into reverse, released the clutch, depressed the accelerator and
shot backwards into something. In the mirror he could just see
the roof of the vehicle, only once he turned his head in panic did
he realise it was another SAPS patrol vehicle. With an ambulance
behind that was blocking most of the road. He ground through
the gears and shot forward. If he could go left into Stanley, and
then left again in Grant . . .

But Stanley was closed, police vans, Opels, blocked the street.
Uniforms came running with guns in hand.

'Fuck,' said Steven beside him.

Barry said nothing. He stopped the bakkie and lifted his hands
slowly off the steering wheel and held them above his head.

'He's coming with me,' said Rachel Anderson as they carried
her to the helicopter on a stretcher. She pointed at Griessel, who
walked beside her holding her hand.

'There's no room,' said the paramedic.

'Then I'm not going.'

'Rachel, I'll be there in a few minutes,' Griessel soothed.

She fought to get off the stretcher. 'I'm not going.'

'Wait,' said the paramedic, 'he can go with you.' To Griessel he
said: 'Where's your car?'

Benny pointed at the van. 'The keys are still inside.'

They loaded her into the helicopter, and Griessel shifted in
beside her with difficulty. 'Wait a bit,' the paramedic said and ran
back into the building. He returned with the toes in a little bag and

passed the gruesome cargo to Griessel. 'They can sew them back on,' said the man. 'Maybe . . .'

In the helicopter she tried to talk but the rotors made too much of a racket.

Once they had landed on the roof of the hospital and when they were ready to wheel her into theatre, the same one where they had operated on Mbali Kaleni and Eben Etlinger, she asked them to wait. She told Griessel there was another thing, last night. After they had cut Erin's throat.

'We'll talk later,' he pleaded, because he had to get back to Vusi, there was a lot of work to do.

'No. You have to know. They killed another man.'

She had seen them cut Erin's throat and she had run blindly in fear and shock back to the street, chose the first possible street away from them. Somewhere not long after that she had seen a building on the left with an entrance through to an inner garden. She wanted to get out of sight. She ran in there.

A big, middle-aged man in a suit, handsome, was standing at a fishpond and watching two other men walk away. He shouted something angry before they opened a glass door and disappeared inside. On the wall was a logo of a bird, she could remember that.

'Please, help me,' she said with huge relief, here was help. The big man had looked at her and the anger on his face had quickly changed to concern. 'What's wrong?' he asked.

'They want to kill me,' she had said and went to stand with him.

'Who?'

They heard their running steps and looked at the entrance, where Jason and the others had appeared. Jason had a gun in his hand now.

'We just want her,' he said to the big man. The man had put his arm protectively around Rachel's shoulders and said: 'Not before we call the police.'

'She stole from us. We just want our stuff back, we don't want trouble.'

'Even more reason to call the police,' and he had started to feel in his pocket, probably for his phone.

Jason pointed the pistol at the man. 'Then I'll have to shoot you.'

The man took out a cell phone.

She realised she was not going to be responsible for another death and she started running again. The big man tried to stop them.

She heard two shots. She looked back. The big man in the black suit fell down.

Then she was gone, around the corner. In the street a municipal lorry had pulled away, a smelly truck transporting rubbish bags. She jumped up against it, saw them coming. The truck picked up speed so that Jason became smaller and smaller. She thought they had given up when she had nearly a half a kilometre lead on them. But then the traffic lights at the top of the street turned red. She jumped off then.

'Two men went into the building just before he saw you?' he asked her as they wheeled her into theatre.

'Yes,' she said.

Griessel followed. 'What did they look like?'

'I can remember only one. He was . . . eccentric. Very thin, his head was shaven . . . Oh, and he had a silver earring,' and then the doctor told Griessel he would have to leave. 'He was dressed all in black,' she called before the theatre doors closed.

16:41–17:46

47

Detective Inspector Vusi Ndabeni finally lost his professional cool in the interrogation room at the Caledon Square police station.

They deposited Steven Chitsinga in a cell. They asked Mat Joubert to question Jason de Klerk in an available office, as Griessel said he couldn't, because if he did he 'would beat the fucker to death'.

Vusi took Barry Smith to the official station interview room. Griessel took charge of Bobby Verster in another office. Verster was the last one to come out of Rachel's torture chamber, the one who had left Jeremy Oerson alone with her. They suspected he was the weakest link.

Joubert got nothing from Jason de Klerk, despite his skill, his intimidating size and the fact that Jason was in agony from his smashed elbow. He ignored every question, just sat and stared at the wall.

To every question from Vusi, Barry Smith mumbled 'Fuck off.' Vusi felt the unease growing inside him, but he suppressed it and asked the next question.

'Fuck off.'

In the other office, Bobby Verster told Griessel he hadn't been on the tour. Last night by chance he had been with Barry and Eben at the Purple Turtle when Jason had phoned. Barry had jumped up and told them to come, and outside they had seen Jason and Steven chasing two girls down Long Street. So they joined in the chase.

Griessel's body was sore, but he was filled with euphoria from the breakthrough and the relief at finding Rachel. He stood up from his chair and approached the table. He looked at

Bobby. Bobby looked away. 'Have you heard the one about the little dog?' Griessel asked.

'What one?'

With suspicion.

Benny sat on the table, folded his arms carefully across his chest and said in a mischievous, playful and friendly voice: 'The one about the young dog that heard the big dogs talking about sex and how good it felt to fuck. "What is fucking?" asked the young dog. "It's the best thing ever, let's show you." The dogs ran up the street and found a bitch on heat. The bitch ran away from the pack. They chased her, around and around the block. After the fourth time around the block, the little dog said: "Guys, I'm only fucking one more round and then I'm going home."'

Bobby Verster didn't laugh.

'You didn't get tired of all the chasing, Bobby?' Benny Griessel asked.

Verster said nothing.

'Not even when they cut an innocent girl's throat?'

Bobby said he was shocked when Jason did it. He had protested. But Steven Chitsinga told him: 'You're next if you don't shut your mouth and help.' It scared him. But he didn't know what the hell was going on with Jason and them.

'So were you forced?'

'Yes.'

'So actually, you are innocent?'

'Yes!'

'Would you make a statement to that effect? Just so we can close your part of the case?' Griessel asked him.

'I will,' he answered eagerly.

Benny shifted pen and paper closer. Bobby wrote. 'Sign it,' said Benny. Once Bobby was finished, Griessel read the statement out loud to him. He asked: 'All this is the truth?'

'It is.'

'Then you are an accessory to murder. You are going to jail, and you will sit there for a very long time.'

Bobby Verster's eyes widened. He protested, just as he claimed he had done the previous night. 'But you said I was innocent!'

'No, I asked you if you were. Come, there's a police van outside that will take you to Pollsmoor.'

'Pollsmoor?'

'Just until the bail hearing. In about a week or two. Three.'

'Wait . . .'

Griessel waited.

Bobby Verster thought for a long time. Then he said: 'You're looking for Blake.'

'Who is Blake?'

'Do I still have to go to Pollsmoor?'

'Everything is negotiable.'

'Blake is the owner. Of Overland. We bring the people in for him.'

'What people?'

'The blacks.'

'What blacks?'

'The blacks they put in the bins under the trailer. From Zimbabwe. But they're not always Zimbabweans.'

'Illegal immigrants?'

'Something like that. I don't know. I've only been helping with unloading about a month, but they won't tell me everything yet.'

'What is Blake's name?'

'Duncan. But we call him Mr B. He lives here in the city, that's all I know.'

'Thank you very much.'

'Do I still have to go to Pollsmoor?'

'Yip.'

Fransman Dekker brought another two uniforms along with him to AfriSound. They walked through the pack of journalists in the little garden. He ignored the questions. One of the two Constables guarding the door opened up for them. Dekker said: 'All of you come with me.' They climbed the stairs in step, the detective in front, four uniforms behind him. They walked through the reception area. Dekker smiled at Natasha. He felt self-confident for the first time today. Down the passage as far as Mouton's office. He didn't knock, he just walked in.

The lawyer wasn't there.

'What now?' Mouton asked.

'The best thing about my job, the thing I enjoy most of all, is arresting a whitey bastard,' said Dekker.

Mouton's Adam's apple bobbed wildly up and down, but he couldn't get a word out. Dekker asked two Constables to keep an eye on Mouton and walked out, beckoned the other two uniforms closer and opened Wouter Steenkamp's door. The accountant was seated behind his computer.

'We know all about last night,' he said. Steenkamp didn't bat an eyelid.

'He doesn't phone anyone, he doesn't move, he just sits here,' said Dekker to the two uniforms. 'I'll be back soon.'

Griessel called Vusi and Mat Joubert. He held a quick meeting in the station commander's office. He told them what Bobby Verster had said. Once the detectives had finished discussing it, Vusi went back and told Barry Smith: 'We're bringing in Mr B. We know everything.'

Barry Smith turned white. 'Fuck off,' he said, with more venom.

'Murder,' said Vusi to him. 'Life sentence.'

'Fuck off, you black bastard.'

The injustices of the day bore down incredibly heavily on Vusumuzi Ndabeni, but he shook them off one last time. Then Barry Smith said: 'Fucking motherfucker,' and Vusi's temper exploded over him like the mighty breakers on the Wild Coast. In one lightning move he reached the young white man, and his fist struck his temple with all the power in the lean, neat body behind it.

Barry's head jerked back and he toppled backwards, chair and all. His head hit the floor with a dull thud. Vusi was there, on him, jerking him up by the collar, shoving his face into Barry's and said: 'My mother is a decent woman, do you hear?'

Then he let go of him and stood back, breathing heavily. Vusi adjusted his jacket, realised his knuckles hurt and saw that Barry's eyes had trouble focusing. Barry got unsteadily to his feet, looked back, slowly picked up the chair, set it right and sat down. He put his hands on the table in slow motion and dropped his head onto them, his palms obscuring his face.

It was quite a while before Vusi realised that the young man was crying. He pulled out a chair and sat down. He said nothing, not trusting his voice: his rage had not subsided, the guilt was just a small dark spot in his belly.

They sat like that for over a minute.

'My mother is going to kill me,' said Barry through his hands.

'I can help you,' said Vusi.

Barry sobbed, making his whole body shake. Then he began to talk.

Dekker sat opposite Mouton. He said: 'I know you didn't shoot Adam Barnard. I know about the girl and the four guys chasing her.'

'Five,' said Mouton, and then looked as if he could bite off his tongue.

'Five,' said Dekker in satisfaction.

'I want to phone my lawyer,' said Mouton.

'Later. Let me tell you what happened. Barnard phoned you, last night, just after nine. You knew we would find a record of the call, that's why you volunteered it so easily . . .'

Mouton's Adam's apple moved, he wanted to say something, but Dekker silenced him with a hand. 'Adam didn't phone you to tell you how silly Iván Nell's accusations were. He was worried. Nell told me Barnard was disturbed. He wasn't himself. He had a suspicion. He had a feeling, he knew someone was fucking with the money. I don't know why yet, but I will find out. In any case, Adam said he wanted to see you. Did he tell you to come to the office, you and Wouter? Or was it your suggestion – keep trouble away from home? So you came in here, probably very worried, because you *are* guilty. What time was that, Willie? Did he tell you to come at eleven so he could look at the figures first?

I know he worked on his computer last night. He was so upset by what he saw that he never turned his laptop off. It was still on this morning. Maybe he loaded all the records on a CD so that you couldn't go and fiddle with them. You sat here, or maybe in his office, and he confronted you. Did you deny everything, Willie? How am I doing so far? Never mind, let me finish. You argued and fought from eleven o'clock to half past one in the night. Barnard must have said something like; 'Leave it, we'll talk more tomorrow.' He must have been tired. Thinking of his drunken wife at home. And you and Steenkamp followed him out into the garden. Argued some more. You went in just when the girl arrived. You got lucky, in more than one way. Because if you had been standing there, you might also have been shot. But then they shot Adam. Problem number one solved. There you two were, looking out the window at the body, and you thought: what now? Your big problem was Iván Nell. Because, whatever you did, if Iván came and told us there was a snake in the grass, you were in trouble.

'So you wondered how you could make it look different, as though you had never been here. Give someone else the blame. Then you remembered about Josh and the Big Sin. And Alexa and the pistol. Fucking brilliant, Willie, I have to tell you. So you carried Barnard to the car. If he was in your or Wouter's car there will be blood and hair and fibres and DNA, and we'll find it.

'Now, I must say, I couldn't figure out the shoe and the cell phone. Until about half an hour ago, when I put the whole story together. The shoe came off when you picked up Adam to carry him to the car. You must have picked him up by the feet. And the cell phone was in his hand when he was shot. So you picked up the phone and you remembered that he had phoned you. So you deleted his call history. And you put the cell phone in the shoe and the shoe in your pocket, or on top of Barnard, we will probably never know. And then when you reached the car and opened the boot, you put the shoe on the roof of the car. Just for the mean time. And then in your hurry you forgot about the shoe. You drove off, Wouter in front with Adam's car and you following.

Something like that. And up there on the corner, as you turned, the shoe falls off and you don't even know it. How am I doing, Willie? I'm telling you, I had a really hard time figuring out that shoe, until I went up there to the corner again. It came to me in a flash. Fucking brilliant, let me tell you.'

Mouton just stared at Dekker.

'You and Wouter carried him up the stairs and you put him down there with Alexa. And you went and got the pistol out of the safe that you installed in the house. Somewhere you fired off three shots. I'm guessing you couldn't do it in the house. Even if you used a pillow or something to reduce the noise, you were too scared of waking Alexa, drunk or not. You must have driven somewhere, Willie. Up the mountain? Somewhere that it wouldn't matter. Then you went back and put the pistol down there. Clever. But not clever enough.'

'I want to call my lawyer.'

'Call him, Willie. Tell him to come to Green Point station. Because this is a warrant for your arrest, and this is a warrant to search these premises. I will be bringing smart people, Willie. Auditors, computer boffins, guys who specialise in white-collar crime. You stole Adam Barnard's and Iván Nell's and who knows how many other people's money, and I'm going to find out how you did it and I'm going to put you and Wouter away, Willie, and that fucking Frankenstein lawyer of yours won't be able to do a thing about it. Or is he also a part of your little scheme?'

Benny Griessel pushed the man through the front door of Caledon Square. His full beard and hair were trimmed short, neat, plain brown turning prematurely grey. He looked fit and lean in denim shirt and khaki chinos and blue boat shoes. It was only the handcuffs on his wrists that showed he was in trouble, his face was expressionless. Vusi was waiting in the entrance hall.

'May I introduce you to Duncan Blake?' Griessel asked, with great satisfaction.

Vusi looked the man up and down, as though measuring him against newfound knowledge. Then he applied himself to Griessel with a worried: 'Benny, we will have to bring the Commissioner in.'

'Oh?'

'This thing is big. And ugly. We will have to send a team to Camps Bay, to a hospital. A big team.'

Only then did a shadow of emotion cross Duncan Blake's face.

17:47–18:36

48

They sat in the station commander's office – Griessel, Vusi and John Afrika.

'I just want to say I am proud of you, the Provincial Commissioner is proud of you. The Minister says I must convey her congratulations,' Afrika said.

'It was Vusi who cracked it,' said Griessel.

'No, Commissioner, it was Benny . . . Captain Griessel.'

'The SAPS is proud of you both.'

'Commissioner, this thing is big,' said Vusi.

'How big?'

'Commissioner, they smuggled people in, eight at a time, through Zimbabwe. Somalians, Sudanese, Zimbabweans . . .'

'All the trouble spots.'

'That's right, Commissioner, people who have nothing, who want to make a new start, who will do anything . . .'

'They must have charged bags of money to bring them to this honey pot.'

'No, Commissioner, not much.'

'Oh?'

'We thought it was just illegal immigrants at first. But Barry Smith, one of the guides, told me the rest. The hospital, the whole thing . . .'

'What hospital?' John Afrika asked.

'Maybe we should start at the beginning. Benny talked to Blake, Commissioner.'

Griessel nodded, scratched behind his ear, paged through his notebook and found the right page. 'Duncan Blake, Commissioner. He is a Zim citizen, fifty-five years old. He was married, but his wife died in Two thousand and one of cancer. In the Seventies he was part of the Rhodesian Special Air Services. For thirty years he farmed the family farm outside Hurungwe in Mashonaland-West. His sister, Mary-Anne Blake was a surgeon at the hospital in Harare. In May Two thousand, the leader of the Veterans' Movement, Chenjerai 'Hitler' Hunzvi, occupied Blake's farm. Apparently, Blake's foreman, Justice Chitsinga, tried to stop the squatters and was shot dead. For two years, Blake tried to regain possession of his farm through the courts, but in Two thousand and two he gave up and he and his sister moved to Cape Town. He brought Steven Chitsinga, his foreman's son, with him and started African Overland Adventures. Most of his staff were young men and women from Zimbabwe, children of dispossessed farmers, or their workers. De Klerk, Steven Chitsinga, Eben Etlinger, Barry Smith . . .'

'And the Metro man you shot dead? Oerson?' the Commissioner asked.

'That's another story, Commissioner,' said Vusi. 'Smith said Oerson was with Provincial Traffic. Two years ago he was working at the weighbridge on the N-seven, at Vissershoek, and he pulled one of their Adventure lorries off the road. It was overweight. Then he began hinting, they needn't pay the fine, and de Klerk was immediately ready to pay something under the table. Oerson took it and let them go. But he began to wonder why the Adventure people paid so easily and so much. He thought about it. They came from the north, through Africa, and he was sure they were smuggling something. He waited for them to pass through again a month later. He pulled them off again. He said he wanted to have a look in the lorry and the trailer, in all the cavities. Then de Klerk said that wouldn't be necessary, how much did he want? And Oerson said, no, he wanted to look, because he thought they had something to hide. De Klerk kept offering him more and Oerson said open up. De Klerk said he couldn't and Oerson said: "Then cut me in, because I smell big money." So de Klerk phoned Blake. And they put Oerson on the payroll. But on one condition, Oerson must apply to Metro, because they needed another man to keep an eye on the Somalis and Zimmers who had already donated organs and were all in the city . . .'

'Donated organs?'

'I'm getting to that, Commissioner. Lots of the people who have already donated have opened street-vendor stalls in the city with the money they were paid. There were a few who threatened to talk if they didn't get more money. It was Oerson's job to shut them up.'

'As in permanently?'

'Sometimes, Commissioner. But never personally, he had other contacts for that. Other Metro people too . . .'

'*Jissis*,' said John Afrika and folded his hands in front of him. Then he looked at Vusi. 'And the organs?'

'Blake started the Adventure business, and he and his sister bought the old Atlantic Hotel in Camps Bay in Two thousand and three, and fixed the place up and started a private hospital. She is the "director" now . . .'

'A hospital?'

Vusi had an idea. 'Excuse me, Commissioner,' he said and pulled the keyboard on the desk towards him, then the mouse. He turned the computer screen so that he could see better, clicked on the web browser icon and typed in the web address.

Google South Africa read the screen.

Vusi typed in the word 'AtlantiCare' into the box and clicked on *Google Search*. A long list of choices appeared. He picked the top link and a website slowly loaded on the screen. It showed a white building on the slopes of the Twelve Apostles, with a banner headline: ATLANTICARE: *Exclusive International Medical Centre*. Another photo appeared – the building from behind, with the Atlantic Ocean stretching to the horizon.

'This is the place, Commissioner.'

John Afrika whistled. 'Big money.'

'Steven Chitsinga said they were big farmers. They owned and rented a lot of farms, there was cattle, tobacco, maize. Big business. There were some investments . . . But the thing is, Commissioner,' Vusi shifted the mouse to a link that said *Transplants*, 'they do organ transplants.' Another web page opened up with the same white building in the banner across the top. Underneath it the heading: *Transplants you can afford.* Vusi read out loud to them. 'The average cost of a heart transplant in the United States of America is three hundred thousand dollars. A lung transplant will cost you two hundred and seventy-five thousand, an intestine almost half a million dollars. Impossible to afford without health insurance, but even if you are covered, there is no guarantee that you will receive a donated organ in time. For instance, the waiting list for a kidney transplant in the USA has more than fifty-five thousand people on it . . .'

'Don't tell me they . . .?'

'That's right, Commissioner,' Vusi said, and he read from the web page again. 'With the most modern medical facilities available, including dedicated, specialist aftercare in a beautiful environment, world-class surgeons and an international network of donors, you can receive your transplant within three weeks of arriving, at a fraction of the cost.'

'That's what they smuggled the people in for,' said Griessel.

'For the organs,' said Vusi.

'*Bliksem*,' said the Commissioner. 'We better get people to that hospital for the records.'

'Mat Joubert is there already, Commissioner. He's got a big team with him.'

'So they bring people in and then they kill them?'

'Not always, Commissioner,' said Vusi. 'Apparently that was the price the people were required to pay for a better life in South Africa. They had to donate a kidney or a lung or part of their liver. Or part of an eye, corneas, and bone marrow as well. I'm still trying to get my head around it. Apparently you can donate a lot of your organs without the consequences being too serious.'

'And the hearts?'

'We will have to see, Commissioner, because the website talks about hearts as well. But the one Rachel Anderson saw, the one that de Klerk and Chitsinga murdered at Kariba, he had AIDS. Smith says they had test kits with them – before they loaded a person under the trailers, they drew blood and then they tested it.

They realised that man had AIDS. So they took him out, and they couldn't afford to just let him go.'

'What kind of people are these?' John Afrika asked.

'That's what I asked Duncan Blake,' said Griessel. 'And he said Africa took everything he had, all his dreams, Africa tore out his heart. Why couldn't he do that to Africa?'

Griessel's cell phone rang shrilly. He looked at the screen, got up and went aside to answer it.

The Commissioner leaned forward, looked at the website, sighed deeply, listening to Griessel making noises of disbelief.

Benny Griessel came back to the desk. 'That was Mat,' he said. 'Commissioner, *this* thing is going to get ugly.'

'Why?' There was a lot of worry in John Afrika's voice.

'There's a government Minister in the hospital records.'

'One of our Ministers?'

'Yes, Commissioner. Liver transplant.'

'*Ag nee, liewe fok*,' said John Afrika.

Fransman Dekker had heard the coloured SAPS computer specialist was genius. So he was expecting someone like Bill Gates. What he got was a slightly built man with the face of a schoolboy, two missing front teeth, a big Afro hairstyle, no sense of humour and a pronounced lisp. 'Thith ith candy floth,' the genius said to Dekker in Wouter Steenkamp's office.

'Excuse me, bro'?' Dekker asked, because he couldn't understand a single word.

'Candy floth.'

'Candy floss?'

'That'th right.'

'How so, my bro'?'

'Illusionth. A PDF pathword ith utheleth.'

'A PDF pathword?'

'No, a pa*th*word.'

'Password?'

'That'th right. People think if you have a PDF pathword then you're thecure. But it'th not thecure.'

'So how did they do it?'

'Thith *ou* . . .' he pointed at the computer, which belonged to Steenkamp, '. . . got the pathword-protected PDF'th for every thinger'th thaleth from the dithtributor. By email. Lookth like it wath hith job to thend it on to the thinger when the money wath tranthferred.'

'Right.'

'The thinger thinkth only he hath the pathword, tho he thinkth the record company can't change the thtatement of THEE-D thales. He thinkth he'th getting all the money.'

'Because it comes from the dith . . . er, the distributor?'

'Yeth, the dithtributor puth the pathword on, but emailth it to thith *ou*. And thith *ou* emailth it to the thinger.'

'Right.'

'But look here . . .' the computer boffin opened a program. 'Thith ith thoftware, Advanthed PDF Pathword Recovery, Enteprithe Edition, made by Elcomthoft. You can buy it from their webthite, the prithe ith juth under a thouthand rand, but then you can do what you like with a PDF, even if it hath a forty-bit encrypthion with Thunder Tableth. It meanth thith ith candy floth, any pathword protecthion.'

'So Steenkamp could get the singer's password and he could change the statement?'

'Exthactly. He copieth and paththeth the PDF tableth into Microthoft Exthell, changeth the tableth, maketh a new PDF, becauth heth got Adobe Acrobat Profethional, the Thee Eth Four edithion, brand new, thtate of the art, and he puth the thame pathword protecthion on again. Tho the thinger thinkth it ith the original PDF, he doethn't know he'th been conned.'

'How much did they skim?'

'It lookth like it varieth, from ten to forty per thent, depending on how much the thinger thells. The big guyth, like Iván Nell, they took up to forty per thent off him on hith latht THEE-D.'

'Fucking hell.'

'My thentimentth exthactly.'

18:37–19:51

49

Precisely thirteen hours since they had woken Benny Griessel in his flat, around 18:37, he told John Afrika: 'Commissioner, I have to be in Canal Walk by seven o'clock, please, will you excuse me?'

The Commissioner stood up and put a hand on Griessel's shoulder. 'Captain, I just want to say one thing. If there was ever a man who deserved promotion, it's you. I never doubted you would solve this one. Never.'

'Thank you, Commissioner.'

'Let Vusi finish up here. Go and do your thing, we'll talk again tomorrow.'

'Thanks, Benny,' Vusi said from the table where the contents of the file were beginning to swell.

'Pleasure, Vusi,' and then he was out of there in a rush. There was no time to change his shirt, but he could tell Anna the story of how the hole came to be there. Then he remembered he owed his son a phone call. Fritz, who had phoned him with the news that he was quitting school, that their band, Wet & Orde, (with an ampersand), had got a fat gig, that they were 'opening for Gian Groen and Zinkplaat on a tour, Dad, they are talking about twenty-five thousand for a month, that's more than six thousand per *ou*,' and Griessel had said: 'I'll call you back, things are a bit rough here.'

He got into his car, took his cell phone's hands-free kit out of the cubby hole, plugged it in and drove away to Buitengracht and the N1.

'Hi, Dad.'

'How's it going, Fritz?'

'No, cool, Dad, cool.'

'Six thousand rand for each *ou* in the band?'

'Yes, Dad. Awesome, and they pay for our meals and accommodation and everything.'

'That's fantastic,' said Griessel.

'I know. A professional musician doesn't need Matric, Dad, I mean, what for, why must I know about the sex life of the snail? Dad, you and Ma must sign this letter, because I'm only eighteen in December.'

'Bring me the letter, then, Fritz.'

'Really, Dad?'

'Sure. A guy doesn't need more than six thousand a month. Let's see, your flat will cost you about two thousand a month . . .'

'No, Dad, I'll still stay at home, so . . .'

'But you will pay your mother rent, won't you? For laundry and cleaning and the food?'

'You think I should?'

'I don't know, Fritz – what do *you* think is the right thing to do?'

'Sure, Dad, that sounds right.'

'And you will need a car. Let's say a payment of about two thousand, plus insurance and petrol and services, three, three and a half . . .'

'No, Dad, Rohan picked up a Ford Bantam for thirty-two. A guy doesn't need a grand car to start with.'

'Where did he get the thirty-two?'

'From his father.'

'And where are you going to get thirty-two from?'

'I . . . er . . .'

'Well, let's say you save two thousand a month for a car, then that's only fifteen months, a year and a half, then you'll have your Bantam, but we are already at expenses of four thousand, and you haven't bought any clothes, or airtime for your phone, strings for your guitar, razor blades, aftershave, deodorant, or taken a chick out for dinner . . .'

'We don't call them "chicks" any more, Dad.' But the first signs of understanding crept into his son's voice and the enthusiasm had begun to wane.

'What do you call them?'

'Girls, Dad.'

'When the tour is over, Fritz, where will the next six thousand a month come from?'

'Something will come up.'

'And if it doesn't?'

'Why do you always have to be so negative, Dad? You don't want me to be happy.'

'How can you be happy if you don't have an income?'

'We're going to make a CD. We're going to take the money from the tour and make a CD and then . . .'

'But if you use the money from the tour for a CD, what are you going to live on?'

Silence. 'You never let me do anything. A dude can't even dream.'

'I want you to have everything, my son. That's why I am asking these questions.'

No reaction.

'Will you think it over a little, Fritz?'

'Why do I have to know about the sex life of the snail, Dad?'

'That's a whole other argument. Will you think about it?'

A slow and reluctant 'Yeeeaah, sure.'

'OK, we'll talk again.'

'OK, Dad.'

He smiled to himself in the car on the N1. His boy. Just like he was. Lots of plans.

Then he thought ahead. To Anna. His smile faded. A feeling of anxiety descended on him.

She was sitting outside where she could see the water. A good sign, he thought. He paused a moment in the door of Primi and looked at her. His Anna. Forty-two, but looking good. In the past months she seemed to have thrown off the yoke of her husband's alcoholism, and there was a youthfulness about her again. The white blouse, blue jeans, the little cardigan thrown over her shoulders.

Then she spotted him. He watched her face carefully as he approached her. She smiled but not broadly.

'Hello, Anna.'

'Hello, Benny.'

He kissed her on the cheek. She didn't turn her head away. Good sign.

He pulled out a chair. 'You must excuse the way I look, it's been a crazy day.'

Her eyes went to the hole in his breast pocket. 'What happened?'

'They shot me.' He sat down.

'Lord, Benny.'

Good sign.

'Luckiest break of my life. Only an hour before, I put a Leatherman in my pocket, you know, one of those plier thingies.'

'You could have been killed.'

He shrugged. 'If it's your time, it's your time.' She looked at him, running her gaze over his face. He ached for that moment when she would put out her hand, like in the old days, smooth his ruffled hair, say, 'Benny, this bush . . .'

He saw her hand move. She put it down again. 'Benny . . .' she said.

'I'm sober,' he said. 'It's been nearly six months.'

'I know. I am very proud of you.'

Good sign. He grinned at her in expectation.

She took a deep breath. 'Benny . . . there's only one way to say this. There's someone else, Benny.'

50

In his car, Fransman Dekker took out the list of names and telephone numbers. Natasha Abader's was first on the list.

What woman can look at you and not think of sex?

Time to see if she was a bullshitter.

He entered the number in his cell phone.

It's a drug for the soul. I think they have an emptiness inside here, a hole that is never filled, it might help for a little while, then in a day or two it starts all over again. I think there's a reason, I think they don't like themselves.

His own words, to Alexa Barnard.

He had a wife at home. A good, beautiful, sexy, smart woman. Crystal. Waiting for him.

He looked at the small green button on his phone.

He thought about Natasha Abader's legs. That bottom. Her breasts. Small and pert, he knew what they would look like, he could picture the nipples, particularly. She would be a handful. In every meaning of the word.

There was something broken inside him. A hurt that had come a long way with him, that never went away completely; every time it came back, worse, but the medicine helped less and less.

Some time or other he would have to stop this nonsense. He loved his wife, for fuck's sake, he couldn't live without Crystal, she was everything to him. And if she found out . . .

How would she find out?

The fever was in him. He pressed the button.

'Hello, Natasha.'

★　★　★

'This is Vusi Ndabeni. The detective from this morning, at the church.'

'Oh, hi,' said Tiffany October, the pathologist. She sounded tired.

'You must have had a busy day.'

'They're all busy,' she said.

'I was wondering,' Vusi said, feeling his heart thump in his chest. 'If you would like . . .'

The silence on the line was deafening.

'If you would like to go and have something to eat. Or drink . . .'

'Now?'

'No, I mean, any time, maybe another day . . .'

'No,' she said and Vusi's heart plummeted. 'No, now,' she said. 'Please. A beer. A Windhoek Light and a plate of *slap* chips, that would be wonderful. After a day like today . . .'

He drove down the N1, thinking ahead. He would draw money at the ABSA autobank at the bottom of Long Street near the offices of the Receiver. He had given the last of his cash to Mat Joubert for the Steers burgers he had brought. Then to the bottle store up in Buitengracht, it was open till eight. He would buy a bottle of Jack and a two-litre Coke and then he was going to drink himself into a coma.

There's someone else, Benny.

He had asked 'Who?'

And she said: 'It doesn't matter. Benny, I'm so sorry, it just happened.'

Fuck that. Things don't just happen. You look for them. She demands that he give up the booze for six months, and then off she goes looking for a man. He would blow the fucker *moer toe*. He would find out who it was, he would fucking follow her and shoot the bastard between the eyes. Probably some or other boy lawyer where she worked, too shit useless to get a girl of his own, showing off with his BMW and his suits to a policeman's wife. He would kill the bastard, then we'll see.

He had stood up. 'I'm so sorry, Benny, it just happened.' He sat down again and just stared at her, waiting for her to say she wasn't serious. He refused to accept the full impact. They were here so she could say that, because he had quit drinking, he could come home. But she just sat there with tears in her fucking eyes, so terribly sorry for herself. There were a thousand things in his head. He'd nearly died today. He'd fought the craving to drink for one hundred and fifty-six days, he'd paid maintenance, he'd looked after them; he'd done everything right. She couldn't do this, she didn't have the right, Jesus, but her teary eyes had looked back at him with bewildering finality, until the full weight of all the implications crashed down on him like a badly built house. He got up and left.

'Benny!' she called after him.

Benny was going to get drunk, that was what he should have told her, but he just kept walking, out of the fucking restaurant, to his car, with his torn shirt and unkempt hair, he saw nothing, heard nothing, just felt this, thing, this anger, it was all for nothing, all for fucking nothing.

He drew R500 and saw how much he had left for the rest of the month. He thought about Duncan Blake sitting there in the interview room and saying: 'How much for all of this to go away?'

'I'm not for sale.'

'This is Africa. Everybody is for sale.'

'Not me.'

'Five million.'

'How about ten?'

'Ten can be done.'

And he had laughed. He should have taken the fucking money. Ten million would buy a lot of booze; ten million and he could have bought a fucking BMW and smart suits too, and a R150 haircut and whatever it was Anna saw in the little shit.

He would buy some booze.

His cell phone rang as he walked back to his car. He didn't look at the screen, just answered.

'Griessel.' Sullen. Brusque.

'Captain, this is Bill Anderson . . . Is this a convenient time?'

His first thought was that someone had taken Rachel again and he said: 'Yes.'

'Captain, I don't know how to do this. I don't know how you thank a man for saving your child's life. I don't know how to thank a man who was willing to put his life on the line, who was willing to be shot at to save the daughter of someone he's never met. It's not something I have any training for. But my wife and I want to say thank you. We owe you a debt we can never repay. We're on our way to South Africa – our plane is leaving in two hours' time. When we get there, we would like to have the honour of taking you to dinner. As a gesture, of course, as a small token of our immense gratitude and appreciation. But right now, I just want to say thank you.'

'I . . . uh . . . I was just doing my job.' He couldn't think what else to say. The call had come too suddenly, there was too much going on in his head.

'No, sir, what *you* did went *way* beyond the call of duty. So thank you. From Jess, Rachel, and myself. We would like to wish you the very best, for you and your family. May all your dreams come true.'

He sat in his car in front of the autobank. He thought about Bill Anderson's words. *May all your dreams come true.* His only dream had been that Anna would take him back. Now he had fuck all.

Just the dream of getting drunk.

He started the car.

He thought about Fritz's words, his son's dream. *Wet & Orde.*

And Carla, who had gone to work in London, because she wanted to come back and buy a car and go to university, and both of them dreamed of a sober father.

He turned the car off.

He thought about Bella, and Bella's dream of owning her own business. Alexa Barnard who said she had dreamed so long of becoming a singer. Duncan Blake: *Africa took everything I had, all my dreams . . .*

And Bill Anderson. *May all your dreams come true.*

He opened the cubby hole, took out the cigarettes and lit one. He thought. Of many things. Lize Beekman's lyrics ran through his head. *As jy vir liefde omdraai.* If you turn around for love.

He sat like that for a long time while the world raced past down Long Street. Then he turned around.

Benny Griessel blew the R500 on flowers. He delivered the first bunch to Mbali Kaleni's ward. They wouldn't allow him in. He wrote her a message on a card. *You are a brave woman and a good detective.*

Then he went to Rachel Anderson and put a bunch of flowers down on the bed beside her.

'They're beautiful,' she said.

'And so are you.'

'And those?' she asked about the other bunch of flowers in his arms.

'These are a bribe,' he said.

'Oh?'

'Yes. You see, I have a dream. I'm going to start a band. And we are going to need a singer. And I happen to know a great singer who's right here in this hospital,' he said.

'Cool,' she said, and he wondered whether he could introduce her to Fritz.

51

From: Benny Griessel [mailto: bennygriessel2@mweb.co.za]
Sent: 16 January 2009 22:01
To: carla805@hotmail.com
Subject: Today.

Dear Carla

Sorry I am only writing now: My laptop wouldn't connect with the Internet, it was a lot of trouble, but it's fixed now.

It was a long day and a difficult one. I thought about you and missed you. But I did meet a famous singer and I was promoted. Your father is a Captain today.

ACKNOWLEDGEMENTS

Researching any book is like a voyage of discovery – your success is determined by the knowledge, insight, experience and goodwill of the guides who accompany you. With *Thirteen Hours* I was privileged to travel with brilliant guides, to whom I owe much gratitude and appreciation:

- Theuns Jordaan, the true gentleman of the Afrikaans music industry, and the embodiment of all that is good and right in it. Despite a busy schedule, he spent precious hours answering my endless questions with immense patience – even once backstage before a show. Without his input, *Thirteen Hours* would have been much the poorer. Many thanks to Linda Jordaan, who arranged these meetings with such professionalism and hospitality.
- Albert du Plessis, founder and managing director of Rhythm Records, surely one of the sharpest intellects in the music industry, who revealed its secrets to me.
- The peerless Captain Elmarie Myburgh of the South African Police Service's Psychological Investigation Unit in Pretoria. I could never give her enough praise, recognition and thanks.
- My world-class editor, Dr Etienne Bloemhof. This is the sixth novel of mine that he has played a giant part in. How does one say thank you for that?
- My agent, Isobel Dixon, for her professionalism, support, encouragement and impeccable judgement.
- My wife, Anita, for her love, patience, support, wisdom, management, organisation, photography, cuisine . . .
- Andries Wessels, for reading and excellent advice.

- Anton Goosen, Anton L'Amour, Richard van der Westhuizen, Steve Hofmeyr and Josh Hawks of Freshlyground, who contributed through informal discussions.
- Neil Sandilands, who unwittingly planted the seed of the story.
- Jill Quirk of the English Graduate Office, Purdue University.
- Dan Eversman of the Hodson's Bay Company in West Lafayette, Indiana.
- Judy Clain in New York.
- The staff of Carlucci's Quality Food Store in Upper Orange Street.

I would also like to credit the following sources:
- The Media24 database at http://argief.dieburger.com
- LitNet (www.litnet.co.za)
- Gray's Anatomy (www.graysanatomyonline.com)
- http://world.guns.ru
- Review: *Standards Employed to Determine Time of Death*, Jeff Kercheval, VICAP International Symposium, Quantico, Virginia.
- www.baltimoresun.com
- www.eurasianet.org
- www.africanoverland.co.za
- http://goafrica.about.com